2022:

P9-DNU-580

9/22

A
Small
Dark
Place

A
Small
Dark
Place

A NOVEL

MARTIN SCHENK

VILLARD

New York

All rights reserved under International and Pan-American Copyright Conventions. Published in the United States by Villard Books, a division of Random House, Inc., New York, and simultaneously in Canada by Random House of Canada Limited, Toronto.

Villard Books is a registered trademark of Random House, Inc.

LIBRARY OF CONGRESS CATALOGING-IN-PUBLICATION DATA

Schenk, Martin.
  A small dark place: a novel / Martin Schenk.
    p.   cm.
  ISBN 0-375-50074-X
  I. Title.
PS3569.C4828S6   1997   813'.54—dc21   97-18666

Book design by Lilly Langotsky

Random House website address: http://www.randomhouse.com/

Printed in the United States of America on acid-free paper

24689753

First Edition

For my brother Matt,
never forgotten

ACKNOWLEDGMENTS

If I were to list all the selfless supporters of my arcane creative endeavors leading to the publication of A *Small Dark Place* I would produce a document longer than this book. In particular, I thank Mom, Pop, my brothers and my sisters for pushing me to pursue pipe dreams. I thank Daniel Waters for financing my future during the lean years with the smallest of sighs. I am indebted to the Scott family, Charley, Nicole, Kelly, David, Gary, Jill H., Jill E., Stacie and Irene for propping up my chin when life or love gave me a sucker punch. I owe a debt of gratitude to my high school art teacher, Ms. McCulloch, for her deep frustration with my procrastinated talents, thereby causing me to suspect I actually had something to offer. I thank Brian Witten for creating that vital nexus to my brilliant agents. On the West Coast I genuflect to Howard Sanders and Richard Green and I anticipate deft counsel from Scott Schwimer; on the East Coast I applaud the cordial genius of the inimitable Theresa Park. Finally, I wish to thank Peter Borland for his sincere interest, and my editor, David Rosenthal, for his invaluable insight and gentle coercion.

Book
ONE

ONE

FIFTEEN YEARS AGO

Peter Wiley of Wishbone, Kansas, looked around this place he called home and sensed the swelling decay with more than his eyes. He could smell the suffering mildew, and everywhere he touched he felt the creeping grime of an existence uncomfortably close to the bottom.

Almost anywhere else other people did better.

Across a wobbly dinner table stained by uncounted spills, Sandra Wiley glared at her husband, Peter—the living relic of her high school beau, the one-time star quarterback of the Wishbone Wagoneers who nabbed nearly every vote for Most Likely to Succeed. Much fallen from her own glory days as the seniors' choice for Most Popular Miss, Sandra wondered for the hundredth time how low he would let them go.

"I can't do this anymore." She forcefully pushed back from the scummy table and stood. With every pace, grease-clogged linoleum tiles squealed beneath Sandra's feet. "Who are we? Who wants to know us? We're nothing! We're nobodies! Do you know what I'm saying? Where is this taking us?"

Peter looked to his riled Sandra and held his tongue. Every stride he had made since their bleak and unlovely wedding six days after their high school graduation failed to satisfy Sandra's quest for higher social latitudes. Her only wish was to be somebody.

Eight years later, Peter had to admit she was farther than ever from getting that wish.

Peter turned from Sandra's agitated glare. He looked out the cracked kitchen window of their two-story farmhouse to the scrubby plot of scratch, five acres wide and four and a half acres deep, from which they had broken backs and spirits to tear loose a meaningful harvest. Outside, near the lightning-struck oak surrounded by fallen leaves, five-year-old Andromeda played with her precious Barbie. Peter had found the scuffed doll while scrounging an outlaw dump at the end of a mud track just beyond the Wishbone town line. Andromeda's older brother, Will, four months younger than Peter and Sandra's marriage, stood dutifully nearby to make certain Andromeda came to no harm.

Just past eight years, Will was old enough to remember the days when Sandra and Peter spoke with hope about the expected harvest, days when Peter would bend Sandra in a tango dip to kiss her near the kitchen sink. But Andromeda, at five, had known only the pessimism that had finally and fully unseated that hope.

In eight years the Wiley family had seen nothing but locusts, moles, ants, crows, beetle larvae, fungus, frost and hail. In eight years their only harvest and one that arrived with formidable bounty was pure and undeniable misery.

Peter swung his gaze back to Sandra, seeing no hint of the tenderness she once held out to him.

"What do you want me to tell you?"

"I want you to tell me what it is we do with whatever it is we got." She spoke slowly, locking eyes with him to make sure he heard what she had to say next. "I want you to tell me if we're going to lose the farm."

Will and Andromeda tromped into the house, stopping as the rusty screen door swung shut. Beyond Will and Andromeda, who dropped to the floor to remove her dirt-filled Keds, the sky darkened as clouds poured across the level landscape, heralding an impending storm.

"Dad, I think it's going to rain. Should I pull in the tractor?"

"It's out of gas. Why don't you and your sister go play upstairs. Your mother and I have something we need to take care of."

"All right. Come on, Andie."

Andromeda stood in her now bare feet and followed Will up the stairs, stopping for a moment on the matted green shag to call to her mother in the kitchen.

"Mom, can we have fish sticks for supper?"

Sandra kept her gaze locked on Peter.

"We're having navy beans and ham hocks."

"Navy beans taste like dirt."

"Well, it's what we're having. Now go upstairs."

"I hate navy beans . . . "

They waited for Will and Andromeda to climb the stairs and close themselves in the upstairs playroom. Sandra exhaled a sigh, indicating she was ready for Peter's answer.

Peter felt the answer climbing his throat as if it were a living being with legs of its own. He coughed it out because there was no denying the truth.

"I think maybe we will."

Andromeda hated the dark.

The dark sheltered all kinds of horrors, like spiders, dead flies, toenail clippings and mummified mice dispatched by unremembered dimestore traps. As a matter of course, dark came easier than light throughout the whole universe. The dark could not be stopped, it could only be held at bay.

Andromeda hated the dark under her bed and she hated the dark at the bottom of a nearly empty cereal box. She even hated the dark between her two little palms when she cupped together her hands. Although she was only five years old she knew and remembered absolutely why she hated the dark.

When she was two years old she had locked herself in the cabinet under the bathroom sink, lured inside by a smiling Mr. Clean, a cracking plunger, and a toilet scrubber. Her father, mother, and brother, amid the knee-high cornstalks, did not hear her screams and did not find her for three hours. In the way a child will fear swallowing pills after choking on a gumball, so Andromeda began to hate and fear the dark after her three-hour stint in the cobwebbed cabinet under the leaky sink in the downstairs family bathroom.

Near her bedside, plugged low into the wall, was a little Mickey Mouse nightlight smiling to shoo away the worst dark of all. At the end of each day when that really bad and scary dark fell and her mother tucked her in, when local hounds bayed at rustling critters in the fields, Andromeda lay at the center of her bed under army surplus blankets and stared at Mickey. His dim light picked out the familiar objects of Andromeda's world and gave them a warm and happy glow.

Mickey made Andromeda feel safe.

Andromeda's bed held the indecipherable odor of some hard-to-place antiseptic, like the industrial scent sprayed by the gallon onto train and bus seats that hid the stench of a million passengers and a million miles. The aroma entrenched within the small mattress had failed to weaken since its purchase from the Salvation Army three years earlier, but Andromeda had long since gotten used to it. The smell now meant home.

Her chipped and scratched dresser, her damaged wall mirror, her cat-scratched braided throw rug, her optimistically large toy chest and her tweaked metal shelving were all landfill and roadside retrievals. Swept clean of spiderwebs and possum poop, they were placed in Andromeda's own room, the one family luxury she never saw as such.

Everywhere throughout Andromeda's house there lived creaks and groans from warping floorboards, dry-rotted steps, rusted hinges, loose doorknobs and sticking windows. The plumbing barked loudly, rocking the house every time Mommy stood at the kitchen sink to wash their secondhand kitchenware.

Its exterior blasted to bare graying wood from countless dust storms, its rooftop a mélange of crumbling shingles of various colors and shapes, the house was two stories with an attic and a basement. The attic was barren and neglected, used solely for fort purposes by Will. Its only permanent inhabitants were spiders and the nomad mouse searching for that lethal piece of trap-sprung cheese.

The basement was used by nobody.

Never completely dry, even in the middle of the driest and hottest summers, the basement was a relinquished world. The door leading down to it had been padlocked shut by Daddy to make it official. He had long since lost the key.

Often filled with a stagnant swill of mud and brackish water, the dirt-floored basement was the domain of snakes, salamanders, black widows and pond scum. As if holding down the dank and moist earth, white roots, none thicker than a thumb, strafed the basement floor and scaled the crumbling inner walls to peek out the basement windows. No leaf or flower grew from the roots to identify their source. No bud appeared to hint at an oak or a maple or even some pesky but familiar weed. The fleshy white roots were the final extensions of some unknown beast that found life best where the sun never shone.

The roots scared Andromeda almost as much as the dark.

Sometimes Andromeda would play in the semicircular brick-lined wells sunk into the soil next to the foundation that allowed light to spill down through the dirty panes of the basement windows and into the basement itself. Sometimes Andromeda would drop into a well, wipe away the dirt on the window and peek into this forgotten world that sat right beneath her home, just a few inches beneath her very own bedroom. Every time she did she would see the roots in the dark and get a chill up her spine, not merely because this was a place of cold mystery all to itself, but also because she felt she was being watched. She felt she was being watched by the roots. She would not be surprised if a root monster hand suddenly broke through the glass and yanked her inside to eat her or turn her into a root monster herself. Andromeda the monster would then have to wait in the basement, for years maybe, until the next stupid little girl climbed into one of the wells to wipe away the dirt for a peek into her own surprising doom.

Andromeda could gaze into the gloomy, root-laced interior of the basement for only a few seconds before the terror got to be too much and then she would scream and scramble out of the well, running as far from the house as she could before turning around to make sure no drooling goblins were loping along in pursuit. Panting from her fright, she would wait a long while before venturing back to the house where a monster lived in the basement.

Andromeda lay in her bed and stared at bright Mickey as he shooed away the dark. In her stomach she could feel the tasteless weight of the unwanted navy beans meagerly flavored by ham off the hock. She lay staring at Mickey and wondered about the silence that prevailed more and more often between Mommy and Daddy.

Tonight was no exception and in fact had been the worst episode yet.

Mommy and Daddy hadn't said one word to each other. Andromeda sat as Will sat, head bowed, eyes fixed on the meal. She chewed her navy beans in silence, feeling like a sinner in church. She wondered if she had somehow been the cause of the silence that enshrouded the Wiley household. She knew Will felt it too and wondered when he would explain to her what it was all about.

The loose frames of the double-hung window rattled slightly in the dying wind from the weak storm that had passed over the Wiley farm in the early evening. Through the gaps in the window the newly lain moisture wafted fresh and earthy vapors to Andromeda as she lay staring at Mickey. The familiar vapors soothed her, making her feel safe and calming her distress over the worrying silence between Mommy and Daddy.

Mickey and the vapors helped to calm Andromeda so much that a few minutes later she closed her eyes and fell right to sleep.

Andromeda heard the voice.

It was loud enough to wake her.

She sat up slowly, groggy from sleep, and listened. The voice was cold and low. The only thing Andromeda knew for sure was that it was in her room.

Andromeda held her breath to listen. What was it saying? What did it want? Why wouldn't it just say what it had to say, shut up and go away?

The voice appeared nine months earlier at the end of a terrible three-day argument between Mommy and Daddy over something called a "morgage." Since then, the voice surfaced in different parts of her room— the light switch, a stuffed toy giraffe on her bed, even a pair of shoes tossed on the floor.

The voice showed up without notice during the night, mumbling Andromeda awake and then quickly quieting, leaving her to fall back into a troubled slumber.

After each of the first four visits Andromeda ran to tell her parents, thinking they would make the voice go away or at least identify it. She was told each time that she was imagining something she positively knew she was not. When the fifth visit came and went, Andromeda decided to keep the news to herself.

This current visit was the sixth. Again it followed an argument between Mommy and Daddy, and again Andromeda would do the same as she had before. She would keep silent.

Andromeda tried to judge where the voice was coming from. Maybe this time it would turn out to be the corner of her metal shelving or maybe it would come from the fractured plastic paperweight with the dandelion puff inside that sat on top of her dresser. Usually the voice was a man's, but it could change midcourse and be that of a little girl, a little boy and even an old, old woman. Whatever form it took, it always spoke just below the threshold of intelligibility.

As Andromeda tried to pinpoint the source of this latest visit, it quickly dawned on her that this one was different. It wasn't just that the voice seemed to come from all over, sounding like many people at once or that after more than a few minutes the voices were still talking.

What was different on this sixth uninvited visit was that Andromeda's room was utterly dark.

In all directions she saw nothing but pitch black. She couldn't see her closet, she couldn't see her toy chest, she couldn't see her windows, her bed or even her hands. She couldn't see anything and she was beginning to get scared. This was the darkest dark she had ever seen, and in this dark there was one thing she could not see at all that she always expected to see.

Where was Mickey?

The question was pushed aside as slowly, and without real notice, the dark lifted and was gone. Andromeda blinked the dark from her eyes and saw she was standing on a plain like the ones outside Wishbone—the last remnants of the buffalo stomping grounds that once stretched unbroken all the way into Canada. A cool and featureless cloud cover filled the sky, taming the light of the hidden sun.

Each breath Andromeda drew came with effort. The air seemed oppressively heavy, as if it were part cotton. Spinning around in her pajamas, Andromeda saw nothing to break the monotonous landscape of stone-still grass.

Yet even though it was dead, dead quiet, she felt she was not alone.

"Mommy?"

And suddenly it was there.

A tornado rode the horizon, tearing down from the solidly overcast sky. At first it was tiny and far distant, but as Andromeda watched, it drifted left, then right, and then it began to head straight for her. The wind began to rage and grass shoots flung themselves over the plains like needle-thin arrows.

Andromeda began to run.

Feeling the dried coarseness of the grass on her bare soles, she pushed through the stinging prairie, her hair whipping past her face. Her pajamas stretched forward, flapping madly in the suddenly howling gale, and her body was pushed along by the invisible force of speeding air.

Andromeda ran to escape the step of the wind giant. But no matter how fast she ran she could feel the howling giant catching up. She looked back over her shoulder to see how close the speeding twister had come. What she saw made her stumble and fall. This cyclone was not the usual swirl of dirt, debris and some neighbor's battered barn.

It was a towering spiral of shining, scarlet, liquid blood.

Amid the slick and dark fluid that rose from earth to sky, popping out in terrible clarity, were hundreds of heads and arms and legs, all roughly severed and torn as if rent by a beast of astounding ferocity. Ripped apart were men, women and children of all ages, all grotesquely lathered in matted blood and mutilated innards. Ragged scars cleaved skin in vivid streaks. Flayed muscles and ruptured organs spilled from skulls and chests in pulsating drains. The odor of a thousand maggot-eaten corpses flowed over Andromeda and filled her nostrils with the taste of decay.

There was a viscous gluttony to the cyclone, a terrifying greed.

It was hungry.

As the twisting carnage bore down on Andromeda, clearly intending to suck her in, the blood-splattered faces of the severed heads, their neck veins and accordionlike esophagi dangling freely at the rip of tissue and bone, suddenly turned her way to wail a unified shriek of torture and grief. Wide eyes fixed on Andromeda, staring out from terrified faces real and knowable, faces that seemed so helplessly ordinary, and in those eyes Andromeda saw the final fright of prey in the mouth of the predator.

The damned horde screamed, and in that hellish chorus Andromeda heard a tragic sorrow.

It was a terrible sadness more profound than anything little Andromeda could have possibly encountered in her short life, the kind of haunted melancholy left by a vanished people over a span of centuries, with roots infinitely tangled through time and history.

The sorrow bit deep, digging through Andromeda's feeble defenses to plant a festering clone hard in her heart. In an instant Andromeda knew their pain.

It was fresh but primordial.

It was eternal.

Weeping, not just for herself but in empathy and pity for the poor unfortunates swallowed by the vortex that would spin down on her at any moment, Andromeda looked up and suddenly recognized her own severed head amid the jellied mass of churning flesh.

She finally decided to scream.

. . .

Will raced downstairs and reached Andromeda before Peter or Sandra had fully awakened. He flicked on the lights and rocked his little sister by her shoulders, holding her tightly to still her piercing screams.

"It's okay! It's okay! Andie! It's okay!"

Andromeda suddenly looked Will in the face and knew him. She cried and dropped her head onto his shoulder. Peter staggered in, rubbing the sleep from his eyes as Sandra slogged halfway down the steps to call over the railing, "What's going on?"

"Andie had a nightmare."

Andromeda sniffled, her sobs diminishing.

"It . . . it wasn't a nightmare. It was the voice. He . . . he was here again. He was mean."

Peter sat between his two children on Andromeda's bed. He yawned deeply and worked to stretch loose the knot formed in his neck by sleeping on a lumpy pillow and a sagging mattress. Then he put a reassuring arm around his frightened daughter.

"Honey, there isn't a voice—"

"There is! It's a man or sometimes it's a lady and this time it tried to get me, and I never did anything to it! How come no one believes me?" Andromeda renewed crying and put her face in her hands. The tears worked through the cracks between her fingers. "There *is* a voice."

"Then tell me where it is and I'll get rid of it, okay?"

Andromeda lifted her face to Peter's, wiped her eyes and scanned the room.

"It was everywhere."

As Andromeda scanned her room, again trying to decide what object or corner or part of the wall was the source of the voice, Peter looked to Will.

"Have you ever heard anything?"

"Uh-uh. All I hear at night is crickets and stuff." Will's face contorted in concern, showing a desire to believe his little sister. "Maybe whatever it is, is in the basement. Andie's room is right over it. Maybe somebody's sneaking in at night. Maybe that's what she's hearing."

Andromeda stiffened.

"The basement?"

Peter stood concerned, suddenly thinking Will might be right.

"I'll have a look."

Watching Peter leave, Andromeda turned to Will and clutched his arm. "I don't want Daddy in the basement. I don't want the basement."

"Why, what's in the basement?"

Andromeda spoke in her tiniest whisper.

"The monster, Will. There's a monster down there."

TWO

THE BASEMENT

It was a whole lot harder opening the door than it had been shutting it. For one, Peter had to dig up a pair of bolt cutters to break the lock. Following that, he found the years had swollen the door impossibly tight in the frame, and he labored with a lever bar to break its grip on the jamb. When the door finally began moving, it screeched like a wounded crow. Both Andromeda and Will, standing in the hall behind Peter as he huffed and labored with the stubborn door, shivered at the screech.

Fifteen minutes after he started, Peter took hold of the doorknob and drew the basement door open for the first time in seven years.

Once free of the jamb it swung without friction, slowed only by trailing cobwebs and a single, pale root that had climbed the staircase to encircle the inner knob. Andromeda shrank from the closeness of the dreaded root, the ivory finger of the root monster below, and hid behind her big brother.

It was cold and pitch black beyond the first few steps, utterly devoid of light. Peter reached in to find the light cord that ran through eyelets to the bare bulb hanging somewhere in the dark below. Suddenly, Andromeda snapped.

"Nooo, stop!"

She shoved her face into Will's back. Peter leaned back to Andromeda.

"Honey, I'm just going to turn on the light."

He played his hand along the underside of the joists, wary of black widows and such. Still remembering the placement of the cord after seven years, he found the braided cloth ring and gave the string a tug.

It broke and the light did not go on.

"Shit—I mean . . . it broke."

Peter pulled the long string back and balled it up.

"You two stay here; I'll get the flashlight."

Andromeda fidgeted.

"Hurry."

As Peter left for the kitchen, Will and Andromeda looked down into the dark. Will tried to keep his voice light.

"Boy, it sure is dark . . . down . . . there. . . ."

He suddenly felt its presence in the dark.

It made no noise, it moved no air, but it was suddenly real. There really was something in the basement.

Will felt a dark chill unlike any temperature drop he had ever experienced. The cold held desire. It was looking for someone, and the first person it had found after years of isolation was Will.

An electric fear shot through Will, slamming through his neck and flooding his body. He stepped back, pinning Andromeda between his back and the wall opposite the basement entry.

"Will, you're squishing me."

Will's throat closed up. He felt a wincing panic he had never before known. Time slowed even as his heart raced wildly, filling him with the urge to flee. Yet he couldn't get the message through to his legs. He suddenly realized whatever was in the basement was on the move.

It was starting up the steps.

When he heard one of the lower steps bowing as if under a tremendous weight, as if a rhino were stepping on a thin plank of pine, Will found movement and reached out to slam the door.

Peter caught the door on its swing back as he returned with a flashlight. "What're you doing?"

"Dad, we don't need to see anymore. Close the door. *Close the door.*"

"I want to see. I haven't been down there in years."

Peter clicked on the flashlight and aimed it down the steps.

Andromeda and Will gasped, expecting to see some lumbering, murderous, fanged and clawed beast crawling up the rotting staircase. But all they saw were tangled roots and scattered bits of rat dung. They eased closer, cautiously intrigued. Peter kicked the roots out of his path. Where the roots broke, pink sap dribbled out and wetted the bone-dry steps.

"Looks like some tree's been making itself at home."

Peter pushed hanging webs from the doorway and started down the steps in a stoop, carefully testing their load-bearing ability before descending.

"Just stay up here until I get the light going, all right?"

Peter hit bottom, his soles sinking a bit into the damp, mottled turf, pushing up small bubbles of long-entombed air. The hairy roots wove a lacy mat of albino tendrils, which crawled from cracks in the dirt cellar wall to run in low-lying, nearly flat meanders to the other side of the room. The roots were veiny white tributaries and capillaries, the smooth wet earth almost like skin. Peter pulled the chain running directly to the light-bulb. Still the light would not work. He glanced back up.

"I'm going to check around."

Peter stepped away and disappeared from Will and Andromeda's view. The ambient glow of his flashlight grew dimmer as he moved farther back in the basement. There was silence. Then Peter's light went out.

A slight breeze crept up from the basement and rustled Will's hair. His spine again shuddered. He knew what it was. Andromeda felt it too. The monster was back.

She screamed.

Will strained to look down the stairs, unable to pierce the black void as the steps began to clap and groan. Something was coming up. It was big and heavy and it was moving fast.

It was almost there.

Will began to cut loose his own scream when Peter's face suddenly broke into the light from the dreaded darkness.

"What are you two screaming at!"

Sandra, disturbed once more from a restless sleep, called down from upstairs, "Goddammit! Peter, what're you doing down there!"

Peter yelled up.

"It's all right! Christ . . ."

As he heard Sandra grumble back to bed, Peter put his shoulder into the basement door to close it tight and turned a compassionately stern face to his two kids. He spoke in a near whisper as he banged his malfunctioning flashlight against his palm. It suddenly flared back to life.

"Now, I checked the whole place out and there's nothing down there anywhere. There's no footprints, the windows are all locked tight, and the outside entry is nailed shut and all grown over. What you two have to do is quit letting your imaginations get to you."

Will was red with embarrassment.

"Sorry, Dad."

Andromeda, however, was not.

"I think it's bad here now."

Peter's expression was blank. "Will, why don't you let Andie sleep with you tonight."

"Okay, but we're not going to move, are we, Dad?"

Peter shuffled up the stairs to his bedroom. He spoke wearily as he turned from Will's worried look.

"I think we will. . . ."

Will stood motionless for a beat after his father went back to bed. Then he took his sister by the hand and backed away from the closed basement door, starting up to his bedroom as the shock settled in.

His father had just said they might move. It was more than Will could consider. Even with the scary basement this house was the center of his world.

The Wiley farm was Will's turf, the only home he had ever known. Besides two day trips to Wichita and one long weekend to Corpus Christi for the only family vacation he'd ever known, he had never been anywhere beyond it.

In his years on the farm Will had learned the secrets under every rock, up every tree and behind every barn in a half-mile radius. He could identify a place by its sound and even its smell. He knew his land intimately, as only a curious boy could. He knew the residence of every snapping turtle, every muskrat, every groundhog, every fox and every cottonmouth in the region. He knew the best places to find cans, old dinnerware, books, arrowheads and Old West artifacts, and he knew how much his finds were worth, trading the most interesting items for a needed family utensil or two at the Wishbone Trading Post. A Teflon-coated skillet might not be as glamorous as a dented pewter mug either dropped or tossed by a forty-niner heading for the gold rush, but it had a day-to-day value no relic from the past could presently have for the Wiley clan.

Will tried not to complain; he tried to smile when his mood asked for a frown. He did what he could.

On the rare occasion when Will was invited to dinner by one of his few friends he noticed how this friend's parents watched his every move, as if he would pocket an ashtray or the *TV Guide*. He noticed how they stared while he ate, probably believing that as one of the poorer kids in town, he was capable of devouring everything in sight.

Will especially noticed that if the host family felt like arguing, they would just go right at it in front of Will as if he were not even there, as if his presence did not merit any special restraint or respect.

He reacted by taking less food than anybody else. He refused dessert even if he was still starving, and he sat still and silent while the arguments raged. For his actual innocence, he still left feeling guilty over his poorness and wondered if he had not been the cause of the argument.

Will saw a different knowledge in a home where existence was predictably secure, where success was taken for granted. For one, the names that came up in conversation were mostly unfamiliar. Still, Will knew a lot of the places they mentioned. He knew the Azores were part of Portugal. He knew the Acropolis held the Parthenon. Beyond that, Will knew the red spot on Jupiter was really a gigantic storm on a planet of cloud. He even knew comets were big balls of dirty ice. It was knowledge that made Will feel he might someday have a chance to take success for granted too.

For all this knowledge he had his father to thank.

Peter Wiley taught Will about that red spot on Jupiter, the Valley of the Howling Winds in Antarctica, and the Battle of the Little Bighorn, where an arrogant Custer met the last roar of a proud but vanishing race. He taught Will how to build a fire, tell a mole track from a field mouse track, put up a tent and use a hammer. He taught Will about life.

Will's father was stronger, smarter, tougher and quicker than anybody else's dad no matter who they were, including the president. Will knew this was true because he watched his father.

He watched his father get up at five in the morning every day and work the fields until sundown. He watched his father searching for weeks through junkyards for the right gear to fix a broken axle on the tractor. He had seen his father mending fences in three feet of snow during a blizzard.

Will revered his father and believed he always would.

But he had just been told by his revered father the worst thing he could possibly imagine.

The Wileys might move.

It was worse than Andromeda's dreams about the voices because it was real and it was happening.

Leaving the farm had just become Will's living nightmare.

THREE

REGRET

The night passed without another disembodied voice popping up or nightmare calling or whatever it was that pestered Andromeda, and in the morning Sandra was able to make it through breakfast before shuffling back to her room.

In her room, Sandra stared in the mirror as she combed her long hair and wondered what had happened to Sandra Henderson, belle of the ball and Most Popular Miss?

The question had a ready answer.

For the ten thousandth time Sandra recalled the night in early January of senior year when she and Peter left a mid-year pep rally and hiked into the gully nearby. What happened next they couldn't even blame on booze. In a moment hidden beneath a cover of clumsy passion, an egg was pierced and cells began to divide. Receiving verification from a Wichita doctor, Sandra managed to keep it from showing long enough to win Most Popular Miss.

At the prom, as the last special night she would probably ever know wound to a close, she decided to tell Peter he would be a father. Peter staggered off the dance floor and took a seat at the top of the empty bleachers to appreciate for the first time all he had risked in the gully gamble. But for the love of his life he would do what was right.

Peter and Sandra graduated and six days later they married. Four months later, at the end of September, Will was born. Now, more than eight full years had passed, and all Sandra felt for conception night and the marriage that followed was something approaching total regret.

Sandra loved her children but couldn't help thinking that as a result of their two births her life was heading nowhere at a pace that seemed both terminally slow and ruefully short.

Every day she saw more weatherbeaten farmer-lines streaking across her temples, creasing open with exacting familiarity every time she squinted into the sky to see what evil would befall her next. She had become the kind of person a dream Sandra would look right past. The dream Sandra sat on a carved sofa before a detailed fireplace in a room lit by crystal chandeliers. The real Sandra sat on a rickety stool before a cracking vanity in a room where the lights always flickered.

Sandra looked around at her pit of a farmhouse and hated everything about it. She hated the idiots dead for a hundred years who built it in the first place. She hated the whole idea of farming and living off the land because it was all a big lie. As jokes go it wasn't funny at all. Sandra would swap it for an urban dive anyday. She'd take the noise, the pollution, the traffic, the lost privacy, the confined space, the rude people and the random crime and she'd take them gladly. At least she'd be in a place where things were happening.

She was only vaguely aware that when she considered such a fantasy swap she mostly saw herself alone.

All Sandra currently saw as she looked out at the place fate had made her home was a dead end. The harvest, as it were, had come and gone and even though the buyers said it was the sweetest corn they had ever tasted, the total income from the sale was half what the family needed to break even.

The best corn some people had ever tasted and the Wileys couldn't afford to see a movie.

Sandra's eyes tried hard to change what they saw. There was no limit to how much she despised the Wiley farm. It was stealing—and had already stolen—the best years of her life. The home and farm had no equity, only bloated debt and it was all overdue.

And the only thing Sandra knew for sure was that it was about to get even worse.

FOUR

DEBT

Peter worked to keep calm as he stared across the massive desk at a grown-up Denny Sharf. He wondered how it was possible that the nerd who was such an annoying chump in high school, who was always getting spontaneous nosebleeds and who Peter barely knew existed could now possess the key to the Wiley family future.

Not only was it possible, it was true.

Eight and a half years after graduating at the height of his popularity, Peter sat in Denny Sharf's richly paneled office at the Wishbone Savings and Loan and begged Denny for a time out on his life.

"Come on, Denny, you can't tell me there isn't something we can't do."

"Peter, you owe everybody in town, but mostly you owe the S and L. We carry the paper on the farm and at this point I'm pretty sure we're going to have to call it in. That's how I see it."

"But if I could just get a big enough crop . . ."

"No offense, but when have you ever had a full crop? You only get half what you should out of your acreage. I mean, how could you get a full crop the way you farm? You grow without fertilizer because you think the produce tastes better—"

"It does, and it's better for you. You use natural fertilizers and natural pesticides, you find crop strains that resist frosts and all, you let your crops defend themselves; you let them work naturally."

"You let your crops take care of themselves? Now, see, that cuckoo talk has gotten you just where you are now. You bring in a bunch of ladybugs instead of dusting like everyone else does and what do you expect is going to happen? The bugs fly away and leave your harvest for weevils and locusts."

"There's a market for organic produce that's—"

"Full of worms? Half chewed by fruit flies and maggots? I mean, who's complaining about the clean, high-quality produce we already got? I had a salad today and it tasted just fine. Anyway, face it, it just isn't good business to create a product, especially one that won't last more than a few days, for a market that only you think exists." Denny leaned back in his padded leather swivel chair. He picked something from his teeth. "Speaking frankly, you just aren't the farmer type."

"If I could get one full crop I could get everyone paid up; I could at least get back to zero."

"You're not hearing me, Peter. What I'm telling you is if you want to get back to zero it'll be on somebody else's seed." Denny leaned forward to make things even clearer. "The bottom line is your farm is worth less now than the day you bought it, a lot less, and when you lose I'm the one who loses. Old times' sake is one thing, but I have to do my business, Peter. They just made me president so I have to perform. Twenty-seven years old, the youngest president ever . . ."

Peter saw that Denny had paused to allow a comment.

"Twenty-seven . . . That's great."

"Yes, it is. But listen, forget a *new* loan; I need something back on what you already owe, and basically I need it right now. I'm keeping track, and you're so far behind, if you're telling me you don't got it, well . . ." He again leaned back in his luxurious seat, a slight smirk saying it all.

Peter picked at a dried splatch of mud on the knee of his jeans. Watching Denny's prematurely widow's-peaked face glancing in displeasure to the sprinkle of dirt on the immaculate carpeting under Peter's chair, Peter caught himself and put his hands in his lap. He couldn't believe what he was hearing.

"You're telling me you're going to foreclose? On my home? On the place where my family and I live? You know there's only one place we can go and that's to the streets. Come on, think about it."

Denny thought about it.

Denny Sharf, in all his years of schooling, had been a distant satellite to Peter's social center. Denny and his friends were the geeks who read comic books and picked zits and who did not date because they were too intimidated by the opposite sex and its mysteries. Denny had been secretly jealous of Peter then and he was secretly gloating now. Peter Wiley, the big man on campus, was down and out on the farm, and now his entire future hinged on a yes or no from the lips of Denny Sharf.

Peter, who in his nervousness had once again begun to pick at the dirt on his jeans, continued to look to Denny with pleading and hopeful eyes.

"Come on, Denny, just this one last time."

Seeing big man on campus Peter Wiley so desperate made Denny feel like he was the Incredible Hulk. He could do as he pleased and there was no stopping him. Yes or no. A future for Peter Wiley or no future at all.

A future for Sandra Wiley.

Denny replayed a special memory from senior year when the boys were learning to waltz with the girls during physical education class. Eventually Denny was paired up with Sandra Henderson, not yet Wiley.

Sandra's hair, so soft and sweet smelling, brushed against Denny's cheek as he gave her a twirl. At one point her right buttock in all its toned glory bumped into Denny's hip. At another point Sandra's left breast pressed against Denny's left shoulder. Denny was positive he could sense the contour of a nipple.

He soon felt a familiar stirring in his pants.

Denny and Sandra danced closer, Sandra completely unaware of Denny's painfully excited arousal. She danced politely, even though Denny could tell she was not enjoying his company.

As Denny spun and twirled Sandra Henderson across the floor, he thought this secret erotic moment would give him one of his greatest nightcap fantasy sessions to date. Then the moment came that forever de-railed that plan. Jason Coombs and Ron Faith, both tackles on the foot-ball team and pals of Peter's, sneaked up behind Denny and yanked his shorts and athletic supporter to his ankles. Denny fell trying to yank up his shorts. But as he fell he saw that Sandra was looking directly at his crotch and his bobbing adolescent erection.

She saw all of it.

The moment lasted only a second or two before Denny got his shorts back up and got back to his feet. As Coombs and Faith laughed their heads off with the rest of the class and guffawed about the pimples on Denny's ass, Denny waited for Sandra's reaction, knowing she had been the only one to witness his excited condition. He quickly rushed through the up-coming scenarios.

Sandra would laugh at Denny and tell everyone then and there about it, or she would talk about it later and Denny would spend the rest of the year hearing giggles and snickers behind his back as he walked the halls. Sandra might scream and call Denny a pervert and Denny would be brought before the principal to face disciplinary punishment. That would be bad.

Or maybe, just maybe, Sandra would be turned on by the sight.

Maybe later that night she would knock on Denny's window and she would crawl into his bedroom to get naked, lying down on his bed with her legs spread to let Denny enter her perfection as he explored every inch of her perfect body. At that thought Denny could feel a new pressure on his athletic supporter.

"Uhhh, Sandra, I, uhh . . . "

"I don't think we should dance anymore, Denny."

Sandra did not laugh, she did not scream, she did not show up at Denny's for a midnight rendezvous and she did not talk about it later. Denny was never subjected to giggles and whispers in the hall. If he was, they were only about the pimples on his ass. All Sandra said was that one sentence to Denny and then she never said another word to him again.

It was the cruelest punishment possible.

As the days passed, Denny began to want Sandra to tell her girlfriends about his boner. At least it would have proved she had seen it, verifying their shared erotic moment. But her silence made Denny and his boner feel totally irrelevant. He wasn't even good enough for a joke? His boner wasn't interesting enough for giggles and snickers? Denny was sure Sandra never thought another thing about him.

He despised her for it.

Denny looked across to Peter, the simpering idiot who did not know the love of his life had gazed upon the wide-eyed weenie of Denny Sharf.

Peter tried to keep from picking more dirt from his knee.

"I know Sandra would appreciate it even more than I would."

That bitch. Denny decided right then and there.

"I wish I could help, I just can't. I'm sorry."

"Not even—"

"Look, Peter, I can't help you, okay? Better luck next time."

Peter stood slowly in stunned disbelief. The entire clod of dirt on his knee fell to the carpet. He looked down at it and dropped to begin picking up tiny bits of dirt with one hand, depositing them in the palm of the other. Denny stood and peered over the edge of his desk as Peter knelt on the floor.

"Forget about it. The night maid'll sweep it up. That's what we pay her for."

Peter again stood, his hand now full of dirt, and looked about for a place to toss it. Not seeing anything handy, he shoved both hand and dirt into his pocket. With eyes downcast and mind racing, he started out the door.

"Sorry to bother you."

Denny moved to the front of his desk and sat on the edge.

"You got two weeks, and then I'm afraid there's nothing else I can do. And don't think I'm not sorry as hell about it." Denny wasn't; he wasn't sorry at all. In fact, he felt even more satisfaction as he watched Peter's shoulders sag farther. "Say hi to the kids, and give Sandra my love."

"Sure. I'll see you around."

Denny watched through the glass pane of his office door as Peter shuffled past the teller windows and left the bank. It wouldn't take a detective to see Peter Wiley was a man with a serious burden. And Denny had just doubled it.

Denny smiled and thanked God for his wonderful, wonderful job.

Peter scraped the corrosion off the battery terminals to start his truck engine, climbed in to sit on a seat held together by long stretches of duct tape, grabbed the cracked steering wheel and backed out onto Main Street for the drive home. It would be the longest drive of his life.

He could picture exactly the look he would get from Sandra. It would be the look given somebody who has unconditionally failed you.

What a change from the adoring looks Sandra gave Peter in high school. Back then, before the zygote took root, Peter could do no wrong. He was the most eligible of eligibles, and Sandra was at the top of her form. She won Peter's heart and together they became the envy of all.

Now all Peter could think was, *What a crock.*

Who gave the first shit now how far he once threw a pass or how much twinkle he once had in his eye? Sandra sure didn't. She told him so every single day.

Through the defensive wall Peter had reluctantly constructed to ward off Sandra's contempt, he knew what he really wanted was to again hear her happy laugh and to see her bright smile. He missed the look of respect she used to turn his way. He missed it more than anything. Just once he wanted to make her glad she had chosen to stay with him. Just once he wanted Sandra to feel proud she was married to Peter Wiley.

With a hard finality, Peter knew today would not be that day.

"So that's it."

With that said, Sandra rose from the dining table and moved to the sink to finish cleaning the lunch meal of hard potato pancakes off the skillet. Peter looked at her strong back as she scrubbed the pan with a pad of soaped steel wool.

Sandra's reaction to the news that the Wiley family would be homeless in less than two weeks was eerily restrained. Peter was cautious.

"Where are Andie and Will? I should tell them."

"They're in the barn." Sandra set down the pan and turned to Peter, wiping her hands on her apron. "Peter, why don't you just let them have a few more nights of not knowing. There's nothing they can do about our situation; no reason to tell them until it's time for us to . . . until we have to go."

Peter nodded, appreciating that he and Sandra were, for this instant at least, in total sync.

He thought it might be one of the increasingly rare moments, grown so hard to identify, when he could get through to Sandra, when he and she could talk in the patient and calm way they once did as a matter of course.

He took the chance that this was such a moment.

"I really thought I did everything to make sure we didn't come to this, Sandy. I run it through my head and I don't see what else I could have done. I know I'm right on this thing. People want foods that are grown chemical free. I know they do." Sandra continued to look at Peter with an attentively blank face. Peter took it as a sign she was willing to hear more. "We just have to get more crop per acre. We just have to get past this bad luck that keeps hitting us."

"The only luck we hit is the kind we make ourselves, and we've been making it for more than eight years." She took a few breaths in silence. "So he wouldn't say anything—just two weeks, that's all he said?"

"That's all."

"That Denny is such a piece of shit. He's really going to toss us out of here? He's going to toss us out just because we're a few months behind even though he knows there's nobody on earth who wants this place?"

"I want this place."

"You know what I mean." The patient calm began to dissipate. Sandra started to huff again. "He's such a piece of shit."

"He's just doing his job."

"His job? You know we're paying four points more in interest than anybody else in town? You know that, don't you? That four points is what's killing us, and the only reason we pay it is because that piece of shit Denny knew we couldn't get a loan anyplace else. Maybe we didn't do the greatest job on this place, and you know how I feel about your organic thing. . . . All I'm saying is that little prick didn't do us any favors."

"Well, whatever. What we have to do is figure out what we're doing next. I thought maybe we should go down Monday to talk to the people at the welfare office."

Sandra stiffened.

"You can't be serious. We're not doing welfare."

"In two weeks we're going to be on the streets. We need help and we won't get it from anybody around here. If we do the welfare for a month or two—"

"I'm not going to see us on welfare, Peter. I'm not going to go into town to pay for things with food stamps. I couldn't . . . and I don't even want to hear about us standing in lines with a bunch of lowlifes waiting for a handout. We're not one of those people."

"Fine. I'll get a job and I'll get us a new place, but that won't be happening right away unless we get some help. If we keep the truck, we got maybe three hundred bucks when I sell whatever Denny doesn't own. How long can that last? Another two weeks? A month? Then what?"

Sandra didn't know. All she knew was that however this equation turned out, she would retain what she had left of her dignity.

"I don't take handouts."

Sandra and Peter glared at each other from their sadly familiar corners as opponents. Peter stood and moved to the coatrack, grabbing his jacket. Sandra was not yet finished with her say.

"Where are you going?"

"To town. If we're not going to get help, then I don't have any time to waste looking for that job, do I?"

"All right, but don't apply for anything that'll make us look bad."

"Like what?"

"The hamburger stand or the car wash. We don't want people seeing every day how bad off we are. My husband does not flip burgers."

Out of breath from playing in the window wells, believing more than ever in the basement monster, Andromeda skipped up the porch, into the house and into the kitchen. She found her two parents standing as far apart as the small room would permit.

"Dad, can I sleep with you and Mom tonight?"

"Ask your mother." Peter put on his jacket and walked out of the house.

Hearing her father clomp to the truck, start it up and peel out of the gravel drive, Andromeda knew something was wrong and was no longer sure if she should ask. But her mother was standing right there and had heard everything.

"Is it okay?"

Sandra turned to Andromeda and didn't alter her hard expression in the slightest.

"Is what okay?"

"If I sleep with you and Dad tonight. I'm afraid of that voice."

"Andie, there's no voice, and since there's no voice there's no reason for you to be crowding us out of our bed. And don't ask Will either. You're old enough to sleep alone and you're old enough to know when a dream is just a dream. Understand?"

She didn't but decided to say she did.

"Yes."

"All right, now take yourself outside; I need to clean up in here."

Andromeda turned glumly and left, frightened by the prospect of sleeping by herself and receiving another visit from the voice.

For Sandra's part, as she grabbed the broom to sweep and watched Andromeda go, she found herself casually wondering how different life would be if Andromeda and Will had simply never existed in the first place.

Now, that was a real dream.

FIVE
FACELESS

At Vale's Chevrolet Peter was turned down because former mayor Tommy Vale, who was running against current mayor Donald Moser, had many fine mechanics working for him already, including his two sons. Tommy slapped a hot pad with the former mayor's smiling face printed on both sides into Peter's palm. A caption beneath the photo on one side read, A VOTE FOR VALE IS A VOTE FOR VICTORY! The caption on the other side was a promo for the next model year of Chevy cars and trucks. It read, YOU'LL FIND WHAT YOU NEED AT VALE'S, INDEED! Before Peter could give his thanks, Vale abandoned him to close in on a potential customer just walking in the door.

Peter stepped out, moved between all the shiny new Chevrolets in the lot, stopped at the street edge and wondered where to go next.

He had tried just about every business in town where manual labor was needed. Disregarding Sandra's objections, he had even applied to flip burgers at the Giant Burger. There were no openings anywhere and as the day went on Peter discovered his own predicament was preceded by a long line of economic heartbreaks. Farmers he had always thought were doing okay he now learned were bankrupt and homeless and taking jobs at places like the car wash and the burger stand.

Peter began to realize the first thing he was going to need to get a job in Wishbone, Kansas, was something along the lines of a miracle.

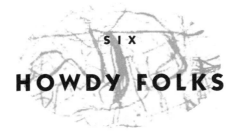

SIX

HOWDY FOLKS

Mary Hayworth Downes was the richest person in Wishbone.

Mary owned a liquor store, two clothing stores, the Wishbone Trading Post and the Tumbleweed Pub. She also owned the Wishbone Historical Museum, a sort of library, artifact exhibition hall, souvenir shop and hot dog emporium that took up the entire first floor of city hall and the chamber of commerce. Tourists coming into Wishbone who wanted to get some information on the town's history needed to pass Mary's enticing displays before heading upstairs for the free pamphlets happily given out by Jason Coombs's mother, Dottie. Mary, who ran the museum in person while leaving her other businesses in the hands of Vincent Proctor, Wishbone's chief resident lawyer and accountant, often made a sale due to the fact that the stairs were at the back of the building and most tourists opted to send only one family member up while the others stayed below to browse.

A direct descendant of Wishbone's founding father, Lieutenant Jeremiah Hayworth, Mary told the tent-slept tourists in from Nebraska or Quebec that she was also a direct descendant of Belle Starr, the western outlaw's guardian angel, who died at the hands of an unknown gun, even though a simple flip through any of the western histories on Mary's own shelves would expose her colorful fib. Mary dressed the part in a red-and-white buckskin jacket and skirt loaded with silver buttons, clasps and baubles. She wore a white felt rodeo-queen hat with white leather gloves and white leather boots, all broadly trimmed in red.

At age forty-seven Mary had a slightly less maintained version of her once fine physical shape and all-around good health. She ate quickly and forgot flavor as she chewed the first bite. She saw no tragedy while experiencing no happiness. Since the loss of her husband, Emerson Downes, to a withering bout of pneumonia twelve years earlier, Mary lived a life of sighing blandness.

She was a widow who did not relish the role.

She had been a rambling soul in her youth, leapfrogging county and state to discover the direction of her future before meeting Emerson in the personnel office of a now defunct south Texas oil prospecting and drilling outfit. She fell in love. Emerson sincerely loved her back and asked Mary to be his wife. Luck smiled on them when Mary's Aunt Clarisse passed away and left a fortune about which Mary had been only dimly aware. Mary and Emerson made their way to Wishbone to accept the inheritance and found they practically owned the town. Their new wealth allowed a few good years together before Emerson was torn from Mary by the killer in his lungs.

Mary had long since moved beyond loneliness. She knew only a featureless space populated by an unending nothingness. She met new faces by the thousands yet they all blurred into Average Joes and Average Janes with their Average Kids. Distinction was lost on Mary as she internalized her universe and showed the outside world a happy mask, telling jokes and asking, "Where y'all from?"

Her happy mask was smiling as Peter Wiley walked in, and Mary saw in Peter's face the same sort of aimless desperation Mary often felt as she sat alone at home listening to the needling silence that worked to overpower the companion ticks of her numerous appliances. Peter had the same evident need that Mary had struggled so mightily to hide, making it obvious he had yet to build his own happy mask.

He asked her for work. Any work.

"I can sweep up, I can clean the gutters, patch the roof, whatever you need. Just pay me what you think the work is worth."

Mary had heard this same mantra from too many others who'd hit bottom long before Peter had even begun his fall. In each case she gave the same response.

"Already got a handyman. Can't help at all."

Peter nodded quietly.

"Sorry to bother you, Mrs. Downes."

"No bother. Good luck to you and yours."

As Peter started off, Mary pictured little Will and remembered how the hard-working boy had always been a good source for local antiquities. She did not wish to see the boy suffer just because his two parents were morons at farming. But there was nothing she could do. She would not put her neighbors on the dole. Still, advice was free, so she offered it.

"Peter?"

Peter stopped and turned.

"Yeah?"

"I was you I might think about headin' to where the work is."

"I've been in Wishbone all my life. Same as Sandra, Will and Andie. Not ready to think about moving to another town—"

"Or even another state. Think it over. I just don't wanna see y'all hangin' on when there most likely won't ever be anything for ya here. It ain't just solitary folks who are hurtin'. This dog's lost its bite."

"What do you mean?"

"I mean Wishbone ain't a place you aim for no more. This here, this is just a stop on people's way to something else. You see it like that, you'll see what I mean. Don't make this place your end, Peter, make it a stop."

"I'll think about it. Be seeing you."

Mary watched Peter go for a moment before aiming her happy mask at the next wave of tourists, possibly European, now passing through her saloon-styled doors. Then she folded herself in a narcotic envelope of sameness and routine and gave them a big, wide smile.

"Howdy, folks! Where y'all from?"

SEVEN

THE WRECKING BALL

As the days passed and the moment of eviction drew nearer, Peter and Sandra did their chores as if there were nothing out of the ordinary. But as their two children watched them packing up whatever the family could fit into the truck when it left for parts unknown, Peter and Sandra understood the subject had to be broached. They sat Will and Andromeda down and told them they had to leave.

Will was, predictably, most injured by the news.

"Where will we go?"

It was such an obvious question, yet neither Peter nor Sandra had prepared a response. All either could do was mutter an answer that reassured no one.

"We'll see."

Andromeda accepted the news gladly. In seconds she was back climbing the lightning-struck oak. Betrayed by Andromeda's casual dismissal of the only home the family had ever known, Will did what his emotions allowed.

He ran away.

It took Peter five hours of tromping through the creeks and gullies of Will's turf to discover the impressive cave fort Will had built from construction scrap, into the hillside of a long abandoned and overgrown quarry. Peter swung open the door to the fort and saw Will hunched in the corner.

"Will? What are you doing?"

"Sitting." He raised a face filled with suspicion and dismay to his father's. "Why do we have to go?"

Peter crouched and passed into the well-engineered interior. He sat next to his son.

"I'm sorry, Will. I really am. Your mother and I know how much you love the farm. We've been trying to hold on, but we . . . we can't do it anymore. The farm is too much."

"So you sold it."

"We never owned the farm in the first place. It belongs to the bank, always has. And now they want it back."

"But we live here."

"Lots of people live in places they don't own. And sometimes it costs a lot of money to live in those places."

"It cost a lot to live where we live?"

"Not as much as some, but . . . well, it cost more than we had. So we have to find another place. I'll get some other work; we'll get this whole thing settled. Then we'll see about getting our own place, one we own, so the bank can't ever tell us to leave. How does that sound?"

"I guess it's okay. When?"

Peter ran through a scenario in his head where everything went his way; the date when he would own a home was still years off. But now was not the time for bald truth. The lie continued.

"We'll be in a new home before you know it."

The red Cadillac with white leather interior navigated the stretch of gravel leading to the Wiley front porch and Denny Sharf emerged with foreclosure papers in hand. Sandra excused herself, opting not to greet Denny. She shut herself in her room as Peter opened the door to a guest for the last time and sat in the kitchen to relinquish the ownership and keys to the Wiley home. Denny struggled to appear sympathetic.

"I hope you don't hold this too much against me."

"Denny, look, I'd rather not even talk about it. Just tell me where to sign."

Denny pointed to lines on the papers.

"Here, here, here and here, and make sure you date it."

Peter scrawled his signature where directed and remembered to date it. He handed the papers back to Denny. Denny placed them in an accordion file, which Peter could not help but notice was full of similar papers for other Wishbone families. Peter wondered if Denny wasn't getting some satisfaction from lording his position over his less fortunate neighbors.

Denny didn't wonder because he knew he was.

There were a lot of people who used to ignore him who now had to pay him their fullest attention. Old Man Jones, who used to run the drugstore but who now occupied a closet-sized cubicle in a nursing home in Dallas, used to give Denny the evil eye over some argument Jones had with Denny's stubborn father when Denny's father ran the S & L. Denny called in the loan on Jones and handed the bank a drugstore, which they sold for a tidy profit to out-of-town investors who quickly tore down the structure that had stood since Wishbone's founding and put in its place a bright and shiny Bob's Big Boy.

That wouldn't be the fate of the Wiley farm. It wouldn't get a Bob's.

Denny would divide the Wiley land into quarter-acre lots, creating a mini-subdivision of single family homes. The fact that the rear of the property bordered a creek made the idea more attractive. He would call the place Royal Oak Gardens, even though there was barely a tree in sight.

But first he had to clear out the current occupants, and with the signed papers in hand he was ready to do so. He held out his palm for the keys.

"You're giving me all the sets, right?"

"You get everything, Denny."

Peter handed Denny the keys and then moved into the living room. Andromeda and Will sat on the couch, Will more glum than he had ever been in his life, Andromeda impatient to go. The truck was loaded, the kids had gone potty and Peter had their room at the Red Cottage Lodge off the interstate paid up for their temporary stay. There was only one thing he needed to get.

Peter called up the steps to Sandra.

Denny stifled a thrill as Sandra stepped out from the upstairs bedroom and descended the staircase with her head held high. Sandra didn't even look at Denny as he stood waiting for a greeting. She addressed the kids.

"Get in the truck. We'll be out in a minute."

Andromeda happily skipped out to the truck, but as Will left he gave Denny a look of pure hatred. Denny ignored it. Instead, he continued to stare at Sandra as she and Peter gathered up the last of their things.

Denny's eyes strayed over the curve of Sandra's back and down to her still shapely rear. As she turned to grab a suitcase, Denny let his eyes fall on her breasts and he noticed she was not wearing a bra. Just a hint of what lay beneath the cotton fabric poked through and Denny again felt the hot flush of fantasy.

Sandra gave one last look around and faced the door.

"Let's go."

Peter did not say a word as he followed his wife out to the truck. He just climbed in as she climbed in, started the truck and drove away from the only home they had known for the last eight years.

When the sound of the truck died down, Denny turned to survey his acquisition.

The house was hopelessly tattered so it was clear there would be no point in trying to move it off the land. This was a definite tear-down. But it did have at least one charm. Seconds earlier it had been the home of Sandra Wiley, née Henderson, Most Popular Miss. The aroma of her presence still filled the air.

Denny decided to soak up whatever remained of that presence.

He stood triumphant in the master bedroom. He licked his drying lips as he imagined Sandra in the nude lying on the now stripped bed, maybe playing with herself, maybe squeezing her breasts and pinching her nipples, maybe thinking of Denny as she did.

Moving into the bathroom Denny grew even more excited. On the floor he found a few hairs, long straight ones and short, thicker curly ones in Sandra's color. These special artifacts were not simply from Sandra, they were Sandra herself.

Unable to contain his arousal, Denny checked the farm perimeter out the window and then climbed out of his clothing as he expanded his rape of Sandra Wiley's misfortune. As he stood naked in Sandra Wiley's bathroom with his recurrent boner, Denny brought Sandra's private hairs to his nose and sniffed.

"You little twat."

Gripping his boner as if it were a dousing rod leading him to ecstasy, Denny first stopped in Sandra's bedroom to roll around on her marvelously worn mattress and savor the notion that here he lay naked where only hours earlier Sandra had done the same. As he continued his delighted tour, running through the house to work toward climax over his possession of Sandra's world, he tried to find the right spot to plant his conqueror's flag.

Denny made his way through the living room, the dining room, the kitchen, the mud room, peeking into the first-floor bathroom, a closet, Andromeda's old room and another closet. He checked out the entire first floor until he found himself passing the open door to the dank and gloomy basement.

Three steps later he stopped.

His first thought was that the door to the basement had been closed when he entered the house. Turning around, he could not deny its current gaping suction. Denny cautiously moved to the mysteriously open doorway and peered down.

In the very dim light seeping in from the well windows he could only make out that the dirt floor was laced with white roots. But the cold mustiness that crawled up the steps and caressed Denny's naked body suggested a certain sensuality, beckoning him into the womb below. Denny thought running naked in the basement would be like running naked out in the open. It was illicit; it was seductive and forbidden. As another waft of chilled air tingled the hairs on his body, Denny decided running naked in the basement was something he would do.

He started down the steps. They creaked with each ginger descent. He could barely contain his excitement and massaged himself with a new vigor.

"Yes . . ."

And then his bare foot caught on a root that casually crossed the steps.

In a poorly executed flip, Denny tumbled five steps to his naked back and landed hard in the middle of the steps. With the full force of his weight thudding with so direct an impact on steps that had been breakfast, lunch and dinner to generations of woodworms and termites, the entire structure of the basement staircase riotously joined Denny in his collapse. As Denny continued his roll to land face first in the muck, the staircase gave way and crashed to the side, groaning loudly as it crumbled in a pile of splinters and rusty nails.

Feeling real pain, as if his tailbone had been snapped free, Denny lifted his face from the muck. Bubbles of trapped air rose up and burst open, releasing a foul, rotten stench. Denny took in a lungful.

Staggering to his feet, feeling a sick fear and embarrassment more intense than any he had felt in his life, mud-covered Denny spun to look toward the open doorway. It was now out of his reach.

"Oh no, oh no . . ."

The muck oozed between his naked toes. He felt more than naked. He felt exposed.

Without a thought for his waning boner, Denny began to wonder how he was going to get out.

He allowed self-pity as he rushed to the foundation wall beneath the open doorway and began leaping to reach the lip. But each leap missed and compressed the root-laced muck even further.

There was no way he could be found like this. If he was found naked in the Wileys' basement there would be no believable excuse. He would be revealed, and this time he would face true shame. This time there would be much more than mere snickers behind his back about the pimples on his ass.

This time he would be outcast for certain.

Denny stood naked in the muck, witnessing the final nosedive of his already challenged reputation. And in this moment of quiet, painfully lonely but highly lucid reflection, it suddenly chose to hit.

Without warning, Denny was no longer alone.

Invisible and formless, a malicious nausea swept over Denny, filling him with an urgent and indescribable fright. Denny, who had been afraid often, was suddenly afraid like never before.

His rational brain told him this fear had nothing to do with his captivity, yet he could not fight its coming. He was assaulted by an alien terror honed to its sharpest edge.

The terror cut deep.

Denny crumpled to his knees, and his hands sank into the muck. Shivering with fear, he began crying in an uncontrolled rush. His stomach chewed itself as the acids boiled to bursting.

"Wha . . . w-what's h-happening?"

He looked around but there was nothing to see. He was alone in the basement. The door above was open; no madman had shown his face. Yet Denny knew he was dying of fright.

He wondered if he was having a heart attack. Too frightened to scream, he dizzily lifted himself to his feet and staggered in blind circles around the basement floor. His skin was breaking out in a cold sweat, and he labored to breathe the still, stale air. His ears rang and his head throbbed. In another minute he positively knew he would be dead. He had to get away from this smothering doom.

Something in the basement was trying to kill him.

"H-help . . . help!"

His muscles spasmed. His left arm was going numb. He guessed his right arm would soon follow and he would be trapped for sure.

Denny scoured the basement for an avenue to escape. Reaching down to the collapsed staircase he struggled to tear free some plank or post he could stand on to give him the lift he needed to set himself free. But the nausea blitzing his now weak stomach made him swoon with the effort and he again collapsed in the stinking muck.

It would take days for them to find his naked and bloated corpse. The shame in his discovery would cross county lines and be told as a campfire tale along with stories about people losing fingers, arms and faces in accidents that could happen to anyone. The name Denny Sharf would become the local pseudonym for "sicko pervert."

Prone in the muck, Denny feebly glanced toward the dirt wall of the basement beneath one of the windows. Here many roots emerged. Denny, thinking past this harrowing battle against things unseen, realized that he might use the roots as handholds to lift himself to the basement window.

Fighting hard to keep from vomiting, he again stood and moved to the wall, dragging roots and muck. He took hold of the roots and pulled to test their strength. They held. Denny began climbing the wall with the last of his strength, feeling it fading with each grab. His feet slipped often in the climb and he repeatedly slammed into the wall.

"Come on!"

But slowly, as the cold sweat slipping from his pores mingled with the foul muck coating his naked body, Denny made progress. He reached the window and the roots still held. He held himself tight in place with one hand as he undid the latch on the basement window and swung it up.

The fresh air from outside acted like a shot of adrenaline. He reached out and pulled himself into the brick-lined well.

He was free. The fear vanished as rapidly as it had come.

Denny sat for a moment to catch his breath. He glanced into the dark of the hated basement and wanted nothing more than to get as far from it as possible. He needed to get away now. He peered over the edge of the well to make certain nobody was in the vicinity. Seeing that the coast was clear, he scrambled out to run, muddy and naked, back into the house.

Retrieving his clothes from the upstairs bathroom and quickly pulling them over his filthy body, Denny ran back down and staggered out of the house, tripping off the porch to fall flat on his face in the stinging gravel. Once outside, his guts finally let loose and splashed his lunch to the ground.

He made his way to his car, fumbling his keys free. He would drive home, clean up and then vow never to tell a soul exactly what had happened to Denny Sharf in the basement of the Wiley family farm.

He looked back at the hateful house with its hateful basement and did not think of Sandra or his fantasies. All he thought now was that he never wanted to see the place again.

He decided right then to make certain he never would.

It was a patch of soil that had not seen sky in more than a hundred years.

As the bulldozers and backhoes ripped apart the former Wiley home, tearing off great chunks, a window here, a slice of eave there and finally the kitchen floor, bits of sunlight crashed into cool turf that had lain undisturbed in such soothing solitude for so long. The venous roots crisscrossing the basement floor drew back from the onslaught, their finest and most delicate extensions withering seconds after exposure.

In a matter of hours the house disappeared.

All that remained was a gaping pit where the cellar once lay. It was scoured and gouged by the claws of the backhoe bucket, every inch of its earth upturned to dry and crack in the sunlight. The decapitated ends of the pearlescent root system stuck out all along the raked walls, dripping pink droplets of moisture onto the rough-clawed turf.

The workmen shut down their machines, dusted off their pants and called it quits.

When they arrived in the morning they faced a home that had survived every disaster for more than a century: Tornadoes, prairie fires, lightning strikes, hailstorms, blizzards, termites—all had been unable to topple it.

In a mere eight hours Denny Sharf reduced it to memory.

Denny moved back to his Cadillac, climbed in and drove out the short gravel drive. As he turned onto the two-lane blacktop leading into Wishbone, he glanced toward the beautiful new sign he had mounted just off the road. ROYAL OAK GARDENS. Colorfully painted and lettered to convey a feeling of tranquil elegance, the sign showed a home in a surrounding of fine country living. Where the Wileys and all the families before them had fought tooth and nail to scratch out a living, Denny Sharf was now offering a place to rest. In a matter of months the phoenix from the ashes of

Sandra Wiley's home would manifest itself in split-level glory, with central air, a wet bar, a pool and a backyard Jacuzzi.

Blaming Sandra and Peter for his experience in the basement, thinking they must have somehow booby-trapped the staircase or dumped foul toxins into the basement soil, Denny had wiped clean every sign of their presence. After all those years he had finally exacted his revenge against Sandra Wiley.

Now more than ever, he felt that she was his.

EIGHT

BABY CARLOTTA

Sandra heard about the wrecking ball destroying her former home and thought, with a relieved sigh, *Now there's no going back.*

Outside the window of their first-floor room at the Red Cottage Lodge, Sandra kept an eye on Andromeda and Will as they played in the emptied pool. Her other eye she kept on the TV screen.

In all the TV viewing she'd put in during the week since they'd left the farm, a week she'd had to herself, as Peter left each morning and stayed out late trying to dig up a job, Sandra noticed that on TV everybody was doing fine and had lots of money. Maybe some didn't seem so happy, but Sandra figured if she had a tenth of what most people on TV had, she'd be plenty happy. All she wanted was to be happy. She was convinced being happy was not too much to ask.

Sandra switched the TV channel from a soap to an old black-and-white Kirk Douglas movie. It was called *The Big Carnival.* Kirk played a somewhat unscrupulous and hungry reporter who manipulates a big story by delaying the rescue of a man trapped in a mine-shaft collapse.

Munching Doritos, Sandra watched as Kirk broadcast the man's sad story from within the shaft itself and caused millions across the country to pray for a heroic rescue. Sandra was struck by the realistic way in which the movie's story unfolded. She watched as swarms of onlookers and volunteers descended on the site to be a part of history. Donations poured in, massive equipment was brought in—nothing, it seemed, was spared to save this one poor soul from a death wedged between hard slabs of cold earth. A man gets stuck in a shaft and the whole world stops to set him free. Sandra saw the truth in it.

"That's just how it would happen."

Like bus plunges in India, people getting stuck in shafts and causing rescue frenzies were events that happened with a certain regularity.

Sandra remembered an event from her grade-school years, a little girl in Pennsylvania falling into an old well. She remembered how the trauma of it filled everyone's thoughts. The story grew hard to avoid as the national press gave it coverage, reporting on the girl's condition and the progress of her rescue in hourly updates around the clock. To heighten the human drama, to make the potential tragedy seem so much grander than it really was in a world where millions die violently in far less than a lifetime, the press gave the girl's name a saccharine appendage. She was old enough to talk and walk, a fact that led to her plunge in the first place, yet the press chose to diminish her age. They called her Baby Carlotta.

It was a grand success.

People everywhere found themselves glued to their televisions and radios, hoping to hear any moment that Baby Carlotta had been pulled from the well and all was fine. And exactly like Kirk's movie, where crews from around the country offered their expert services, crews from across America flew to Pennsylvania to dig a second shaft alongside the one clutching Baby Carlotta in a desperate bid to set her free.

In Sandra's church the preacher asked for a special prayer to save the endangered waif. At school the teacher asked Sandra and her classmates to send "We're praying for you" cards along with a Care package containing money and clothes to Baby Carlotta and her tearful parents. On the street it was a subject that could open a conversation with any stranger. Invariably the response would be something like "I just pray to God they get that little girl out in time," or "She's such a brave little thing," as if falling into an open hole and not dying right away demonstrated some sort of courage.

Most of all Sandra remembered how she felt at night when she slept safely under her covers. She really pitied the little girl, stuck down there, cold, wet and frightened, never knowing if she would make it out alive. Sandra knew hers was not the only heart that sank when news arrived that Baby Carlotta was more deeply stuck than anticipated or when it was revealed that she could no longer eat the food lowered down on a rope. After four days spent trying to effect her rescue, doctors gingerly began preparing the national audience for the worst. A cloud descended over America as it grew clear that Baby Carlotta would die if she was not rescued in the next day.

That whole night Sandra and millions more did not sleep, caught up as they were in Baby Carlotta's tragedy. If empathy and prayer alone had the power to raise Baby Carlotta from the well's grip, the amount directed her way would have lifted her to the sun.

Sandra in the end fell into a short and uneasy sleep. Upon waking, the first thing she wanted to know was how Baby Carlotta fared. Running into the living room she found her mother, her customary bottle of bourbon barely touched but standing by, crying an ocean before the Magnavox. Sandra's heart dropped to her feet.

"Oh, Mom, she's dead."

Sandra's mother turned her wet face to Sandra, and Sandra was surprised to see a wide smile.

"No, she's alive! They saved her! She's alive!"

On the tiny TV with its tenuous vertical hold, Sandra and her mother watched as rescue workers lifted Baby Carlotta from the second shaft and placed her in an ambulance. When a reporter shoved a mike her way and asked what she wanted, Baby Carlotta smiled a smile bright enough to crack the hardest hearts and said she wanted a pony.

Hugs and handshakes filled the screen as Baby Carlotta's family thanked as profusely as possible the people who had saved their child. Doctors quickly answered the question on everyone's mind and declared Baby Carlotta to be the bravest of girls and in remarkably good shape. There was no reason to think the experience would leave her scarred in any way. As the reporter, fighting back his own tears of joy, turned to the camera, he reported that an anonymous donor had called in to say he would donate not just one but two ponies to Baby Carlotta's family. In an outpouring of charity, other donors called in to match or outdo previous donations. When all was said and done, Baby Carlotta and her family were healthy, happy and more than a hundred thousand dollars richer.

More than a hundred thousand dollars.

In her mind Sandra laid out the sum in one-dollar bills. If one bill was six inches long, one hundred thousand of them would create a string fifty thousand feet long or almost nine and a half miles in length. If she spent one dollar a day it would take nearly 274 years to go broke. Realistically, if the family's daily expenses were twenty-five dollars, it would still take almost ten years to run out of cash. In that many years their whole world could change.

But Baby Carlotta's tragedy and salvation had occurred nearly twenty years earlier. That hundred thousand dollars, translated from those earlier dollars to more inflated dollars, would now be two hundred thousand at least, maybe more.

Being conservative, Sandra considered the doubling of that precious number. Two hundred thousand dollars would not only pay for the basics, it would cover some tasteful luxuries as well.

With that kind of money they could buy a home with a swimming pool. They could throw dinner parties. They could fit in.

Sandra broke her contemplation to return to the movie. She saw that in this cinematic tale, the ending was not so happy as was Baby Carlotta's. The current scene showed a downtrodden Kirk Douglas as he learns the subject of his story has died in the shaft. The crowds surrounding the shaft entrance filter away until all that remains is a lot of litter, a guilty Kirk and the quickly forgotten family of the dead miner, a sad group left with nothing. It was clear to Sandra that the movie version was a cautionary tale about how the victim himself was the first to be forgotten as the crowds moved on with their lives.

Not wanting the movie's sorrowful ending to ruin her financial fantasy, Sandra flicked off the TV and stood to check on Andromeda and Will. The two kids still ran around the banked walls of the empty pool.

Two hundred thousand dollars and maybe more was an awful lot of money for a few days of misery. Sandra wondered if Baby Carlotta, now in her mid-twenties, looked back on her experience in a different light. Maybe she felt it was the turning point that led to a lifetime of success. Certainly there had to be some good in knowing so many millions had been rooting for you. Sandra could see that, having survived, Carlotta would do proud all those people who had worked to save her life. She would do more and work harder because anything less would demean the grand effort that had led to her resurrection. Sandra could imagine that Carlotta, with the finances to attend the best schools and armed with a confidence bred from her survival, had gone on to a bright future. She was probably a compassionate and strong woman who was a friend to many and the envy of all.

Carlotta was in the well for five days, sixteen hours and thirty-three minutes. But for some bruises and a scrape or two, she had come out without real damage. Although her discomfort could not be underestimated, and some residual psychological difficulty was to be expected, time and one hundred thousand dollars probably did much to make things better.

In the long run Carlotta probably decided her fall into that well had been the best thing that ever happened to her.

Outside, running up and down the sides of the pink pool bottom under a pale October sky, her arms outstretched to imitate the wings of a plane, Andromeda seemed the happiest girl on earth. Envious of her oblivion to the family's dire state of affairs, Sandra nevertheless knew Andromeda's innocent bliss was one bright spot in a sea of gloom. Her happiness was the last precious cargo from a legacy of soured hopes.

Sandra knew it would take the support of a strong family to help a child through the experience of getting stuck in a shaft for five days. Looking to her two children, she wondered how they would handle such an experience. Andromeda was a willful girl but she was absolutely terrified of the dark. The experience of falling into a shaft for even a few hours would wreak havoc with her worldview. Andromeda did not make a good candidate for a successful rescue.

But then there was Will.

Will was an explorer. Sandra knew there was almost no place on earth Will would not be willing to go. Will had little fear of the dark, and what fear he did have he was able to control by the force of his own will. If his actual discomfort was minimized, he would probably come through falling down a shaft okay. The scrapes would fade and the memory would be soothed over by an infusion of riches, by new opportunities and by the knowledge that so many cared. Knowing Will as she did, Sandra thought he would probably endure the experience like a trooper, even believing it was a sort of adventure. For certain he would not give up or succumb to panic. He was too strong for that. Weakness wasn't his way.

Even though Sandra was just engaging in idle speculation, nothing more than a daydream, she guessed that if all went well, Will might end up thinking it was the best thing that ever happened to him.

DEAD ENDS

With his latest employment rejection minutes old, this time at the hands of the sympathetic owner of the local septic tank cleaning service, Peter stepped out the door of the Honeypot and onto Main Street with a view to nowhere. The Honeypot had been his last hope for a job in Wishbone. He had been everywhere. Now there was nothing left to do but look beyond Wishbone's limits.

Standing before the headquarters of the Honeypot, smelling the faint odor of sewage from the nearby pumping truck decorated with a smiling bee, Peter looked east down the length of Main Street and knew he had finally run out of options.

The relief that he expected when reaching rock bottom, a point where the only way to go is back up, did not materialize. Peter felt more anxious than ever. Upon reaching rock bottom he realized that there were actually two routes to travel. The preferred route was obviously back up. But the other route, the one that was more commonly taken as a result of sad fate or resigned choice, was to stay at the bottom. It was possible to say, The best has come and gone and a life of nothingness is here to stay.

Rock bottom with nowhere to go.

Peter felt there should be some sign of momentous revelation, maybe a dirty halo over his head that said to others, There but for the grace of God go I. But as his gaze met that of his wary friends and neighbors, Peter knew he didn't need a halo or a sandwich board to symbolize avoidable failure. He already carried the stink of ruin. Yet when so many were failing around him, he didn't even get the luxury of being unique in his failure.

Peter stepped onto the narrow bridge spanning the creek that cut the ground beneath Main Street. He leaned over the railing and looked down at the murky water flowing out the arched culvert.

This was the same stream that ran along the edge of Peter's farm. If Peter were a fast fish he could swim up this stream and arrive at his farm in less than ten minutes. The water flowing by carried in solution soil that had felt Peter's weight and been nurtured by his hands. It was soil that would now be buried beneath layers of sod and asphalt, pierced by sprinkler systems, saturated by chemical brews and peppered with clone houses in approved colors. Upstream at his former farm, bulldozers were carving roads and cul-de-sacs in fields he once hoped would grow the finest organic vegetables.

As he watched the waters flowing even muddier, picturing a bulldozer plowing down his carefully raised fences and corrupting the native thickets along the stream banks, Peter knew at last how stupid his plan had been.

There was just not enough of a market in a farming community for organically grown foods. If his neighbors were truly concerned, they could grow them themselves. For local sale and personal consumption, many already did. Peter saw the key deficiency in his plan. He had not delivered his higher-priced produce to the people he was sure would buy it. If he had devised a distribution system so his produce could cheaply reach urban centers, where health concerns were more ritualized, he might have stood a chance.

Might have, if, should have, could have. Peter tried to shake off the regret.

It was done. His experiment had failed. He could see many of his errors and he was positive he would discover more as time went by. But his immediate concern was to face a future without farming.

He turned from the creek that carried his much-loved soil and headed back into town. He made it only thirty or so yards before Denny's red Cadillac pulled alongside. His wide-collared shirt open to reveal a gold chain around his hairy neck, Denny pulled off his sunglasses and called to Peter.

"Hey, Wiley! I've been looking for you. We need to talk."

Peter sat in the Straight Line Cafe across from Denny Sharf and his lawyer, Vincent Proctor, the very same man who ran the enterprises of Mary Hayworth Downes, and couldn't believe his ears. Denny wore an expression that said, I have been wronged. Peter couldn't see how.

"You can't be serious."

"Do I look like I'm joking? You poisoned that soil and I'm not the one who's about to pay for the clean-up."

Vincent Proctor, a large, almost completely bald man who was always sweating and who was always wiping his brow with a monogrammed hand-kerchief, waved his pudgy hands to stop the discussion from getting ugly.

"Now let's keep this civil. We don't know what's going on; we just know we have a problem."

"What is the problem?"

"It seems there's something leaking from your former cellar, Mr. Wiley."

"Vince, you've been calling me Peter since I was two. Calling me mister makes me nervous."

"I'd rather keep us focused on the business here, Mr. Wiley. Now, in the terms of your foreclosure, you are bound by certain obligations, one being that you leave the property in a healthy state. Mr. Sharf claims he was stricken by—what was it? Fumes?"

"Fumes. That soil is toxic. I took one whiff and puked out my guts. God-dammit, I'm going to have to haul away half the topsoil."

Peter narrowed an ever angrier glare on red-faced, righteous Denny.

"That soil is the cleanest in the county. Everyone in Wishbone knows I never had even a pound of chemicals on my land."

"You mean *my* land."

Denny, who knew the guilty soil from the basement had already been dumped into the creek and had by now been washed down to the Missis-sippi, enjoyed the spectacle of turning the screw on Peter Wiley.

In the days that followed his terrible experience, Denny came to the au-thentic conclusion that Peter and Sandra were too naive to booby-trap the basement. That sort of malice was Denny's realm. But it still did not spare them from his desire to make someone pay. Why not Peter? Why not San-dra?

He decided to test their breaking point.

If Peter broke, maybe Sandra would realize she had other options. Maybe she would see Denny in a new light. He could do a lot for her. If she did something for him, he would buy her clothes, set her up in one of his foreclosed homes, maybe even get her a car. She would recognize her folly in marrying small-minded Peter Wiley.

Denny would be Sandra's savior. He would rescue her from the nothing life Peter had built for her, and she would be grateful in the most extreme and erotic fashion. But before any of this could occur he needed to break Peter, to expose his cowardice to Sandra so whatever respect she still had for him could finally die.

This fictitious lawsuit was Denny's final trump.

The lawsuit that Denny had slammed in Peter's face would lead nowhere. Denny already had the soil checked and it was as Peter said. It was the cleanest in the county. It was so clean Denny considered bagging it and selling it by the pound. But the process of countering the lawsuit would drive Peter to the edge of despair and beyond. Peter would not be able to put up a fight. Without support he had to collapse. And in that collapse Sandra would have nowhere to turn but to Denny.

Denny flashed Peter a stronger sneer.

"When you signed those foreclosure papers you signed a statement saying everything was fine with that land, and that just ain't so. You put something in that land and it's in my way. You're setting me back weeks on Royal Oaks. I'm telling you right now, whatever this whole business costs, it's coming out of your pocket."

Proctor wiped his brow.

"Mr. Wiley, the first thing you need to do is get yourself a lawyer. After that I'm afraid you'll have to pay for a soil specialist to do an on-site investigation. That means there'll be fees not just for his visit but also for lab work, making up reports, filing with the court. I know I'm not supposed to do this, but I'm willing to suggest a few names out of Wichita. Good men who should be able to help us all come to a compromise."

"I can't afford a lawyer. I can't afford any of this. How much will this cost, anyway?"

"Oh, I'd say maybe five or six hundred. Shouldn't be more than that. Of course, if it does turn up that you got some toxins in that soil . . . well, hauling off forty or fifty tons of dirt isn't cheap."

Peter sank back in his chair.

"I don't believe this."

Vincent Proctor dropped a few bills on the table to cover the coffee tab and stood with his client Denny Sharf. He wiped his brow.

"Get a lawyer, Peter. It's the first thing you've got to do."

Sandra took the news badly.

"That sonofabitch! That fucking sonofabitch!"

She kicked a chair across the room and into a shared wall, an act that caused their Red Cottage neighbors, a pair of Vietnamese newlyweds, to call the management, which soon arrived in the form of a pregnant seventeen-year-old who asked through a lit cigarette for Sandra and Peter to keep it down.

Will and Andromeda, out on the lodge's swing set, gladly kept their distance as Peter and Sandra battled it out.

Sandra continued to pace, trying hard not to kick anything else or the one thing she wanted to kick most, her pathetically incompetent husband.

"This is a bunch of bullshit and you know it. Denny Sharf is doing this to get back at you and that's all there is to it."

"Get back at me for what? I never did a single thing to him."

"You married me!"

"Yeah, so . . ." Peter began to understand. "You mean he's doing this because I married you."

"Why else? He's had a thing for me ever since grade school."

"Lots of guys did; that doesn't mean they make it their life's obsession. It has to be more than that."

"Why does it have to be more than that? Think about who we're talking about. This is Denny Sharf!"

"So it's Denny, so what? I mean, why would he put so much effort into screwing us up just because he had a school crush on you and you ended up with me? It's ridiculous. Nobody does that."

"Denny does. Denny is the type who has nothing better to do."

Peter looked at his wife and wondered.

"It just doesn't make sense, Sandy. There has to be more to it." What he was thinking he knew would sound unbelievable, but under the circumstances, he felt he had to consider it. "You never . . . you never gave him cause to feel he had an attachment to you, did you?"

Sandra stopped pacing.

"Peter, what are you asking me?"

"I'm just trying to find out if this is all based on something that happened between you two."

"Between me and Denny? I haven't said a word to the little creep since high school."

"I know, and I always wondered why."

Sandra looked down at her husband and dredged up an image of Denny Sharf lying on his back on the gym floor with his shorts pulled down to his feet. Even now she could picture the sick smile Denny directed her, knowing she had witnessed the hairless protuberance from his groin. Yet even now Sandra refused to give it any distinction.

"Because he's Denny Sharf; do I need another reason?"

"I think you do."

"Why don't you just say what you're thinking? You're thinking I somehow encouraged him."

"Maybe. Maybe you did."

"Oh, my God. Do you think I did something with him?"

"I don't know. Did you?"

Sandra's face reddened and tears welled in her eyes.

"You mean did I fuck him? How could you ask me that? How could you even think it?"

Peter suddenly knew he had crossed the line. In a flash he suddenly understood that through thick and thin—mostly thin—Sandra had always remained faithful to him. He quickly tried to recant.

"I didn't mean that. Jesus, I don't know what I'm saying."

"I've never once . . ."

Peter stood and tried to embrace Sandra. She allowed his arms to encompass her but she did not lift hers to return the hug. She merely cried into his chest.

Peter felt as guilty as he would feel dropping a neighbor's baby.

"I'm sorry, I'm sorry. Sandy, I didn't mean that. I didn't. I know you never would."

Sandra's sobbing softened into sniffles.

"He's going to win everything and we're going to let him."

"He won't win. We won't let him. We'll find a way out of this thing."

Sandra pulled her face from Peter's chest.

"I want it to be nice again. I haven't been happy for so long. I want us to be happy again, Peter."

"So do I."

"Then, we have to do something. We have to do something big."

"I'm doing everything I can. Tomorrow I'll head down to Sterling and see what's available there."

Sandra pulled away from Peter, suddenly angry again.

"No! No more! You're not going to find anything in Sterling or Dodge or anywhere around here! We need to do something big!"

Peter sat back on the bed. Too tired to fight anymore, feeling guilty at the shambles he had made of their lives, he decided in that moment that his best option was to let Sandra direct their course.

"Like what?"

Sandra began pacing again. At the end of one of her paces she glanced out the window and saw Will hanging by his knees from a monkey bar. He was the picture of a happy and confident kid.

She felt the idea coming on like the flood from a broken dam. Even though her heart was squeezed in the twisting grip of conscience, she couldn't stop it, she couldn't keep from hearing what it told her. What it told her was the answer to all their problems was right this minute hanging upside down pretending he was a monkey.

Will had the power to make things right.

Sandra decided the time was ripe to propose an alternative to a lifetime of failure.

"Something big."

TEN

SOMETHING BIG

Peter sat alone in his truck with his forehead against the steering wheel. Out the windshield he watched Sandra's back heave up and down from her nervous breath as she sat on the bumper. He could tell she was crying. But her tears were not his immediate concern. His mind churned with one issue only. Peter's ears rang from the conversation shared with Sandra in the privacy of the truck, following her statement that they had to do "something big."

It was insane. More than that, it was criminal.

What they had discussed for the last two and a half hours was nothing less than the torture of their child.

It was all that TV she was watching, Peter told himself. As a result of watching people win the publishers' sweepstakes or hearing about some overnight sensation who is suddenly set for life, Sandra was now looking for a quick fix to lifelong problems.

The fix Sandra had proposed was pure evil. Parents did not do to their children what she suggested, and any parents who did should be taken out and hung by their ankles from rusty meat hooks. They should be skinned alive. Peter knew he was right to be revolted, he knew he was right to be shocked, he knew he was right to say no way, not now, not ever.

But what stopped him from piling the kids in the truck and ditching Sandra to race for the hills was the potential. Peter found he could not deny the potential in Sandra's proposal.

It held the potential for salvation.

Sandra had a plan. The plan was heinous and it might not work. A risk had to be taken by one special individual within their family. It was not a small risk. It could mean some physical injury. It would definitely entail a high degree of emotional trauma for all concerned. If it didn't work it would mean public scorn, jail time and the breakup of the family. He didn't even want to consider the worst-case scenario.

But if it did work . . .

Peter pictured fields filled with ripened vegetables growing from the richest organic soil. He envisioned workers transporting his crops to distant markets where grateful consumers clamored for his goods. Peter saw Will and Andromeda in a new home, in new clothes, in large, clean rooms filled with the best furniture and the best toys. He saw them excelling in private school because their home life was so secure. And then he saw Sandra.

Peter saw Sandra smiling at him with eyes filled with respect. His heart ached as he remembered the sincere admiration she once held for him. In this dream it had returned.

Was this perfect vision really so close? The bigger question, the one framing Peter's current struggle, asked if a long future of financial security was worth a moment of hellish chaos.

Peter had to face his true prospects before the question could be answered. Although he believed in organic farming, he knew the success of a new venture would require more capital than he could ever hope to earn through manual labor, assuming he could find even that. As far as credit went, he had none. He would never again receive a loan. At minimum it would require many hard years before the family reached even the bottom tier of middle-class life. What this meant was that they had to continue to tighten their belts for another three or four years at least.

The way things were between he and Sandra, he knew their marriage would not survive another year of poverty. Sandra would leave him. She was a beautiful woman; she could easily remarry her way into a higher tax bracket. If Peter did not show her that there was light at the end of the tunnel, it was almost certain in the spirit of self-preservation she would do just that.

If they divorced, where would it leave Andromeda and Will?

Peter hated to think how heartbroken the children would be if their family were divided. He could imagine them growing sullen and rebellious, making their way into adulthood cynical and bitter, feeling as if nothing was secure and nothing and no one could be trusted. They might become delinquents, they might start using drugs. This was not the future

Peter wanted for his children, but it was a future that seemed as likely as any.

Sandra's proposal offered a different future. She had practically promised that a heaven on earth would rise from one bad experience. Her words still rang in his head.

"This could save us, Peter. In less than a week we could be fine."

"What if everything you say happened exactly like you say it's going to happen? How could you live with yourself?"

"At least I'd be living."

"Well, I'd never be able to look Will in the face again."

"Do you think this is easy for me? I'm his mother, for chrissakes! Don't you dare accuse me of caring less for him than you do! Don't you dare!"

Peter turned level eyes on Sandra.

"Then don't even think about doing this to him. There's no way we can do this . . . no way. We can get by some other way." Seeing he was not swaying Sandra in the least, Peter brought out more ammo. "He'll get hurt, you know he will."

"He doesn't have to. We can make it so he doesn't."

"He'll be scared to death."

"You know him better than that. Will is tough, and we'll be with him every minute. We'll be with him all the time, twenty-four hours. I'm not going to abandon my baby."

"What happens if he just comes right out?"

"We have to see that doesn't happen. We need three days."

"Three days! Jesus!"

"Maybe more."

Peter shook his head, overwhelmed by the idea of it.

"I can't leave him in there for three days, Sandra, I just . . . I mean, three days."

"It has to make the national news. I figure that's three days. After it goes national we can get him out anytime."

"But what if they don't care? I mean, who the hell are we to anybody? We're nobody. You said it yourself."

"We're exactly what they're looking for in a human interest story. We're hopeless. We have problems beyond what would be happening to Will. That's what they like."

"You talk as if we already decided we're doing it."

Sandra did not blink.

Peter slumped back and wrung the truck steering wheel.

All he could picture was how Will adored him. Will and Andromeda were the only two people on earth who still did. Their love and respect was the only real treasure Peter had left. Going through with Sandra's plan meant he would risk losing it.

He swung back to face Sandra. In her pleading eyes he suddenly saw a hint of the long-lost respect she herself once held for him. In this moment he was again her hero. In this moment Sandra needed him. But the moment came with a clause. It would not continue and it would never again return if Peter did not come through for her. Her eyes growing moist, desperate for Peter to do the right thing by her, Sandra was offering a way to revive her respect forever.

In the end Peter could not resist.

"We'd have to make it look real."

Sandra expelled her held breath before exiting the truck to cry on the bumper. "That's where I'm counting on you."

At three in the morning Sandra excused herself from the king-sized bed in their room at the Red Cottage Lodge, gently lifting Andromeda to the side, and made her way into the bathroom, where she locked the door behind her. Climbing into the dry bathtub, she sat and brought her knees to her chest. In seconds she felt tears streaking her cheeks.

The urge to commit suicide was suddenly real. At a moment like this she understood how a person could say life was not worth living.

She still could not believe she had actually proposed what she had proposed. The woman who spoke to Peter through her mouth was a stranger to her.

Sandra had carried Will for nine months and pushed him into the world after thirty-seven hours of aggravated labor. She loved Will as any mother should, despite some resentment for a birth that had led to her present sorry state.

Sandra's own mother, an alcoholic living off the pension from her dead veteran husband, was exactly the kind of mother Sandra tried not to be. But even her drunk mother, who during a vodka binge had accidentally given a seven-year-old flu-stricken Sandra a near-fatal dose of sleeping pills to help her stop crying at night, would never purposely put her child in harm's way. So how could Sandra?

Neither she nor Peter had families to count on. Peter's parents had their own troubles and to this day had seen Will on only two occasions. They had never even met Andromeda. They had never asked to. Looking to their families for help was a dead end that had not been explored during this latest and greatest crisis because history had already proven its futility.

If there had only been some option.

The list of quick financial fixes leaned to the sleazy side. The most honorable of the bunch was to hit it big in Vegas. From there the options took a dark dip. Sandra wondered if stealing or selling her body was any less honorable than what she intended to do to Will.

The answer was no. What she would do to her little boy was the most despicable act imaginable.

A huge part of Sandra told her to accept a life on the streets, taking handouts and eating from trash cans, anything to avoid what she was planning for Will, but Sandra could not keep from drifting back to the idea that this one thing could fix everything for life.

Tears like acid ran into her mouth and she sobbed in short breaths so as not to awaken the others. The thing had gone beyond Sandra's control. Once the proposal had been aired, there was no going back. Peter would never look at her in the same light. The only way either of them could hope to find a new common ground would be to go all the way and hopefully come out together on the other side.

If all went well they just might make it.

If it went really well they might make it big.

As Sandra tried to rationalize what she had proposed to Peter, knowing he would give up his life rather than put his children in danger, she found her only excuse was that every family member had to do his or her share.

She just prayed that Will's contribution wouldn't leave too many scars.

How to engineer it: that was Peter's first problem.

How to live with it was the second. The first seemed surmountable but the second did not.

Will would be put through hell. This wasn't a brief *Boo!*; this was an ongoing event, a festival of terror.

Peter's disbelief and disgust at how low he had sunk, to a point where he would risk his innocent boy's safety and sanity, drove him from the cramped motel room early each morning in an effort to avoid facing his little son. He returned as late as possible, when he knew Will was asleep, for the very same reason. As far as Will and Andromeda knew, their father was staying out late scouting for jobs. But Peter and Sandra knew he was really out scouting for the place to do the deed.

It took a week and a half of searching, but Peter finally found it.

In a shallow depression between eroded, grass-covered slopes, in a wide space littered by rusting and rotting refuse from bygone industry, Peter found the ideal shaft. It sat in a tortured landscape that mirrored his mood.

The soil in the area was blackened from heavy oil spillage and had hardened into a kind of glossy tarmac. Whatever vegetation there was fought to sprout through an earth assaulted by intense fires and lathered with debris from years of drilling. Old bulldozed mounds were covered in patchy grass and weeds; old pits were filled with slimy water, or had been, and were now basins of artfully cracked muck. Links of heavy chain, parts of tools, old, bald tires, bottles broken and intact, oil-coated buckets, sheets of corrugated roofing, gears, cogs and cams were embedded all over the eerie and desolate scene. The derricks were gone. The only remaining structure from an operation that at one time must have been loud and full of life was a small tin shack. Its bullet-riddled sides held up a torqued metal roof that shielded inner walls inhabited only by hibernating mud dauber colonies.

It was a lonely place, forgotten and dead. The tall grass that hid the length of the old road leading into the site confirmed this was a place that had few visitors.

It was exactly the place he needed.

Peter kicked aside the splintered piece of plywood that some careless worker, lazily deciding it was sufficient cover, had placed over the shaft opening. Whoever it was who had left the hole so inadequately sealed as he turned out the lights on the defunct operation had either not cared or had thought they would soon be back. Since all relevant machinery had been removed, the latter prospect did not seem likely. This field of wells had run dry. Many had never produced, including the well Peter now faced. For Peter's purposes a clean shaft was a major requirement.

He pulled out a tape and measured the width of the hole. It was a foot and a half wide. Too small for an adult but a wide enough fit for an eight-year-old child. Shining down a flashlight he could see the sides were nicely smooth. The shaft ran straight but dipped at a slight angle. That was good; it would slow the descent, lessen the chance of injury on the way down and relieve some pressure when Will stopped. The fact that the hole was as wide as it was, when most of the old oil wells were only a few inches wide, told Peter this particular well was dug for some other purpose. What that purpose was, he had no way of knowing. All he knew was the purpose he had in mind.

Peter pulled out the videocamera he had locally rented with some of the last of his money, tied a long rope to its handle, turned on its light and lowered it into the hole. As he played out the rope that he had prepared by marking out one-foot increments in Magic Marker, Peter kept convincing himself he was just humoring Sandra and that she would realize the insanity of the idea, maybe not until the last minute but at some point, and they would agree to call the whole thing off. But the countdown was two days to homelessness, and neither had said a word about aborting the plan.

The rope went slack. The camera had reached the bottom of the well. Peter took up the slack and checked the rope. It read ninety-six feet deep.

Ninety-six feet wouldn't seem so far above ground. You could walk ninety-six feet in a matter of seconds. But ninety-six feet nearly straight down was a long, long way.

Peter pulled up the camera, untied it and attached to the freed rope a small cage that contained a chirping canary with plenty of seed and water. He lowered the canary down to ninety-six feet and tied off the rope. In a couple of days he would retrieve the canary, and if it was still chirping he would know the well was free of gas.

Moving to his truck with the camera, Peter rewound the tape and peered into the eyepiece to see on the teeny screen what it would reveal when he played back the tape.

On the puny image Peter saw that the sides were smooth all the way down. A few pale roots like those that had found a home in their former basement stuck out to add slight texture to the shaft walls, but no single root was thick enough to impede anything that might fall in. Viewing the part of the video that showed the bottom, Peter was able to see plenty of things had already done so. Desiccated skeletons of mice and a snake were mixed with blown-in twigs, grasses, a crumpled cigarette pack, a yellowed newspaper and a paper cup.

It didn't present the daintiest or even safest landing, so Peter made a mental note to arrange for padding. Shredded burlap, a lot of it, should do the trick.

Another requirement for success was keeping Will down there long enough to necessitate a real rescue operation. He had to slide past some obstacle that would not injure him during the fall but that would prevent him from being pulled back up. Peter needed something that allowed an object to pass in one direction only, and whatever device he ultimately came up with had to remain immovable within the shaft and not seem planted. It was just one of the big challenges presented by the task at hand.

The task at hand was inhumane and cowardly. Using a child for such a purpose was immoral beyond question. Even considering such a thing should be a crime. Peter constantly struggled to understand how he could be contemplating doing to Will what Sandra had proposed.

It always came back to the money.

The money was the thing.

From soaps and supermarket tabloids, Sandra had an excellent sense of the scope and form of American sentimentality. Americans were by and large a sappy lot. They loved the edge-of-your-seat excitement as the clock ticked down on some stranger's tragedy. If the tragedy was newsworthy enough, if they could say "aw" in its witness, they felt obliged to partici-pate in the rescue. From their living rooms a thousand miles from the scene they could write letters to the key players and give emotional sup-port that said, Keep your chin up, we're on your side out here in Anchor-age or Des Moines or Atlanta or Phoenix. Then again, they could offer more direct support. They could send money.

A lot of the time that was just what they did.

Maybe it would be five bucks. Maybe it would be twenty bucks, no great sacrifice to anyone. Twenty dollars was, in fact, a terrific bargain. For twenty bucks you could buy yourself a sliver of heroism, a karmic pass on future sins. If enough people around the country felt it was worth five or twenty bucks to be a hero, the final tally could easily run into the multi-ple thousands. It was a scenario by no means far-fetched, and Sandra was probably right to give the American heart the better odds.

In the aftermath of the rescue Peter and Sandra had predetermined that Will would receive special treatment. This whole episode would be made up to him. If a pony would help him forget, then a pony it would be. One thing Peter and Sandra both knew was that Will, and Andromeda for that matter, could never know. For the children the tragedy had to forever re-main an accident.

There were both practical and selfish reasons for keeping it a secret. For practical reasons Will had to be as convincing as possible. Will had to be an authentically terrified little boy.

For selfish reasons Peter could not let Will or Andromeda know he had done this to them. He would accept life on the streets and a perpetually hungry stomach before risking their admiration.

But as he coiled the rope and headed back to his truck, he understood he was risking their admiration right this minute. He was risking it because Sandra's plan was an undeniably simple long-term fix for a set of unyielding problems.

Peter prayed with every cell in his body that nothing would go wrong.

ELEVEN

NINETY-SIX FEET

On the morning of the day Peter, Sandra and their two children were forced to leave the Red Cottage Lodge, the day when the money at last ran out, Peter drove to the abandoned well site to check on the canary. He found it alive and well. It had passed the test; it had served its purpose. Opening the cage, he set the bird free.

Peter turned to another item that could not be checked until it had served its purpose.

Wearing gloves to avoid leaving fingerprints, Peter removed the simple contraption from his truck that would be the architect of Will's capture. The trap consisted of three ordinary items nailed together. A square of plywood was nailed as a base to the bottom of an eight-foot-long two-by-four. At the top of the two-by-four a slightly curved piece of metal sheeting eighteen inches wide and three feet long was also nailed on. It bent back down the length of the two-by-four to act like a flap. Together, the whole thing looked something like an inverted **J**.

There was nothing unusual about the joining of these three items. It didn't look like anything at all and that was the idea. This purposeless union of common materials could easily be the product of a child's first use of a hammer. Heavy-gauge nails driven at an upward angle through the two-by-four's length, protruding out the side opposite the flap of sheet metal, heightened the impression that this bit of junk was a child's first foray into pounding construction. Peter carefully tied his measured rope to a sharp jag of metal on the back side of the two-by-four. He carried the trap to the shaft, where other gear stood ready.

He tossed the pile of shredded burlap into the shaft until he was satisfied enough had made it to the bottom to create a cushioned pad. Grabbing a well-used hand pump sprayer, Peter began sending a stream of fine oil down the hole. He watched as the slick oil coated the sides of the shaft. He then lifted his contraption. First lowering in the end with the nailed-on plywood square, he carefully held down the sheeting flap, through which he had drilled numerous air holes. He guided the device into the shaft. As it dropped into the darkness, Peter knew the curved metal sheeting would act as a scoop to allow anything past that might head its way.

At eighty feet the rope went slack. Since the two-by-four was eight feet long, that fact told Peter that the burlap had created a landing pad eight feet deep. The drop into the shaft would not be a free fall, there would be friction, so an eight-foot-thick pad should be more than enough. Clutching the rope tight, he gave it a sharp tug. He staggered back as far below the rope cut itself loose from the sharp jag of metal. Peter quickly coiled the rope from the hole and placed it along with all the other gear in a trash bag, which he would dispose of when he headed back to town to pick up the others.

The next step was to camouflage the opening. Gathering drifts of the dead grasses and weeds surrounding the site, Peter moved to the hole and constructed a thin mat over the dark shaft. Stepping back, he was satisfied it did not look obviously arranged. He was also satisfied that it would take close observation to tell there was a hole beneath the three-inch-thick grass layer.

Near the base of a tree dead for decades, Peter set up the faded and stained canvas tent that would be the family home for that night at least. Eyeing a line from the tent to the hidden shaft opening, he made note of a spot just beyond. Grabbing a battered cooler, he carefully walked around the hidden shaft and set down the cooler on the spot he had noted. Looking back to the tent he could see that the hidden opening fell right on an imaginary line between cooler and tent.

Surveying the scene, double checking that nothing was forgotten, Peter saw that everything was ready. Now all he had to do was pray a miracle would come along so he could forget the whole thing.

Peter stepped back to his truck and climbed in. Glancing at the gas gauge he realized he had barely enough fuel to gather the family, return to the soiled basin and drive for help when the tragedy began.

As usual, it was down to the wire all the way.

· · ·

Sandra, who had selfishly avoided viewing the place where she would commit her greatest sin, saw it now and felt it was an appropriately grim vision. The darkening sky heightened the vision as blood reds, flaming pinks and rich purples from the setting sun splashed the crisscrossing clouds.

Will, in contrast, thought the place was paradise. The junk and flotsam littered all over, the dead trees to climb, the baked dump truck lying on its side halfway down a hillside and even the mud dauber–infested tin shack presented new and exciting exploration opportunities. Who knew what might be found here?

"Dad, look what I found!" was an expression followed by the gleeful presentation of some indescribable piece of unknowable machinery useful only for a found-art piece or as a paperweight.

Knowing what he was planning to do to his happy boy, Peter struggled to sound normal.

"You kids stay by the tent. We're almost ready to eat."

Will couldn't contain his excitement and it broke Peter's heart.

"I just want to see what's over that hill."

"There's nothing over that hill but another hill. Now come on, we're going to eat."

Andromeda sat on the open blanket that Sandra had spread before the tent and commented on the surrounding land.

"This place is poop ugly. Are we really going to stay here?"

Sandra also tried to sound normal as she handed Andromeda a plate that held a peanut butter and jelly sandwich and a handful of potato chips.

"For a little while."

"And then where will we go?"

"Honey, just eat, okay? Don't ask so many questions."

"Why not?"

"Because I said so, that's why. Will, please come and get a plate."

With an eye on the magical hill over which he was certain were more treasures, Will sourly trudged to the blanket and accepted his plate of food. When he sat his two parents followed.

Peter and Sandra ate in silence with heads lowered in shame.

If Will or Andromeda felt the tension between Peter and Sandra, they did not let on. But if the tension could manifest itself as an electric charge, what now passed between the tormented couple was enough to light a city.

How could they do this? How?

The plan called for Peter to ask Will to fetch a drink from the cooler. Will would typically oblige and would typically choose a straight line as the shortest distance between two points. He would walk for the cooler, his step would land on the hidden hole, the thin mat of grass would give way and he would slide in. He would plunge. Simple physics would then ensure his capture.

Will would slide past the top of the two-by-four and the curved metal sheeting that descended farther into the shaft. Will's feet and then his whole body would be scooped by the flap of metal down the length of the two-by-four. Once past the flap of metal, Will's feet would then hit the square of plywood. The impact would yank down on the two-by-four. It would tip toward the shaft center as it fell with Will. The bottom edge of the metal flap would dig into the shaft wall. It would then crumple in the cavity and form an impassable lid. To further ensure Will's captivity, the nails protruding through the back of the two-by-four would dig into the sides of the shaft as the two-by-four tried to spring back up, following its cushioned impact with the pile of shredded burlap. The two-by-four would be impossible to move, the corrugated sheeting would be hopelessly caught in the hole and Will would be trapped beneath. It would take a major operation several days to effect his rescue. That was the plan.

Peter, on the verge of vomiting, suddenly knew he could go no further.

He would not do this thing.

If he went through with the tormenting of Will, the only way he could live with himself would be to slice open his wrists until every last drop of blood had run from his body. The only way he could find peace would be in death.

He wondered if Sandra was feeling the same. One look at her gave him his answer.

His eyes met hers and he knew she was also incapable of going through with it. With mouths half full of difficult-to-swallow food, they knew they did not have it in them to do what they planned to do. No words were needed to express the agreement. It was a telepathic communication between two people who suddenly remembered their morals.

Peter voiced what Sandra was thinking.

"We should go."

Sandra nodded.

"We should go now."

Peter and Sandra stood. Will sat at their feet polishing off his sandwich. Peter suddenly realized Andromeda was not sitting beside her older brother.

"Where's your sister?"

Will crunched down a mouthful of chips.

"She went to get drinks."

It was such a simple sentence but for Sandra and Peter it felt like knives of dry ice had just been shoved between their ribs. They spun to look toward the cooler. It sat exactly where Peter had set it. It sat unopened. And in between was nothing. Andromeda was not to be seen.

Sandra was suddenly shaking.

"Peter, no . . . no!"

Peter dropped his plate and ran for the hole, praying beyond hope that the grass mat stood intact. Sandra ran up behind and they saw at the same time that the mat had indeed been pierced. The shaft hole was fully exposed.

Something or someone had fallen in.

Peter dropped to his stomach and looked down into the dark opening. He held out hope that whatever had broken through was not his daughter, that maybe it had been a possum or maybe a raccoon. With intense apprehension he called down into the hole.

"Andie?"

His heart was slammed in a vise as Andromeda cried back.

"Dad-dy! I fell . . . I fell down a hole! Get me out! Get me out!"

Sandra collapsed to her knees and clutched her face. She screamed.

"Oh, God, no . . . Andie!"

All the blood ran from Peter's face.

His trap had finally been sprung, but on the last person Peter and Sandra wanted to take the bait.

TROUBLE EVERY DAY

Sheriff Chuck Austin and his two deputies, Fred Zinneman and Bart Currie, would sometimes respond to break-ins, acts of vandalism, bar fights, thefts of farm gear and crops, an occasional rustling, domestic squabbles and once even a murder when a ninety-year-old man decided sixty-eight years of a bad marriage should end by cutting his wife in two with both barrels of his twelve-gauge shotgun. But mostly they had little to do until the next time they would be called to address crime on its back end.

Wishbone was not Mayberry and Andy Griffith was not its sheriff. It was a real town no different from any other real town; as the economy plunged the crime rate rose. These days Sheriff Austin, who believed when he joined the force eighteen years earlier that the duty of a cop was to put all things in order so crime did not occur in the first place, saw what it really meant to be a cop.

He was a janitor.

All he could do was clean up the mess.

There was no stopping a carload of white kids from doing cookies across the lawns of any of Wishbone's black families if that's what they had a mind to do. There was no stopping a husband from pushing his wife down the stairs. There was no stopping the wife from refusing to press charges. People sped, people drank too much, people argued, they lied, they stole, they spit, they littered, they started fires and they sought revenge. All these things happened regardless of Austin's commitment to law and order.

What he longed for was the sense of honor he once assumed was part and parcel of his job. But the world he had to deal with in America's breadbasket had so much mind-boggling stupidity of the get-your-arm-caught-in-a-candy-machine-while-trying-to-steal-a-Snickers variety that doing anything for honor now seemed a ludicrous concept.

Austin was a cop because he wanted to be a hero. Every now and again he had the chance. He delivered a baby in the backseat of his car, he saved the life of a bicycler struck in a hit-and-run, and every few months he gave a shut-in a ride to the doctor. But there had been a heroism drought of late. It had been over six months since he had even helped pull a cat down from a tree. Austin was hungry for noble action. It was the only thing that made the job worth doing.

When Peter Wiley burst into the station with his clothes disheveled, his eyes and face wild in panic to shout for Austin's help in saving his little girl, who had apparently fallen down some sort of hole, Sheriff Chuck Austin got the chance to once again be the cop he always wanted to be.

"Zin, get Timms and his fire guys on the horn. Have them meet us out there with a truck and an ambulance pronto. Currie, grab some flashlights, as many hanks of rope as we got, the block and tackle, a couple ladders, a wheelbarrow, buckets and enough shovels for a team of diggers. Oh, and load up with those two-by-twelves stashed in the shed in case we need to do some shoring."

As his two deputies leapt into action, Austin pulled out a pad and paper to officially take down Wiley's report. Wiley, pacing like a madman, his face dirty and streaked from crying, was babbling.

"We gotta get her out, she's . . . she's . . . she's never . . . Andie can't, she . . . she needs to be out of there. We have to get her out!"

"Now try to stay calm and tell me what happened."

Peter was so agitated he thought he might explode. His mind was colliding orbits of thought and emotion. But through it all he knew he could not reveal that he himself had set in motion this horrible accident.

"She . . . she fell. We were camping near the wells and she went to grab a drink from the cooler and . . . she . . . she disappeared, and we . . . we . . . How long is this going to take? She's down there right now!"

"Can't say until we see what's what. So she fell in a well. Did you notice or could you tell if it had any water or oil in it?"

"It's dry. I think it's dry."

"Sorry to say that's pretty standard for these parts, but in this case it's good. Could you reach her or if she raised her arm could she reach you?"

"She's down a long way."

"How far would you say? Just take a guess."

Peter knew how far to the inch but this was a fact he had to fudge.

"Maybe ninety feet . . ."

"Ninety feet? God Almighty." As Austin wrote he spoke without looking up. "What were you doing out there at the wells, Mr. Wiley?"

"I told you, we were camping. We lost our home a little while back and we don't have the money for a motel anymore, so . . . It was just a place to spend the night."

"Funny choice. I can think of at least ten other places a whole lot nicer and safer. You used to quarterback for the Wagoneers, isn't that right?"

"A long time ago, yeah."

"I remember you had a hell of an arm. How come you never tried to go pro?"

"Never thought I was that good."

"Sure you were. I'm surprised none of the colleges picked you up. You get any offers?"

"One from Alabama. One from Texas."

"So how come you didn't move on? Boy like you could have gone places. The way you tossed that stuffed pig, man, that was your ticket out of here."

"Something came up."

Austin remembered.

"That's right. Your boy, Will. Nice kid. He out there at the site with your wife?"

Peter nearly choked, knowing the whole family was out there precisely because Will was the original target of the shaft plunge.

"Yes."

"I keep saying we have to cap these damn things or blow them shut. Anything else you think I need to know?"

Peter could think of a lot of things the sheriff would like to know if he had a clue as to what was really going on. Instead of giving him that clue, Peter shrugged his shoulders.

"I don't know what."

Austin finished writing and put away his pad. Outside, the sounds of fire truck and ambulance sirens raced past in a Doppler roar. The flashing lights momentarily blasted through the police station windows as the vehicles sped by. Zinneman and Currie returned to Austin.

"All set."

Further convinced by Peter's sorry choices that athletic talent and brains did not go hand in hand, Austin nodded to Peter, who stood.

Sheriff Chuck Austin over the years had grown fairly jaded to happy endings. Truly happy endings, he had seen, were a rare commodity. But duty called for an optimistic face.

"We'll get your girl out of there. She's going to be fine."

An hour earlier it had been just Peter, Sandra, Will and Andromeda eating a pauper dinner under a scarlet sky. Now the well zone, which had probably seen no activity like this for thirty years or more, was all business. Two fire trucks, an ambulance and three police cars were parked alongside Peter's battered pickup. A huddle of firemen discussed tactics with Sheriff Austin as Bobby Timms, Wishbone's craggy and energetic fire chief, ordered his men to clear the vegetation and debris from around the hole.

"Now, goddammit, let's put up some barricades here! I don't want nothing more falling in that hole." Timms tromped to where Sandra and Peter lay on their stomachs at the opening, trying to stay in contact with their trapped daughter. "Ma'am, sir. Could I ask you to step back from the hole?"

Sandra, her face puffed and moist from crying, did not want to move.

"She's my baby. She needs me."

"Well, just right now we can't have you at this hole. You want us to get her out, we have to see what's keeping her in."

Peter stood and pulled Sandra to her feet.

"Come on, let's let them see what they can do."

Timms flicked on a large and intensely powerful flashlight.

"Thank you. Now why don't you both go over there and sit with your boy. I'll have my people send over some coffee."

Peter and Sandra backed away from the trap they had planted. In their anguish all they could see was the terrible irony of how well it had worked.

Will sat wrapped in a blanket beside one of the shiny fire trucks.

"Are they going to get Andie out?"

Peter turned to Will.

"Sure they will. All these people here, she'll be out in no time."

"I don't see how. They're too big. No way they can climb down to get Andie."

"Maybe they won't have to. Maybe they can just drop her a rope and lift her right up."

Will remained suspicious. "Maybe . . ."

Peter and Sandra sat with their son and watched as Timms took a position at the hole. Timms shone his bright light down into its depths. What he saw far below appeared to be a crumpled layer of metal, completely covering the bottom. If the girl was in the hole she had to be somewhere underneath.

To himself he muttered in a voice of doubt and surprise, "Damn . . ."

To Andromeda he called out in a voice filled with optimism, "Andie? Little girl?"

The sound of faint sniffling came to his ears. It was followed by a tiny voice, muffled by the crumpled metal barrier.

"Yeah? Who is that?"

"My name is Timms! I'm a fireman! I'm here to get you out! I want to ask you some questions! Can you answer a few questions for me?"

"I suppose . . ."

So far, so good.

"Honey, are you caught on anything? Is your leg stuck? Does anything hurt?"

"My bottom hurts, and I peed my pants."

"I think I'd pee my pants too if I fell in this here hole."

"Big people only pee their pants if they're really old. You must be really old."

Timms smiled. The kid was holding up.

"Andie, tell me if you're stuck."

"I don't think I am."

"You can move your legs?"

"Yes."

"And your arms too?"

"A little."

"Do you think you're cut anywhere? Do you think any of your bones are broken?"

"My bottom is scraped. My feet feel ouchy, but my bones are okay."

It was looking better all the time.

"Can you see my light shining down?"

"I can see it through the holes."

"You mean you can see the piece of metal over your head, the metal with the holes."

"They look like stars."

"Is there anything between you and the metal? Can you reach it?"

"There's nothing, but . . . but I can't reach it. It's too far."

Timms could hear Andromeda's sniffles returning.

"Andie, that's okay. We'll reach it for you. What else is down there?"

"Just a big piece of wood and another piece of wood. That's what I'm standing on. And there's some branches sticking out."

"You mean roots."

"Yeah, roots."

"Okay, Andie, listen. I'm going to leave for a minute but I'll be right back."

"Don't take the stars! It's too dark already! I don't like the dark!"

"I won't take the stars. Just hold on a second."

Keeping his light trained into the hole, Timms yelled over at his nearest man.

"Rig up a spot and shoot it down this hole! On the double!"

His men quickly rushed to offload a light and stand. They brought it to the hole and aimed it down as another firefighter hooked it to the truck generator and fired it up. The bright light illuminated not just the depths of the shaft but most of the surrounding area as well. Timms turned off his own light and called back down to Andromeda.

"How's that?"

"It's okay. How long do I have to stay here?"

"I don't know, Andie. We're trying to get you out of there as fast as we can."

"Hurry. My legs are tired."

Timms stood and motioned to Peter, who walked over.

"How is she?"

"She doesn't seem injured and she says she isn't caught on anything. What I need to know from you is if she has any medical condition that I should know about. Is she diabetic, does she have epilepsy, is she on any medication?"

"No, nothing."

"Good. I know you both want to stay by your daughter and that's understandable, but I can only have one of you near the hole at a time. I don't know what we're dealing with yet, so the less pressure we put on the opening the better. I don't want to see this thing collapse."

"Just tell us what to do. We want to help."

"That's what I like to hear. You say she just fell in this hole."

"We didn't even know it was there."

"That's not surprising. This whole area is full of ankle busters. There *is* one thing that really, seriously bothers me. I don't get how she fell to the bottom of a hole that's blocked so far down by a piece of metal. How do you think something like that could happen?"

"It was probably already in there."

"I don't see how. From the looks of it the thing is jammed in tight all around. Anyhow, we have to get past it. If we do, we ought to be able to just hoist her up and out."

"What's it going to take?"

"We can't get a man down that hole. It's too tight and, besides, even though your daughter made it down okay, the walls of these old shafts are notoriously so-so. We mess with the shaft itself we could end up bringing down the whole deal. 'Course, that metal piece is good that way. It should protect her a little from the normal crumble that happens in these things. I'm thinking it'd just be quicker to dig us another shaft alongside."

"But she's ninety feet down. How long would that take?"

"Three days, maybe more. At minimum she's in there for the night."

With a terrible sense of déjà vu, Peter realized he was hearing Sandra's predicted timeline for such an event to make the national news. It was appearing appallingly likely they would find out if her theory was correct.

"In the meantime I'll work on getting past that piece of metal," Timms continued. "Might be able to lower down a heavy magnet on a line, might pull it free. Can't know until we try."

Peter meant his response with every fiber of his being.

"Try."

THIRTEEN
THE SQUEEZE

Andromeda could, with some effort, squeeze her arms up and down past her body. But she could not sit and she could not climb. She could only stand or slump. The scrape on her bottom hurt but it took too much effort to try to reach back to rub out the pain. What made her most uncomfortable was the wooden board digging into her back. The stupid board took up so much space it made it hard for her to move at all.

She was able to move up and down on her toes, and in doing so she realized the ground beneath the wood square was soft and spongy. She couldn't see what it was made of but it felt like she was standing on a pillow.

Her head was the freest part of her body. She could look to both sides and even up but in the darkness, pierced only by thin rays of light streaming down through the scattered holes in the metal, there was little to see. It hurt her neck to keep looking up to the points of light, which reminded her of stars, but the alternative was to stare straight ahead into cold earth and the creepy-looking white roots etched along its length.

She hated to look at the roots. They reminded her so strongly of the roots from her lost basement. They reminded her of the voices and the nightmares.

They reminded her of the monster.

At least she was not cold. The shaft was, in fact, on the warm side. Although the air was stale and smelled of something musty, like the smell that came from opening the pages of an old soggy book, something Will might have found, it was at least breathable.

Andromeda could hear distant echoes of the activity outside, but where she stood at the bottom of the shaft it was mostly silent.

In the silence she began to think she could hear her own heartbeat. It was very, very faint, but as she forced her ears to focus she thought she heard it distinctly. *Poom-poom, poom-poom, poom-poom.*

Andromeda decided the sound of her own heart would be her companion in the hole. She would think of it as a separate being whose one wish was to make sure Andromeda stayed safe.

She rested her neck from looking up at what she told herself were real stars to stare ahead into the dank shaft wall. Her heartbeat was her companion, the pinpoints of light were real stars, maybe even planets, where there were cities and farms and oceans with mermaids and talking fish. The springy floor was a cloud that held her up, and under the cloud was a bright kingdom where unicorns ran through fields and huge butterflies landed on flowers that had faces and sang funny songs. The board in her back that made things less comfortable than they could be was now the prow of a glorious ship sailing through a magical sea, and Andromeda was the carved woman mounted to the prow who made sure the ship avoided all rocks, sea serpents and icebergs.

In every other direction Andromeda was able to find an alternative to reality. But straight ahead, looking at the whitish roots lacing the entire inside of the shaft, she found she was unable to come up with a substitute. To Andromeda they were just white roots that reminded her of the monster. Try as she might, she could not see them as anything else.

The only positive she found in the roots was that the effort of turning them into something nice might be enough to distract her from counting out the passage of time between now and the moment they pulled her out.

With the rest of her life waiting for her beyond the hole, Andromeda hoped the end of this squeeze in the dark was not too far off. How much she could stand was a question she prayed would never have an answer.

FOURTEEN

THE SCOOP

The *Wishbone Review* had two rooms. One was where its two writers did their writing and the other was where the printing press sat, turning out a newspaper once a week that almost never ran longer than thirty pages. Of those thirty pages nearly twenty-seven were taken up by ads for places like Lola's Beauty Salon, the Whistle Stop Inn, the Fourth Street Bowlarama, Prairie Value Real Estate, Coast to Coast Hardware, Glencoe's Drug, Woolworth's, Piggly Wiggly, Ben Franklin and Amy's Stop 'N Go.

Right in the center of town, the *Wishbone Review*'s office sat above the Wishbone Savings and Loan in a brick building that carried the same air of stable permanence one could find in all of Wishbone's similarly styled structures. The office enjoyed a view up and down Main Street as well as a kitty-corner view of Courthouse Square Park.

As Wishbone's true center, the one-block-square park was populated by tall elms, oaks, maples, wrought-iron benches, a bandstand and one grandiose bronze statue of a westward-gazing Lieutenant Jeremiah Hayworth. The park sat directly before Wishbone's pioneer courthouse, a place that had its glory in the dying days of the Old West, when farmers fought cattlemen, tycoon fought tycoon, and the air in Wishbone carried the acrid scent of seared gunpowder.

Howard Clark, with his feet on his desk, looked out his window at the *Wishbone Review* to Courthouse Square Park. Since Wishbone was a farming town, at seven in the morning the place would be hopping. But seven o'clock was still an hour away, and at six the streets were positively dead. The only person Clark could see was Melba Ashford. Still in her pink bathrobe and with her nearly blue hair still bound by green curlers,

Melba tossed bread crumbs to Wishbone's resident flock of pigeons. Opportunistic squirrels also joined the action as they darted for crumbs, filled their mouths and rushed off to hide the bounty. In Wishbone the event almost passed for news: OLD LADY FEEDS PIGEONS AND SQUIRRELS. In truth it had nearly the same impact as most of the items Clark and his staff partner, Julie Fletcher, were forced to call news. But Clark did what he could with the material at hand, writing articles about chickens on the loose with wit and flair not seen outside Manhattan or D.C. Still, Howard Clark wanted more.

Howard Clark wanted a scoop.

Clark was one of those people who had a core confidence that someday he would reach the pinnacle of success and fame. He kept a journal in lifelong preparation for the eventual publication of his memoirs. The fact that absolutely nothing memorable had yet happened to him did not dissuade Clark from scratching down each day larger thoughts about his rightful place.

Clark lifted this week's issue to be delivered later in the day. The headliner was WAGONEERS BLITZ PANTHERS 27–13, an article that belonged in the sports section, if the paper had actually had sections. Other items on the front page: WATER MAIN BREAK, CATHOLIC CHURCH ELEPHANT SALE, FENDER BENDER ON THIRD AND CHEYENNE. From there it just got worse.

Julie Fletcher, a housewife in her mid-forties, had been at the *Review* since high school. Five days a week she arrived promptly at eight in the morning and left promptly at four in the afternoon. She came because she truly enjoyed telling people about bake-offs and fireworks shows and charity auctions.

Howard Clark, on the other hand, was a twenty-four-year-old recent college grad from Iowa State. Inspired by all the journalistic greats, he had majored in journalism, beginning his hunt for the big story. Following graduation, he had applied to all the majors—*The New York Times*, the *Chicago Tribune*, the *San Francisco Chronicle*—but even with his collegiate distinctions, all they would counter with were intern positions, where he would clean out garbage cans, fetch coffee and pick up laundry.

Howard Clark did not fetch coffee.

Clark did a six-month stint at a paper in Prineville, Oregon, covering only the local high school sports. It was six months of pure boredom in a land of thorny scrub and tobacco chew. When he found out about an opening at the *Wishbone Review*, he threw his stereo, his box of clothes and his cat into his compact Chevy, a graduation present from his parents, and headed southeast to Wishbone. It was now a year and counting into his stint at the *Review,* and in his esteem he had still seen little news worth printing.

He had missed Wishbone's last murder, where the old man shotgunned down his wife. Covering the remaining petty crimes, which each received about twenty words in the *Review*'s crime blotter, took about fifteen minutes of labor, requiring only a stop at the sheriff's station to pick up the neatly typed list produced each week by Fred Zinneman. To return Zin's favor, Clark ordered the *Review*'s two layout and pressmen to enlarge the ad for the shop owned by Zin's wife, Amy's Stop 'N Go, a strangely mixed shop that sold everything from hair products to chess sets from India to those little golfer statues made out of nuts and bolts. Clark by now knew that no matter how large he made Amy's ad, business at her funky shop would probably not improve.

Clark's phone rang.

Believing it to be a wrong number—who else would call the *Review* at six in the morning?—Clark took his time lifting the receiver.

"Yeah?" he said, fully expecting the person on the other end of the line to ask, "Is this Younger's Seed and Feed?" But this is not what the voice asked, and the voice did not come from some fumbling stranger; the voice was that of Fred Zinneman.

"Howie?"

"Zin?"

"I thought you might be there. Listen, I got something for you. You know the Wileys? Pete and Sandra?"

"Yeah, he used to be some Wagoneer stud, she used to be some Wagoneer betty. I got them on a list of recent foreclosures. What of it?"

"One of their two kids, the little girl—well, she fell down an old shaft. We got all the services out there right now."

Clark swung his feet down from his desk as his newshound nose began to sniff a story.

"How long ago?"

"Sometime last night, maybe around eight or nine."

"Is she dead?"

"No, doesn't sound like she's even hurt. Just stuck. But boy, she is way down."

"So what's the prognosis?"

"Huh?"

"How long until you get her out?"

"Timms is telling the parents a day or so, but between you and me, this thing could take too long. She's got no water, she's got no food—"

"So this little kid might die down there."

"Just might."

"That is so sad."

Clark did not feel sad, however. For once it was bona fide news. Clark suddenly grew protective.

"Anybody else know about this?"

"Nah, you're it buddy. We've been out there digging all night. Couldn't get to a phone until now. I mean, I just came in for doughnuts and coffee. Fact is, I have to head back."

"First, wait—tell me where it is."

As Zinneman gave directions and as Clark scribbled them down, he began to frame how he would handle the saga. First thing he had to do was knock WAGONEERS BLITZ PANTHERS 27–13 and FENDER BENDER ON THIRD AND CHEYENNE to the back where they belonged. At least the front and back pages would have to be reprinted. A couple of ads might shrink to accommodate this breaking story. But since this was real news and not the daily crapola about a bat living in the school gym, Clark would do what it took to give it the prominence it deserved.

He grabbed a tape recorder, extra pens, his camera and his trusty notebook and rushed out the door.

On the street he piled into his Chevy, revved its puny engine and sped down Main Street, causing Melba Ashford's pigeons to take to the air. He didn't care. He was on the trail of a story worth telling.

News, glorious news at last!

The sun creeping up the sky cast long shadows from the trucks and equipment surrounding the open shaft. Sandra lay on her stomach near the entry. Half dozing from fatigue, she hummed a song down to her daughter in the hole. Peter lay in the shadow of the largest fire truck, tossing in fitful sleep. Will sat awake.

He had not slept a minute since his sister had fallen into the well. His eyes were dry because he had not wanted to blink. He felt if he did not constantly stare at the hated opening that had swallowed Andromeda, it would suck her in farther. So Will did not blink and his eyes were now red and sore.

He had been offered a turn to sit by the hole but he had refused. He refused out of shame. Andromeda had gone to fetch drinks from the cooler for both of them. If he had been the one to fetch the drinks instead of Andromeda, then he would be the one in that hole right now. Will knew he had let his sister down; he knew her falling in was his fault. He should have gone for the drinks himself. He wished he were the one who was in the hole.

He had no idea how close he had come to getting that wish.

Will fought to stay awake, to make sure his gaze propelled the police and firemen to do everything they could to remove Andromeda from the shaft. Twenty feet from the side of the shaft, the sheriff and the man named Timms directed other men to dig a hole. The hole was now eight feet deep and ten feet wide. They lined the sides of the hole with wood planks and kept digging, pulling out the dirt and rocks in buckets tied to ropes. Using picks, the men worked hard to crack the tough earth, but in ten hours they had only made it eight feet. Will could do the math. A little more than nineteen feet each day meant it would take five days to reach Andromeda. He knew his little sister; he knew how scared she was of the dark.

He knew she would never make it.

Rising to his feet and tossing aside the blanket, Will felt he had to make the need for speed more clear. He marched to Sheriff Chuck Austin and pulled on the sheriff's shirt. Exhausted from a lack of sleep but getting a second wind from the coffee and doughnuts brought in by Fred Zinneman, Austin turned to Will Wiley.

"What is it, son?"

"You have to go faster. Andie won't make it if you don't."

"Son, we're working as fast as we can. This is hard ground here. It doesn't give way without a fight."

"You have to work faster. I mean it."

"Listen, you can do everybody, including your sister, a big favor if you just keep out of our way and let us do our job. Okay?"

Will turned for a moment to watch as a light blue Chevy pulled in and a lanky young man with wild red hair stepped out carrying a camera and notepad. Will turned back to the sheriff.

"What about food and water? If you guys are hungry and thirsty, then so is she."

Austin stopped midchew. The boy was right. Austin swallowed the last chunk of custard-filled doughnut and called over to Timms.

"Hey, Bobby, what can we do about getting some food and water down to the kid?"

Timms walked over. Will noticed the redheaded man, who had begun taking pictures of the scene, was now paying their little huddle some attention. Timms looked perplexed.

"How am I supposed to get food or water past that sheet of metal? She can't reach it and none of the holes are big enough to feed anything through."

"Well, we have to try something."

"What I'm trying right now is to get that damn sheet out of there. Boys are hooking a heavy magnet on a cable right now. Electromagnet. Strong enough to lift a car. Let's give that a shot first, and if it works we'll be feeding her bacon and eggs at the Whistle Stop."

Coming out of his fitful sleep, Peter saw Will standing with Timms and Sheriff Austin. His bones aching and his head sore from the emotional storm, he whistled to Will, who walked to him.

"What's going on?"

"They're talking about getting Andie some water and stuff."

In the original plan, Sandra and Peter would have asked Will to carry a bag to put in the cooler when they sent him to fetch drinks. The bag would fall with him down the hole. In the bag would be candy bars, apples, sandwiches and a half gallon of water.

Andie, who was not given the chance to carry the bag, had nothing. No food, no water. That fact alone caused Peter his greatest desperation. He would jump off a cliff onto a plain of knives right this second if it would stop Andromeda from suffering even one more minute.

He could see the fatigue in Will's eyes.

"You been awake this whole time?"

"I can't sleep."

"Will, if you want to be on your toes here, you have to sleep. Now, why don't you just lie down and take a nap."

"I want to watch when they try the magnet."

Will nodded to the fire truck nearest the shaft. Timms and his men had the ladder extended nearly horizontal. On the end of the ladder they mounted a block and tackle. On the end of the line running through the block and tackle was a saucer-shaped magnet, out of which ran a heavy-gauge power cord.

Timms walked to the shaft opening.

"Mrs. Wiley, ma'am, could I ask you to step back?"

Sandra, bleary-eyed, looked up at Timms and merely nodded. She moved back with muscles on the verge of crashing to join Peter and Will. Timms took Sandra's place at the hole, lying on his stomach. He called down to Andromeda.

"Andie? It's Timms. Are you awake?"

In the bottom of the tight shaft, unable to sit, in the stuffy dark with the musty smell and the white roots and with her pants soaked by urine, Andromeda had not been able to sleep. As her anxiety grew so did the drumming volume of her heartbeat. The *poom-poom, poom-poom* was almost audible over Timms's voice. She lifted her weak head and spoke through lips cracking from thirst.

"I'm thirsty."

"We know, Andie, and we're going to do something about that. But first I want to let you know what's going on. I'm going to have to turn out the light for a little while; it's going to get dark for a few minutes. Can you handle that?"

"I don't know. I think so."

"That's a girl. When I turn out the light I'm going to send down a big magnet and I'm going to try to pull that metal thing out from above your head. It might be a little bit noisy and a little bit of dirt might fall on you, but if we can get it out we should be able to pull you right up, okay? Wouldn't that be nice?"

"I don't like it here. I want to go."

"And we want you to. Now, I'm going to turn off the light and then I'm going to send down the magnet, okay?"

"Okay."

Andromeda looked back up at the stars in the metal and watched as they suddenly went out. It was now pitch black in the hole. She could not help but grow more worried. The dark, which now closed in completely, reminded her of so many terrors, like madmen under her bed or ghosts in the attic or roots in the basement. But Timms said the dark would last only a few minutes, so she tried to be strong like she knew Will would be if he were the one in here.

Outside, Timms and his men swung the truck ladder until the pulley with the magnet was right over the hole. With great care they lowered the magnet into the hole, and the saucer disappeared in the dark. Using his flashlight, shining it down the hole, Timms gestured with one hand for his men to keep feeding out line and power cable. He watched until the magnet was an inch or so above the sheet of metal and then he brought his fingers together in a pinch of air to let his men know how close they were. An inch more line and cable, and Timms made a motion to cease. He leapt back to his feet and nodded to his men to flip the power switch.

Beneath the metal sheet Andromeda had heard the approach of the magnet. She heard it coming closer as it swung from side to side down the shaft, kicking loose small bits of debris that tinkled down on the metal. It finally came to a thudding stop on the sheet. For a moment nothing happened, but then the metal seemed to suck itself against the magnet thing and Andromeda heard the metal groan. The sound of her heart, the *poom-poom*, grew even louder.

At the top of the well, all eyes focused on what was going on at the shaft. Howard Clark clicked off a few more establishing shots, then stepped closer to the Wiley family and stuck out his hand. Peter, his mind unfocused, absently took it and shook it.

"Mr. Wiley? I'm Howard Clark, with the *Review*. I'm sorry to hear what's happened to your little girl. I want you to know the whole town is behind you on this."

Sandra had the quickest doubt.

"The whole town? How do they even know?"

"Word gets around. Could you tell me, sir, what's happening right now?"

Will spoke first.

"They're going to get my sister out with a magnet."

"Really? I've never heard of that happening before."

Peter gave a more specific answer as he considered his role in Andromeda's entombment.

"There's a piece of metal"—*a piece of metal I put there*—"that's blocking access to our daughter"—*who might starve or die from thirst*—"and they need to get that out before they can pull out Andie"—*from the trap Sandra and I set.*

Clark scribbled in his pad.

"Is that her name? Andie?"

"Short for Andromeda."

"Daughter of Cassiopeia, chained to a rock for offending the gods with her incredible beauty." Clark responded to their uncertain looks. "From Greek mythology—your daughter's name."

"Oh, we got it out of a science book. It's one of the constellations."

"Would you happen to have a picture of her?"

"What for?"

"Well, I'd like to run the story with her picture."

"For the paper? You're writing a story about this?"

"When something like this happens to one of Wishbone's own, I'd be derelict not to. People in these parts want to know what's happening to their neighbors."

Peter thought with cynicism bred from experience that just yesterday those very same neighbors hadn't given a damn what happened to the Wileys. But Clark's presence and his desire to write a story brought Sandra halfway back to the original purpose of the shaft fall.

"Next you'll want to bring in TV cameras." She said it almost as a suggestion.

Clark suddenly realized he did want TV, if he could figure out how to maintain control. He scanned his mental-strategy banks and discovered a way.

"Some people don't read the *Review.*"

Sandra nodded. "I have some pictures in the truck."

Peter was growing concerned.

"Sandy . . ."

Sandra took Clark by the elbow and began leading him to the family truck. She briefly looked over her shoulder to Peter but she did not stop.

"In a minute." To Clark she asked, "What kind do you need?"

Sandra was sending Clark signals that told him he could dispense with beating around the bush.

"Something innocent. She should be smiling."

"I know just the one."

Will and Peter watched as Sandra and Clark yanked down a box from the back of the truck. Sandra opened the box for Clark, pulled out a Kmart photo of a smiling Andromeda and handed it to Clark. He smiled in satisfaction.

"Perfect." Clark placed the photo in his notepad. His eyes gleamed at the rest of the family photos. "Mind if I look through these? I might want some snaps of the whole family during happier times to contrast with the ones I'm getting here. It'll make the story more complete."

"Help yourself."

Sandra left Clark and rejoined Peter and Will. Peter didn't like what he was seeing.

"Doesn't seem like this is the time for that."

"This is exactly the time, Peter. Besides, Timms said it himself; we'll probably have Andie out of there in a few minutes and then we can put this whole thing behind us. There won't be any story to write and that's what we're hoping, right?"

Still uncertain, Peter turned with his family, all three heavily anxious, to watch as Timms gave the signal to begin raising the magnet.

"Slowly! I don't want it jerking!"

The crew took up the line and cable slack and began to pull.

At the bottom of the shaft, Andromeda felt the two-by-four at her back shudder, and, the metal above her head groaned more loudly. The metal and the two-by-four began to rise up the shaft. The square of wood on which she stood began to shudder also and at first hinted that it would lift her too, attached as it was to the bottom of the two-by-four, but it suddenly dawned on her that the board at her feet was actually beginning to tip down. It was being torn loose from the two-by-four.

That fact did not startle her so much as did the precipitous amount of dirt and debris that the mobile metal had begun tearing loose from the walls of the shaft. The nails sticking up from the back of the two-by-four also cut loose a lot of dirt, nearly all off which tumbled onto Andromeda's neck and then into her clothing. So much dirt had begun raining down on Andromeda that she was forced to lower her head and close her eyes. It was getting hard to breathe. The cavities around her body were being filled. When a series of softball-sized chunks broke loose to jam into what little free space remained, Andromeda decided it was time to scream.

With an ear to the shaft opening, Timms heard her scream first.

"Stop! Hold it!"

His men stopped. Timms quickly swung his flashlight back into the hole. He could see the metal was not giving way and was instead just gouging its way up the shaft, tearing loose enough material from the shaft walls so that the metal now had piles of dirt all around its edges. He could see that dirt had plugged some of the precious air holes. In other spots dirt was spilling down through the holes, presumably landing on Andromeda's head.

"Andromeda! Are you okay?"

Andromeda was bawling now.

"There's . . . there's dirt and I . . . I can't move my legs!"

Timms sighed in frustration. The metal sheet had moved only a foot but had torn loose enough material to pack Andromeda's legs in tight. Andromeda shrieked in frightened anger.

"I want out! I want out now! *Mommy!*"

Sandra, hearing her daughter's shriek, turned and buried her head in Peter's chest. Clark quickly raised his camera to capture the poignant shot of Sandra turning to her husband for comfort. As he tried to frame the shot, thinking he wasn't getting enough of Sandra, he noticed that Sandra seemed to turn Peter slightly, a move that presented more of her face. Clark had to wonder if she had not done it on purpose, because now the shot was perfectly composed. He clicked off four frames and zoomed in for a close-up.

Timms circled his arm in the air and his men shut down power to the electromagnet. They pulled it from the hole and swung it aside. As they reinstalled the light that was Andromeda's only illumination, Timms walked to Peter, Sandra and Will.

"Won't work. I'm sorry. We'll have to keep digging."

Peter was near tears. Sandra was already crying. Will was too stunned to know what to do.

Peter spoke through a cracking voice, "This is really taking too long."

"That's because we're doing it by hand. This ground is a lot harder than I thought it'd be. I say we ought to try to bring in a drill."

"What do you mean, *try?*"

Sheriff Austin stepped up to answer.

"We'll have to see if we have the budget for it. This thing is already tapping the well big-time, so to speak. Any outside gear we bring in has to be paid for. That means it has to come out of the budget, which means we have to check with the city council and the mayor for a go-ahead."

"And how long will that take?"

"If it was up to me, one phone call and it'd be on its way—we'd figure out how to pay for it later. But these guys are politicians. How long does it take any politician to make up his mind?"

Timms tried to reassure them.

"We'll pressure them to give it the stamp. We'll get that drill, don't worry."

Peter did worry; he worried a lot.

"What about getting her some water at least?"

"I'm going to run a thin-gauge copper pipe down there and try to fish it through one of the holes. We can deliver her some water and maybe even some soup."

Will chimed in.

"She likes tomato."

Timms, a father five times over and aware what this experience had to be doing to this family, gave Will's neck a gentle squeeze.

"I'll cook it myself."

Armed with a set of Wiley family photos and his camera filled with shots of the ongoing rescue, Howard Clark sped back to his office. He pulled into a space next to a red Cadillac. As he jumped from his car, he nearly ran into Denny Sharf as Denny opened the Savings and Loan for the day. Denny was curious about Clark's haste.

"You look like you got someplace to go."

"That's because I'm going places, Sharf. By the way, I was considering doing a piece on all your recent foreclosures. A bigwig like you deserves to have his face in the paper."

"You said *was*."

"Something else came up. Lucky you."

"I foreclose because it's business, Clark. It's not personal. It gets personal because that's how they want it. They want everyone to say, Oh, ain't he the bad guy because he won't let us live on his land for free."

"Who is *they*?"

"You know. They. Them. The trash. All those who think the world owes them something and who want to live on my dime. It's all these slackers who're holding us back."

"Like the Wileys?"

"Yeah, the Wileys. Wiley is a fool and he had no business putting me out the way he did."

"How'd he do that?"

"Polluted my soil. I had to file a lawsuit. It's on record, go see for yourself. Maybe you should do a story about that."

"Maybe I will. So you don't think much of Peter Wiley, his wife, Sandra, or their kids, Will and Andromeda?"

"Don't know the girl but that boy is a garbage picker. You know that's how they made a living? Sent their kid out to pick through garbage."

"Is that on the record too?"

As the curly hairs on the back of Denny's neck stood on end, he suddenly realized he was being pushed into a corner.

"On what record?"

"For my story on the Wileys. You've been a big part of their life lately; I think you should have a chance to tell your side of it."

"Why would you be writing a story on the Wileys?"

"Their girl fell down an abandoned shaft outside town. Only reason she's in there is because they needed someplace to camp. Only reason they had to camp is because they don't have a home anymore. Only reason they don't have a home anymore is because of you." Clark gave Denny his best have-a-nice-day smile and started up the steps to his office. "Anything else you want to tell me, Sharf, you know where to find me."

Without knowing exactly why, Denny suddenly felt sick.

The first person Clark got in touch with was Julie Fletcher. She drove in right away to receive the numerous calls Clark expected they would get as the day progressed. Running through his Rolodex, Clark's fingers fell on the card that held the second number he chose to call.

He got through to Rayna Higgins at KCBS in Los Angeles. Higgins was an Iowa State alumna who had gone much farther than Clark in her own journalistic career and who was suddenly a tremendous asset to know. Now a segment producer for the CBS affiliate in Los Angeles, Higgins was Clark's ace in the hole.

"Rayna? Hey, it's Howard Clark. . . . New York? Shit, I wish. No, I'm living in the sticks working for the hicks. . . . I know, I know, we definitely should talk more often. . . . yeah, I know. Anyhow, listen. I got a story I'd like to pipe through you. It's a human interest thing about a good family on some bad ropes. . . . No, it's not about a family going homeless; well, part of it is, but there's more to it. Just let me tell you. They went homeless a few days ago and now their five-year-old girl fell ninety-something feet down an abandoned oil well shaft. She's stuck tight. Going to take a lot to get her out. Could be we got another Kathy Fiscus, Floyd Collins or even a Baby Carlotta on this one." Clark flashed on his most unique idea ever. "Could be we got a Baby Andromeda."

Clark held up the Kmart photo of Andromeda. In the semiprofessional portrait Andromeda, with a ribbon in her hair and wearing a spring dress, sat before a cloth backdrop on pillows and held a teddy bear as she gave a bright smile. She was the paragon of a sweet little girl.

"Helps us big-time that the kid is very seriously cute. . . . No, she's not black, she's white, they're all white. . . . I thought you'd think so. By the way, I carry the paper. I'm on the inside and they're only talking to me. . . . Is that binding? . . . Good, because I'm taping this conversation: You'll set it up so I get CBS? You're a goddess. I'll work the AP here so you handle the camera crew and all. . . . Hey, now, my hair is fine. Just send out the boys. . . . Okay, see you soon. Bye-bye."

Clark hung up and hit the "memo record" button on his answering machine to end the recording of his conversation with Higgins. He spun and took a look at himself in a mirror. He ran his fingers through his shock of hair and then turned to Julie before he made his next call, to the Associated Press.

"Set me up an appointment for a cut. I could use a trim and maybe see about toning down my color a little."

"But we're in the middle of this story. Why now?"

"Got to get ready for my close-up."

FIFTEEN

THE CIVIC PRIDE

By one-thirty the debate was in full swing.

With all five members of the city council assembled, Mayor Donald Moser, who was in the midst of a nasty reelection campaign against former mayor Tommy Vale, took his customary role of Switzerland.

"I have an estimate on bringing in this big drill. The total from start to finish ends up being nearly a quarter of this month's budget. Before we start, let me say we can't afford that and we all know it. So if you want to do this thing, you figure out where the money comes from. We already got a big overtime tab on our boys working out there now. Just keep all this in mind before you decide to bring in outsiders."

Allison Larkins spoke first. "Why do we even need to discuss this? Let's bring in the drill and get that child out of there."

Janice Piasecki spoke next. "That's the shortsighted talk that handed us our budget mess in the first place. Where are we going to get that money? We're losing mom-and-pop operations every week. Our tax base is shrinking. This keeps up, downtown is going to be a ghost town. What do we cut from the budget? School lunches? Books for the library? Funding for the fire department? What? I'd like to know."

Larkins responded. "We give up one of our parades. That's a chunk of change right there. We can give up George Washington and Abe Lincoln. We're talking about a little girl—"

"Who doesn't even live in our town." Frank O'Connor, a corpulent man with a squared-off buzz cut, leaned back with his usual imperial air. "Why should we pay for this rescue when these people don't even have an address in Wishbone? We have a fiscal duty to the people who actually pay their taxes, which we will seriously violate if we stupidly spend their money on every man jack looking for a handout. In my opinion, we should hand this over to the county board."

Kelly Mahon, who held Frank O'Connor responsible for ending a taxpayer-financed summer camp for local kids, a turn of events that meant Mahon and his wife now personally had to shell out the cash to get rid of their kids for a few blessed weeks each year, always took up a position contrary to O'Connor no matter what the issue.

"We all know Pete Wiley and his girl Sandra are Wishbone through and through."

Piasecki edged in. "Not *are, were*. It's an important distinction. They took themselves off the roster. Our responsibility for them ended the day they said good-bye. Frank is right; we should pass this over to county. It's more a county issue anyway. That land where the girl fell is unincorporated."

Larkins was incredulous. "You are such a hypocrite, Piasecki. Just last week you sat here and rallied us to get that very section annexed into the town limits. You people . . ."

Piasecki grew defensive. "What do you mean by that? You always do that, Larkins — 'You people . . .' It really ticks me off. I want to know what you mean by it."

The mayor sought calm.

"Janice, you know she didn't mean anything by it."

"No, I don't know that. I can tell when I'm being insulted."

"You're being paranoid."

"See, I find it insulting that you would say that, Mayor."

"Look, I'm not going to waste this council's time and my time tiptoeing around your ego, Piasecki. Now, it's clear we got two for and two against. We still haven't heard from Cullman."

All eyes turned to Cullman Shermer. Leaning back in his chair with the back propped against the wall, wearing his traditional faded overalls and work boots, Shermer, a leather-faced rancher who fought his way onto the city council over a water rights issue that caused many a nerve to be pinched, relished his role as the tie breaker. He took his time speaking.

"I'd like to see the girl come out of there."

Larkins and Mahon smiled. Larkins looked directly at Piasecki.

"So that's three against two. We vote to save the girl."

But Shermer, in his slow way of talking, was not finished.

"I said I'd like to see that girl out, but I'm wonderin' how we're gonna pay for it. We gotta give up something. Miss Larkins says give up a tradition we been honorin' for more than sixty years now. Maybe she don't have a problem dishonorin' two of the finest Americans who ever lived, but I'll wager the rest of the town don't feel like she does. I'll wager the rest of the town wants their presidents' parade. I don't know what kinda liberal hooey she's tryin' to hand us here, but for your information, Miss Larkins, here in Wishbone we don't burn the flag."

Now it was Piasecki who smiled. "So it's three against two we vote to save the girl but without breaking the bank by bringing in a load of high-priced gear."

Allison Larkins was stunned.

"You people!"

SIXTEEN

BABY ANDROMEDA

His tie loosened and his sleeves rolled up to give the impression he was part of the rescue team, Howard Clark stood holding a mike as he faced the waiting TV camera. His once-red hair was now more brown, and it was cut and combed into an appropriately conservative coiffure.

The CBS crew out of Wichita had arrived at eleven in the morning. Receiving the elements from Clark, they began an on-site editing of a segment to be played later. By five o'clock, just in time for the first evening-news broadcast, Clark was out of makeup and ready to roll.

It had been a busy day. For Howard Clark it was turning out to be the best day of his life.

Before his haircut Clark had written a quick article for the *Review*, which Julie Fletcher quickly handed off to the pressmen, who in turn churned out a double run, which in turn hit the streets to be read by an energized populace stunned that such a tragedy was happening right here in their very own town. Everybody seemed to have some tale to connect them to the Wiley family. The baker: "I sold the little girl and her father some day-old bread just last week." The grocer: "I gave Andie a lollipop the last time she came in with her mother. They bought a roll of toilet paper and a can of Hormel tamales." The dentist: "I filled one of Andie's molars just last year. I was going to tell her mother she's due for a checkup." A little boy: "Andie might marry me."

But the most common phrase one could hear when discussing the topic everybody was suddenly discussing was "Oh, the poor thing."

Wearing an earphone, Clark ran his fingers through his hair to slightly mess it up, as if he had seconds earlier manned a wheelbarrow. He quickly reached down, grabbed some dirt and rubbed his arms with it to complete the effect.

Through the earphone he could hear the anchorman at CBS's Wichita affiliate station, KWCH, as he set up the ongoing tragedy for the viewing public. Clark looked to the side of the camera as the field producer counted down with her fingers. Clark took one last nervous gulp before the field producer waved him to fame.

"This is Howard Clark reporting from Wishbone, Kansas. In this desolate place on the outskirts of a town hit by hard times, we stand by as a tragedy unfolds for a family already pressed by misfortune. Their only daughter, their Baby Andromeda, has, in a terrible turn of events for the recently homeless family, fallen more than ninety feet down an abandoned shaft. Firefighters and local engineers have worked through the night to effect Baby Andromeda's rescue, but as of this minute they are not expected to reach her for a matter of days. I've spoken with the family and here is what they have to say."

Clark breathed a sigh of relief as the producer made the cutoff sign. On a nearby monitor showing the live-news broadcast, he could see himself interviewing the Wiley family as the prerecorded segment took over. Behind the camera on another, larger monitor shaded by a taped-on piece of cardboard, the three Wileys watched the live broadcast of their tragedy. Will was astounded.

"That's us! Man, Andie should see this."

Peter Wiley, who in the prerecorded interview was the more nervous of the two parents, took a backseat to the more confident Sandra. Clark had to admit that Mrs. Wiley, a highly attractive woman in any crowd, had a photogenic flair for the camera. Sandra looked into the camera and her tears flowed on cue.

"Andie is so afraid of the dark. . . . We just want our baby back safe."

The interview was followed by a sequence narrated by Clark that showed the family photos, shots of Peter as a star quarterback, shots of Peter and Sandra, at that time a Henderson, smiling in finery at their senior prom, the Kmart shot of Andromeda, a photo of their old farm and a current video of bulldozers carving roads beyond a glossy sign that read ROYAL OAK GARDENS. There were a couple of man-on-the-street interviews with Wishbone residents who related how the Wileys were good, good people who didn't deserve what was happening to them. The segment ended with an ominous push-in shot of the hole itself, run in slow motion effect to increase the sense of danger.

The tale Clark presented so digestibly was exactly the tale he hoped to tell. Hearts would be tugged by this one. The Wileys were more sympathetic than he could ever hope.

Clark was satisfied with how quickly he had put the whole thing together with a lot of help from Rayna Higgins and the crew she had sent out from KWCH. Word from Julie Fletcher that the Associated Press had run with his story was the capper. The name Howard Clark would head an article that would probably run in the very same papers that had previously decided all he was good for was fetching coffee. Come tomorrow, Clark would have to send Julie out on a souvenir hunt as she bought every paper known to man.

Clark prepared for his wrap-up. The countdown came and then the wave. "This is Howard Clark, reporting from Wishbone, Kansas."

"And we're out. Nice work, Clark. You're a natural."

Of that he had never had a doubt.

Clark handed back the mike and glanced at the monitor to see the two KWCH anchors chatting about the tragedy. They both seemed sincere in their concern.

"It always seems to take an incident like this to bring people together."

"Let's just pray the story of Baby Andromeda has a happy ending."

"We can only hope. In other news . . ."

Clark walked over to the Wiley family and placed a hand on Sandra Wiley's firm shoulder.

"You did great, all of you. Now the whole world is on your side."

Peter, who noticed the way Clark's hand squeezed Sandra's shoulder almost lovingly, was too distraught to dredge up the energy to be jealous. He thought about what Clark had just said.

The whole world was on his side.

Would they be if they knew he had planned all this?

He knew they would not. After they burned Peter and Sandra at the stake they might still try to rescue Andromeda, but he believed their efforts would not be so directed—they might not work so hard for a family of liars. They might not get Andromeda out in time.

Thankfully the lie that Peter was just an innocent victim of a terrible accident had the appearance of truth, because the face of distraught innocence was a mirror image to the face of guilty anguish. The only two people who knew how to tell the difference were he and Sandra, and they would never, ever tell.

SEVENTEEN

POOM-POOM

he stars in the metal sheet had diminished since the magnet episode. Now there were half as many as there used to be, all clustered in the center. The soil that had fallen around Andromeda's waist and legs now held her tight. She could not move her feet, which was just as well because she was certain the wood square upon which she had previously stood had completely broken loose from the two-by-four and had dropped to a farther depth. Wiggling her toes, Andromeda could feel only empty space below. She had been down in this place so long she had been forced to mess herself, and she cried for hours in displeasure. But the situation was improved in two regards.

The first improvement was the speaker and microphone the TV people lowered down to the metal sheet, which allowed her to talk to her mother and father more easily. It made them seem so much closer, almost within reach. The TV people asked Andromeda a few questions and she was happy to answer, knowing her answers would be on TV and might be seen by people who actually knew her.

"I want to be a animal doctor when I grow up, or—no, wait—I want to fly a plane, maybe to the moon."

She could hear people chuckling at her answers, but she could tell they weren't laughing at her and were instead laughing with her. The speaker and microphone constituted her first comfort.

The second was a thin metal tube that had been fished down to her. After a prolonged effort to snake the end through one of the holes in the metal, they lowered the tube to where she could reach its end with her mouth and on request she was sent down its length enough water to quench her thirst. They also poured down some tomato soup, but Andromeda was unprepared and it mostly just splashed on the front of her shirt to make her even more uncomfortable.

It had been twenty-three hours since her captivity began and Andromeda, who did not want to miss anything that was going on above, who was physically miserable, could no longer stay awake. She closed her eyes and nodded off to sleep.

In her dream Andromeda was with Will and her parents on a picnic. They sat on a blanket on the bank of a sparkling stream that cut through a narrow valley. Ringed by cliffs of sculpted granite, the valley was lined with trees whose leaves had turned every autumn shade of red, orange and yellow. Puffs of cottony seeds drifted through the air and all seemed tranquil. There was no one but Andromeda and her family, and in the dream it seemed just right.

Her mother's dream self, who looked like her mother but somehow did not feel like her mother, handed Andromeda a plate of food. Andromeda took it and saw that it was all sweets like cookies and cupcakes and candies. As colorful as it was, she didn't care to eat it. She knew she should be eating real food, like carrots and celery and maybe an apple. She watched as Will, her mommy and her daddy, with their backs to the stream, greedily ate the piles of sweets from their own plates.

Andromeda looked past her family to the sparkling stream. The sound of the water moving was the typical gurgle. But as she listened she heard something beneath the water's song.

The familiar chorus of sad voices, the men and women, old and young, was subtly hidden beneath the gentle flow. Andromeda couldn't discern words, as usual, but this time she could discern meaning. She felt their message. And the message said one thing.

Leave.

Leave now.

Andromeda's gaze was suddenly forced back to her family. She watched as roots punctured the ground beneath Mommy, Daddy and Will and began racing up, curling around limbs and consuming flesh, which itself turned into root. The roots were thick and brutish near the ground. Higher up, consuming with every second more and more of the family flesh, the roots were much more delicate. The faces of Andromeda's family expressed sweeping agony as they were completely devoured.

Where Will had sat there now stood an inverted-root being, like a massive sea anemone on land. Its highest roots were wispy white and waved as if blown by some gentle wind. Two other root beings sat where her parents had sat, their white tops also blowing gently. The scene was surreal, and in a way even beautiful. At least it would be if Andromeda did not feel now more than ever a seething predation aimed her way. The roots tipped toward her and their tops opened to reveal in each of their centers a bulbous and pulsating bloodred organ, like a heart the size of a beach ball, heavily veined and spotted with disease. Their masses beat together with the sound of a single heart and the voices were no longer heard.

Poom-poom, poom-poom, poom-poom.

The sound had weight and force and it caused Andromeda's dream vision to swirl and swoon, overcome by a blanketing suffocation. A darkness descended and the beating of the heart grew so tremendously loud that Andromeda could not hear herself shouting over it.

She awoke to darkness.

She was still in the shaft.

And she could still hear the beating of the heart.

Andromeda quickly looked up and saw the stars were still there. She could faintly hear the men above still digging. Nothing had changed except that the sound of her heart was so loud.

Poom-poom.

With her arms free she moved her hand to her chest to feel if her heart was going to come right out of her body. It only took a few moments of feeling her own rhythm to realize the *poom-poom* did not come from her.

Her eyes fully adjusted to the dim light, Andromeda leaned closer to the network of white roots lacing the shaft wall. As she listened to the *poom-poom* she saw that the roots were pulsating ever so faintly with the same rhythm.

"Eewww."

Andromeda did not like worms, snakes or anything icky so she detested the image she saw only inches before her eyes. The roots were alive in a way she had never known possible. She had never been taught that plants had hearts that beat.

But the very act of her focusing on the roots caused the *poom-poom* to diminish to its previous background level. It was still present, but it no longer commanded attention.

"Mommy?"

"I'm here, sweetie."

Her mother's voice through the TV people's speaker quickly soothed Andromeda. The speaker, a bit on the tinny side, again squawked to life.

"What do you need, Andie? More water? Do you want to try some more soup?"

"Can you hum to me?"

"What song?"

" 'It's a Small World.' "

Andromeda's mother began humming for the twentieth time a song that reminded Andromeda of her beloved Mickey Mouse light, her great protector. The calming effect was immediate.

Andromeda tried for an hour to stay awake, not knowing if it was day-time or nighttime above, but then she fell back to sleep and dreamed no more dreams.

EIGHTEEN

DAY TWO

On the morning of Baby Andromeda's second day of captivity, after her story had been broadcast the previous evening to local stations and then to the nationals for the just-completed morning newscast, a full day earlier than Sandra had expected, things began to happen fast.

Under a vocal siege by Bobby Timms, who made overt threats to bring their heartless refusal to the attention of the media, the city council voted four to one, with Cullman Shermer still saying no, to fund the delivery and operation of an earth-moving drill. A beaming Janice Piasecki, now saying no expense was too great to save the life of a child, hogged the limelight to make the announcement before cameras that represented all the major networks.

"This is what we in Wishbone do for one of our own."

At nine in the morning the drilling company made a big TV splash as it promised to arrive by four in the afternoon, looking heroic but not cutting its rate a dime.

"We're very, very proud to be a part of this rescue."

After receiving a descriptive death threat, a fact not relayed to the media, the drilling company announced at nine-thirty that it would arrive by two in the afternoon and that its fee would be zero.

"We feel donating our services is the, uh . . . appropriate thing to do."

Cheering went up all around.

Miners, engineers and regular folks drove to the site and offered their services. Kids on bikes and churchgoers in family cars drove up with shovels and casseroles to lend a hand. They all got in line to haul dirt and work the picks.

"Tell me what to do. I'm here to help."

Stan's RV Center arrived with a brand-spanking-new motor home to house the Wiley family for the duration of the crisis.

"It comes with a full kitchen and two double beds."

The Whistle Stop Inn pitched in with regular deliveries of hot coffee and sandwiches for the Wileys and the workers. They presented the Wileys an invitation to drop by the Whistle Stop for one free meal a week for the next six months.

"We're there for you."

The manager of Wishbone's Woolworth's stopped by with a selection of discount toys for both Will and Andromeda.

"Every boy wants a Wookie."

The Bowlarama sent over passes for unlimited bowling one night a week for a year.

"Except for league night, come in anytime."

The Wileys received children's books from the House of Titles, a portable stereo and a selection of tapes from Ben Franklin, free groceries for three months from Piggly Wiggly, and from Joe's Garage a rebuilt transmission for Peter's truck whenever he had the chance to bring it in.

It had all been orchestrated by Howard Clark. He had Julie Fletcher calling every business in town to get a bidding war going to show who cared the most. All around town yellow ribbons appeared on oak trees. A drive through Wishbone, which was trying to hold on when other towns were failing, would tell even the most lazy-eyed observer that this was a town that cared.

Everybody who actually helped was given a golden lapel pin showing a bird flying before a sun, and they wore them proudly. The pins were not created for the occasion of Andromeda's rescue but were actually an overstock item from Amy's Stop 'N Go, castoffs from an aborted Earth Day celebration several years past. Wearing the pins, people stood straighter and smiled more often because they now had tangible proof that they were good. They were all helping out a little girl who was in a really bad way.

Clark added dimension to the story so it was no longer just about a little girl in a bad way because lots of little girls were in bad ways. In other countries little girls stepped on land mines or were kidnapped, beaten and killed, or were sold into prostitution or were intentionally starved by dictators draped in gold. Even in America there were plenty of little girls who needed help. Maybe they were homeless, maybe they had no parents at all, maybe they were abused by trusted friends, neighbors and family members. Maybe they were seized by strangers. Maybe they had a crippling illness requiring a lifetime of attention. What they all had in common was baggage, which the story of Baby Andromeda did not.

The first thing that worked in the case of Baby Andromeda was that it had a built-in ending. She would either be saved or she would die and either of these outcomes would happen in that brief period that was the American attention span. There was no long-term commitment to follow the story. If she was saved there was no reason to think she would not be just fine. If she died, then that would be that. People could tune in with gusto because they knew they would not be called on to pay attention next week. Their obligation to care was finite.

The second thing in her favor was the nature of the disaster. Falling in a hole had no messy attachments like those found in the cases of child abuse or chronic illness or political quagmires where the little girl might be one of millions who suffered, a number too big to grasp in any personal way. There was no partisanship to whether or not a little girl falling in a hole was a good or bad thing. Everyone knew this was bad. Everyone wanted to see her come out.

The third thing was the fact that Andromeda was a beautiful little girl with good-looking parents and a good-looking brother. They appeared to be people you'd call friend or invite to dinner or ask to stay for the holidays. Andromeda's parents were articulate, decent and honest people who gave the impression they would die for their girl, an image reinforced by shots of Sandra and Peter Wiley taking turns at the hole so their daughter would never be left alone. If the viewers bought it in Kansas—and they had, by all accounts—the rest of the nation would follow.

The media, which would never admit it, were also satisfied with the color of the Wileys' skin. If the Wileys had been black or Latino or Asian, skin colors rarely represented in those old safety flicks where an accident such as this would star a girl who might look just like Andromeda, then a tragic portion of the audience might say through closeted prejudice, "This always happens to those people. Those people are always getting into that kind of trouble." For the media it would just make things messier than they needed to be. Better to completely avoid turning it into a race issue.

The final thing in their favor was their economic plight. While there were plenty of recently homeless families, especially among the farming community, the sheer volume overwhelmed most people's desire to create a personally focused concern. With all the bankruptcies they could plead, "I'm just one guy, what can I do?" The Wileys, who had wanted only to work their tiny plot of land and who wanted only to make a decent living and who weren't asking for the world, could be the one family to represent the plight of all farming families. A handful of names attached to photogenic faces allowed the American public to say, "I've felt bad about this whole farming thing but I haven't known how to help. Now I know." They could help the Wileys of Wishbone.

Clark worked to draw parallels between what was happening to the Wileys and what was happening to farmers everywhere. He identified the culprits. The government was only in business for the wealthy. Interest rates for farmers were too high. The government was allowing too much business to head out of the country, and so on and so on.

But while Clark for the most part made it an Us versus Big Brother tale, he did choose to name one actual person as a chief baddie in the Wiley plight.

NINETEEN

PEEPER

Denny Sharf had never in his life encountered so much hostility. Everywhere he walked he received sneers. People coming into the Savings and Loan to do reluctant business purposely glared at him through his office window, and he had been forced to draw his shades. When he went out to his car to fetch a file left in his big red Cadillac, he found two freshly cracked eggs dripping down the hood. He quickly splashed them off with buckets of water before the paint was blemished.

Even his own tellers were short with him. He might ask, "How's everything?" and instead of getting the toady response he was accustomed to, he received an unsmiling and curt, "Fine."

He tried to counter with a defiant glare himself but he was inherently not a master at defiance. Denny stood up from his desk, opened his door quietly so as not to draw attention and whispered to Lois Knowles, the nearest teller, to come into his office. Lois, a shapely woman in her mid-thirties with a street-smart style who chain-smoked and bar-hopped and who could shoot a fast game of pool with the best of them, and who had already been divorced twice, glumly closed up her station and followed Denny's orders.

She stood before Denny with arms crossed.

"What is it?"

Denny tried to seem humble and kind.

"That's what I was hoping to ask you. What's with everybody?"

"You mean why does everybody seem like they might say yahoo if you fell off the edge of the earth?"

"I guess that's what I mean."

"The Wileys. Now can I get back to work?"

"Just a minute—what about the Wileys?"

"If you don't know by now you never will, Denny. Think about it. You put them on the street. Because of you their little girl is at the bottom of that terrible hole. What do you expect people to do, shake your hand and slap your back?"

"I was merely doing my job."

"Cut the crap, Denny. We all know you've had the hots for Sandra Wiley since she was Sandra Henderson. You've been trying to get back at her for not jumping your bones since day one. We're not stupid. We've all seen it even if that dummy Peter hasn't. We knew it the minute you suckered him into signing a fixed rate four points higher than anybody else. Hell, that much more interest alone would nearly pay my mortgage."

"He didn't have to accept the deal."

"Of course he did. You were both right out of high school. Nobody else would have given him credit, and it would have been better for him. He'd probably have something to show for his life by now."

"Well, how long is this whole business of everybody sneering at me going to go on?"

"Well, let's see. You overcharged them on their mortgage so badly they were doomed to fail, then you took their home and set them up so their kid could fall down a hole, where she might even die. You've been jerking off to Sandy for years and we all know it, and now you filed a crock-of-shit lawsuit everybody in town knows is a crock of shit just to rub it all in. My guess is the rest of your pathetic little life."

"Listen, missy, talk like that could get you fired."

"So fire me. I'll take the whole office with me, you stupid little grease-ball. You don't think I can, just give it a shot. In one hour I could get this whole town to pull every last penny out of your stupid little bank and then where would you be? Maybe you'll be falling in a hole next, how about that?"

"Okay, okay! Jesus Christ, you people are all insane!" But Denny could not face it any longer. "What can I do?"

"Give them back their home."

"I can't. It's gone."

"Well, then, face it. You are chum to the sharks." Lois started out the door but turned back at the entry. "And you can plug your little peephole into the women's crapper, Denny. The show is over. You try any of that shit again, we'll kick your balls from here to Pittsburgh."

She slammed the door so hard as she exited that Denny's windows rattled. With his own nerves already rattled, he barely noticed.

He suddenly realized that in one fell swoop his cover was blown.

TWENTY

THE GLITCH

The massive drill arrived as promised, and within an hour it was erected over the secondary shaft. The drilling began in the late afternoon of the second day. As the drill raucously cut into the earth at a speed measured in feet per hour, creating a three-foot-wide shaft in the process, an obvious wave of relief passed over the assembled crowd, now grown to over a hundred.

People were coming not simply from all over the county but had even driven in from nearby states. Most had come to help but a few, still a small percentage but growing, had come just to watch the disaster unfold, some secretly hoping for a tragic ending so they could seem more important for having witnessed it, as if the tragedy were partly theirs. When somebody told a story about how a coworker fell off a roof and impaled his leg on a fence, they would be able to say, "That's nothing. I saw Baby Andromeda die."

To meet their needs, vendors in mobile trucks set up at the edge of the site to sell hot dogs, Cokes and umbrella hats. In the makeshift camp of newspeople and TV vans, which grew in population by the hour, music blared from several quarters. The anticipation was thick.

Sandra and Will slept as well as could be expected within Stan's luxurious loaner RV. At the heart of the disaster, near the shaft, Timms and Sheriff Austin reassured Peter Wiley as he took his turn manning Andromeda's intercom system. Watching the lofty drill grind away, Timms was particularly proud.

"With this baby we'll be down there at the outside by tomorrow afternoon."

Peter still had doubts. The presence of the drill had not, for some reason, caused him to feel any more secure.

"I don't know, I just . . . What if something goes wrong?"

Timms spoke with less tact than he might have.

"You should be a little more positive here, Wiley. You got the whole world watching. You want them to say you're looking a gift horse in the mouth? Why don't you try acting like you're part of the team for a change?"

Deciding he had business elsewhere, Timms stomped off. Sheriff Austin gave Peter a shrug and followed. Peter had only a moment to wonder if he or Timms was right.

"I didn't—"

He was cut off as a woman in a business suit walking with an officious stride approached with briefcase in hand and shoved a business card in Peter's face.

"Mr. Wiley? My name is French, Diana French." Peter glanced at the card. It read, DIANA FRENCH, CHILD PSYCHOLOGIST. "I'm here to offer my services."

"What services?"

"You have two children who are suffering from, A, a sense of inferiority as a result of your financial state and, B, a sense of insecurity as a result of this continuing trauma. They're going to need help, Mr. Wiley. Will and Andromeda need to feel safe again."

"No offense, but I don't need you to tell me that. Sandra and I can—"

"I'm sorry, you've misunderstood me. I am not here to supplant your role as a parent. I am only here to support you in restoring their faith and confidence. We would naturally work closely together to bring about the healing these beautiful children of yours will need to move on with their lives. This whole trauma has to be an external event, just something that happened, not something they end up feeling they caused or deserved and that they'll carry around their necks for the rest of their lives. I'm sure you'll agree that neither Will nor Andromeda are feeling as secure as you'd like."

Peter had to admit the truth in that. "No, they aren't."

"And you do want them to grow up confident, healthy and happy?"

"Of course."

"Then we should get started. Where is Will?"

"He's in the motor home. But, listen, he's—"

The intercom speaker on Peter's end squawked.

"Daddy?"

Baby Andromeda was calling.

The TV cameramen, always on the alert, rushed forward and flicked on their cameras as Peter grabbed the mike. Eight cameras jostled for prime position to peer over Peter's shoulder. Diana nodded to the intercom control and gave Peter a reassuring smile.

"Answer her. I'll check on Will."

As Diana headed toward the motor home before Peter could protest, Andromeda's weak voice again came through the intercom speaker.

"Daddy?"

"Yes, honey?"

"The ground is shaky. Are they almost here?"

A cameraman, vying for a better view, shoved his lens forward until it hit Peter on the back of the head. Peter turned, annoyed.

"Hey, do you mind?"

"Sorry, pal."

Andromeda again called up.

"Daddy, are you there? Daddy?"

"Yes, sweetie, I'm here. They'll be there in a while, honey. You have to stay patient for a few more hours. Just be patient, honey, we're coming."

"I'm so tired. I hurt."

"I know, Andie; we know."

"I hurt all over."

"You won't hurt much longer. I promise."

"That's all."

The intercom fell silent.

"Andie?"

But there was no response. The cameramen, seeing the show was over, flicked off their cameras and retired to their deck chairs a car length back from Peter. One industrious cameraman kept filming, moving around Peter, covering Peter's blank stare from every possible angle before turning off his camera and sitting back down.

Peter set down the mike and stared back into the hole.

After five live TV broadcasts in one day, broadcasts seen coast to coast and even in London, where the story of Baby Andromeda was slotted between one item about the latest civil war in postcolonial Africa and another detailing some new scandal involving Britain's royals, Howard Clark now considered himself a veteran.

At ten o'clock in the evening of the second full day of Andromeda's capture, more than forty-eight hours after her plunge into the shaft, Clark worked the phones and watched his mug on the news.

"See, I'm looking for a home. You've seen my work. I just—Hold on, I have another call. Can you hold? This'll just take a second. . . . Hello? . . . Ah, gorgeous Rayna. Are you coming out? . . . Uh-huh, uh-huh. What do you mean it's slowing down? . . . Sure, it'd be better if we got another couple days on this but what am I supposed to do about it? The drill is there, they're going to get her out tomorrow morning. Well, you gotta do what you gotta do. Look, let me call you tomorrow. . . . Okay, great."

He switched buttons.

"Sorry about that; phones are off the hook. So what I'm saying is your organization attracts me and if we can talk about my coming aboard . . . I'm sure it is a competitive world. All I'm saying is I'm here to compete."

Clark leaned back as he worked to extract from someone else's misfortune a brand-new future for himself.

At eight forty-five on the morning of the third day, at a depth of sixty-one feet, the drill hit the pocket.

Sandra and Diana French had been sitting before the motor home under a wide awning, sharing a gentle laugh as if they were old friends. Will tried to take up his customary position to stare at the hole and anybody who was supposed to be working on it, but Diana, supported by Sandra, had seduced him to pay attention to himself. She asked Will many questions in a soothing voice and Will felt the determined frown in his forehead ease.

After an extra-long turn at the hole, Peter snored within the motor home, having left instructions to awaken him if anything happened.

The news vans had begun the process of wrapping things up, fully expecting that sometime that day Andromeda would be pulled from the secondary shaft and all would be well. They wanted to be ready to speed away from the site to cover the next story, whatever and wherever that might be.

Timms and Sheriff Austin, along with a multitude of volunteers, watched as the impressive drill and its crack crew dredged up earth and stone that had last felt air in the age of the dinosaurs. It all seemed so easy.

It all seemed so positive. The sun was out, a cool breeze wafted prairie fragrances into appreciative nostrils and, high above, lazy planes droned out peaceful rhythms. The day of Baby Andromeda's rescue could not be more perfect. Everything, absolutely every last thing was a go.

Until the drill hit the pocket.

Andromeda, who had found nourishment over the past sixty hours on only three occasions when a thin consommé was sent down the tube, knew she could not hold out much longer. She was too weak to speak much and in fact really had nothing much to say. She was beginning to feel too weak to even care anymore. She had been forced to soil herself repeatedly but now she had grown so numb it no longer seemed to matter. The vibrating earth that entombed her had a lulling effect, keeping her, for the most part, in a netherworld of consciousness. She could not really call it sleep, but she could not say she was actually awake. She just was.

Peter had ordered that he be rousted before the drill made it to Andromeda's level, but when the drill hit the pocket he was up in a flash. When the motor home rocked from the blast, he flew from the soft mattress and smacked his head into the bathroom corner. He barely noticed that his head was gashed open as he rushed outside to see what had happened.

The drill, which had moved with such blissful smoothness through the densest earth, at fifty-eight feet began cutting through rock veined with flint. At sixty-one feet the tip cut into a pocket in the rock filled with prehistoric gas. A spark off the flint ignited the cloud. The resulting explosion rendered the end of the drill a useless mass of twisted metal. But what happened above was worse.

The segmented drill's drive shaft lifted from the hole it had cut, buckled wildly in the supporting sleeve and broke loose to send fragmenting shards spinning into the surrounding crowd. Blue flames rushed from the depths of the hole and rose in a lofty inferno some sixty feet into the air like a geyser on the surface of the sun. The drill operator had every hair singed off his face and head as he dove for cover. Others in the crowd ducked and dove behind anything they could as the ground shook massively with the force of a mighty earthquake. People lost their footing; others tripped and fell.

The hot shards found a few victims.

Bobby Timms, standing so close, was both seared by the flames and struck in the thigh by a softball-sized piece of ragged steel. As he went

down in agony, his leg broken in a compound fracture, he rolled reflex-
ively and put out the flames that clutched the fabric of his shirt and pants.
Others were cut and scraped by smaller bits of metal. A piece whistling
past the diving heads of Sandra and Diana French imbedded itself into the
front tire of Stan's RV, flattening it in a blink, while other shards pocked
holes and punched dents into the motor home's once flawless paint job.

Cameras rolled in all quarters. For the quick-thinking news crews it was
a video feast.

Screams and the silence of open-mouthed shock replaced the cool satisfaction that had ruled the day just minutes earlier. But the first person to
think of anybody beyond himself was Peter Wiley. As he burst from the
motor home, his forehead bleeding badly, he shouted out the name that
reminded all of them why they were here.

"Andie!"

Peter rushed for the hole, snapped up a flashlight on the run and aimed
it down the opening. Dust rising from the hole made the attempt a useless
one. He screamed into the clouded depths.

"Andie! *Andie!*"

Sandra ran for the intercom and yanked up the mike.

"Andie! Can you hear us!" She turned to the chattering and crying
crowd. "Everybody shut up!" Back into the mike: "Andie, if you can hear
me, please answer. Honey, say something!" She looked to Peter with a face
filled with helplessness. "Not now, not after all this. . . ."

Suddenly a voice coughed from the intercom speaker.

"Mommy? What happened?"

Choking back a tearful rush, Sandra kept it together long enough to answer.

"Andie, oh baby . . . We . . . we had an—"

Diana shook her head, whispering, "Don't tell her about any of this, just
say it's a delay," as she made a gesture to encompass the stunned, singed
and cut people lifting themselves to their feet or rushing to help Timms
and the drill operator.

Sandra tried to sound normal.

"We have a little delay, sweetie. Tell me if you're okay."

"Everything shook a lot in here and now there's dust and I'm even dirt-
ier."

"But did you get hurt, honey?"

"No, but I think I slipped more down."

Sandra, Peter and even Timms, who was crowded by his concerned fellows, suddenly paid even more attention. Peter was particularly concerned.

"What does she mean?"

"Honey, what do you mean you slipped?"

"That metal thing, with the stars, it's farther away and I don't got the wood in my back anymore. If I reach up I can touch the bottom of the wood thing."

Sandra and Peter did notice Andromeda's voice seemed more distant as it came from the speaker. Knowing the two-by-four was eight feet long, Peter guessed that Andromeda must have dropped another six feet at least. How that was possible he didn't know, since it would put her lower than what he thought was the lowest depth, unless . . .

The bottom was not the bottom.

Peter grabbed the mike from Sandra.

"Honey, it's Daddy. Can you feel anything with your feet?"

"Umm . . . no. I can't feel anything."

His fears were confirmed. He now had no idea how deep that shaft might be. If the bottom had truly fallen out, then Andromeda was only kept in position by the dirt that had filled in around her body. If that dirt should begin trickling down, if Andromeda should come free, she could fall for who knew how long. Andromeda called back up. "Now how long will it take?"

"It might take a little longer than we expected, Andie. Can you hold on for us?"

"I don't have anything else to do."

Peter handed the mike to Sandra. As Sandra continued talking to their daughter, Peter walked to Timms, who, with his leg tourniqueted, was being loaded onto a gurney.

"Did you hear?"

Through his pain Timms worked to stay focused.

"I heard. I haven't . . . I haven't been able to find any records at all on this shaft. Too big for oil, maybe drilled for water . . . don't know. I wish I could tell you she can't fall . . . much further, but for all I know that shaft goes down another mile."

Peter just nodded as he pictured Andromeda dangling over a mile-long plunge.

"What do we do now?"

"We'll have to . . . leach out the gas before we can start digging again. We're also going to have to bring in a new machine. This doesn't set us back to zero but it costs us. A day, maybe even two. I don't know what more . . . what more I can tell you." Timms grimaced a moment, but the face that came out of the grimace was apologetic. "I didn't . . . mean what I said earlier. I had no right. I'm a father too, I just . . . Well, I don't know what I was thinking. I just know I was out of line."

As the paramedics began carting Timms off, Peter let him know there were no hard feelings.

"You've been a lot of help."

"I'd rather hear that from your little girl."

So would I, Peter thought. *So would I.*

TWENTY-ONE

BREAKING NEWS

The exciting destruction of the drill, luckily captured by one prolific news crew, together with the news that Baby Andromeda had slipped farther down into a shaft that seemed to have no historical record anywhere and that no living human being could attest to having worked on, was just what the doctor ordered to give the story a kick start. The story of Baby Andromeda riveted the nation. It now ran as the top story on every major network.

More and more people decided they wanted to be a part of saving this poor little girl, a girl who had remained doggedly optimistic in the face of so much bad news and who was hanging in there like a trooper. A second drill and a team of mining specialists raced to the site late in the evening of the third day as children all over the USA wrote letters of support. In many a church, office and school, donation boxes were set up to help the Wiley family pay for any expenses incurred during this disaster. Like the rubber drives of World War II, the drive to help Baby Andromeda gave some meaning to a country that many felt was morally spinning its wheels. She was fast becoming an icon. If the trend continued, her name had the potential to become permanently installed in the folk lexicon.

Howard Clark could not believe his luck. It amazed him what fifty cents' worth of natural gas had done for his career.

Even though the journalistic field was now crowded, he was widely considered to have the ear of the Wileys. Other reporters, famous faces from famous networks, consulted him for the inside poop as they coordinated their take on the ongoing tragedy. Clark freely offered his services and they freely compensated him for doing so. He was soon thinking, Chevy, bye-bye; BMW with black leather interior, hello.

After the explosion Clark was the only reporter allowed inside the motor home to interview the Wiley family. It was Clark who captured on tape the heavily envied moment when Will Wiley turned to the camera and said, "I'd die for Andie, that's what brothers do." It was a sound bite that played in Paris, France, and Paris, Kentucky. Around the country when talking of the Wileys, people more often than not called them by their first names. "Will is such a great kid." "Peter is such a great father." "Sandra is a wonderful mother." They had become de facto celebrities.

Clark's office, under the guardianship of indomitable Julie Fletcher, was the address to which all donations and correspondence were sent. Thanks to the sympathetic postal service, letters to the Wileys were given special attention and were forwarded as rapidly as possible, delivered several times daily. So much mail had already arrived that Julie had been forced to bring in the Wishbone Quilting Club to open and sort it all. The vast majority were simply letters of the keep-your-chin-up variety. But an important minority, upon being opened, dispensed checks and cash. No total had been arrived at, but the sum promised to be something more than tidy.

A few examples of the psychotic underbelly of the American psyche also appeared—letters hailing Satan, letters hailing God and raging about how the sinful Wileys had brought this on themselves, letters enclosing pornographic photos of men lusting after Sandra or women and men lusting after Peter. Some told of conspiracies and advised the Wileys to watch out for UN troops, aliens from outer space, troglodytes from inner space, fluoride in their water, evil crystals, Scientologists and even Santa Claus. Lois Knowles, having told Denny Sharf she was taking the day off to help and if he didn't like the idea then too goddamn bad, saved the best wacko letters and photos for personal consumption with her similarly satiric friends.

As the money came in, Julie Fletcher saw the need to open an account in Andromeda's name, yet even though the Wishbone Savings and Loan was directly beneath her feet, she was loath to give any business to the man who was responsible for the Wileys misfortune in the first place. Julie Fletcher, who had never uttered a profanity grander than *darn*, who had never said an unkind word about anybody, told everybody she met that Denny Sharf was "a real asshole."

It appeared there were plenty of people who agreed.

TWENTY-TWO

RABBIT FEVER

Denny Sharf was more frightened than a rabbit in a foxhole. People he had always considered friendly to him now let him know in no uncertain terms that he was the first name on their shit lists. His social leprosy was working overtime.

Wilda Palozi, a widow miser who still drove an immaculate forty-year-old Buick, the first car she ever owned, a woman who had every bit of furniture in her home covered in clear plastic, a woman who used handfuls of coupons to buy groceries, who saved string, who made garden windmills from plastic milk containers and who picked up stray pennies on a regular basis, waltzed up to Denny—forced by a record number of tellers calling in sick to man the windows himself—and said, "I want to close my account."

Denny begged her to reconsider. "You've had an account with us for fifty-three years, Mrs. Palozi. Why leave now?"

"I don't bank with perverts. Give me my money."

"But the closest bank is thirty miles from here."

"Don't make me call the cops. Just give me my money."

Denny, seeing no use in arguing, took a look at Wilda Palozi's balance and did a mental whistle. The sum totaled many thousands of dollars.

"We don't have this much."

"You don't have my money?"

"Not in cash, not right now. I can write you a cashier's check. It'll be safer for you anyway."

"Write it."

As Denny began making out the check, he noticed that a line was forming behind the Widow Palozi and that not one of the waiting faces was smiling.

He handed Mrs. Palozi a cashier's check and closed out one of the oldest accounts in town.

"We'll miss your business, Mrs. Palozi."

Wilda Palozi turned as she stuffed the check into her thirty-year-old purse. "You detestable man. Never speak to me again."

Denny waved to the next customer. It was Mike Serven, the butcher, called Ike by his friends.

"What can I do for you, Ike?"

"The name is Mike. I want to close my account and don't give me any lip or I'll bust it open."

"S-sure. . . . Could you hold on a second?"

"Make it snappy, creepo."

Denny locked the bars on the teller window and slipped into his office. Closing the door, he quickly picked up the phone and dialed.

"Dad? You gotta get down here! They're making a run!"

After a long and loud tirade from the retired man who had entrusted the Savings and Loan to his theoretically trustworthy son, Denny was told to handle it himself. Denny hung up the phone and peeped out his shades. The line was now to the door and more glum types were lining up every minute.

While still not seeing anything wrong in his secret desires, while still not feeling guilty for peeping on the female employees, while still feeling no guilt for purposely orchestrating the Wiley family downfall, he was at least feeling bad about getting caught. As a wave of self-pity washed over Denny, he knew the first order of business was to save the business.

The vault was closed and the cash drawers were locked and inaccessible behind the locked teller windows, and knowing this Denny felt there was only one way to save the bank.

Climbing out his office window, he hit the sidewalk and headed for parts unknown.

TWENTY-THREE

DAY FOUR

It was noon of day four. The day was Saturday.

The mood surrounding the rescue of Baby Andromeda had shifted. There was a general air of depression among the crowd, enhanced by the fact that the previous day's gloriously blue sky had given way to a blanket of chilling clouds that stretched horizon to horizon. All present had little to do but stand by and wait.

More spectators had arrived and more vendors had followed to support them. The first T-shirts appeared with a photo of Andromeda on the front and a caption that read, IN OUR HEARTS. BABY ANDROMEDA. Other wares were sold. One enterprising vendor sold vials of dirt dug from the secondary well. He hawked it like a circus barker, and even though a nearby dirt pile twenty feet high was there for the taking, he racked up many a sale to those passing through who did not want to get their fingers dirty. Vendors sold hats, drinks, sunglasses, fans, binoculars and even sports paraphernalia for Kansas teams, both college and pro. There was something for everybody.

Mayor Don Moser made an appearance and proclaimed that the outpouring of goodwill that would soon effect Baby Andromeda's rescue was a sign that Wishbone was a town that worked. He stated with practiced sincerity that as mayor, his first and only duty was to the good people of Wishbone, and that he would create more jobs, help out suffering families like the Wileys and make sure that the stores stayed open for prosperous business.

Ten yards from Mayor Don Moser, former mayor Tommy Vale also made an appearance. But Tommy Vale, who was unseated by Moser over the perception that Tommy was primarily concerned with conducting personal business via the mayor's office, brought along something Mayor Moser could not.

Tommy Vale brought a prop.

With keys dangling high for all the news cameras to see, Tommy presented the Wiley family with clear title to a brand-spanking-new Chevrolet pickup truck. His only requirement was that the Wileys give him in return their old battered pickup so he could have something to preserve the sentimental moment.

The cameras rolled as Peter Wiley almost reluctantly took a short spin. When he came to a stop he thanked Tommy and handed over the keys to his battered truck. Tommy immediately had his son Randy drive it away.

It came as no surprise to many when the Wileys' truck appeared later that day raised onto a platform in Tommy Vale's showroom. A huge sign in front of Vale's Chevrolet promised to all who entered a chance to sit behind the wheel of history in the making. To accommodate the influx, Tommy brought in additional salesmen, who pointed out the lack of features on the Wiley truck, something you could not say of the option-heavy Chevrolets surrounding it. Brochures were handed out with bright smiles.

Bumped from the limelight, Mayor Moser slunk away from the site with a vow to return. He never would.

Sheriff Austin, in charge in Timms's absence, chewed his nails as the imported mining experts undertook the laborious process of remotely drilling pilot holes to open any more hidden gas pockets. So far they had approved the next ten feet for drilling. They stood aside as the new drill took its place over the secondary shaft to dig out the next ten feet.

Sheriff Austin was feeling impotent. He had proved woefully inadequate for this hero job. All he had been able to do since Timms was rushed to the hospital was add an extra six feet of copper tubing to Andromeda's water pipe so she could still slake her thirst at her new depth. Austin vowed that when this was over he would prepare himself so the next time a heroic opportunity presented itself, he would not automatically assume the role of fifth wheel.

Dressed in new clothes supplied free of charge by Marshall Field of Chicago, Will looked up at the darkening sky. A reporter from *The New York Times* nodded up to the same sky and spoke to Will.

"Looks like it'll rain."

Will, the farmer's son, sniffed the air.

"Not yet."

Sandra sat with the intercom mike near the shaft entry and tried to keep her little girl going.

"Andie? Do you want me to sing 'It's a Small World'?"

Andromeda's voice came back in a weak rasp.

"No."

"Well, do you want me to sing something else?" She waited through a long pause. "Andie?"

"No."

"Honey, is everything okay?"

What came back was unintelligible.

"Mmrrggphh . . ."

"What? I didn't understand."

"I don't want anything."

"Let me know if you do, okay?"

She heard no response.

Diana French, having calmed Will, came to Sandra and knew her anguish. Sandra was grateful for the sympathetic ear.

"She's feeling abandoned. I know she is."

Diana, the professional, gently took Sandra's hand.

"You're doing everything a mother could. Even if she doesn't answer back, you have to keep letting her know you're there for her."

"You've been such a help, Diana. Thank you so much."

Taking notes for an eventual book on the incident, which she intended to call *Answer the Light,* and fully intending to oversee Andromeda's mental rehabilitation following her rescue, Diana squeezed Sandra Wiley's hand in comradeship.

"It's why I'm here."

Mary Hayworth Downes had until now remained on the sidelines during the Baby Andromeda fiasco. But as the quantity of tourists coming into her shop exploded over the course of the last few days, she found she could no longer stay neutral. People would not pay attention to her shtick about being the descendant of Belle Starr. The only thing the tourists wanted to know was how did they get to where they were digging out Baby Andromeda and where was the Wileys' old house and did Mary know the Wileys and what were they like? Mary tried to be as polite as she could, but the overwhelming tide of eager strangers eventually forced her from her own shop. She asked Dottie Coombs to take over and Dottie, who was naturally talkative, happily stepped in.

Mary retired to the silence of her home.

She sat at the kitchen table, where she and Emerson had shared loving chuckles after nights of passion and tenderness. In the years since Emerson's death Mary had learned to keep her concerns to herself. She did not want anything from her neighbors and she did not want them to expect anything in return. She was a true loner; all who knew her recognized that Mary was basically unapproachable.

But this thing with the Wiley child was stirring feelings Mary had thought were lost for good. Mary was feeling for the child in the hole. Even though she had promised to keep her life and business separate from all others, she could not help but empathize with little Andromeda, a girl she actually knew.

Mary pulled a file from a drawer in her home office and laid it open on the table full of memories. The file contained deeds to all of Mary's properties. Unfolding each deed in turn, Mary found she had actually forgotten she owned some of the local properties. She went through each deed one by one until she found what she was looking for. She read it over to make sure.

Forty-nine acres of flat land, no structures, unfenced, no well, no electricity, no services whatsoever. It was a plot that had remained fallow for decades. Mary was dimly aware of its location and decided it was the place where boys on noisy dirt bikes ran tracks in the dirt and constructed plywood jumps to hone their acrobatic skills.

Folding the deed into her jacket pocket, she decided those boys would just have to find somewhere else to play.

All three Wileys sat in the motor home and said not a word as they tried to eat the tasty meal sent over by the Whistle Stop. They had endured another day of media scrutiny and had grown utterly jaded to having a camera or mike shoved in their face. They were so disinterested in the exposure that they now declined any of Clark's offers to watch some new segment he had produced for television consumption.

It was nine o'clock in the evening; Andromeda had now been in the hole a full ninety-seven hours. The last conversation with her had been one-sided, with Andromeda replying in nothing more than weak grunts. It was imperative that she be saved soon.

The leach-gas-and-then-drill-a-little-farther process had accomplished a fifteen-foot gain during the day. That left twenty or so feet down and another twenty feet sideways to reach Andromeda. Working through the night, it would be another full day until the moment they broke through the shaft to reach Andromeda. But with assurances pouring in from engineers and experts all around, it did finally seem that the end was in sight.

Knowing Andromeda had nothing to fill her belly but water and thin broth, neither Peter, Sandra nor Will in particular wished to feel free from hunger. So they ate little and spoke less.

As the one person on earth most attuned to Andromeda, Will felt he knew things about her past, present and future that nobody else could. What he felt now was that Andromeda was slipping away. His frustration over the slow pace of the rescue would sometimes build to moments where it burst forth as a physical twitch, as yet unnoticed by the watchful eye of Diana French. Will looked to his parents, who did not eat but instead moved their food around with their forks.

"May I be excused?"

Sandra didn't bother to look up.

"Just stay away from those reporters. I'm tired of the way they keep asking us questions. The whole world thinks it has to know every goddamn thing about us. Well, they don't, so don't go offering any information, understand?"

"Okay. I mean, I won't."

Peter looked up as Will reached for the motor home door.

"Will, I really think you should say something to Andie."

"Dad, I don't want to—"

"I mean it."

Will sensed a new urgency from his father. This wasn't an order, it was a plea.

"Okay."

Will stepped outside the motor home and the cameramen and reporters camped nearby suddenly stood at attention en masse. Lights lit up on the cameras and Will blinked at the bright corona, protecting his eyes with an upheld hand. A voice called from the wide glare that followed him as he walked for the hole and the intercom.

"Hey, kid, is there anything new?"

"I'm just going to talk to my sister." Will stopped and turned, well aware the pack was following. "Alone, okay?"

Sheriff Austin barked at the pursuing reporters, "Let the kid talk to his sister!"

The lights went out on all but a couple of cameras. Will raised his fist to the two cameras that refused his request and lifted his middle finger. Their lights went out too.

Will nervously took up the intercom mike and lay down next to the hole to peer into the opening. He cleared his throat.

"Andie?"

After the customary pause the speaker spit out Andromeda's feeble voice.

"Will?"

"Yeah. It's me."

"I miss you, Will. Where . . . where were you? Did you fall in a hole too?"

"No, I . . . I was afraid."

"Why?"

"I should have gone for the drinks myself."

"But then you would be down here. I don't want you down here."

Will suddenly could not hold back his emotions. He began softly sobbing into the mike. Andromeda was the voice of calm.

"Will, what's wrong?"

"Andie, don't die. I don't want you to die. . . ."

Andromeda waited a moment for Will's sobs to pause.

"I won't. Will I?"

"No, you won't."

"Will?"

"Yeah?"

"Tell me a story about me in a nice place."

"I don't know . . ."

"Please? I need it."

Will racked his head for a decent story. He remembered how much Andromeda loved Africa.

"Okay. There was this princess and she lived in a big castle on top of a mountain right near a jungle in the middle of Africa—"

"Are there monkeys?"

"There were lots and lots of monkeys. . . ."

As Will told his sister a story about talking monkeys and friendly zebras, Peter looked out the window of the motor home and gave a sigh of relief.

He and Sandra had done all they could to prop up Andromeda's flagging spirits. Will, the person they knew Andromeda loved more than anyone else, was their last hope to keep Andromeda going for the remaining hours.

"He's telling her a story."

"Finally."

Alone for the first time since the disaster began, Peter and Sandra shared a nervous and uncertain look. Without understanding exactly when it had happened, they knew something had been lost between them. They now saw each other through a wall of suspicion and doubt. The subject they most needed to address, their shared guilt, was a cancer eroding their trust. Even knowing this, they tried to squelch it, pretending that if they could just get through it, all would be back to normal.

Peter imagined a future in which he and Sandra did not communicate, and he saw a frightening image of his own embittered parents. He decided to risk being the fool.

"Sandy, we should talk this thing—"

A knock came at the door. Sandra stood, relieved by the interruption.

"Hold on."

"It's just another reporter. Tell them to go away."

Sandra opened the door, and standing there was Mary Hayworth Downes.

"May I come in?"

"Mrs. Downes, hello. Peter, it's Mrs. Downes."

Peter stood out of respect for a woman who deserved it. Mary stepped in and smiled softly.

"Hello, Peter."

"Mrs. Downes, have a seat. Can we get you some coffee?"

"No, I'm just stoppin' by for a minute. I just had somethin' to say. Could you both sit?"

Mary Downes, Peter and Sandra all sat at the small table. Mary took her time getting started.

"You know how I feel about gettin' involved in other people's business. I'm no busybody; I don't lean against my fence to get the latest gossip from my neighbor. I frankly don't care who in this town is screwin' who behind whose back. The truth is, I don't much care about anything. Now, I know that sounds harsh but I'm bein' honest. When I lost my Emerson I lost somethin' inside. . . . I don't know. It probably sounds silly, but one day I was complete, the next—the next day I'm this." Mary could see neither Peter nor Sandra had a clue what she was talking about. She smirked. "You don't know what I'm talkin' about."

"No, we . . . well, no, not really."

"I'm talkin' about finding something I lost. Now, I know you; I know both of you for years. I know your boy Will real well. He's a dear, dear boy. If I had a son I'd pray for a boy half as kind and sincere." Mary tried to avoid sounding sappy but this was something she felt she had to say, if only to have it out in the open. Once said, she would be forced to deal with it, as she hadn't done since the day she lowered Emerson into the ground. She had come to banish old ghosts, not knowing, however, that she would do so in a loaner motor home from Stan's RV.

"It's a precious thing to feel complete. We're complete when we're children, assumin' we grow up with loving parents, which I know you two are. Will and Andie wouldn't be who they are if you weren't. When that innocence goes, we let a whole lot slip away. We say a lot more easily, 'I can't do it, it's too late for me, my time is over, I'm done for.' I don't want to see that happen to Andie. I want her to keep that light of joy. I want her to keep what I lost."

Peter thought he had the gist of the conversation.

"We appreciate that, Mrs. Downes—"

"Mary."

"Mary. It's nice of you coming by here to tell us that. To be honest, we've always thought you were one of the smartest people in town, and not just because of your money and stuff. Will was always talking about how sharp you handled things. You've been sort of his mentor."

"That's a sweet thing to say, Peter."

Thinking the conversation was over, Peter stood.

"I'm glad you came by, we both are. It means a lot."

Mary did not move.

"What're you doin'? I ain't finished."

"Sorry, I thought—"

"Just sit." She put both her elbows on the table as Peter sat. "Let's just put our cards on the table for a moment. When this thing is over, it looks like you might come out okay. You got a new truck, you got new clothes, toys, things. . . . I know for a fact a lot of money is comin' in from all over. My guess is you'll at least be set for a while. I gotta ask one question, though. What're your plans?"

"Well, we . . . we don't really have any just yet. We really haven't had much time to—"

Mary waved him quiet.

"That's fine. I have an offer. My offer is this. I want you to stay here in Wishbone, I want to see you do well and I want to see your kids do better. I don't have a family, I don't have anybody to leave anything to, probably wouldn't even if I did. But I'd love to be able to look in the mirror and say I did somethin' for somebody. The reason I'm choosing you is because I owe it to you."

"I don't see how."

"I'll tell you how. For the first time since I can remember, Andie falling in that hole made me feel sorry for somebody other than myself. It may not sound like a big deal to you, but it is to me. This whole thing made me remember how to feel. That's why I wanna give you this."

Mary removed the folded deed from her jacket and slid it across the table to Sandra, who cautiously opened it.

"What is it?"

"Well, right now it's a messy bunch of dirt trails, but with the right hand it could be forty-nine acres of corn, lettuce, parsley, you name it."

Peter was stunned.

"You're not giving us this."

Mary smiled her first truly happy smile in such a long, long time.

"I am."

"Forty-nine acres!"

Mary stood as Peter and Sandra pored over the deed.

"It ain't all a free ride. You gotta put up a house, you gotta put in a well, there isn't a lick of fence anywhere, no running water, no sewage, no nothing. Whatever it's going to be, it's up to you two to decide."

Sandra stood and gave Mary an unexpected hug.

"Oh, Mary, thank you so much."

Unpracticed at such close contact, Mary gave Sandra's back a few pats.

"There, now, you're welcome."

Peter stood and shook Mary's hand. Thinking it wasn't enough, he gave her a hug too and then planted a kiss on her cheek.

"This is the nicest thing anybody has ever done for us. I . . . I don't know what to say. I don't know how to repay you for this. How could I?"

"Tell you what. When your first harvest comes in, you handpick me a few bushels of whatever it is you're growing and we'll call it even."

"It's a deal."

Peter and Sandra waved as Mary Downes left the motor home and made her way past inquisitive reporters who wanted to know who she was. Mary didn't hear them. In the cool night she felt free. Her step was so light she felt she could almost skip.

But even though she felt more alive than she had in years, she knew no piece of paper could cure what ailed that sweet little girl in that deep, deep hole. She knew that no matter how powerful Andromeda's support, the bright light of her innocence would be dimmed by this experience.

She prayed as best she could that Andromeda got herself rescued before the light went all the way out.

TWENTY-FOUR
ILL WIND

It was ten-thirty in the morning of day five and Howard Clark, on site with Rayna Higgins, who had flown in from Los Angeles on her way to New York, was worried about keeping the story fresh. The sky was even darker than the day before and the breeze that blew was moist and cold.

"It has to be today. If they don't get her out by three at the latest, we won't be able to put together the wrap-up in time for the five o'clock."

Higgins was less circumspect. "It's today or they'll get bored. Come tomorrow it'll be 'next.' "

Clark agreed. The story was at its peak. Everybody was watching. The time was ripe for the coda, good or bad.

Sheriff Austin, on the phone with Bobby Timms, explained the progress.

"They're down to eighty-three feet. . . . Me too. They're only going to be able to get one guy down there at a time. . . . Right. . . . Sure, I'll let them know."

He hung up and spoke to the foreman of the drilling crew.

"Timms thinks we should send a man down to start cutting a slanted shaft toward the well."

The foreman thought for only a second.

"Wondering when you'd make that call."

With a consensus reached, the drill was shut down and backed away from the secondary shaft. The foreman lowered one of his men down the hole in a sturdy harness, toting an air-powered jackhammer. When he reached the bottom a compressor topside was powered up, and eighty-three feet below in very cramped quarters the worker began the laborious process of cutting a slanted shaft to link the world to Baby Andromeda.

Will sat at the hole. Andromeda, he knew, was asleep. In the twelve hours or so since he first spoke to her he guessed she now did more sleeping than waking. The reporter from *The New York Times* walked up and again looked at the sky.

"Don't tell me, no rain yet."

Will sniffed the air. He hadn't even noticed it coming. Leaping from his chair, Will ran to the motor home and tore open the door.

"Dad! *Dad!*"

Peter and Sandra, trying to stay alert through unbelievable exhaustion, staggered from the motor home. Will was frantically pointing to the sky.

"Look!"

Peter sucked a deep draught of air through his nose. He could smell what was coming.

"It's a storm. A big one."

He looked around for Austin.

"Sheriff!"

Sheriff Austin spun around, just missing a flash of lightning on the horizon.

"What is it?"

"We got rain on its way. A lot."

Austin took a whiff and frowned deeply. "Oh sweet Jesus." He quickly rang up Timms. "Timms, we got rain coming. It's a storm. . . . Hell, I can see it! We're still at eighty-three feet. We just started the slanted shaft. If we're lucky we're two inches closer! . . . Uh-huh. . . . Okay, gotta go."

Austin hung up and rushed for a knot of spectators standing near the hole who appeared to have little to do.

"Get some shovels and dig a trench two feet deep four feet from this hole! I want sump pumps in that trench and I want them ready to go now! You and you, get some of them shade tents and cover both holes. The rest of you stand by!"

"For what?"

Austin looked to the now-broiling sky. Sheets of rain poured down on distant plains. Flashes of lightning connected sky to earth.

"God only knows."

It was a downpour of epic proportions.

Spectators and newspeople alike rushed for cover as the raindrops, some as thick as a thumb, smacked into the dry earth. All along the two-lane blacktop at the edge of the site, people scrambled for their cars parked up and down the shoulder and shut themselves in to peer out at the gray torrent. A half second under the deluge and everything everywhere was completely soaked.

Down in the secondary shaft the man at the jackhammer continued to toil while up above workers and volunteers fought to alter the course of muddy rivulets that instantly came pouring down the low hillsides, heading straight for Andromeda's hole. The sump pumps in the encircling trench worked furiously to keep up with the raging waters. Peter and Sandra joined others to shovel out water as fast as it came in.

For the newsfolk it was an inconvenient filming arrangement but one that offered the highest drama. In the dry comfort of Rayna Higgins's rented Mercedes, Clark watched the footage being shot by their man from KWCH on a small monitor. It was worth its weight in gold.

"We are in the saddle."

In the motor home, Will stood alone at the window. He saw what no one else could see.

"She won't make it. She has to go now."

In the secondary shaft the jackhammer operator planted his feet for a better stance when he heard a splash. Looking down he watched as brown water began filling the shaft in inches per second.

"Damn . . . Pull me up! Pull me *up*! It's flooding!"

As the man was quickly pulled to safety by his crewman, the news that the fully covered secondary shaft was filling with water told Peter the same thing it told everyone else.

"It's coming through the ground."

He raced for the intercom mike and screamed to his daughter.

"Andie, what's happening down there!"

But Andromeda was in no position to answer.

TWENTY-FIVE
THE MONSTER

It had been days and days of nothing but immobility, pain, thirst and hunger. There had been headaches, leg aches, backaches and even finger aches. Andromeda's skin had felt gross and dirty for eons now. It was hard to breathe and her neck was so weak she could not even call up the energy to look to the stars.

Sometime in the night, after she had spoken to Will, Andromeda felt an odd pull, as if something was telling her she could end all this if she just followed the pull. The offer was tempting and it didn't feel like much effort was required to accept. Andromeda believed all it would take was a moment of relaxation. All she had to do was say, "Okay."

But she thought about how disappointed her parents would be if, when they finally got down to her in this hole, she had already left. Andromeda knew that if the tables were turned, she herself would be very upset. If she did leave without her parents and Will, they might never want to see her again. As they were the three people who truly mattered to Andromeda, that was something she could not face.

She refused the pull. That's when things started going bad.

The *poom-poom* from the roots grew loud again and it beat faster, the way a heart would if it was running or scared. The next thing that happened was the water.

It started with a trickle emerging from where the metal sheet had cut a groove in the shaft wall. At first Andromeda thought it was a flow from another pipe sent down by the people above, but as the trickle grew in strength, as it began to soak not just her clothing but also the soil packing her into the shaft, she suddenly knew otherwise.

The soil around her legs, weighted by the water leaching in from above, began to drop free in clumps. In a matter of minutes Andromeda's legs were free and she could indeed tell that there was absolutely nothing below to stand on.

"No, no, no . . ."

She felt herself beginning to move, but in the wrong direction. She was moving down. In a beat the last soil holding her in the shaft fell free and Andromeda began a new slide down the shaft, its sides slicked for speed.

"*Noooo!*" she cried.

Expecting to fall for miles and miles until she burned up in the center of the planet, Andromeda was shocked when after a fall of only ten feet or less she came to a gripping halt. She didn't stop because the shaft narrowed or because friction returned. She stopped because something had stopped her. Even though it was pitch black she knew right away what it was.

It was roots.

Roots had stopped her.

Andromeda could sense that she had fallen into a sort of chamber, not large, but wider than the shaft. And in this chamber hundreds, maybe even thousands of roots, all fine and fleshy moist, wove themselves into a deep and dense mitt that now clutched her to stop her fall.

She was in the middle of the *poom-poom*.

She was in the belly of the monster.

She began struggling like a fly caught in a spider's web but the roots stuck and clung, and with each flail toward escape, Andromeda found she was clutched even tighter. Bands of root wrapped her wrists, her feet, her legs and her waist. She felt roots encircle her neck. She felt their cool slickness constricting into a firm collar that began to choke her. Her breath came only with a struggle even as she began to hyperventilate in new terror. She felt herself once again peeing in her pants as this terror told her what was happening.

Her terror told her the root monster was trying to kill her.

"N-no!"

As she slid into the far recesses of consciousness, as she felt all over the *poom-poom* from the hated roots, as she was held helpless in the hated dark, Andromeda felt her spirit being devoured. Chunks of will and determination were swallowed whole. She was losing the fight. She was moving beyond terror to numb acceptance. She would die, she would be eaten by the root monster and there would be nothing to find if and when they ever made it down to her tomb. There would just be the roots and maybe some dust that others would brush off on their pants, not knowing the gray dust was all that remained of the little girl who fell in the hole.

Andromeda cried salty tears and called out for the person she needed most as the roots closed the door on her awareness.

"Mommy!"

And then she saw no more.

TWENTY-SIX

ANSWER THE LIGHT

Will could not stand it any longer.

He rushed from the motor home, fighting his way through the still blinding rainstorm, soaking himself in an instant, and yelled to his father as he fought to bail out the trench by the hole. Lightning and thunder cracked the sky.

Will tossed a long hank of rope to the ground.

"I have to go down!"

"What?"

"They'll never get her out in time. Somebody has to go down the hole. I'm the only one who can fit. I'm going down!"

"No way. Forget it, Will! We're not losing both of you!"

Will's face showed his sudden dismay.

"So you're saying she's already lost?"

Sheriff Austin and the drill foreman, witnessing the argument, stepped closer.

"What's this he's saying?"

"He wants to go down the hole."

Will was energized.

"You can tie the rope to my ankles and send me down headfirst. I can cut through the metal with some snips and then I can pull her out."

Peter vigorously shook his head.

"No way, Will. It's crazy! Right? Come on, it's crazy!" Both Sheriff Austin and the drilling-crew foreman demonstrated that they didn't think it was such a crazy idea after all. Peter couldn't believe it. "Look, we're not sending my son headfirst down that hole! That isn't happening!"

"Well, what else are we going to do? Face it, our time is up."

Will grabbed his father's attention as he lifted the rope and presented it to him.

"Dad, I can do this. I've been in smaller holes before." It was a lie but in the howling rain it would be hard to tell. "Let me get Andie! I need to!"

Sheriff Austin agreed.

"He's all we got left."

Sandra had to be given a sedative as the firemen rigged a suitable harness to safely lower Will down the shaft headfirst. Placing two bright head-lamps on his head and tucking three lashed pairs of tin snips in his pockets, they looked to the boy with hope and dread in equal measure. The newspeople clamored for pole position, soaked but getting the footage of a lifetime.

It was beamed live to millions.

Will asked his father to man the rope. As they stepped to the hole, Peter bent to give his son a firm hug.

"Bring her back."

"I will."

Will took one last look around and then slipped into the hole. Supported by Sheriff Austin and many others, Peter slowly fed out line and Will vanished down the shaft.

Inside it, Will had less difficulty with the fit than he had expected. The first thing he had to deal with was the dizziness he experienced when all the blood rushed to his head. But hanging upside down, a playground antic he had utterly perfected, was something he knew he could handle.

The intense light from the two headlamps kicked shiny gleams off the trickles of water running out from cracks in the walls. As he smoothly slid lower and lower, growing nearer and nearer to the hated piece of metal that had kept his sister entombed for days, Will noticed the walls were covered everywhere with a mat of fine white roots. Touching one of the root networks as he passed, he was certain he saw it withdraw in the same re-flexive way a Venus's-flytrap will close upon a landing fly. But he did not have time to tell for sure as he reached the metal sheet.

He pulled the signal line, signaling *stop*. Up above they held the line fast.

Will called through the holes in the metal, "Andie! It's Will. I'm here to get you out!" No answer. "Andie!"

There was still no answer.

Will reached out and grabbed the metal sheet. Trying to budge it proved fruitless. It was wedged tight. He pulled free a set of tin snips and began cutting a line from hole to hole.

On the outside Howard Clark and five other reporters stood in the massive downpour to give their live broadcasts of the latest twist in the saga of Baby Andromeda.

"This is Howard Clark speaking to you live to bring you this dramatic development in the continuing rescue of Baby Andromeda. William Wiley, the eight-year-old son of Peter and Sandra Wiley, has volunteered to climb into the shaft himself to bring his sister to safety. Just minutes earlier he went down the shaft headfirst and has now been lowered to a depth of some eighty feet. Over the last few days we have grown accustomed to some bold attempts to rescue Baby Andromeda, but in this reporter's opinion, nothing so far has even come close to matching the daring we're seeing here now!"

Will heard none of it. In the close quarters, where he struggled to cut the metal with the snips, he heard only his breathing and the beating of his heart. The fact that his heartbeat was so loud just told him that way too much blood was pumping around his ears.

The snips cut through a section from one hole to the metal edge, and the sheet moved. It was loose. Suddenly realizing it might fall on Andromeda, Will reached out and grabbed it as it tore loose from the shaft walls and dropped.

Outside, the sudden weight gain caused by Will's seizure of the metal and two-by-four caught the men off guard and they lurched forward a step. But control was reinstated and two tugs from Will's signal rope told them to let down more line. Sheriff Austin voiced what the now-hopeful faces were thinking.

"He made it! He's past!"

Will slowly lowered the metal sheet and the attached board down the shaft. As he dropped, he noticed something reflective approaching below.

"Whoa . . ."

He suddenly dropped into a small chamber filled with a tangled mass of white roots. He gave the signal rope a tug that told those above to stop.

Up above, the men grew excited.

"He stopped somewhere!"

Peter peered down the hole. He could only see a circle of white far, far below. Other helpers crowded closer to peer down as well.

"Does he have her?"

"I . . . I can't tell."

Will could tell, and the answer was that he did not.

He hung at the end of the line in the center of the small chamber either carved or eroded out of the rock. It had no exits but the one he had come in by. Turning his head from side to side, Will was almost blinded by the reflected glare from the mass of pale roots, most as dainty as a doily. Poking out of the root mass here and there were pieces of torn burlap, a few rodent skeletons, a paper cup, a crumbled-up cigarette pack, an old paper, twigs, grasses and a square piece of wood with nails sticking out. What was conspicuously missing was the one thing he had come looking for.

Andromeda was nowhere to be seen.

"Andie?"

As he tipped the metal and wood contraption into the small chamber to move it out of the way, Will hung twisting at the end of the rope, trying to figure out what was going on.

"Andie? Andie!"

Her absence was the last thing Will expected. She should be here. She had to be here. Andromeda could be nowhere else.

Will panned his gaze over the dense mass of roots. As he squinted against the glare he noticed a depression in the center of the mass, directly beneath the shaft opening out of which he now hung. As he stared into the depression he noticed it was moving up and down, in an inhale and an exhale, as if the root mass itself or something hidden below was breathing.

"Andie?"

Will reached down and began tugging at the roots, trying to tear them open to reveal what lay beneath. Despite his full strength the roots were tough and stringy. They put up a good fight. As they were torn open they withdrew as if singed, oozing out pink sap, just as Will thought he had seen them do in the shaft. Will pulled out his snips to cut faster.

As he pulled aside a flap of severed roots he saw the upturned and pale hand of his sister.

"No!"

Will cut faster, severing the roots in a circle. As he sliced away he saw Andromeda's arm and then the top of her head and then her face. Andromeda's eyes were closed as she lay cocooned by the roots, deathly silent, her face whiter than a blank canvas. But for the gentle flush of her breath against the daintiest roots, Will thought she might be dead.

Knowing she was not, he reached into the roots and pulled on his sister's arms.

"Come on!"

The pink sap dribbling from the severed ends was sticky like syrup and it matted Andromeda's hair to her face, giving her an even ghastlier aspect. Will huffed as he called forth every erg of power his wiry muscles could deliver.

"Let her go!"

With a final heave Will lifted Andromeda free and she slipped from the living envelope.

She was pale and lifeless, the only color on her face produced by the speckled droplets of the pink sap. As Will lay his inert little sister into the root mass and pulled free a second harness to strap her to his own, he gently tapped her face.

"Andie? Can you hear me?"

Andromeda's eyes fluttered open.

She looked at Will. She did not speak. She did not blink. She just stared.

She stared the coldest stare Will had ever seen.

Water continued to trickle down the shaft above and into the chamber. Will quickly fitted Andromeda into the harness and lashed her harness to his own.

"I'm getting you out, Andie. It's going to be okay."

Andromeda's unspeaking stare out of her ghoulishly white face suddenly made Will nervous. The look she gave him was not one of recognition. It was an alien stare, as if she were looking at a beetle on a pin. Her look made Will feel examined. He tried to shake his nervousness.

"It's going to be okay."

Will tugged on the signal rope.

On the outside the reaction was immediate.

"He's coming back up!"

"Does he have her?"

"I don't know. I can't tell. Just pull!"

They pulled.

As Will was lifted up the slick shaft, still dangling upside down, the face of his sister as she rose beneath him continued staring, now inches from his face. Her stare penetrated and laid bare all that Will kept hidden, the self he called his own. He felt revealed and vulnerable. He felt cornered by the stare of his sister.

He felt afraid.

There was no turning from Andromeda's chilling stare for the hundred-foot ascent to freedom, and in that ascent Will began to wonder who it was he was working to save.

TWENTY-SEVEN

TOP STORY

It was a rescue seen by hundreds of millions. It was legendary.

Baby Andromeda was alive and well.

In homes and pubs, in offices and in cars going to and from work, people heard the news and thought that finally, good things were happening to good people. Tears of joy were shed by many who had followed the tragedy from its inception. Things could not have worked out better.

The news replayed over and over the amazing shots of Baby Andromeda being pulled from the shaft by her remarkably brave brother. Still images of that very moment would be plastered on the front page of that night's late edition and tomorrow morning's paper.

The whole saga made people who might have been feeling lost and directionless reconsider their pessimism. If there was one image that demonstrated the American can-do spirit, it was Will Wiley bringing his baby sister to freedom. It was what life was all about.

Andromeda knew none of it.

Recuperating in a Wichita hospital, outside of which the media were now camped, it was said she was suffering from dehydration, exposure, a severe skin rash, infected cuts and lacerations, and a catatonia brought on by the stress of being trapped in a dark shaft for nearly five days.

Everyone prayed for her speedy recovery.

So many flowers and stuffed toys were sent to Andromeda that the hospital had to ask the Wiley family to publicly request that the practice end. The Wileys asked instead that the stuffed toys and flowers be distributed to all the children in the pediatric ward and to anybody else who could use a lift in their spirits. It was a generous compromise.

Back in Wishbone, Howard Clark had done what he could to make sure the Wiley family's best interests were served. He engaged Vincent Proctor as their attorney, and Proctor, who no longer represented Denny Sharf in his abandoned lawsuit against the Wileys, worked closely with Julie Fletcher to make certain there were no improprieties in the handling of the Baby Andromeda fund.

Clark had done even better to make certain his own interests were served. As a result of his sterling performance during the crisis, he had staff position offers from numerous stations around the country, and several leading dailies had expressed interest in giving him a shot. Clark decided he would milk the Baby Andromeda story for a few more days and then he would head to Cancun for a two-week vacation, possibly with Rayna Higgins, before accepting whichever offer promised the most.

The positive fallout of the happily ended tragedy was seen everywhere.

Wishbone put itself on the map with real distinction, and everybody did their best to see it stayed there. They knew the drain was open, they knew the crowds that flooded the town during the crisis would dribble out in a day or two at best, but what they hoped the bounty of visitors would leave with was a favorable impression of the place. If even twenty new families moved into Wishbone, it would mean twenty new sets of consumers for things like toothpaste and gas and new tires and dinner downtown.

Those seven days, which constituted the eventual run of the crisis and cooldown, had dumped enough money into local business that the townspeople felt it was possible for the first time in a long while to make holiday plans or ask relatives to come for a visit. Everybody had been part of Andromeda's rescue, everybody wore the bird pin from Amy's Stop 'N Go, and for a while they would be friendlier to one another. They would engage in less gossip, feeling a sweet afterglow, as if it had been an especially nice Christmas.

The Wileys, whom most used to regard as idiots and business dotards, were now considered one of Wishbone's leading families. They had open invitations to dine with the already acknowledged civic leaders, who were delighted to count the Wileys among their very best friends.

The fact that the Wileys still had no actual home was not lost on the townspeople. Denny Sharf's escape to prevent a run on the bank—an act patently illegal—put him between a rock and a hard place. On the Monday after Andromeda's rescue he was brought to face the Baby Andromeda fund by his furious father, a onetime army sergeant who could not believe the Milquetoast he called son had actually sprung from his loins. Promising to come out of retirement until the whole Savings and Loan debacle was settled, Denny's father told all assembled that his son had something to say.

Everyone listened as twenty-seven-year-old Denny spoke through a mouth that had evidently been solidly slapped.

"It has come to my attention that an oversight may have been committed by the Wishbone Savings and Loan against the Peter Wiley family. It seems they were unfairly overcharged in their interest payments over the last . . . eight years—"

The whole crowd "tsked." Denny continued.

"—and this will be rectified."

A voice piped up from the back of the crowd. It was Mike Serven, the butcher.

"How, you dumb bastard? You tore down their house!"

Denny turned with pleading eyes to his father, who merely glared back.

"Well, umm . . . yes, we tore down a house but, well . . . houses can be rebuilt, and so will theirs! The Wishbone Savings and Loan is proud to announce that it will pay its restitution to the Peter Wileys in the form of a brand-new home!"

Denny pulled aside a cloth covering a board on an easel. On the board was the same beautifully rendered drawing of the lovely home seen on the Royal Oak Gardens sign. People from the audience began asking questions, as if they themselves were buying for the Wileys.

"How many bedrooms?"

"It has to have three at least."

"It should have a spare too, so that makes four."

"I'm sure Sandra would love an island in the kitchen."

"I have a trash compactor; she should have one too."

"With all they've been through, the place should have a pool!"

"Definitely, a pool and a Jacuzzi!"

"Has to have a playroom."

"What about the barn? What about all that?"

"It'll need a silo or two."

"What about it, Sharf?"

Denny looked out on the angry faces. He again glanced back at his father, but his father only shrugged.

"It's your game, boy."

Denny turned back to the crowd. Buying the Wileys a family home was going to kill him. It meant he would have to sell his own home. He would have to rent. In time he would make it up. After all, the Wishbone Savings and Loan still had substantial holdings and he was still the boss, but the interim would be years of living low. Still, some lean years were preferable to no years.

"They can have the bedrooms, the pool, the Jacuzzi—"

"The trash compactor? She needs one, I'm telling you."

"—and the playroom. But no trash compactor, no barn and no silo. That's the deal."

Denny waited as the crowd fell into a hushed discussion. Mike Serven, who earlier threatened to bust Denny's lip, a feat later accomplished by Denny's own father, acted as the spokesman.

"We'll take it."

Denny exhaled. It cost him a lot but the worst was over, and in the back of his mind he was beginning to see how the best might be yet to come. Before he had even stepped away from the easel he began to concoct a plan on how to install a hidden camera in the Wileys' new master bedroom.

Will Wiley was rightfully hailed as a hero, but in his usual humility he refused to accept the tag. Standing at the foot of Andromeda's hospital bed he knew why.

What had he saved? The body lying in the bed, so pale, so still and silent, with those piercing eyes, had no resemblance to the warm and happy girl he used to know. This person gave Will the creeps. She seemed so . . . *old*.

That was the word he had been searching for.

Andromeda, physically still five, seemed in essence far older. A look into her eyes received in return the sense that those eyes had witnessed lost worlds, that they had seen armies battling on plains, that they had seen ships afire on distant oceans. Her eyes were bright but the color had changed. Will was certain Andromeda's eyes used to be hazel. Now they were a blue that seemed to have more depth, as if subtly transparent tones were laid one on top of the other to create an intangible hue. He suddenly remembered that he had seen those eyes before.

They were the eyes of a wolf.

They were the eyes of a carnivore.

It had been a week since Will pulled Andromeda from the shaft, and she had still not spoken. When he spoke to her, all she did was follow him with her clinical eyes, as if examining him for later dissection.

When he professed his concerns to his mother and father, he was rebuffed.

"Will, your sister has been through a lot. It's normal that she should be suffering from—"

Diana French, now a constant presence, filled in the blank.

"Post-traumatic stress syndrome. She shut down. It's a common reaction to shock of this sort."

"See, it's normal."

Will was unswayed. He brought up another point of contention.

"What about the roots?"

Peter was growing tired of Will's story about man-eating roots.

"Listen, you're not being helpful. How will this talk about monsters help your sister get better? Use your head, Will. Scaring her with this talk is the last thing she needs."

Diana offered to intervene.

"Maybe I should have a chat with Will. Maybe he can tell me what he thinks he saw."

"I don't think anything, lady—I know."

"Will, you apologize right this instant to Diana. You don't call people 'lady' and you know it."

"Sorry."

Diana smiled and caressed Will's hair.

"Would you like to talk?"

"Nobody believes me, nobody wants to send a camera down the hole to see what I saw, nobody wants to see if I'm telling the truth. Forget it. I didn't see anything, okay?"

Peter, who had already perfected the very camera technique that Will now suggested, had never before seen his son so adamant about anything. He was sure Will had seen something but he couldn't believe Will had seen it right.

"Will, we can't do that even if we wanted to. They plugged the hole, filled it with concrete."

Will was flabbergasted.

"When did they do that?"

"Yesterday. No one'll ever get in that hole again."

Diana French gathered her things and prepared to leave. Back at her hotel room she had already finished the third chapter of her book chronicling her time with the Wileys and Baby Andromeda, and she was anxious to start the fourth.

"I'm making it my mission to help Andie out of this. We'll use every resource at our disposal to see your daughter healthy and happy."

Sandra wiped a tear from her eye. Later that day she would choose interior colors, tile patterns, trim styles and carpeting for the four-bedroom home with pool and Jacuzzi that the Wishbone Savings and Loan was building on their free and clear forty-nine acres.

She gave Diana a hug.

"Getting Andie back is all we want."

Will felt a buzzing sensation creeping up his arms. Like the warning hairs that tell a cockroach it's about to be mashed, the sensation told Will he was being watched. He turned to look through the open door of Andromeda's private room. Andromeda lay exactly as she had lain for a week. And she stared. She stared at Will with the eyes of a hunter.

Will stepped out of the line of sight of the thing that was not his sister.

"Can we go now?"

TWENTY-EIGHT

REVIVAL

She had existed for more than a week in a state of silent observation, mutely witnessing the machinations of doctors, counselors, interns and nurses who worked to bring her back to the speaking world. She was probed, she was sampled, her tongue was depressed, her temperature was checked. She was scanned and documented. Patient and gentle hands had examined her and applied medications to heal wounds. But what all the attention had so far failed to accomplish was any success in breaking Andromeda out of her shell.

The nurse who attended to Andromeda's daily needs, who had seen all types of injuries and felt she was incapable of being shocked, gave Andromeda, a girl who had such a strong way of staring, a standard sponge bath. She leaned Andromeda forward and ran the wet sponge up her back. She washed Andromeda's face and then moved the sponge down her arms. Andromeda sat emotionless throughout the entire operation.

The nurse had bathed Andromeda every day since the poor child had been placed under her care. In that time, the nurse grew accustomed to an ordinary routine with this girl who had survived an experience so extraordinary.

Nine days after Andromeda was pulled from the hole, the nurse fell victim to the end of routine.

As she ran the sponge around Andromeda's neck with the same tender manner she had applied without incident for the last nine days, Andromeda suddenly jerked up straight and let out a full-volume shriek. The terrified nurse stumbled back, knocking over the bath pan and three bouquets of the many flowers filling the room. Andromeda continued to scream as loud as she could, and the nurse slipped on the soapy water, tumbling in a loud racket over metal trays, carnations, roses and daffodils. Orderlies, doctors, nurses and mobile patients rushed to see what was happening.

Andromeda sucked in more air and screamed from the bottom of her soul.

Having sent Will off with Sandra and Diana French, Peter had stayed behind to arrange for Andromeda's in-home care if that need should arise. Hearing Andromeda's scream, he rushed into her room.

"Andie?"

When Andromeda saw her father she stopped screaming and cried with her arms open, "Daddy!"

His eyes filling with tears, Peter rushed to his daughter and took her in his arms.

"I'm here, Andie, I'm here."

"Don't leave me . . . don't ever leave me."

"I won't sweetie, I'll always be here."

Andromeda's doctor rushed in along with too many others as Andromeda screamed, and saw that the dam had finally broken. Waving the spectators out and following behind, he left father and daughter to renew a healing contact.

Peter held Andromeda tight.

"It's all right, you're safe; you're *safe*."

Andromeda pulled away to look past her father.

"Where's Mommy? Where's Will?"

"They went home."

"Home?"

"Back to Wishbone."

Andromeda was suddenly trembling.

"I'm not going back there, I'm never going back there!"

Andromeda again hugged her father with all her strength. Peter was surprised to see how strong she had become in the space of a week and a half. She held him so tight he could hardly breathe.

"Honey, you're cho . . . you're choking me."

"Don't take me there. Promise you won't. Promise."

It was the only thing Peter could say under the circumstances.

"I . . . promise."

Andromeda's death grip softened and she laid her head on Peter's shoulder. As he rocked his daughter and thanked God for her return, he did not see the cold light filling her eyes. Slumped over his shoulder, Andromeda looked past her father with a vision of things no girl her age could possibly see.

What those things were, it was too early to know.

TWENTY-NINE

BIG BROTHER

Mary Hayworth Downes sat with Will Wiley at her kitchen table and smiled at the boy she now considered one of her closest friends.

"So, little man, fill me in."

Will drank his milk and munched down a plate of fresh brownies.

"We're supposed to have this hero-dinner thing this weekend. That guy Timms is going to be there, a bunch of people who sent us money, the sheriff, a bunch of other guys. It's going to be on TV again, I think."

"I know, they sent me an invite."

"Oh yeah, I forgot. You're really supposed to be there."

"And you? Are you going to be there? I mean, you're the real hero."

"Yeah, me."

"What about Andromeda?"

"She's saying something from the hospital. They're going to show it on a big screen. She's not coming home anyway. They're sending her to some special school with that French lady."

"Andromeda's not coming home?"

"She can't, at least not for a while. Something about coming back to where it happened. She gets too scared. She even gets sick."

"I'm sorry to hear that. I'll bet you're sorry too."

Will wasn't sure how sorry he was.

It was just possible Andromeda scared him even more than the hole. He had seen her since she came out of her catatonia and she talked the same and laughed the same but somehow she was not the same. One particular look from Andromeda made Will feel small. It made him feel expendable. He didn't want to be around her as long as she had that flash in her eyes.

But it would sound mean-spirited to say that, since he pulled her from the hole, he preferred her absence.

"Yeah, I'm sorry. I miss her."

That much was true. He did miss Andromeda, but he missed the old Andromeda, not this new and strange version.

In some ways Will felt Andromeda, the version he knew and remembered, was still at the bottom of the hole, that she had never come out. If this was the case, he should be grieving her loss; he should be in mourning. But all his senses told him he had not lost her. He could see her, he could hear her and he could touch her. Yet even with all this physical evidence he could not help doubting her identity.

He could not convince himself that she really was Andromeda.

The question had haunted Will every waking moment since he had pulled Andromeda from the clutches of the white roots—in Will's opinion the chief cause of Andromeda's later strange behavior, but one that no one wanted to believe. His father, his mother, even Andromeda herself thought he was lying when he mentioned the roots that had held Andromeda tight.

Andromeda's denial stung most deeply, and Will could not help but feel betrayed by her answer when he asked if she remembered the roots.

"I don't remember any roots, Will. I really, really don't remember."

Will knew she was lying; he just couldn't understand why. His baby sister, who used to adore him and said she still did, would not lie to her big brother. She never had in the past. Why should she now?

She would lie because she was trying to conceal whatever it was in the hole that had put that flash in her eyes. She would lie because she was no longer who she seemed to be. She would lie because she was no longer Andromeda.

As far as Will was concerned, his Andromeda had died in that hole and whoever it was who smiled out of her familiar face was a deceptive intruder. Will could foster no trust for the thing that had switched places with Andromeda. The way he felt right now, he believed he never would.

Before he pulled his sister from the hole his greatest wish was to have her safely nearby for the rest of his life. Now his greatest wish was to keep her as far distant as the planet would permit. Will had gone so far as to check a globe, deciding St. Paul Island in the Indian Ocean was Wishbone, Kansas's, polar opposite. Having Andromeda live on St. Paul Island was an option Will kept to himself, but one that he thought with a solid measure of guilt would send him a lasting relief.

Will finished his milk and stood to go.

"Well, I have to head out. I have to get back and help my dad figure out where we're going to put the barn."

"You don't stop, do you?"

"Nope. 'Bye, Mary!"

" 'Bye, honey. You come by anytime!"

"Okay, I will!"

As Will climbed on his new bike and rode off, Mary thanked the fates for the restoration of the Wiley family and for handing her a role in their restoration, which had encompassed her own lonely world. But now she had learned the restoration was not yet complete.

She had heard about little Andromeda's troubles, she had heard about the residual effects of her trauma, and now Will had completed the story by telling Mary that Andromeda would not be coming home anytime soon. It was the only blemish to a tragic story that had ended so well for so many.

It was so often said that time had the ability to heal all wounds. In Mary's case, it was finally coming true. She was again and at long last feeling a joy toward life she had so mightily lacked in all the years since Emerson's death. She told herself the same would be true for little Andromeda Wiley. It would take time to heal her deepest wounds.

Yet it would take Andromeda herself to explain how severely she had been wounded. The scars most deep would not be seen. They resided beyond reach in a place small and dark, where horror found an echo. And the echo sang a song she would not easily forget.

Poom-poom.

Poom-poom.

Poom-poom.

Book
TWO

THIRTY

TODAY

Will Wiley, at age twenty-three, had become a man.

Six feet tall and strong from his years of working the family farm, Will was the definition of a Wishbone local. Where he stepped he had stepped hundreds of times before, and other locals he encountered knew him in an instant as one of their own. He felt safe and complete in this little town in the middle of nowhere, where everyone knew his name.

Each day he woke early to check the fields and then drive for a cup of joe at the Straight Line Cafe — the precise spot where a flame of love two years earlier bonded him to Lisa Benson, a sweet and sincere soul who was herself a lifetime local. Will downed his daily dose of Straight Line java over a plate of waffles and talked farm talk with men and women he'd known his whole life before heading home to work by his father's side.

He often felt his life was practically perfect.

Yet even in those soothing moments when his breath came easy, a ghost from the past haunted his tranquil vision. A dark cloud of history, grown fainter over time but still present and still shielding Will from the full glare of good fortune, hung over his perfect world. He knew this cloud intimately because it shared his blood. He knew it because it had a name.

Andromeda.

Will's perfect world seemed forever doomed to fall under the shadow of his sister's legacy.

It had been fifteen years since Andromeda's fall into the shaft, and it had been just as long since she last set foot in her hometown, or even stepped within a thousand miles of Wishbone. The memory of her trauma, the thing that kept her distant, had a radius of trespass larger than most countries. Andromeda to this day refused to enter that radius. More specifically, for the past fifteen years she had steadfastly refused to come home.

Will had by now spent far more time apart from his sister than he had spent with her, and in that void Andromeda had become a stranger to him. If he now thought of her at all, he felt what one might feel for a distant cousin or a grandparent who never comes to visit. Whatever emotional connection Will once had to his younger sibling had long ago dissolved into a thin bond whose daily relevance was nearly nonexistent.

Five years earlier, the last time Will had seen Andromeda, she was a perky teen living on The Campus in Vermont, still counseled by Diana French, still working past the trauma of her experience in the hole. Andromeda talked happily about her friends, her new interests, places she had visited and places she intended to visit. She demonstrated that a decade on The Campus under the tutelage of Diana French had produced a young woman who was creative, intelligent, vibrant and eager to experience life. Andromeda seemed utterly healed, yet every request from their parents for her return to Wishbone was met with a response that she needed more time. Now five more years had passed, and at age twenty Andromeda was still a no-show in the fair burg of Wishbone.

Will cautiously accepted some of the blame.

In his limited and awkward encounters with Andromeda since she left town, in those brief sojourns when the family made the trek to Vermont to see her at The Campus, Will tried to dissuade Andromeda from coming home. He painted a dead-end picture of the town he loved. He made it seem as if coming back to Wishbone was a failure. Even so, Will sensed that she was on to him, that she could see through his clumsy machinations and was fully aware that he simply did not want her around.

There was a reason why Will did not want her around. That cold light in his sister's eyes, that lupine gleam—better controlled as she aged but still quietly present the last time he saw her—was what caused him to shun her. Will had convinced himself there was a shadowy alter ego hiding within Andromeda.

Logic screamed for Will to come to a different conclusion, to accept that she was nothing more than a normal girl who had survived a harrowing experience. It was crazy to think she was anything other than who and what she appeared to be. It was crazy to see dark menace in a girl who had never hurt a fly.

Yet in her presence he felt fear, plain and simple.

It was fear that was not imagined.

There was nothing false about the way Andromeda's stare caused Will's guts to twist. Her gaze tore to shreds the protective shell around his core self. He was left naked and weak and utterly vulnerable. When Andromeda's cold eyes first met Will's, she could have killed him with a wink.

But the years and a growing maturity had nevertheless begun to produce doubt. Will had not felt anything approaching the intense fear he'd experienced immediately following Andromeda's rescue, when she stared at him from her hospital bed. In truth, he had rarely given Andromeda the chance to repeat the episode.

He meticulously avoided making direct eye contact with his sister in all his diminishing visits to The Campus, and after the first few years Andromeda seemed to cue in on it. Although she never said anything directly, when speaking to Will thereafter she always looked at his shoulder or his chest. Without complaint she complied with his unspoken request, even though Will could tell her feelings were hurt.

The whole issue of Will's relationship with his only sibling stirred in him such a complex brew of emotions that he felt the only way to deal with it was to avoid it completely. He shut his sister out, accepting lost joys as he exiled Andromeda from his heart.

But try as he might, he could not avoid her completely.

Andromeda's fall into the shaft shined a lasting light on the town of Wishbone, and in the intervening years since it had occurred, the entire town had capitalized on the event. In restaurants, in diners, in Laundromats and in hotel lobbies, framed pictures showed in crisp detail the dramatic and heroic rescue of Baby Andromeda. Will could scarcely walk anywhere in town without seeing some memento of the occasion, and people constantly reminded him that the story of his little sister would be forever entwined with his own.

Will would always be Baby Andromeda's brother.

He could not help but feel some resentment. He wanted to be free from the story and free from his part in it. He wanted to be plain old Will Wiley. Most of all, he wanted to shake the memory of what he saw when he pulled his sister from the hole. But he understood this was a wish that would never be granted.

Will would be forced to remember Andromeda in exchange for her permanent absence.

To this day, he considered it a bargain.

THIRTY-ONE
A LETTER FROM ROME

The letter from Rome arrived on a Tuesday.

Reading it, Peter realized his entire life was about to change.

He rubbed his chin under his short-cropped salt-and-pepper beard and read the letter once more. It was short and to the point, but it carried more weight than many volumes.

Andromeda was coming home.

Folding the letter and returning it to its envelope, both written on the same delicate stationery Andromeda had used for the past fifteen years, Peter stuck it on the refrigerator with a magnet made to look like a hamburger.

Stepping back, he stared at the letter as it hung between recipes, reminder notes, event invites and photos of Will in the midst of a skydiving free fall. It was as if in staring, he might rearrange the words into a message that made more sense.

It wasn't that Peter did not want Andromeda to come home—having her home was without a doubt his greatest wish. It was that he simply didn't believe it.

Fifteen years earlier, Andromeda suffered a traumatic experience when she spent five days at the bottom of a hole. As a result of that experience, the Wileys were handed a second chance to grab the brass ring, but that chance was tied to the town of Wishbone. Because of her experience, Andromeda could not accept that tie. In the beginning she could not even hear the word *Wishbone* without getting physically ill. It was an extreme reaction that eventually subsided, but her fear of the place never did.

She would not come home.

As difficult as it truly was, Peter and Sandra decided to place their little Andromeda in a special school where her mental and emotional rehabilitation would be overseen by Diana French, the celebrated author of both *Seeing Beyond*, a book on near-death experiences, and her first best-seller, *Answer the Light: The Restoration of Baby Andromeda*. The expensive private school, blandly named The Campus, sat on lush grounds in forested countryside in central Vermont. The run from Wichita to Montpelier was an exhausting one, often requiring transfers, stopovers, delays, hours on the tarmac and the occasional in-flight turbulence scare, but Sandra and Peter made it a point to spend at least one week every three months by Andromeda's side. Months turned into years, and still Andromeda would not return to Wishbone.

As the foundation was poured for the Wiley family home on the forty-nine acres of land given to them by Mary Downes, as the barn was raised, as the silos went up and Peter began the laborious process of turning hard-packed soil into an airy loam, he and Sandra told themselves Andromeda's stay at The Campus was temporary and that she would indeed come home. They readied a room.

The room was still ready.

Plugged low in the wall of Andromeda's room was her old Mickey Mouse nightlight. Its plastic was now yellowed and some of its color had faded, but it still worked, it still cast its tender glow. When Andromeda was first shipped off to The Campus, Peter asked her if she wanted to take Mickey along, but she didn't seem to know what Peter was talking about. When she finally remembered she said, "I don't need it."

His girl had changed and it stung Peter deeply because he had set the change in motion. Since that moment out near the abandoned wells when Will casually stated that Andromeda had gone for drinks, when both Peter and Sandra first faced their brutal error, he could not consider himself without disdain. He had committed a mighty sin. He would never forget it.

When other farmers called it quits after twelve hours of work, Peter put in sixteen, eighteen or even twenty hours, falsely believing if he burned himself up through hard labors he might be able to purge the demons. In the end all he was able to do was keep them caged, and the side effect of his industriousness was the surprising reality that he was now one of the most prosperous farmers in the region. His initial forty-nine acres had grown to more than thirteen hundred, all of it no-till organics. Where it had been just himself and little Will in the beginning, there was now a corporation. His produce was admired from California to New York.

He had even failed at failure.

Yet while Peter dwelled each day on things he could never change, Sandra lived a different life.

She had said nothing about her crime. She still smiled, she still laughed and she exuded more confidence than ever. She lived her life well because she refused to discuss what they had done to Andromeda, and the marriage suffered, blooming into cautious mediocrity as Sandra danced around their shared guilt.

Sandra would take the news of Andromeda's return well; Peter was sure of it. Will, however, was another matter, and Peter's first concern when reading Andromeda's letter was how he would break the news to his son.

Andromeda would not have survived without Will's brave dive down the hole. It was an act fully consistent with a brother's love for his sister. But Will's behavior following Andromeda's rescue, when he grew distant from her, was not consistent at all.

It was through no fault of Andromeda's. She had asked for Will's company from the beginning of her recovery. Fifteen years later, she still asked how he was doing with sincere concern and interest. The division between sister and brother was entirely and inexplicably Will's doing.

Will's visits to Andromeda were spaced farther and farther apart until they stopped altogether. Whenever Peter delved into the matter, Will responded with shrugs and mumbles, unwilling to expand on behavior that defied reason. As the years slipped by Peter stopped asking.

Now Peter's patience was at an end.

Whether Will liked it or not, Andromeda was coming home and Peter vowed to make her feel welcome. He would fill the house with fresh-cut flowers, he would cook the most lavish meal and he would stack presents to the ceiling. If Will had a problem with Andromeda's being home, it was just too damn bad.

In the middle of Peter's ruminations Will walked in. Opening the refrigerator, he pulled out a soda and popped the top.

"Hey, Dad. What's up?"

Peter watched as his strong son guzzled down the soft drink before throwing the can in the recycling bin.

"Good question." Peter yanked the letter from under the hamburger magnet. "She's coming home."

"Who? Mom?"

"Andromeda."

Will fell mute. Then: "When?"

"Two weeks."

Will's eyes scanned the room for something to stare at as he considered the news. His eyes landed on the trash compactor.

"Great."

Then he abruptly turned and left the house.

Peter heard Will start the ATV, and he looked out to see him racing for the ragged fields of recently harvested corn. He sighed.

News that should normally cause unbridled rejoicing was instead causing consternation and conflict within the Wiley household. But as Peter watched his son racing off, trailing a streamer of brown dust, he decided that nothing and nobody, not even Will, would stop the story of Baby Andromeda from having a happy ending.

THIRTY-TWO

ANDROMEDA'S TOMB

Driving past fields of corn and grain, crossing the flats of central Kansas, anything vertical tended to catch your eye: a radio antenna, a grove of trees, a silo, a house with a widow's walk, a tornado siren, a billboard or even a joke mailbox twenty feet high that says AIRMAIL on the side. If you weren't always looking you might only catch these things out of the corner of your eye and say, "What was that?" as you sped past at seventy miles per hour.

Upon entering Wishbone, Kansas, however, was a sight impossible to miss.

At both ends of the main drag into and out from Wishbone, identical concrete archways resembling gigantic wishbones were built over the road, tall enough to allow a semi and trailer to pass underneath. Mounted on the vertical lengths of the bone-colored arches were welcome badges for the Kiwanis, the Daughters of the American Revolution, the Rotary Club, the Lions Club, the Toastmasters and more. Professionally rendered three-dimensional metal scrolls in the act of unfurling were installed horizontally across the tops of the huge arches. The colorful scrolls read in a florid script, WELCOME TO WISHBONE, KANSAS. In smaller letters directly beneath sat a second caption.

HOME OF BABY ANDROMEDA.

Few tourists were aware as they drove beneath the big wishbones and entered Wishbone country that Baby Andromeda, now a twenty-year-old woman, had not lived in Wishbone for fifteen years. But Andromeda herself was not what drove the tourists into town. What brought the crowds was her Midwestern saga.

The saga of Baby Andromeda was aided tremendously by an interactive tourist center erected upon the site of Baby Andromeda's five days of terror. Inspired by places like Flintstones Village and Trees of Mystery and the Oregon Vortex, icons of roadside Americana, Andromeda's Tomb was a place that promised at least twenty minutes of delight between one long stretch of road and another.

Pulling into the parking lot, the very spot where news vans and disaster gawkers had camped out those five days, detoured tourists first saw the large drill damaged in the gas explosion. It was set on a circular concrete platform ringed by a thick layer of red lava pebbles, ringed by a railing, as if the busted drill were Michelangelo's *David*. The drill was the free part of the exhibit, and a plaque mounted to the railing explained technical details about the drill that almost nobody cared to know. Tourists universally gave it a perfunctory look upon discovering there was nothing you could do with it, no levers to pull or doors to open or wheels to spin, like an old cannon in a town park good only for climbing on, something they wouldn't even let you do here. They lost interest and moved for the pathway leading to the main building itself.

The building sat beneath large bright, three-dimensional letters in a cartoony font that read, ANDROMEDA'S TOMB. For some associative reason, the building was shaped to look like it had been thrown together from construction-site objects. The effect was not altogether unappealing.

The roof appeared to be a haphazardly strewn stack of oversized concrete slabs sporting large rusted eyehooks. The supporting walls were held by poured concrete pillars rising at all sorts of funny angles. A wide tunnel of concrete cylinders, actual sewer segments, led visitors into the lobby, where they would pay five dollars for adults and two dollars each for kids to be let past a turnstile into the "museum" portion of the exhibit.

The museum itself was shaped in the form of a figure eight. A front circular bulge narrowed to meet a rear circular bulge. Both rooms were designed to seem like chambers in a cavern, with foam and plaster stalactites and stalagmites dripping from the ceiling and rising from the floor.

In the first cavern room, along the curved walls, were enlarged photos of the rescue operation. There were photos of Peter and Sandra Wiley looking worried. There were photos of Sheriff Austin standing beside fire chief Bobby Timms as they directed the rescue. There were photos of the explosion and the injured. This portion had videos, which the tourist could watch by pushing buttons on display cases.

In one vertical case behind glass was a lifelike mannequin of Androm-eda as a girl, dressed in the actual clothing she wore during her five days in the hole. The face of the mannequin wore a look of terror, crunched as it was into an authentic-looking cross section of a dirt shaft made from fiberglass. The clothes were stained and torn, and children always pointed out with snickers the stains where she had obviously gone potty.

Another case held sections of the copper tube used to feed Andromeda water and soup. The picks, shovels and buckets used in the rescue, the outfits worn by Sheriff Austin and Bobby Timms (Timms's complete with a huge gouge in the pant leg where the shrapnel struck) were all on dis-play. There was also a reasonably lifelike mannequin of Will Wiley in the actual outfit he had worn, tethered to the very harness used in the rescue. Behind the glass of this case, Will's mannequin face showed determina-tion as he prepared to crawl into a fiberglass hole.

The centerpiece of the first cavern room, forever protected from the el-ements, was the secondary rescue shaft, still open. Its upper sides were lined with the two-by-twelve planks brought in by Sheriff Austin. Visitors could walk over a small bridge that allowed them to look down into the eighty-three-foot shaft. For safety reasons a thick, clear piece of Plexiglas enclosed the shaft after a depth of about ten feet. Beneath the transpar-ent cover, the shaft extended way, way down. At certain points along the way, illuminated arrow signs sticking from the shaft walls marked each day of progress. One sign told visitors where the explosion occurred. At the bottom stood a worker mannequin lit by a caged handy light. The stiff mannequin, also in the clothes of the actual rescue worker, aimed the actual jackhammer into the unfinished, slanted portion of the actual shaft.

But the second room held the main attraction.

In the center of the second cavern room, dramatically lit by an appar-ent hole in the cavelike ceiling (actually a frosted skylight), was the con-crete plug beneath which lay Andromeda's tomb itself. There was no railing or lava-pebble landscape to keep visitors away. They could sit on the plug to absorb the frightening chill that most certainly hid beneath. It was one of the prime photo opportunities.

Set into the wall behind the plug was another prime opportunity. Here stood another fiberglass incarnation of the well shaft, but this time there was no glass to prevent access. Here you were encouraged to try to squeeze into the cross section to have your photo taken. Tourist families giggled as too-fat Mom or Dad tried to squeeze in and couldn't. But children could and did with nervous and excited glee.

The tour naturally poured out into a gift shop, where you could still buy those vials of earth taken from the secondary shaft. You could also buy shot glasses, key chains, Viewmaster cards of Baby Andromeda's rescue, water-filled pens that when tipped showed a little Andromeda moving in or out of the shaft, and T-shirts with all sorts of captions. A favored one was I GOT THE SHAFT. You could also buy Indian crafts, kachinas, crummy arrowheads made in Korea, some actual Indian artwork that cost more than the average tourist could afford, rubber dinosaurs, Wishbone souvenirs and postcards galore.

Andromeda's Tomb was rarely a main destination for traveling folks but it had acquired the ability to cause tourists to rethink their routes so they could stop in on their way to real destinations like the Grand Canyon or Pike's Peak or Yellowstone. And like Wall Drug in South Dakota, where you saw signs hundreds of miles before you got there telling you how many hundreds of miles you still had to go to get there, Andromeda's Tomb had bold signs plastered on all roads leading to Wishbone, encouraging travelers to come and take a look.

The success of Andromeda's Tomb, fully owned by local developer Denny Sharf, who had given the Wileys a home in exchange for the rescue souvenirs populating his museum, was part of what drove the town of Wishbone to reinvent itself over the past fifteen years. The town was becoming a destination in itself.

For decades an obscure cattle, farming and sheep-ranching town, Wishbone wisely decided to emphasize its connection to the Old West. Boardwalks were built, horse rails were put up, stagecoach rides were offered around town, a fake saloon put on a honky-tonk act and gunfight show, Indians in period garb staffed the travel office, and every store in the downtown quarter had its front redesigned with old-style colors and old-style signs. Stores boarded up fifteen years earlier were now collectibles shops, antique shops or Western-themed restaurants. Old West hotels opened in buildings that had formerly been vacant dustbins.

On any given weekend, particularly in the summer and fall, the boardwalks were packed with tourist families looking for a taste of the way things were, or at least the way things were as they liked to think they were. Historical details such as mounds of horse and cattle shit, rivers of sheep piss, toothless whores and flat-on-their-face drunks were conspicuously missing from this sanitized version of the way things were.

Julie Fletcher, now head of the *Wishbone Review*, dressed in a period costume to give tours of the old press, still used to print the weekly paper. For a few dollars she printed out "Wanted" posters with your picture in the space and your name on the bill. If your tastes went to more refined arts, you could cross the street and head south to O'Connor's Gallery. Stepping in, you would find wood crafts, leatherwork, metalwork, paintings, ceramics, drawings and sculptures produced by local artisans. Frank O'Connor, still on the Wishbone city council, would step forward and tell you the story behind every overpriced item in his shop, as if each local artist had international renown and was famous in Hungary and Botswana. Farther down was Amy's Stop 'N Go. Tourists walking into her strange shop, which looked like it sold the pickings from every bad garage sale in the country, knew they had reached the limit of the fun section of Wishbone and immediately backtracked toward Courthouse Square or Piasecki's Polecat Pub and Eatery.

Baby Andromeda was not forgotten in the revival of Wishbone's center. Photos of the rescue operation were on walls in nearly every eating establishment, and as people wolfed down a banana split or a Macho Taco, they could look to a framed picture above their booth and see Andromeda's face as she was pulled from the well by her brother Will.

Andromeda had become a welcome part of Wishbone's tradition. Even though she was now twenty years old, to the citizens of Wishbone, she would always be their poor little girl who fell in a hole.

THIRTY-THREE
VÌA KANSAS

All Will said to Lisa was "Andie's coming home."

Lisa then told her parents, who told their bridge partners, who told the gas station attendant, who told the next customer, who told Julie Fletcher, who then printed the news in the *Wishbone Review.*

BABY ANDROMEDA RETURNS! was the headline.

"Oh, Christ" was Peter's reaction when he read it.

Sandra, handling the news better than anybody, shrugged it off as she walked into the mudroom.

"Who cares? So what if they know? They'd find out soon enough."

"I don't want Andie coming back to another frenzy like she had before."

"It's been fifteen years, Peter; nobody cares anymore. They know Andie's a private citizen, they won't bother her."

Peter continued reading the article in the *Review.* It produced another reaction.

"Oh, shit."

Having returned from her artful labors in her barn studio, Sandra cleaned her sable brushes in the mudroom sink and tossed her colorfully splotched artist's apron into a hamper.

"What now?"

"They want to throw her a parade."

"You're kidding."

Sandra and Peter considered for a moment what that might mean. Sandra quickly decided it meant nothing.

"I think it's fine. Andie needs to get reacquainted with the town. It's a nice way to do it."

"To parade her around like she's one of the local attractions?"

"Well, isn't she? Look, just let Andie decide. If she doesn't want to participate, she doesn't have to. End of story. Did you want me to pick her up when she comes in or do you want to go?"

"I thought we'd all go."

"Including Will?"

"He should."

Again Peter and Sandra paused for a moment of thought. Sandra broke the silence.

"I'm nervous about all this. It'll be okay, won't it?"

"I hope so."

Sandra walked off and left Peter to finish the *Review*. He scanned the rest of the articles. Most were notices about keeping your dog on a leash or buying tickets for a Cub Scout spaghetti dinner. He tossed down the paper and considered what was coming.

Since her early graduation from high school at age seventeen, when she accepted a scholarship to study abroad, Peter and Sandra watched as Andromeda attained a level of sophistication they could never have imagined. Her letters home were now flavored with foreign phrases, and her tone gave the impression that she was a young woman wholly comfortable with herself and the world.

Peter could tell that Andromeda's sophistication somehow intimidated Sandra, whose education had ended a few days before their marriage had begun. To compensate, Sandra studied art, she read Keats, she read Hardy and she tried to understand the worldviews of Eliot and Sartre. She learned enough French to pepper her conversations with a phrase or two. When asked if she had information about something which she did not, rather than just saying, "I don't know," Sandra insisted on saying, "*Je ne sais quoi*." No longer could the family have simple coffee in the morning; it was now a *latte*-this or a mocha-that. Instead of good old Oreos and Chips Ahoy!, the snacks were now hard-to-pronounce *biscottis* and dry, crackerlike wafers that crumbled to dust on the first bite.

At age forty-one, Sandra was engaged in an eternal catch-up. She needed to know what was hot and who was in and what to wear and which exercise or which herbal medicine would do the best job of keeping her body trim and in shape. She was at the crest of the wave, and that's where she strived to stay. With her radar out for the next trend, she had become a guru to all the other local seekers of enlightenment and firm fannies.

With a great deal of conscious effort, Sandra had finally succeeded in regaining the title of Wishbone's Most Popular Miss.

Watching Sandra struggle with a canvas as she tried to copy the style of Monet or Degas, Peter dreaded having to compliment her muddy and unskilled handiwork. He resented her devotion to her personal needs because he felt they were meaningless and shallow; they had nothing to do with the lifetime of penitence that was he and Sandra's burden to accept.

But at the moment he was not thinking about his guilt or Sandra's penchant for saying *c'est dommage* every time she saw something out of sorts. There was only one thought that filled Peter's mind.

Andromeda was finally coming home.

Julie Fletcher, who had an endless supply of enthusiasm for community affairs, again read the letter she had received from Andromeda Wiley and came to the conclusion that she could not agree more.

Little Andromeda, all grown up, had written to Julie Fletcher from Turkey of all places to let Julie know she was returning to Wishbone, something Julie already knew and had already printed in the paper, and would Julie please see about organizing a reunion of the principals involved in Andromeda's rescue? Well, if Andromeda wasn't thinking exactly what Julie had already been thinking, then Julie didn't know what. Asking the principals, some of whom no longer lived in Wishbone but most of whom still did, to return for a reunion was an obvious extension of Julie's parade inspiration.

With fingers spinning the dials of a continually updated electronic Rolodex, Julie Fletcher began the process of making the calls.

"Howard, you have a call on line two."

Howard Clark spun from his office window with its view down Madison Avenue and spoke into his headset.

"Who is it?"

His assistant in the outer office, where the hubbub from the magazine staff was loudest, answered his query.

"An Andromeda Wiley."

Clark did a double take. He was not sure he had heard correctly.

"Andromeda Wiley? Are you sure?"

"That's what she says. You want me to tell her you're out?"

Clark was as stunned as he was intrigued.

"No way, no—put her through."

Clark fixed his tie as if he could be seen through the phone and licked his lips as a young woman's voice came on the line.

"Mr. Clark?"

"Yes?"

"It's Andromeda, Andromeda Wiley. I'm not sure if you remember me—"

"Of course I remember. Baby Andromeda. I don't believe it! What are you, like twenty years old now?"

"Yep. My teenybopper days are over."

"So how have you been? Fill me in."

"Actually I don't really have time for that right now. I'm in Giza and the phones here are kind of iffy. I'd hate to get cut off in the middle of my life story."

"You're in Egypt?"

"Yeah, I can see the pyramids right out my window. Listen, the reason I'm calling is because I'm returning to Wishbone, where they're planning on having a sort of reunion for everyone who helped me out. I know it sounds silly and it's probably the last thing I need, but I figure I owe it to the town to go along."

"I can see that."

"Good, because I'd like to ask you to join us. I mean, I'll understand if you refuse because I know you're a busy editor these days."

"Yeah, I am busy, but . . . "

Clark was suddenly thinking there might be a story here.

He was curious how the girl from the hole had turned out. If *he* was curious, a lot of his readers might be curious. Telling his readers how Baby Andromeda had become a healthy and happy woman was the perfect coda to a famous near-tragedy. Clark decided he could afford a few days back in Wishbone to see if it was true.

"I'm there."

"Really? Truly? Oh, I'm so glad. Hey, do you think there's any possibility you could get that friend of yours, Rayna Higgins, to come too?"

"I don't see why not. After all, she is my wife."

"Wow. I didn't know that. Well, congratulations. So you'll both come?"

"Just say when."

As Andromeda Wiley gave Howard Clark the relevant details of her upcoming reunion, Clark allowed himself a flashback that encompassed the fifteen years following his breakthrough story about Andromeda falling down a hole.

After his television exposure, he had received offers from so many branches of journalism that he found he was able to select the area that interested him most. Although he had carried himself well as an on-camera reporter, he found it was not a job that suited him for the long haul. He could see doing it once in a while, but as a career he decided to pass.

Clark came to the conclusion that what he really wanted was to focus on one story at a time, allowing his storytelling abilities to be pressed to their fullest. He discovered the perfect format as a staff writer for *Insight*, a magazine in the vein of *Harper's* that gave its journalists free rein to track down and explore virtually any story of personal interest. Clark had not yet found his Watergate but he had acquitted himself well during his fifteen years at *Insight*—so well that the owners eventually appointed him editor. He now oversaw the operation of a highly respected, sometimes inflammatory but always incisive monthly. It was exactly where he hoped he would be, covering real news—at the opposite end of the spectrum from his dog days at the *Wishbone Review*.

He said his good-byes to Andromeda and ordered his assistant to arrange first-class passage for himself and his wife to Kansas.

On the streets of Wishbone banners were strung up that read, WELCOME HOME BABY ANDROMEDA! Tourists passing through Wishbone were excited to learn that Baby Andromeda herself would be returning to the site of her tragedy after a fifteen-year absence. Many made plans to return to see for themselves how she had turned out, as she sat atop a float.

The slow daily pace of Wishbone's vendors kicked into high gear. Parade floats had to be taken out to get holes patched and engines tuned. Some decided the occasion provided reason enough to build brand-new floats.

Mayor Tommy Vale decided it was the perfect occasion to build a float that featured papier-mâché versions of his new Chevrolets. He further decided he would lead the float in his jet-black Hummer and have two or three Wagoneer cheerleaders do a routine on the roof rack. Thinking bigger, he decided he might also bring the Wileys' old truck out of the storage yard, where it now sat rusting away between a houseboat the Vales took to Lake Powell one year and all the junked muscle cars collected by

Tommy Vale's two sons, Randy and Pat. Tommy thought it might be peachy to have a few of his employees drive the old Wiley truck through town, passing out maps to Vale's Chevrolet. Since the parade was a civic affair, he decided the taxpayers would subsidize the needed repairs to get the old truck up and running, naturally done by his own mechanics.

Janice Piasecki saw the opportunity to advertise her new arcade room, filled with games guaranteed to delight the youngsters. She would add a burger to her menu, on which the diner could already find a quarter-pound Baby Andromeda with cheese. She would add a fried egg to the Baby Andromeda and call the new burger the Lady Andromeda. Cullman Shermer, operating the Wishbone Stage Lines, offered a ride in his six stagecoaches drawn by pairings of tired nags for the small fee of six dollars. He decided he would rig up a few buckboards and offer special-occasion hayrides for seven dollars a pop. Frank O'Connor decided he would commission some artwork relating to Baby Andromeda and offer it for immediate sale. Reese and Rita Vosker, owners of the Pony Express Hotel, a couple who had moved into Wishbone years after Andromeda Wiley's fall but who had lived in the town long enough to feel it was their right to seize a piece of the Baby Andromeda pie, decided to give their place a new paint job. As a sitting councilman, Reese, having replaced Allison Larkins, who moved elsewhere and was long forgotten, believed as Tommy Vale did that this parade was a civic event, so he sent the painting bill to the city accountant.

Wishbone was ready to go, old-timers and newcomers alike—almost everybody was excited about getting into the act.

Almost everybody.

Will drove through Wishbone with Lisa at his side the same as he had done for years and shook his head as decorations went up and posters were tacked to telephone poles.

"This is such bullshit."

"Why are you so against this?"

"I never said I was against it."

"If you're not against this, then maybe it's her you're against. Seriously, I can't remember you saying more than a sentence about Andromeda since we started going out." Lisa looked out as a bright red Cadillac zipped past and parked before the Wishbone Savings and Loan. A bald man with a potbelly, a store-bought tan and prescription sunglasses emerged with shiny shoes and entered the Savings and Loan. Lisa looked away from

Denny Sharf and set her eyes on Will. "What did she do to make you hate her so much?"

"I don't hate Andromeda."

"But you don't like her."

"I don't even know her."

"And that doesn't bother you?"

"Andie wouldn't come back to Wishbone after the accident—that wasn't my fault. She lives all the way in Vermont. And now she's been in Europe, going all over the place. It's not like she's been right next door or anything."

"Your mom says you never wrote her even once."

Will stopped at the red light and sighed. He had not written Andromeda even once because he had nothing to say and there was nothing he cared to know.

"It's just something that happened. She's there, I'm here. Look, I really don't want to keep talking about this."

"What are we talking about? You're not saying anything." Lisa turned to look back out her window. "Whatever." They passed under another WELCOME HOME BABY ANDROMEDA sign. "So when does she get in?"

"Saturday. Mom and Dad're picking her up."

"You're not going?"

Will did not respond and Lisa took his answer to be a negative. She shook her head, clearly signaling her disappointment.

"Nothing like the love of a brother . . ."

THIRTY-FOUR

WELCOME WAGON

The plane set down almost at the promised second. As it navigated the tarmac to the terminal, Peter and Sandra, accompanied by Lisa, stood at the gate window trying to quell their nervous shakes. Will was nowhere to be seen.

The plane stopped, the ramp butted against the plane, and passengers began disembarking. The first passengers stepped into the terminal and as Lisa, Peter and Sandra scanned the exiting faces, Sandra squeezed Peter's hand so hard he had to pull it free with his other.

"Sandy, relax."

"I can't. I feel like I've had a pot of espresso."

"You did. Pull it together anyway."

"What do we say about Will not being here?"

Lisa chimed in. "Let me handle that." She looked out as a young woman with a stylish haircut, holding a leather bag by its strap over her shoulder, strode out with bright and expectant eyes. "Is that her?"

Peter fixed his gaze on the young woman.

"That's her. . . ."

He had not seen his daughter in nearly two years. Then, Andromeda had been a girlish eighteen-year-old. But this person who cracked a happy smile as her eyes landed on Peter, Sandra and Lisa was no longer a girl. She was a woman. The appreciative glances she received from all the surrounding men supported Peter in his belief that she was also a very beautiful woman.

Andromeda dropped her bag and rushed to Peter. She draped her arms around him and hugged him deeply.

"Daddy . . ."

Peter hugged his daughter back.

"Andie."

Sandra fidgeted.

"Do you have one for me?"

Andromeda moved to hug Sandra. Mother and daughter held each other tightly. As Andromeda pulled out of the hug, a tear ran down her cheek and over her moist lips, still shaping themselves into a smile.

"I've missed you so much."

"We missed you too, sweetie. We're so happy you're finally home. It's just been too long."

"Well, I'm here now and I don't think I'll be going anywhere for a while."

Awkward in the moment, Peter moved for Andromeda's bag. He lifted it over his shoulder.

"Let's get your bags."

"I had everything shipped. All my stuff should get here today or tomorrow. Right now that's all I brought."

"Oh, okay. Then let's hit the road."

Sandra pulled Lisa into Andromeda's view as the group began walking from the gate.

"Honey, I want you to meet Lisa, Will's girlfriend."

Lisa shook Andromeda's hand.

"Hi."

"Will's girlfriend? We can do better than a shake." Andromeda gave Lisa a friendly hug. As she pulled out of it she scanned the area. "Hey, where is that brother of mine?"

"Uh, he had to do some stuff downtown. You'll see him tonight."

Andromeda nodded, her smile lessening a bit as she tried to hide her evident hurt. Lisa stifled a rush of anger toward Will. Here he was, a grown man unwilling to meet a sister he had not seen in five years. It was the only immature reaction she had ever seen in Will, but it aggravated her nonetheless.

By any measure Andromeda was a perfectly normal woman, although Lisa was able to see as easily as any how ravishing Andromeda had turned out. A tinge of envy made a quick pass through Lisa as she considered the stylish beauty of her probable fiancé's sister. There was not a curve out of place. Andromeda had the figure women binged and purged for. She had the fluid grace of a top model. The way she moved also showed she was fit and toned. Her skin was flawless and any asymmetries to her stunning face only added to her allure. This was a woman destined to turn heads.

Yet the first impression Andromeda gave of herself was that her beauty was not utilized to curry favor. She was outgoing and friendly in a natural way.

Andromeda chatted brightly as they walked through the airport, telling story after story about her travels through Europe, Asia and Africa. As the group neared their parked car, Lisa came to believe that Will was severely petty to distance himself from his exceptional sister. Andromeda was nothing less than thoroughly charming.

The group stopped in the parking lot at a sparkling Chevrolet Suburban, also courtesy of Tommy Vale but this time bought at theoretical cost. Peter opened the back and tossed in Andromeda's bag. Sandra offered the front passenger seat to Andromeda.

"Honey, you're the guest of honor. Sit up front."

"Okay, but will you guys do me a favor?"

"Name it."

"Can you stop walking on eggshells around me? I'm fine, really. I'm just your same old Andie."

The casual affection Andromeda directed toward her awkwardly nervous mother and father was disarming, and Peter began to believe what he saw.

All the years Peter had pummeled his conscience over what he had done to his daughter were beginning to seem pointless in the simple witness of Andromeda's smile. It was hard to deny what anybody could see and what Andromeda herself was saying.

Andromeda was fine.

He felt a crack forming in the guard he had constructed between himself and gladness. A feeling of calm satisfaction held at bay for fifteen years poked through the thin fissure and washed his heart. He restrained it before it got out of control. Still, he broke his first genuine smile in years.

"It's a deal."

Sandra had to keep from crying as she heard it.

Laughter in her home. Real laughter.

She sat with Andromeda, Peter and Lisa sipping wine before the glowing fireplace as Andromeda told more stories about her adventures abroad.

" . . . I was so tired from three days of trying to get out of Kazakhstan that I could barely keep my eyes open. I stumbled into the communal bathroom and sat down to pee. Suddenly the lights go on and I see this whole group of orthodox priests yelling in Russian and waving their arms at me and then I notice I'm not in the bathroom, I'm in their room and I'm peeing in this big chalice of holy water. Needless to say, I offered to wash it."

As Peter's laughter subsided, his eyes met the gleaming eyes of his brilliant daughter.

"How did you get to be so funny?"

"I kept looking in the mirror. The only two choices were laugh or cry."

Sandra put her arm around Andromeda's shoulder as Andromeda let her face fall into a fake pout.

"Oh honey, you're gorgeous!"

"My nose is crooked and I can't lift one eyebrow at a time. I can't go on living like this. Is there any cyanide in the house?"

Sandra pretended to stand.

"Hold on, I'll go get it."

"Mother!"

Lisa smiled at the warm and tender moment.

"I'd like to make a toast." She raised her glass. "To Andromeda. Welcome home."

They drank and Andromeda grew shy with embarrassment.

"Okay, that was sweet, but that's the end of the fuss over me. What I want to hear about now is—"

The sound of a truck came through the closed windows. Lisa stood and looked out.

"Will."

The sound of the engine died, and then the sound of the truck door opening and closing was followed by the sound of booted feet making their way to the side door. Andromeda bolted up, suddenly agitated.

"Do I look all right?"

Sandra stood and rubbed her nervous daughter's arms.

"You look fine."

"How's my hair?"

"It's perfect, just like the rest of you."

"Ohh, I don't know what to say."

"You'll think of something."

"What am I worrying about? He probably won't talk to me anyway."

Peter worked to control his own anxiety.

"He'll talk. Just be yourself."

Lisa touched Andromeda's shoulder in assurance and headed for the kitchen as they heard the side door open.

"Let me lead him in. I'll be your buffer."

"Okay. Thanks."

As Lisa walked off, Andromeda turned to her parents with a face skewed.

"Catch me if I faint."

She turned back as she heard Lisa reenter with the person wearing the boots. Andromeda turned and looked for the first time in five years into the face of her brother Will. She gave what she felt was her most harmless smile.

"Hello."

Will tried to hold his ground as he looked across the living room to the stunning woman who faced him with a soft-spoken hello. He immediately noticed that Andromeda aimed her gaze not directly into his eyes but toward his chin, proving that their unspoken contract was still in effect. Will cautiously looked to his sister's eyes to see the thing he most feared.

But it was not there.

He did not see the alien flash in her eyes. In her beautifully featured face he saw no carnivorous gleam. Its absence allowed him to continue looking her way. Still, she was so utterly tangible he could not help but gulp.

"Hi."

Lisa pushed Will toward Andromeda.

"Go on, lunkhead, give her a hug."

Sending Lisa a quick grimace of annoyance, Will turned his nervous face to Andromeda as he stepped to her and gave her an awkward hug, keeping his body separate from hers.

"Welcome home."

"Thanks."

Will quickly pulled out of the hug and tried to find something else to give his attention. But his parents had thought beyond him.

"We'll leave you two to chat. Lisa, join us in the TV room?"

Andromeda seemed ready to explode in nervousness. Will tried to protest.

"I thought we were going out to eat or something."

Peter waved Will back into the living room.

"Plenty of time for that. You two have a lot to catch up on."

Peter, Sandra and Lisa left Will and Andromeda standing alone. Andromeda had no trouble sensing her brother's agitation. It was exactly like her own.

"So . . . " Andromeda innocently cocked her head. "So . . . maybe you could show me something."

"Like what?"

"Anything. Everything is new to me here. Show me the farm."

"What part?"

"I don't know . . . What's in the barn?"

"Gear, trucks, my apartment. Mom's studio . . . "

Andromeda scanned the well-lit paintings decorating the home.

"Did Mom paint all of these?"

"If you could call it that."

"They're a little . . . "

"Bad?"

"I was going to say . . . hopeful."

Will felt his face crease into a smile in spite of himself.

"Never thought of using that to describe them." He paused a moment. He decided his sister deserved at least some token effort. "Let me show you the greenhouses."

From the kitchen Peter, Sandra and Lisa watched as Will led Andromeda outside and into the greenhouses. Lisa made the first comment.

"At least they're talking. He hasn't run for the hills yet." She turned to Will's parents. "If you don't mind me asking, why has he been so cool to her for so long? Don't answer if I'm stepping out of bounds."

Sandra crafted what little she could in answer.

"Right after Will pulled Andie from that hole, he just turned himself off to her. We asked Diana about it—"

"The one who wrote the book on Andie."

"Diana French, yes. She couldn't figure it out either. Will just kept talking all this bogeyman nonsense about something that was down in the hole."

"Really? How weird. He never told me any of that."

"At first I thought he might have been a little jealous of all the attention Andie got, but that wasn't Will. Somehow he developed this delusion about how Andie changed."

"Five days in a hole—who wouldn't change?"

"That's what we kept trying to tell him. Anyhow, let's hope that whole silliness is over."

Lisa watched as Will gave his sister the tour of his life's work.

"Judging by what I'm seeing, I'd say maybe it is."

Inside the greenhouse, Will led Andromeda through neat rows of organic herbs. Andromeda stopped and felt the healthy leaves of a basil plant. She smelled the sweet fragrance as she lifted her fingers to her nose. Will gestured to the herb garden.

"Name an herb and we grow it."

"This is all so different from what we had before."

Andromeda leaned against a support post, shuffling her feet as she ran out of conversation. Will leaned into an opposing post and risked a more thorough examination of his sister.

She seemed so accessible, almost vulnerable even. Yet his mind could not shake the image of her trapped beneath those roots and the chilling look she gave him as he set her free. That was an event he positively knew happened. At least . . . he thought he was positive. Staring at his sister he suddenly wondered if he was all that positive after all.

He recalled an occasion when he was nine, maybe a little older, when a bank in Sterling was robbed. In his mind he was certain he heard a reporter say on the radio that the suspects were a circus strongman and two Mexican bandidos wearing sombreros. When he rushed to tell his father to keep a lookout for such an unlikely trio, he was told he was imagining things he was certain he was not.

As an adult, he knew he had to have been mistaken about the descriptions of the bank robbery suspects. Circus strongmen and Mexicans in sombreros do not rob banks. If he was mistaken about the robbers, might he not be mistaken about other things? He began to wonder if he had imagined cutting Andromeda free from a layer of man-eating roots. He wondered if he had been mistaken about the alien gleam in her eyes.

He decided to risk meeting the eyes of Andromeda. It was the only way he could know for sure.

Andromeda sensed Will's eyes locking on her own and she lifted her face to look back for the first time in years. As their eyes met, Andromeda gave Will the sweetest and most affectionate smile he could have hoped for.

He was suddenly flooded with guilt.

There was no alien gleam in her eyes and there probably never had been. Even though the memory of the roots seemed real, he had to have been mistaken. Probably there had been roots of some kind, but what was so strange about that? It was underground, that was where roots grew, and Andromeda had just been tangled, not purposely caught, the way Will's mind remembered. The revelation meant he had kept Andromeda away for no reason at all. When she needed him most he had abandoned her.

But Andromeda, in her quiet and patient way, seemed to be telling Will that she had no hard feelings and could he please be nice to her again, if that was what he wanted.

Will, in that moment, felt it was not just what he wanted, it was what Andromeda deserved.

"I should have gone to see you."

"You didn't have to. You were busy."

"I should have gone." Will began to pace. "Once it got started it got too easy not to go."

"I did wonder . . . "

"What?"

"Why didn't you?" She nervously put her hands behind her back and stared down at her feet. "I mean, you never even wrote or anything."

"I didn't know what to say."

"How about now?"

"I still don't."

Andromeda nodded, seeming to understand Will's struggle.

"Will? What . . . what did I do to you down there? I think the only way you would have acted like you have was if I did something bad to you. I don't remember hardly anything from that time, but whatever it was I didn't mean it. You're the last person I'd ever want to hurt." Tears began to run from Andromeda's eyes. "I loved you so much. I still do. Whatever it was I'm so sorry. I wish I knew what it was. I really wish . . . I'm just so sorry. . . ."

Will tried to stand his ground, but he soon felt tears forming in his own eyes.

Unable to stay distant any longer, he went to Andromeda. He took her in his arms and held her tight as she let loose her pain, sobbing into his strong chest.

"Andie, I'm the one who's sorry. All those years . . . It's all my fault; you never did anything to me."

"Promise?"

"I promise. It was all me."

"So we won't . . . we won't do that not-talking thing anymore? We can talk from now on?"

"If you'll let me."

"I will."

THIRTY-FIVE

MIRROR, MIRROR

Will sat in back with Andromeda and Lisa as Peter and Sandra sat up front to drive the family Suburban into Wishbone. It was smiles all around as Andromeda gawked out the window.

"Hey, what happened to the haberdashery?"

"They turned it into a Starbucks."

"Geez-us, everything is so different . . . "

"You've been gone for fifteen years, honey, of course it's going to change."

"I thought it might change a little but . . . They have stagecoach rides around town? Who started that?"

Peter growled.

"Cullman Shermer, that sonofa—"

"We get the idea, Peter."

"Why, what's he do?"

Peter finished his growl.

"Forget that he and the council wiped out the game reserve and keep handing out permits to whatever business wants to plop here, no matter what it might do to the town; now Shermer's lobbying to bring in a prison, wants to build it on his old cattle ranch. He just wants to exchange one type of cattle for another."

Andromeda stared out as a stagecoach full of tourists looking for excitement passed by, dragged by two near-dead nags. Andromeda's eyes drifted to the banners above the street welcoming her back to Wishbone.

"I wish they would quit calling me that."

"Calling you what?"

"Baby Andromeda. I'm not a baby. *Waaaaa.*"

Everyone laughed as Peter turned the Suburban into a vacant space before Piasecki's Polecat Pub and Eatery. Peter turned back to Andromeda.

"Honey, you sure you want to eat here? We could go somewhere a lot more private."

"Dad, it's fine. They'll see me sooner or later. Might as well get it over with."

"All right, it's your call. But I'm warning you, Piasecki's food is more than borderline lousy."

As the family exited the car, the few locals walking the sidewalks or sitting on benches looked over and recognized the Wileys.

"Howdy, Peter, Sandra."

"Evenin', Bill."

But one person the locals did not know was the stunning young woman with them. Watching the Wileys enter Piasecki's Pub, two older locals working to conform their nightly bench seat to their aging duffs commented on the young beauty.

"You see that?"

"That can't be who you're thinkin' it is. She's some actress or something. I guess those Wileys hang with that sort these days."

"All I know is even if I was half my age, she's the kind of high-class tottie who still wouldn't gimme the time of day."

Janice Piasecki, working a printer calculator behind her desk in her office at her Polecat Pub, looked out her huge see-through mirror and saw Peter Wiley and his family entering. It was occasion enough to warrant a personal appearance by Piasecki herself to guarantee they received the best service. But seeing the Wileys had a guest, a startlingly attractive young woman of about twenty who bore a resemblance to both Peter and Sandra Wiley, Janice Piasecki decided the service tonight would be extra special.

As a teen hostess led Peter and his family to a table resting on a floor covered in hay and discarded peanut shells beneath a ceiling loaded with Western props and buffalo heads, Janice Piasecki closed in, more effervescent than ever.

"You must be Andromeda."

Piasecki shoved out her hand, catching Andromeda off guard.

Andromeda took the hand as the other patrons, having heard as a result of Piasecki's purposeful volume, stopped their eating or game playing to whisper and stare.

"That's the girl that fell in the hole!"

"That's Baby Andromeda? I thought she was a little kid."

"You sure that's her?"

"Man, she's fine. . . ."

Andromeda shook Piasecki's hand and pulled hers free.

"Just call me Andie."

"Andie, then. I just want you all to know this dinner is on me. Christy? Bring some peanuts and a pitch . . . no, wait . . . *two* pitchers of Coke! Carl, come here and get a picture of this!" Carl, a high-school-age roving photographer dressed like Buffalo Bill, stepped over and snapped a photo of Janice Piasecki leaning close to the Wileys and smiling like she was their best friend on earth. She turned back to the Wileys and flashed her polyethylene smile. "Enjoy."

Piasecki walked off and Andromeda glanced around the room. Nearly every face stared back, some blatantly. Andromeda tried to raise one of her eyebrows.

"I just hope they don't ask for my autograph."

As the family ordered and the meal arrived, Andromeda stood. Will asked, "Where are you going?"

"I want to say thanks to Mrs. Piasecki for the dinner. I'll be right back."

Andromeda walked through a gauntlet of eagerly staring patrons. As she passed the bar section, two men in dusted and frayed denim wearing baseball caps rimmed with car grease looked her way. Pat Vale elbowed his brother, Randy.

"Check it out."

Finishing off a pitcher of the cheapest draft, Randy Vale leaned out toward Andromeda and parted his lips to reveal tobacco-stained teeth.

"We got an empty chair right here, Lolita. Sit. Let me buy you a beer."

Andromeda tried to stay polite.

"Maybe some other time."

As Andromeda passed the two brothers, Randy quickly grew surly.

"Snobby bitch . . ."

Andromeda continued to run the gauntlet until she knocked on the door to Janice Piasecki's office at the back of the long hall. Having watched Andromeda's approach through her see-through mirror, Piasecki readied herself and spoke a bubbly greeting.

"Come in!"

Andromeda opened the door and entered Piasecki's office. She saw Piasecki's mirror arrangement.

"Boy, you sure can't tell that thing is see-through from the other side. I thought it was just a big mirror."

"And that's the idea. Is there something wrong with the meal?"

"No, not at all. It's great. Fact is, I wanted to say thanks, just me to you, and not just for the dinner. I kind of left Wishbone before I got the chance to properly thank everyone who supported me when I fell down that hole. I know you were one of those people, and, well . . . Can you forgive me for being fifteen years late?"

"Oh, you are a treasure. It was my pleasure, Andie."

Piasecki sipped from a steaming cup of coffee as Andromeda leaned against her desk. She looked at a picture of Janice Piasecki wearing a hard hat and manning a gold shovel along with Frank O'Connor, Kelly Mahon, Cullman Shermer and Reese Vosker as they broke ground on some new construction.

"You're still on the city council, right?"

"Yep."

"So Wishbone has you to credit for everything that's happened since I left?"

Piasecki took another sip and set down her cup of coffee.

"I wasn't alone in Wishbone's transformation. Everybody had a part in it. All of the merchants."

"Well, it's amazing. This place is happening. Who would have believed it?"

"We've done well."

Andromeda smiled.

"You sure have. Well, I should be getting back. Thanks again for the dinner."

"It was my pleasure."

Andromeda turned for the door and took one last look out the see-through mirror.

"That really is some mirror."

"It's my eye on the world."

"And what a world it is."

Andromeda exited Janice Piasecki's office, and as Piasecki sat, she watched her return to her table through the see-through mirror.

Piasecki lifted her coffee and drank deeply as she considered how she would frame and place Carl's snapshot of her and the Wileys. She decided she would use a frame that had a rope border with burned-in ranching brands. It would sit on the wall next to the bar, just above the Love Tester machine.

She set down her coffee and glanced back out her see-through mirror.

Andromeda Wiley sat at her table. But she did not pay any attention to the lively conversation occupying the other Wileys.

Andromeda Wiley paid strict attention to something else.

As Piasecki moved from one side of her desk to the other, she did not see how it was possible, but it seemed to be happening. No matter how she moved in her office, the eyes of Andromeda Wiley followed her.

"That's odd."

She purposely rolled her chair from one side of her desk to the other and then back again. The bright eyes of Andromeda Wiley hung on her without error.

A dryness seized Piasecki's throat as she grew convinced that Andromeda Wiley was somehow able to see through her mirror, something no one else had ever been able to do. And her stare was so direct, almost a scowl. Piasecki began to wonder if the mirroring had somehow fallen off and that it was now just a clear piece of glass. But then a family stepped to the mirror to check themselves out, a sometimes comical display she had witnessed hundreds of times before. For this family at least, the mirror on their side was still a mirror. They could not see through to Piasecki inside.

For a moment relieved, Piasecki's relief vanished as she looked back toward Andromeda Wiley and saw the girl was still brazenly looking right at her. As a subtle smile rose on Andromeda Wiley's face, she raised a finger to point right through the mirror to a spot directly between Janice Piasecki's eyes, in the center of her forehead. Piasecki felt a spot of heat rise up exactly where Andromeda pointed. She bumped the cup of steaming coffee off her desk. It spilled in her lap. She leapt to her feet.

"Shit! Owww! Shit!"

Quickly grabbing a towel to wipe herself, she tossed a gaze back out through her supposed see-through-one-way-only mirror and saw that the Wileys were leaving. In that moment Janice Piasecki thought she would just as easily prefer they never came back.

THIRTY-SIX

FIRST NIGHT

By the time the Wileys left Piasecki's Polecat Pub, word had spread around town that the grown-up version of Baby Andromeda had arrived. People made their way to Piasecki's to see if they could spot her, and a crowd had formed as Peter led his family out to the waiting Suburban. Locals of all ages who had wondered for fifteen years how Andromeda Wiley turned out now got the chance to see for themselves. The experience left them speechless.

Andromeda Wiley was an amazing sight.

At a glance, pretty much everyone who saw her agreed she was Wishbone's number-one babe. Freshly unseated beauties looked upon Andromeda with a mixture of scorn and envy, even though two days later they would begin copying her hairstyle.

Andromeda smiled in a friendly way as she passed her neighbors and climbed into the family Suburban. As Peter backed the car out, one of the locals, a young man somewhere in Andromeda's age range, was bold enough to step forward and make a comment, evidently prodded by his nervous friends, also college-age males, waiting in the background.

"Uh, hey . . . You, uh . . . you here for a while?"

"I'm here to stay."

"Oh, uh . . . cool."

When Andromeda sent him a platonic smile, the young man knew he had blown his chance at impressing her, a distressing fact because he believed he might be falling in love at first sight. As she drove off he tried to correct his error.

"So maybe I'll see you later!" Knowing he had blown it. "Oh man, she's awesome."

Will gestured back to the hapless stud left with his foot in his mouth.

"In Wishbone, he's the cream of the crop."

"Oh, joy." Andromeda put her arm over Will's shoulder. "Anyway, I'm not even thinking along those lines. There are only two men in my life right now and they're both in this car."

They laughed and chatted warmly as they drove home.

There, before the fire, another hour slipped by as they sipped wine and talked about how things used to be. Andromeda, feeling fatigued, excused herself. She climbed up to her bedroom, readied for her return for fifteen years, and closed herself in.

Freshly showered, Andromeda sat naked on the edge of her bed in the room that had waited so long for her presence. Her window was open and the air drifting in was thin and cold. Goose bumps rose on her skin as she accepted a chilling caress of her naked body. The only light was produced by a faded and yellowed Mickey Mouse nightlight plugged low in the wall.

Andromeda stared at bright Mickey.

With her eyes fixed on the warm glow she grew meditative. A whole history, which she could never separate from who she was, came up as it had every night for years. She could see the hole, she could feel the tightness of the space, she could smell the musty odor. She knew the dark.

The sensation ran through her body like an injected liquid.

It formed in her toes like bubbles that joined together into larger bubbles to move through her ankles and up her legs to come together in her abdomen as one large bubble. The large bubble caressed her gut and her heart and her lungs before moving to her neck, where it tried to force its way higher. In a dam burst it squeezed through her neck and filled Andromeda's skull in a potent rush. Andromeda gasped and quickly stood to her feet as she quaked, blind to the world. Lost to consciousness as the pseudo-seizure short-circuited awareness, the rush passed just as suddenly and Andromeda fell back onto her bed. She stretched catlike as her body felt heated from within, as if she had just completed a mile run.

Andromeda stood and reached down to the Mickey Mouse light to unplug it from the wall. Stowing it away in a drawer, she pulled the curtains shut and the room fell into total darkness. Andromeda crawled beneath the clean and soft sheets and stared into space.

In the dark she considered why she had returned.

In the dark she finally felt safe.

Peter climbed into bed, leaned close to Sandra and pressed his lips to hers. He kissed her deeply as his hand ran up her smooth hip and along her trim ribs. Sandra put her arms around the neck of her husband of twenty-three years and stared into his eyes.

"Don't look at me. I'll cry."

"Why?"

"Because it's been so long and we've . . . we've been together but we've been . . . and tonight you were so sweet. It's how I've missed it being between us."

Peter stroked Sandra's hands as they stayed locked behind his neck.

"We never talked about it. You know I've had a hard time getting past that."

"Can't we just go on from here, like it is right now?"

For years Peter had begged Sandra to talk out what they had done to Andromeda. But it now seemed destructive to continue waiting for Sandra to come to terms with something she would never face. He knew he would always harbor some faint resentment, but he also knew he was being given the best chance he had been offered in such a long time to have the marriage he wanted.

He would have to forgive and forget.

He decided it was the only way.

"We'll never talk about it again."

Sandra pulled Peter close and kissed him with real passion and thankfulness. She ran her hands down his back to pull him on top of her.

"I love you, Peter."

Peter, feeling the return of passion, meant what he said in response.

"I love you too."

THIRTY-SEVEN

BROTHER MEET SISTER

The morning after Andromeda's arrival, Will took his sister out for breakfast at the Straight Line Cafe and tried after a fifteen-year delay to find out who she was.

"So what did Diana French do to you?"

"She just stared sympathetically a lot and said 'I see' all the time. Oh, and she'd always put one hand on her chin and do that half-pointing politician's gesture with her other hand, like this, where the index finger wraps around the end of the thumb. She was trying to emphasize without threatening."

"Did you like staying at The Campus?"

"It's a beautiful place; well, you saw it."

"I don't remember it much."

"We had horses, lots of riding trails, the trees were amazing in the fall, and the snow in winter. In the summer we could swim, canoe on the lake. It's not like it was some loony farm. It's a real school, if you have the money. I was the only genuine wacko there. Diana was one of the staff professors. She decided to make me her private guinea pig."

"So the other students came from families with money."

"The driveway was all Bentleys and Benz's."

"Well, I wish I'd visited you more often. I feel like such a jerk."

Andromeda put one hand on her chin and jutted out her other hand with the index finger wrapped around the thumb.

"I see."

Will backhanded his sister's shoulder.

"Very funny."

"I thought so."

The conversation fell silent and Will stared into his sister's eyes. He felt a growing bond between himself and Andromeda even as he felt grief and regret for all the years he had stupidly pushed her away. He remembered how he once imagined himself as her hero. Seeing her now it was clear she no longer needed him. Andromeda was getting along fine without Will.

Will was a different matter. He could no longer deny that he missed Andromeda, and his regret for all their lost years together was now total.

He never wanted her to leave again.

"Andie, you don't hate me, do you?"

"Why do you even say something as silly as that? I admit in the beginning I didn't get why you didn't want to see me and in a lot of ways I still don't—and I really was hurt—but I'm sure you had your reasons. I mean, you had a reason, right?" Andromeda tried to hide a tinge of anguish. Will saw it anyway and he gulped as he was again washed by guilt. Andromeda reached out her hand and gently laid it over Will's. "Anyway, that's the past. I'm here now and we're together and I couldn't be happier."

"I thought I had a reason. . . ." Will saw that Andromeda wanted him to continue. "When I was pulling you out I thought I saw something in your eyes."

"In my eyes? Like what?"

"After the rescue your eyes changed, like they weren't even yours anymore. I stayed away because of how you made me feel when you looked at me."

"And how did I make you feel?"

"Like I didn't matter. Like I might as well be dead."

Andromeda fell silent as she absorbed Will's comment. She stared at her plate of food for a moment before lifting her face back to Will.

"And now?"

Will stared into his sister's eyes.

"All I see is you."

Andromeda smiled softly.

"Good, because that's all there is, folks."

As Will and Andromeda continued chatting, Will couldn't help noticing how often the men and women in the Straight Line turned to check out his sister. He couldn't blame them.

Andromeda had made herself into something more than she would have been if she had stayed in Wishbone. How much of it was due to Diana French's supervision, he could not say. But the reality was that Andromeda was truly unique in a place where so much was exactly the same.

Andromeda smiled at her brother.

"So how's Timms? I was thinking of dropping in on him."

"Timms . . . you don't want to know."

"Don't tell me—he's not dead?"

"No, he's alive, but I don't know if you really want to see him, Andie."

"Why not? I have to see Timms. He worked so hard to get me out of there and then that accident. . . . Mom told me he has a permanent limp."

"Timms still gets around, when he wants to, which isn't very often. If you want to see him, he's home. He's always home." Will drank his milk to wash down the pancakes. "After your rescue it was like everybody in town got something out of it. I mean, we sure did. We got the house and the farm and, you know . . . Howard Clark went off to New York, Sharf started that bullshit tourist trap, your pal Diana wrote that book. I mean, everybody got something, even that asswipe Cullman Shermer. Timms was just about the only one who didn't get what he wanted."

"What did he want?"

"Honestly? I think he just wanted to be acknowledged, especially by his wife. Guy worked his whole life helping people out; guess he wanted the woman he loved to give him a pat on the back and say, 'Nice work, proud of you.' She divorced him about three months after we got you out. Who knows what the real story was at home. Anyhow, that's when Timms decided to write a book about pulling you out of that hole. He called it *Anatomy of a Rescue*. It takes him three or four years to write it and then he quits the department, puts all his money into trying to get an agent, can't get an agent, and then he tries to sell it himself, buying ads and going to bookstores. I think he sold like two copies. Since he couldn't get a publisher, he had to have Julie Fletcher print it up for him."

"Did you read it?"

"Yeah. He spent most of the book grumbling about how when he worked navy crash and rescue, he couldn't get parts for this or gear for that. It was really whiny. Then he had this whole bit about family and how important family was to a guy in his line of work. He barely even mentioned your rescue. It was just sort of embarrassing."

"Poor man."

"Because of his leg he could retire on disability. Nowadays all Timms does is sit in his house. Remember how nice him and his wife used to have their yard? Man, you should see it now. The place looks like it's abandoned."

"Where'd his wife go?"

"Took the kids and split to Little Rock."

"Does Timms . . . ?" She made a gesture of drinking from a glass.

"I don't think he has the energy for it."

Andromeda and Will finished their meal, reflecting on the sad fate of a man who for one brief period fully directed their lives. Will started to toss down a few bills but Andromeda stopped him.

"This is my treat."

"Only if I buy lunch."

"That's fine because for lunch I always have caviar and truffles."

Andromeda paid the bill and stepped out of the diner with her brother bringing up the rear.

As they walked through the gravel lot toward Will's truck, Will noticed out the corner of his eye that Tommy Vale's two well-oiled thirty-something sons, Randy and Pat, stood at a restored '66 Pontiac GTO. They were talking with two other like-minded greaser buddies who sat in the confines of a canary-yellow '71 Dodge Charger. They all noticed Andromeda at the same time and their conversation died as their eyes grew hungry.

Randy Vale swung his acne-scarred face toward Andromeda as she and Will passed.

"Long time no see, babe."

Will moved to the passenger door of his truck to open it for his sister.

"Save it, Vale."

As Will opened the door, Randy and Pat moved closer. Randy put his hand on the opening passenger door and stopped its progress. The two greasers in the Dodge Charger stepped out with mischievous smiles, anticipating the impending bully routine.

"No time better than the present. Besides, I got something to say to little Miss Celebrity." He turned to Andromeda and leaned close. "You're pretty fine and I'm sure you know it. You're so fine I'm offering to lick you from here to Sunday."

Will quietly moved to position himself to throw the most effective punch.

"I'm telling you to back off, Vale."

"Not me. I like it up close and personal."

The Dodge greasers, filling their role as distracters, began rustling through tools sitting in the open bed of Will's truck. Will barked back, "Keep your hands out of my shit!"

One of the Dodge greasers held up a long pry bar.

"Your shit? This is mine. I been missin' it for weeks."

Randy shoved the passenger door shut.

"Now you're stealing my buddy's tools? What else you got in there?" He leered at Andromeda and looked directly at her chest. "What's the parade queen got in here?"

As the four men surrounded Will and Andromeda, Will's eyes narrowed in defiance.

"Vale, you'll back off, we'll get in our truck, and nobody gets hurt."

Pat shoved Will's shoulder.

"Yo, chumpy, you do not talk to my bro like that, right?"

Randy kept up his role as leader.

"Tell you what. If the princess lets me suck her titties, we'll let you slide."

The Dodge greasers started lifting gear from Will's truckbed.

"But I'm still taking back my pry bar—oh, and this is my skill saw too. Oh, and this posthole digger."

Will decided he would punch Randy in the throat and kick Pat in the nuts before grabbing the ax handle from behind his front seat to take on the Dodge greasers. Will gave Randy his best 'you will be hurt' glare as a final warning.

"You'll never see the end of this, Vale."

"Is that so? Show me."

Hands drew into fists. In a second the men would begin fighting.

Andromeda finally spoke. She turned directly to Randy and looked him square in the eyes.

"You really love your brother, don't you?"

The lurid expression on Randy's face gently slipped away as he seemed to think about it, and was replaced by the soft face of love.

"Patty? Sure. Sure, I do."

Randy turned to his brother and smiled sweetly. Pat frowned in confusion.

"What? What're you lookin' at me like that for?"

"I love you, bro."

"Don't go sayin' that shit to me."

"I don't want to say it. I want to show it."

Randy reached out and grabbed Pat's face tightly. Before Pat could react, Randy laid his lips to those of his brother and shoved his tongue down Pat's throat.

Pat struggled to break free from his stronger brother.

"Mmphh . . . what . . . what the fuck!"

Pat broke free, spitting out his brother's kiss. He jumped back to the Dodge greasers to stand confounded as Randy moved for him with mouth open.

"C'mon, Pat. One more kiss."

"Hey, fuck you! What are you doin', man!"

As Randy advanced on Pat, the Dodge greasers tossed back Will's gear and quickly hustled into their hot rod, disgusted by the change of events.

"This scene is whacked."

Will turned to Andromeda and opened the passenger door.

"We better go."

Andromeda climbed in and Will quickly moved into the driver's seat. Starting the engine, he put the truck in gear and began heading out of the lot. Andromeda raised her hand.

"Hold on a second. I want to see this."

As Will slowed the truck to a stop, he and Andromeda looked out in shock as Randy suddenly yanked his pants to his ankles. Randy grabbed his dangling organ and began flailing it toward his brother.

"Come on, Patty, love me."

Pat began crying as he backed closer to the street.

"Randy, what's goin' on! Why are you doin' this!"

"Because I love you, man."

"No way! This ain't right! It's sick!"

"It's what I want, bro."

"Fuck off!"

Pat spun and ran into the street, his eyes blinded by confused tears.

The Dodge greasers leaned out their windows.

"Fuck both you assholes!"

They revved their engine and peeled out of the lot, kicking gravel. As they fishtailed onto the street, they swerved into the opposing lane.

Will was the first to see it coming.

"Oh, shit . . . "

Andromeda saw it next.

"He'll be hit . . . "

A fully loaded Freightliner, driven by a trucker yawning his way through his fifteenth hour on the road, sped for the Dodge Charger. As the trucker saw the car in his path and opened his eyes wider than they had been for days, his foot slammed down on the air brakes. The truck's tires locked up and clouds of blue-gray smoke from burning rubber billowed out the back. The truck swerved and began to jackknife.

It jackknifed right for Pat.

Standing in the street, Pat turned toward the sound of screeching tires.

"Oh fu—"

His comment was cut off as the truck's front fender clipped him, flinging him aside without effort. The rear tires of the jackknifing trailer hopped over the asphalt and climbed the hood of the meticulously restored Dodge Charger. The greaser occupants screamed as the hood was flattened and the windshield shattered. They shrieked in terror as their prize possession crumpled and heaved, shoved back and pressed into the street. The truck, spanning the roadway and straddling the Dodge, finally came to a stop.

Tire smoke lay over a scene now crowded by stunned patrons from the Straight Line.

As the dismayed trucker stepped down from his rig, and as the Dodge greasers climbed out the windows of their destroyed car, Pat lay in the gravel at the lot's edge and writhed in pain. It was obvious from the abnormal bend in his leg that it was severely broken.

"My fuckin' leg . . . "

"Somebody call for an ambulance!"

Randy looked out and saw his injured brother. He then looked down and saw his pants at his ankles.

"What's happening?"

Will sat with Andromeda and stared mutely at the wreckage, both human and machine.

"Jesus Christ . . . "

As Will opened his door to rush out, Andromeda grabbed his arm.

"Will, you don't need to go. He has plenty of help." Will saw his sister was right. Pat Vale was surrounded by help. Will slowly shut his door as Andromeda again spoke. "We should just go."

"Don't you think we should wait for the cops? I mean, we should tell them what happened."

"What did happen, Will?"

Will thought for a moment.

"I don't know."

"Exactly. Whatever happened it's got nothing to do with us. I really don't care to spend half my day trying to explain something I can't explain, so let's go. If they need to talk to us, they can call us."

"Okay . . . All right."

Will slowly drove onto the street and headed away from the Straight Line. He stared in his rearview mirror, watching the scene recede.

"What the hell was that all about?"

Andromeda stared out her window and watched the quiet town slip past.

"Karma, I guess."

"If it was, it was the most instant karma I've ever seen."

"Seems to me it was a long time coming."

Will quickly remembered how deep a thorn in the side Randy and Pat Vale had been to so many of the locals. They had tormented their neighbors for years. But now, after this incident, they would be out of commission for months, if not years. After coming on to his own brother in front of so many witnesses, Randy Vale might never again show his face.

Will could not help feeling some satisfaction.

"I guess maybe it was."

THIRTY-EIGHT
SIGHTSEER

Will and Andromeda pulled into the family drive and Will stepped out of his truck. In the distance he could see his father directing their field workers as they prepared the soil for the next season's crops. Will stood waiting for his sister, but Andromeda did not move from her seat.

"Aren't you coming?"

"I don't think so. I want to take a drive through town on my own. Besides, I have to meet Howard Clark this afternoon. Do you mind?"

Will handed Andromeda the truck keys as she slid into the driver's seat.

"I have to work anyway. When will you be back?"

"Depends on what there is to see." Andromeda pulled the door shut. "Will, I don't think we should say anything to Mom or Dad about what happened to those two jerks. Mom especially. She'll just get worried over nothing."

"Yeah, probably. I just keep thinking it's weird how Randy went off on Pat right after what you said to him."

"What did I say?"

"Something about loving his brother."

"Oh, yeah, but that was just the first part. If he'd let me finish I would have capped it by saying, 'Then you probably don't want to see him in the county jail,' or something like that."

"No offense, but threats as lame as that don't mean anything to the Vales." Will thought it over for a moment. "Oh, well. Randy Vale was never mister sanity anyway. In a bizarre way, it all makes sense."

"If that was normal, don't show me strange."

Andromeda waved good-bye to her brother, pulled onto the road and headed for her first destination. The drive was only eight miles but she took it as slowly as she could.

As she neared her destination she saw a huge yellow-and-red arrow proclaiming YOU ARE HERE! pointing into the parking lot. She turned the truck in and headed for the large drill that sat on a concrete platform in the middle of the lot. There were few cars at Andromeda's Tomb at nine in the morning, the hour the attraction opened its doors, and Andromeda's truck was the first of the day that did not belong to an employee. One of the cars in the lot was a shiny red Cadillac.

Andromeda parked, exited and gave the drill a perfunctory glance before heading down the concrete tubes into the lobby. The woman behind the ticket window, showing without discretion the deep cleavage of her bionic boobs, giggled for no reason when Andromeda approached. The badge pinned to her ample bosom said LAURA.

"That'll be six dollars for adults."

"I thought the sign said five dollars."

"Oh, shoot, they didn't change it. Well, it's supposed to be six dollars; they just didn't change the sign."

"So how much is it?"

"Five dollars. I mean *six* dollars. Sheesh." Andromeda handed over six dollars and Laura clicked the turnstile to let her in as she shoved a pamphlet out the ticket window. "Oh, here's a program. It tells all about Baby Andromeda and stuff. Let me know if you want anything from the gift shop, because I'll have to unlock it."

Andromeda took the pamphlet and walked into the first cavern room of the museum. She paused to ready herself as she took it in.

She saw the pictures hanging between artful stalactites. She saw her five-year-old catatonic self being dragged from the hole as the rain poured down. She saw eight-year-old Will standing in an intense downpour with so much anguish on his face as she was loaded into an ambulance. She saw the mannequins of herself and Will. She saw the secondary shaft and she stepped forward to stand on the little bridge.

As she stood looking down through the thick Plexiglas, she became aware of a small argument going on in the second cavern. She crossed over the bridge and moved toward the back room.

Denny Sharf refused to hear there was something he could not have.

"I just want the goddamned thing unplugged! What's so hard about that?"

Wayne Deets of Deets and Son tried to squelch the desire to punch Denny Sharf in the face.

"We try to pull out that plug, there won't be nothing left of that hole. Never mind the fact you'd have to shut this place down for a good two weeks or more."

"What about the other hole? What about finishing it?"

"I don't know, maybe we could do it. Won't be easy."

"You mean it won't be cheap."

"These things never are."

"And I wouldn't have to close down?"

"Hell, no, make it an attraction. Watch us finish the shaft. I'd pay extra to see that."

"I just raised the ticket to six dollars."

"You could get six-fifty."

"When can you start?"

"Clear out that Plexi and let me put up my rig. Tomorrow morning."

"And you'll be done in time for the parade?"

"Guaranteed."

"Then do it."

Denny and Deets suddenly noticed that an incredibly beautiful young woman in tight but tasteful pants and a delicate blouse stood watching their conversation. With a hand on a hip, Andromeda cocked her head and a delicate lock of hair dropped over one eye. It was the sexiest of images.

"I'm sorry, boys, I didn't mean to snoop."

Denny Sharf ran his hand over a head that used to have hair. He stepped closer to this creature of exquisite sensual beauty.

"No, you're more than welcome, Miss . . . ?"

"Wiley. Miss Andromeda Wiley."

Deets spoke as Denny fell silent.

"Oh, Lordie . . . "

Denny regained his voice.

"You're little Andromeda?"

Andromeda did a delightful spin to show herself off. In the spin a delicious band of naked midriff and a dainty belly button were exposed, showing the toned flatness of her abdomen.

"Ta-da! In the flesh." She bounced lightly past Denny and stood looking down at the concrete plug, keeping her legs straight and together as she bent low and swayed her hips in a rhythmic bop. "I just came by to see the scene of the crime."

Denny stood behind Andromeda Wiley and let his eyes play up and down her body.

She was even more perfect than Sandra had been in her prime. The perfect stance of Andromeda's perfect legs rose to a tight pair of curves that perfectly filled the butt of her designer pants. Her slim waist rose in a perfect V up her strong back to a graceful neck and perfect features. The ideal breasts that rose and fell with each breath beneath the white cotton of Andromeda's blouse yearned for contact with Denny's hands. He pictured himself stepping to her backside to bring his hands under her armpits, reaching out and around to cup her firm breasts, squeezing them and feeling her nipples harden as he himself hardened and pressed his crotch into the seat of her pants.

Andromeda spun back to Denny with a stylish whip of her hair and bit her lower lip in teasing coyness.

"Did I hear you're going to open this back up?"

"We were considering it. We're probably going to finish the secondary shaft instead, for the celebration, you know."

"How cool. And then you'll close it again?"

If Denny could get even ten minutes to taste what he guessed was under those clothes, he would agree to anything. Even though the prospect seemed an incredible long shot, he decided it was best to keep his options open.

"If that's your wish, that's what we'll do."

"Let me think about it. Will you let me know when you get it open? Pretty please?"

"First thing."

"Okay. Well, thanks. You're both too cute. Be seeing you!"

Andromeda Wiley trotted out of Andromeda's Tomb and left both Denny and Deets staring at her exit in wonder. Her scent hung in the air like a mouth-watering pheromone that said, "Take me." Deets was more blunt about what they had just seen.

"She's the kind who says, 'Come with me,' you don't wonder about leaving your wife, you just go."

Denny, who felt he had more right to think those thoughts about Andromeda Wiley, grew short with Deets, a man who was not anywhere near Denny's social level.

"Just get to work."

"I'll have a whiskey sour and she'll have . . . "

Sitting next to Howard Clark, Rayna Higgins looked over the happy hour drink menu.

"What's a Prairie Geyser?"

The lanky waiter recited the brief ingredient litany.

"It's basically a gin martini with fizz."

"Then I'll have an Irish coffee."

Clark scanned the types populating the afternoon happy hour at the Whistle Stop's saloon. There were middle-aged divorcées looking for romances measured in hours. There was one table of Japanese tourists who kept looking around with a traveler's anxiety, expecting Jesse James and his gang to come bursting in to take their wallets and belt buckles. At the bar sat the regulars, who got their drinks with a wordless nod and who felt their regular attendance gave them the right to comment snidely on every nonregular coming in the saloon. Clark and Higgins received the treatment as they entered, but by now they had been sitting in the saloon for over twenty minutes and were almost regulars themselves.

Clark, the suave Manhattanite, could not help but feel his old neighbors and *Review* readers were a bunch of redneck hicks.

"If Andromeda is anything like these yokels, it'll be a tough sell."

"Lay a few road signs before you go with the body of the story to remind people about her. You should do another 'Whatever Happened to . . . ' segment. Don't go into detail about her, just bring up her name."

"Already thought of that, already did it. I'm not worried about how she is as a person, I'm just worried she doesn't have what it takes to make the story sexy. I'd like to accompany it with some pics. We're not going to get Lev to shoot her if she's a gap-toothed farm girl whose mother might be her sister."

"Well, it won't make or break our careers if the story's a dog."

"I know that, but Baby Andromeda is what put me on the map. I want to tie a ribbon on it and shove it under a tree."

"Well, I guess we'll find out in a minute if that's what's going to happen."

Clark and Higgins downed their drinks and ate drink olives skewered by plastic swords with tiny Conestoga wagons on their ends. They watched the clock tick down. As each solitary female entered the saloon they half rose, wondering if it would turn out to be Andromeda Wiley. But after eight or nine misses she had still not shown.

Clark was ready to pull his cell phone to call and see if she had forgotten, when a lovely image of feminine beauty stepped into the saloon and scanned the faces present. All faces present turned to return the look. Clark couldn't take his eyes off her.

"Oh, let it be her."

The young woman, wearing tight slacks and a delicate blouse, landed her gaze on Clark and Higgins and smiled. She began heading their way.

"Mr. Clark?"

Clark did a mental flip. *Yes.*

He stood with Rayna Higgins to greet Andromeda.

"Call me Howard. Would you look at this—little Andromeda all grown up. You remember Rayna?"

"Actually, we never officially met. I'm happy to meet you."

They all sat and Clark signaled the waiter for another round of drinks.

Rayna Higgins scanned the beautiful Andromeda Wiley and saw in an instant the perfect layout. It would be a black-and-white spread. They would have Andromeda posing in scant clothing before the gaping maw of a huge open pit mine, or possibly they could have her partially buried and she would be straining to break free. At any rate, her expression in at least the first shot would be fearful. They would follow this shot with others showcasing the current confident Andromeda, maybe wearing tight jeans with the top button undone. Maybe she could be carrying picks and shovels and have dirt on her face. Higgins voiced a thought.

"Do you smoke?"

"No. Never."

Higgins decided she would have Andromeda sitting like a man, smoking a cigar or maybe a cigarette from a classic cigarette holder as she turned an expression of total contempt on a group of muscled pretty boys vying for her attention. Higgins saw Andromeda had what it would take to make a very attractive cover story.

"This'll work."

Clark gazed directly at Andromeda's perfect face.

"Man, you are a knockout. What have you been eating?"

"All the basic food groups, if chocolate is considered a food group."

"The formula works." He leaned back for business. "So fill us in. What the holy hell have you been up to?"

"The Cliffs Notes version? After all that business here, I shipped myself off to The Campus in Vermont, I stayed there all the way through high school, after that I accepted a scholarship that allowed me to travel abroad, and that's about it."

Higgins held up her chin with her hand.

"Interesting. Very."

Clark couldn't believe his luck.

"So, listen, we want to do a whole follow-up to the first story. We want to show how exceptional you turned out. My first impression is that'll be a piece of cake. We don't even have to lie. Think you're up for it? Ready to be famous again?"

"What do I need to do?"

THIRTY-NINE

SHERMER'S FALL

Will kicked the dirt from his boots as he stepped into the kitchen. He was met by his mother as she held up a newly completed painting.

"What do you think?"

He scanned the glossy canvas. The muddy browns, yellows and greens seemed to reveal an image of an old two-story farmhouse. Will thought he recognized it so he took a chance.

"It's our old house?"

"I painted it for Andie. Just a little something to remember the old place. Do you think she'll like it?"

"Mom, I'm sure she'll love it."

"Where is she? I want to show her."

"She's checking things out in town."

"Well, that won't do. She'll miss dinner." Sandra thought a moment. "Why don't you drive into town and bring her back."

"She has my truck."

"So take my car."

In minutes, Will found himself climbing behind the wheel of Sandra's Mercedes. After a short drive he entered Wishbone proper and headed down Main Street, scanning for Andromeda.

As the sun set and the lights of Wishbone flared to life, youths in glossy cars and lowered trucks passed Will, cruising Main Street and hoping a wink would get them a date. Girls in provocative outfits rolled their eyes and turned from whistled proposals with hormonal struts calling for a U-turn and a second shot. Sheriff Austin, ever alert for delinquency, explored the avenues in his own cruiser and signaled impending trouble with a meaningful shake of his head if a certain activity was not stopped or a certain grouping of teens did not break it up and move on. The college crowd hit the bars and experimented with such lines as "Aren't you in my class?" and "I don't normally do this but . . . " Fake IDs were produced and the music was turned up loud.

Will reached the end of the Main Street action and began scanning the side streets. In front of Amy's Stop 'N Go he found his truck. Parking the Mercedes, he stepped out and tried to pick Andromeda from the pedestrian hustle. In the jostling crowd he saw at least one familiar face.

Janice Piasecki, walking fast and keeping her eyes to the sidewalk, frowned in frustration and scratched an itching forearm. Will reached out as she moved past and yanked her out of her introspection. She turned with eyes wide, as if frightened.

"Will Wiley. You startled me."

"Sorry, Ms. Piasecki. I was just wondering if you'd seen Andromeda."

Piasecki's frown returned.

"No. No, I haven't. But she saw me, didn't she?"

Abruptly concluding their sidewalk chat, Piasecki turned from Will, stared back at the sidewalk and continued her frowning pace. Will watched her go.

Shaking his head, he turned again to scan the crowd. His eyes suddenly located the object of his search. Several blocks away and with her back to him walked Andromeda. Already well past the downtown crowds and growing more distant, she was a solitary figure moving under the street-lamps.

Will watched as his sister suddenly crossed the street and headed for a huge, weathered barnlike structure. A faded sign above the tall double doors read WISHBONE LIVERY.

Will's confusion was suddenly doubled.

"Shermer's . . . "

"Stupid sonofabitch! Move! Now, git!"

Cullman Shermer spit a mouthful of black phlegm to the ground and glared at the frightened roan horse that refused to leave its stall. In the large Wishbone Livery, where Shermer housed his stagecoaches and buckboards with his twenty Cleveland Bays, Percherons, Suffolks and Belgians, the remaining stalled animals waiting for evening duty snorted in agitation as Shermer took a whip to their unfortunate comrade.

"You'll move when I say you'll move! Now get on out there!"

But the horse, on the small side for a Percheron, just flared its nostrils and edged even farther back into its stall. A cold sweat broke out on the horse's flanks and its scarred coat glistened with liquid fear. Done with being frustrated, Shermer walked to a post and pulled down an electric cattle prod. He slapped it in his hand as he returned to the stall and planted a sharp jolt on the Percheron's rear. It leapt from the shock and found itself in the aisle, where the yoke of the last remaining stagecoach hung ready to hook it up for another evening of toil.

Shermer spit another black splatch into the dirty hay and reached for a chew refresher as he exited the stall and yanked the Percheron into the yoke.

"I'd just as soon sell ya for glue."

As he hooked in the horse next to its equally depressed companion, the tall barn doors opened slightly and a soft woman's voice chirped in.

"Hello? Is anybody here?"

Shermer leaned around his stagecoach and saw a young woman silhouetted by the bright streetlights stepping into his livery. He spit.

"This here's off limits to tourists. Close the door on your way out."

Andromeda continued her entry.

"Mr. Shermer? It's Andromeda Wiley."

Shermer finished rigging the Percheron and stepped out into open view.

"Is that so? Well, I still don't allow nobody in my stables."

Andromeda caressed the faces of the six horses still in their stalls as she continued moving closer to Shermer. Beneath her gentle touch the horses suddenly calmed. They stopped their fussing and slowly moved to the fronts of their stalls to watch in unison as Andromeda closed in on Shermer.

"This is quite an operation. You've done all right."

Shermer saw in growing anger that the Wiley girl would not be stopped, even as he noticed that the livery had fallen completely silent. Not one of the horses was moving. Every single beast stood staring in rapt attention as the Wiley girl stepped right up to Cullman Shermer and stopped. Shermer, not one to be pushed around by anybody, looked her in the eyes.

"I work hard. What do you want?"

"I just wanted to say thanks for your help back when I really needed it.

I know it's fifteen years late in coming and all but . . . I know you were for bringing in that drill to save me and, well, it meant a lot to me. I just wanted to apologize for taking so long to say my thanks."

Shermer, who knew he had voted against the drill, who held a vague ill will toward the whole Wiley family, believing they were less than American because a suggestion was made on their behalf to get rid of a parade salute to two of the finest Americans who ever lived, narrowed his eyes out of natural suspicion. But scanning the girl's face, he could see no hint of deception.

"You're welcome. Now, if you don't mind, I got work to do."

"I understand. I didn't mean to bother you." She turned and took a few steps toward the tall double doors before stopping again. She looked back over her shoulder. "You'll be at the reunion ceremony, won't you?"

Shermer chewed on a wad of cud and leveled his narrow gaze on the impudent girl.

He could see in a glance that she was one of the new "me first" breed, who did not respect duty to God and country, who was only interested in hedonism and glorifying her own existence. She was asking him to waste his time on a parade that said, "The world is such a better place because I got saved and got all this free money and never had to work a day in my life and never had to know what it was like to wonder where I was going to get my next meal." Andromeda Wiley was the seed of mankind's doom. A fornicating, treasonous harlot. Cullman Shermer, God-fearing patriot, did not have time for her kind.

"Can't do it. Too busy."

"Shoot. Well, we'll miss you. Thanks anyway, for everything."

"Yeah. Now, good-bye."

He stood his ground to make sure the annoying girl left him in peace. He watched until she exited the double barn doors and closed them behind her before he turned back to his ready team.

He stood frozen by what he saw.

Every one of his horses stood staring at him with a cold and unblinking expression. Time suddenly wound down to a standstill.

In a strangely hollow moment Shermer suddenly felt himself being drained, as if every other blood cell in his body had vanished. He began shivering uncontrollably. He staggered a step back and nearly fell. Catching himself, he lowered his head between his knees and tried to shake off the instant nausea and wooziness.

He blamed it on blood sugar.

"I n-need something t-to eat."

But it wasn't hunger he was feeling. He was feeling something he thought he was too strong to feel.

Cullman Shermer felt fear.

He forced himself to stand straight and was rewarded as the fear and dizziness evaporated. He felt fine again. The first thing he noticed was that his horses were still staring at him with that same cold look.

Agitated by their stares, Shermer swung out his whip and smacked the stall doors of the closest horses.

"Get on back in there! Shoo!"

The horses moved back at the smack of leather on splintered wood.

Having shown them who was boss, Shermer took hold of the ready yoke and harshly yanked the pair of hitched horses and the trailing stagecoach toward the tall double doors.

"Gimme sass, you two'll work an extra hour each."

He put his hand to the double doors and pushed.

They didn't open.

Shermer leaned into the tall doors and pushed hard with his shoulder. The doors still did not give way.

"Sonofabitch . . ."

He continued to shove his body into the double doors until he felt something creeping over his exposed neck.

Like a heavy cloud rolling up his spine, a waft of musky air, hot and humid, tingled his back. He felt moist exhales blowing his shirt against his skin. He turned.

The door to every single stall was wide open. And every single stall was empty. It was impossible but it was true.

Every last horse, the emotional products of years of physical and verbal abuse by this vicious and vindictive man, had somehow left their stalls and now stood in the aisle inches from Shermer. They aimed prophetic glares at the man who with every shock of his prod called himself "master."

"What the hell . . . What is this?"

But cornered against the double doors by his slave herd, Shermer suddenly knew the answer.

They came to show their hate.

They hated his shrill voice and his twisted spirit. They hated the years of torture he had so readily inflicted on them. They hated his whip and his quick willingness to use it.

They hated his rotten soul.

Shermer met the red eyes of nearly ten thousand pounds of horse and knew their hate. As the horses suddenly rose on their hind legs and surged forward with hooves high, Cullman Shermer realized how they meant to express it.

Three blocks from the Wishbone Livery, Will intercepted Andromeda. Much like Janice Piasecki, Andromeda walked with her eyes glued to the pavement. She gasped in slight shock as Will blocked her path.

"Oh, Jesus, Will, you scared me."

"What were you doing at Shermer's?"

"I stopped in to say thanks."

"For what?"

"For helping me out when I fell in the hole. I'm thanking everybody."

"Well, don't go thanking Shermer. Shermer doesn't give the first shit about you or anybody else, for that matter. He never helped you out."

"But I thought . . . He didn't?"

"Never. You probably spent an extra day down there because of him."

Andromeda frowned for a moment, but then she quickly tossed it off and smiled.

"Oh, well, whatever. What are you doing here?"

"Mom wants you to come home. She's making dinner—"

Will stopped when he heard something banging against the inside of the livery's closed double doors, but as he glanced back the sound quieted. The closed-up livery was the picture of quaint rural serenity.

Andromeda took Will's arm and began walking him back toward the town center.

"I suppose Mom's making a soufflé."

"Believe it or not, she's taking a shot at sashimi."

"Yikes."

As they merged with the evening crowd, Will overheard excited whispers from those who recognized Andromeda. But as intrigued as the crowds were at Andromeda's public appearance, no one took the initiative to speak to her directly . . . until a familiar voice spoke from the open doorway of Watertower Books.

"Hello, Will. And this must be Andie. Lord, how you have grown."

Andromeda and Will turned to see Mary Downes exiting the bookstore with books in a bag. She looked older than Andromeda remembered, having lost all color from her once tidy locks.

"Mrs. Downes? Oh my gosh, I've been meaning to come see you!"

Andromeda gave Mary a loving hug. Mary returned the hug and smiled sincerely as she pulled free.

"After getting all those letters from you over the years I feel like I know everything about you, dear. It's good to finally see your face. Do you two have a minute?"

Andromeda turned to Will.

"Do we?"

"One minute, then we have to go. Sorry, Mary, Mom's making us dinner."

"We'll talk fast."

Mary led Andromeda and Will into Courthouse Square Park, where they sat on a bench directly beneath the westward-looking bronze statue of Mary's ancestor, Lieutenant Jeremiah Hayworth, forever dressed in the U.S. Cavalry's finest. As pigeons who no longer had Melba Ashford around for a guaranteed meal laid another coat of droppings on Jeremiah's head, Mary looked Andromeda up and down.

"Well let me look at you. . . . Honey, you have turned out just right."

Andromeda blushed.

"I blame it on the genes."

Mary nodded and then let out a deep breath.

"Andie? Why'd you come back?"

"Come again?"

"I don't intend that in a mean way or anything, but . . . well, I'm just wonderin'. You done all right for yourself without havin' this place in your life. Why come back now?"

"I wanted to see my home; I wanted to see my family." Andromeda took Will's hand in her own. "I especially wanted to see this boy here."

"And that's it?"

Andromeda hedged a moment before speaking.

"I needed to see it. I needed to see where it happened. I had this hope that if I saw where I fell, everything would be like it was before."

"Hmm. And did you see it?"

"Yeah. Nothing. I didn't feel anything. It was just a place like any other place, except for the six bucks it cost to get in."

Will's brow furrowed.

"Sharf made you, of all people, pay to get in?"

"He didn't know it was me. Besides, some blond bimbo took my money."

Mary chuckled.

"That bimbo is his wife, proving there's even a special somebody for Denny Sharf. Still, I know one soul who might have a hard time finding the right gal, especially after today. I suppose you heard what happened to the Vale boys."

Will responded.

"We were there. We saw the whole thing. Not that I care, but how's Pat?"

"I guess his leg's pretty busted. A rib or two is cracked, but nothin' life threatening, I'm half sorry to say. One thing I don't think either of those two is ever gonna recover is their pride. Last I heard, that Randy freak took all his stuff and disappeared, and thank God. If we never see his sorry ass again it'll be too soon."

Will nodded as he stood. "You don't hear me complaining." He spoke to Andromeda. "We should get going."

"Okay." Andromeda turned to Mary. "I hope I can see you again soon."

"Any day of the week."

Their attention shifted as an ambulance, its sirens wailing, rushed down Main Street, whooping for people to move out of its way. It turned down Platte Street and headed toward the Wishbone Livery. Pedestrians began rushing after it. Mary stood to join Will and Andromeda.

"Looks like somethin's goin' on over at Shermer's."

Will started at the news.

"Shermer's?"

Mary began moving with the crowds toward the Wishbone Livery.

"Only one way to find out for sure."

Mary, Will and Andromeda crossed Main Street and joined the crowd. The only person they passed moving against the flow was Denny Sharf as he tried to make his way to his red Cadillac. Andromeda barely gave him a glance but Denny still stopped with eyes wide and mouth open to watch her go by.

As they neared the livery, Will felt a restless concern building in his gut that touched old fears. He glanced at Andromeda, hoping for an answer, but he could see she was as oblivious as any as to what was going on.

The ambulance was at the open doors of the livery, parked near the cruiser belonging to Sheriff Austin. The sound of horses neighing loudly and men calling "Whoa!" burst from the open doors, and it was clear from the dust accompanying it that there was a great deal of activity happening just inside. Under the bright light of a high streetlamp, two paramedics with arms held high for protection rushed out of the livery, dragging by the armpits what looked to be a man. Sheriff Austin scrambled out and slammed the livery doors shut. He yelled to Fred Zinneman as Zinneman pulled up in his own patrol car.

"Get some handlers down here! These horses have gone loco! And keep that crowd back!"

Zinneman made a quick call on his radio and then moved to the growing crowd that stepped closer every second.

"Folks, now you're all going to have to step back! Just stop right there! Now, I said step back!"

The crowd stopped mainly because they were already close enough to see what had happened. A man who could not be identified owing to the bloody and crushed nature of his face and body lay on the street. The two paramedics, splotched in the man's blood, checked for a pulse and came to the quick conclusion that there was little they could do. A sheet was retrieved from the ambulance and draped over the brutalized body. Sheriff Austin was handed the dead man's gored wallet. He opened it and pulled out the ID.

"It's Cullman Shermer."

Will fixed a disturbed eye on Andromeda.

"You just saw him."

Andromeda stood shocked.

"He wasn't . . . he wasn't . . . not like this . . . "

The crowd began to chatter and murmur.

"Looks like Shermer got run over."

"More like beaten to death."

Sheriff Austin grew annoyed at the chatter.

"Zins, clear them out!"

Fred Zinneman waved his arms at the crowd and made motions in the air as if he were pushing them all back. A few spectators produced video cameras and zoomed in for close-up action.

"Now, you all gotta clear out! Get those cameras out of here. There's nothing more to see." His eyes landed on Andromeda standing in the crowd with her brother, Will, and Mary Downes. Zinneman walked up to Andromeda. "You too, Miss Wiley."

Andromeda shook herself out of her stare.

"Oh, uh, sure . . ."

"By the way, welcome back. You look great."

Sheriff Austin, kneeling by Shermer's body, lifted the sheet for a wincing peek at the destruction heaped on it.

It was clear those sad horses had taken out whatever rage was in their system on every single inch of Shermer's body. There was not one square inch unbloodied and unbroken from the pounding of their hooves. Shermer's bones were hammered to powder. He was now a gaping and jellied stretch of formless flesh, held together only by virtue of his tough overalls. Shermer's skull was cracked open in fifty places. The gray matter that once held his bitter spirit oozed from its sanctuary; the neural mass that stored and processed his ideas about duty to God and country and killing commies was right this minute compressed and smeared under the shod hooves of his formerly oppressed beasts of burden.

Sheriff Austin could not believe the force of their revenge. "God Almighty . . ." He dropped the sheet and hoped the sight of so much gore would not stick too long. He stood and looked up to see his deputy talking to Andromeda Wiley. Austin moved their way as Andromeda, Will and Mary began walking off. "Hold on, there."

Mary, Andromeda and Will stopped and turned. Austin took a good long look at twenty-year-old Andromeda Wiley.

"Andromeda?"

"Hello, Sheriff Austin."

"Well, now, it's about time we saw you again. Are you in town to stay or did you just come in for the reunion?"

"To stay." She looked past Austin to Cullman Shermer lying dead in the dirt. "Sheriff, I should tell you I saw Mr. Shermer only fifteen minutes ago."

"You saw Cullman? Why would you do a thing like that?"

"I stopped in to say thanks and . . . and . . ." Andromeda was clearly shaken. "What happened to him?"

"Looks like he got kicked to death by his animals. At least, there's plenty of evidence to suggest that: bloody hooves and all, scuffs on the door. Let's just say we won't be calling in Columbo on this one. So you saw him fifteen minutes ago? And?"

"And he was alive. He was normal."

"That's always been a matter of debate around here. Did you see anything to suggest something like this was about to happen?"

"Not really, except . . . Well, he didn't seem to be treating his animals too nice. He kept poking this one poor horse with a prod."

"Yeah, we found the prod lying on the ground next to his body." Sheriff Austin sighed. "Normally I'm the last to speak ill of the dead, but the way he treated them horses, them stomping Cullman to death don't surprise me one bit. I'm mainly surprised it didn't happen earlier." Austin made the sign of the cross. He turned back to Andromeda. "Sorry you had to see this. Not the kind of reception we had planned, believe me."

"I'm thankful for that."

Mary grabbed Andromeda's shoulders.

"You'll be all right, dear. Is there anything else, Sheriff?"

"Nope, I'd say it's cut and dried."

As Mary led a shocked Andromeda past remorseless spectators who joked about how the literal shit was kicked out of the late, pancaked Cullman Shermer, Sheriff Austin rejoined his men to scoop Shermer's body into the ambulance, where it was shut in and driven off. Andromeda kept her eyes on the ground as she walked with Mary.

Will lagged a few paces behind them and surveyed his sister. A doubt that had sprung up refused to be squelched. Like an alcoholic freshly off the juice, Will struggled to keep from telling himself the same thing over and over. But he could not resist. He could not stop telling himself the same thing over and over.

Andromeda had something to do with Shermer's death.

In the course of a single day, two bizarre incidents had happened and they both involved Andromeda. Randy Vale, a pure but predictable asshole his entire life, lost it only after Andromeda spoke to him. Now Cullman Shermer was dead and Andromeda was the last person to see him alive.

As if sensing Will's growing doubt, Andromeda turned to him.

"First Randy Vale and now Mr. Shermer. I'm starting to think I'm a jinx."

As Will stared into Andromeda's face, he saw it was twisted in tortured confusion. Her apparent sincerity began eating away at his doubt and he again felt his recent anguish for distancing himself from Andromeda. He took hold of this new doubt before it grew too strong. Stopping its progression, he made a conscious effort to squelch it.

"Just bad timing."

Mary showed little remorse.

"It's the hand of fate. Randy and Pat Vale, Cullman Shermer . . . They reap what they sow, and Shermer reaped it plenty."

Andromeda lifted her head and turned to Mary with a heavy smile.

"I'm glad we got to talk. I hope we'll see you at the reunion."

"I wouldn't miss it for the world."

As Will drove home in his truck and Andromeda drove home in Sandra's Mercedes, he found he was still struggling with a new blooming of mistrust toward his sister. He watched the taillights of the Mercedes directly ahead and tried hard to fight the suspicion.

"Stop being stupid. She didn't do anything."

He wasn't even certain what his suspicion was trying to propose. Was he thinking Andromeda had some power to control fate? Believing such a thing was tantamount to believing in ghosts and alien abductions, and Will believed in neither. So why was he so willing to believe the improbable when it came to Andromeda?

He had no easy answer because his suspicions came not from his mind but from his gut. They were not thought, they were felt.

As Will followed his sister through the night, he tried to tell himself Andromeda was not the director of fate but was instead its victim. Just as she was in the wrong place at the wrong time when she fell in the hole, she had been in the wrong place at the wrong time when Randy Vale tried to make love to his brother. She had not asked to be present; fate put her there. Anything sinister about Andromeda's unfortunate placement at each scene was nothing more than a fabrication of Will's long paranoia toward his sister.

But why had fate also chosen Andromeda as the last person to see the still-living Cullman Shermer?

It was a question only fate could answer.

Fate or Andromeda . . .

Janice Piasecki could see through her see-through mirror, all the way across the expanse of her Polecat Pub and out the open doors, that some commotion was going on outside. She called Carl into her office. Carl yanked free his Buffalo Bill beard as Piasecki gestured toward the action with her thumb.

"What's going on out there?"

"Cullman Shermer got killed by his nags."

"No way. Shermer's dead? When?"

"Just a few minutes ago. They stomped him dead as dead gets."

"You saw it?"

"I didn't, but Eric saw him and so did Betsy, and they both said his whole head was smashed open, his brains and guts and all were—"

"That's enough. Geez, Louise." She shook her head in disbelief. "Well, you better get back out there."

Carl replaced his beard before leaving Piasecki's office. She sat back at her desk and watched Carl through her beloved mirror as he returned to his photographic duties, then lifted the phone and rang up the sheriff's office.

"Yeah, Currie? Hey, it's Janice. What's this I hear about Cullman? . . . Uh-huh, uh-huh. That's so awful. Tell me more. . . ."

As Janice Piasecki coaxed out the gory details of Cullman Sherman's stomping, she absently raised her hand to the center of her forehead and scratched a serious itch.

Cullman Shermer getting stomped to death by the very horses that had hauled Wishbone's tourists for over ten years was the town's main news of the evening. Tommy Vale, still reeling from the embarrassing tragedy involving his two sons, had no desire to comment on the death of a man he practically hated. Julie Fletcher had been notified and was already preparing Shermer's obituary, knowing it would be a struggle to find anyone who had anything nice to say about the man. She decided, contrary to her morals, that she would lie on his behalf. Even Howard Clark and Rayna Higgins had learned of Shermer's stomping. They both thought it made a nifty footnote to the Baby Andromeda reunion story.

But for one citizen the fact of Shermer's demise took a distant backseat to the fact that he had once again seen the object of his desire.

Everywhere Denny turned he saw Andromeda in either picture or print. Her name was on banners strung across the street. Her picture graced the cover of this week's *Review*. Posters on bulletin boards and telephone poles reminded everyone who might not already know that a parade in her honor would occur in three days' time. Yet except for that brief moment of contact when they passed earlier in the evening, she had failed to produce an adequate sequel to her first inspiring appearance at Andromeda's Tomb.

He was tormented by her absence. He was tormented because Andromeda Wiley was the most beautiful creature he had ever seen.

Denny just could not get her off his mind.

Denny began to wish he really had installed a secret camera in the Wiley home, but one that focused on the bedroom of the daughter. As he drove his red Cadillac down the curving and well-lit street to his home in Royal Oak Gardens to meet his wife, Laura—who worked during the first part of the day as the ticket taker at Andromeda's Tomb but who subsequently spent the rest of her day watching TV, eating, ordering items from the Home Shopping Network, chatting with her on-line cyberlovers, and running through her "Buns of Steel" routine before heading to town for her ritual shopping spree—Denny considered how he could arrange a rendezvous with Andromeda Wiley, or at minimum a peek at her goods.

Denny glanced at his reflection in his rearview mirror. He was not stupid enough to believe he was a good-looking man. At age forty-two he had become something less than hideous. The only reason Laura, who at one time had a shot at becoming a Dallas Cowboys cheerleader, had married him and had stuck around was because of Denny's money. Denny knew it and Laura knew it and there was no pretending it was not the case.

Denny knew about Laura's cyberlovers, having caught her in the sweaty act more than once. He even suspected her trips to Wichita to see a fertility doctor, who would help her figure out why she was not getting pregnant, were really arranged so the doctor could get Laura pregnant himself. The thing about his wife's transgressions was that Denny didn't care. If Laura thought she was pulling something over on Denny, he thought it was fine to let her think so. It was a routine that did not create a happy home, but it was a situation that allowed each partner to safely conduct his or her own deceptions. Denny had the freedom to pursue his own interests.

One of Denny's interests was Mistress Wanda down in Wichita. Once a month Denny drove down for a weekend of abuse and domination. He always allowed enough time for the scrapes on his ankles and wrists and the splotches on his butt to fade before demanding that Laura fulfill her marital duties.

Still, Denny was growing bored. He had Laura, he had Mistress Wanda, he had other girls for hire all over the state. But his interests had not been truly piqued for a very long time. Even the fantasy over Sandra Wiley had faded as she crossed into her forties. Denny was looking for something new. He found it in Andromeda Wiley.

Wanting Andromeda Wiley with an erotic passion that boiled over with every memory of her sensual swagger, Denny knew he would draw her to him only if there was something in it for her. He had to discover her angle. What Andromeda's lure could be, he had no idea; he just knew he had to find it.

Andromeda Wiley would be his.

IN FOND MEMORY

They're plotting against me. They want me out. Just like that witch Larkins, they want what I have. They're talking behind my back. They won't win; I won't let them.

Janice Piasecki sat in her usual chair at the city council meeting in the Wishbone City Hall and scratched her itching arm before lowering said arm to scratch her itching thigh. She tried to listen as Mayor Tommy Vale and the city council discussed what to do in the wake of Cullman Sherman's death. Piasecki surveyed the faces of Reese Vosker, Frank O'Connor, Kelly Mahon and Tommy Vale.

They're men so they're in it together. They're out to get me. They want what I have.

Piasecki spun on Mahon.

"What did you just say?"

Kelly Mahon turned to Janice Piasecki and his double chin shook.

"Huh? Oh, I said maybe we could have Andromeda Wiley sit in for Shermer, just temporary, like it's an honorary position."

"Andromeda Wiley is only twenty years old. She is not old enough to sit on the council. Besides, she saw through my mirror."

Frank O'Connor frowned at Piasecki's sudden tangent.

"What are you talking about, Janice?"

"That's not the question, O'Connor. The question is what are you talking about?"

"We're talking about what do we do about Shermer. If you were paying attention, you'd know that."

"I'm paying attention, believe me; I'm seeing all sorts of things."

Reese Vosker, who fancied himself a good-looking man with a sharp wit, could not help but comment on Janice Piasecki's off-kilter state of mind.

"I bet you are."

Piasecki sneered at Vosker. When she spoke it was almost a hiss.

"You better not put peanut shells on your floor, Vosker. That's my idea."

"First off, the Pony Express Hotel does not throw peanut shells on the floor and second, that idea has been around since your granny started to crawl."

"You don't know my grandmother. You don't know that."

Mayor Tommy Vale, still lacking news as to the whereabouts of Randy, was in no mood to tolerate Janice Piasecki's erratic behavior.

"Now, goddammit, take a pill and stow it, Janice. You people—"

"Who told you to say that? It was Larkins, wasn't it? That witch—"

"Okay, stop!" Everyone fell silent as Tommy Vale huffed things back on track. "Now, we got a parade happening here before we know it. We got floats to finish, TV people to take care of, we got newspaper reporters and we got paying tourists coming to see the parade and Baby Andromeda in it. One thing we need going is Shermer's coaches. We also want them buckboard hayrides happening like Shermer promised. Now, who is going to handle that end since Shermer doesn't have one goddamned person on earth who wants to admit they're related to him?"

Frank O'Connor raised his hand.

"I know all of Shermer's drivers. They'll listen to me, so I accept the duty, although I expect to be compensated for my time."

"You get whatever Shermer would have got if he was still around to run the operation. Next order of business: When do we bury Shermer and who pays for his stone?"

Nobody spoke for a moment. Finally Kelly Mahon said, "Why does he need a stone? Ain't a single person anywhere who's going to visit it."

Vosker was in total accord.

"I vote for cremation. No urn. No ceremony. Shermer didn't leave a will because he thought he was going to live forever; that's his tough luck."

Tommy Vale scanned the faces of the council.

"Everyone agreed?"

Every face nodded except for Janice Piasecki's. She stared across the table with eyes unfocused as she scratched her shoulder.

"Shermer stained my napkins with chew spit."

"Uh, yes, that's fine. . . . So it's unanimous. Cremation, no urn and no ceremony. Who scatters the ashes?"

O'Connor looked up.

"Let's get off this subject, Tommy. No one cares, okay? Shermer never married, he's got no family and none of us liked him much, am I right? Let's just toss his ashes in the creek and be done with it."

"Is everyone agreed? We dump Shermer's ashes in the creek?"

Again, every face nodded except for Janice Piasecki's.

"The creek has water. Plants like water."

"That's true. . . . All right, so we cremate Shermer—"

Vosker interrupted, "Today. We don't want to be dragging this into the ceremony."

"We'll call as soon as we adjourn the meeting. We cremate Shermer, we toss his ashes in the creek, O'Connor runs Shermer's stage lines until the Baby Andromeda ceremonies are over, he is compensated for his trouble by drawing out of the proceeds no less but no more than Shermer's usual profit, and when all this business is over and we settle what we need to settle, we put Shermer's ranch and stage lines up for public auction."

O'Connor raised the question on everybody's minds.

"Sealed bids?"

Tommy Vale, who felt he might care to join the bidding himself, thought sealed bids would unfairly handicap his chances of winning.

"We'll make it an open auction."

O'Connor continued.

"No need to make it too open."

Tommy concurred.

"We'll type up a notice and pin it on the courthouse bulletin board."

"In a small font."

"Whatever keeps it legal. Meeting's adjourned."

FORTY-ONE
THE ANALYST

Diana French and Kathleen Saunders drove to Wishbone in a chauffeured limo following their landing in Wichita. The long drive through flat country swung Diana's thoughts to a time fifteen years past.

She had been on a sabbatical from her labors as a professor at The Campus, looking for something, anything to make a splash in her chosen field of child psychology. Even though it was no small feat to teach at The Campus, she wanted more. She wanted more than just peer recognition.

She wanted household fame.

She had toured the super-rural hamlets of West Virginia and studied the psychologies of boys and girls who came from seriously dwindled breeding stock. She had swung into lower Alabama and stayed with a black family to study the effects of poverty and racism on their worldview. She had interviewed homeless children and illegal-immigrant children to find out how they saw themselves, to gauge their levels of self-worth. Certainly she had discovered some intriguingly affected psychologies, but in every case she knew she was breaking no new ground.

Then she heard about Baby Andromeda, the girl in the hole.

The girl was trapped by poverty; that was bad enough. But she was trapped physically as well. This was a child who would have unique features to her psychoses. And if that wasn't enough, her story had become familiar to the man on the street.

Baby Andromeda was famous.

Diana rushed to greet the Wileys and offer her services before anyone else could. She made it in time.

As she expected and as she in fact hoped, Andromeda emerged from the

hole with severe emotional trauma. She was at first catatonic. She later refused to return to her hometown. She had irrational paranoias and delu-
sions. She spoke for a very short while about voices and monsters in the
basement.

She was perfect.

Diana spent the next four months completing her book on the subject
of Baby Andromeda's ongoing recovery. When her book was published it
reached a respectable number on the best-seller list. Diana did the book-
signing circuit and met other authors, who treated her as an equal. She
gave peer speeches, she appeared on several talk shows and she reaped impressive financial rewards from her book sales. The Campus administra-
tors asked her to accept a tenured position and she did so with the
stipulation that she would have great leeway in pursuing outside projects.
It was granted.

Baby Andromeda herself was given the best attention money could and
did buy. The Campus paid for Andromeda's stay in full as part of their ne-
gotiated deal with the now-celebrated author of *Answer the Light*.

Diana French, who had not married because she gravitated toward the
company of capable women, currently gravitating toward her assistant,
Kathleen Saunders, considered Andromeda's recovery a success even
though she knew that most of Andromeda's gains were accomplished in
spite of Diana's interventions.

Andromeda had healed herself; Diana was certain of it. But Diana did
not refuse the credit when the public chose to give it.

She had watched Andromeda grow confident and capable for twelve of
the last fifteen years, before Andromeda left The Campus to continue her
education abroad. She had studied Andromeda thoroughly and intimately. She felt that after twelve years of daily contact she should be able
to reasonably predict Andromeda's behaviors and reactions. But she could
not. After twelve years all Diana knew was that she would never know the
true mind of Andromeda Wiley.

She thought she had been studying Andromeda, only to discover that
Andromeda had been studying her.

It was Andromeda's eyes, beautiful at a first glance, dauntingly mysteri-
ous at a second, which made Diana feel so impotent and so studied. Even
at five and six and seven, Andromeda looked to Diana French, her supposed emotional savior, with eyes that knew far too much.

Diana struggled for twelve years to break through Andromeda's gaze to the suppressed trauma she knew had to live there, to exert her rightful control and foster Andromeda's dependency. She never could. Andromeda refused to let down her guard; she refused to reveal how she really felt behind her poker-faced amiability.

Diana was considered one of the leading popular child psychologists in the country. She had given good, solid advice to millions of parents via articles for *Family Circle* and *Parenting*. She resented the fact that one of her perceived great successes, the recovery of Baby Andromeda, had nothing to do with her teachings. Andromeda did not practice any of the healing rituals or therapeutic meditations that had worked so well for her other youthful patients. Andromeda had followed her own course and in the end had turned into a young adult smarter, wittier, stronger and more confident than anyone could have thought possible.

Andromeda Wiley intimidated Diana almost from day one of her recovery and Diana didn't like it. She didn't like it one bit. Andromeda should owe everything to Diana French, but in reality owed her nothing beyond room and board. That fact inspired Diana to feel something she would never be able to admit.

She hated Andromeda Wiley.

She hated her completely.

Kathleen Saunders turned to her boss and lover as the limo pulled up to the front of the Whistle Stop Inn at precisely two o'clock.

"We're here. How quaint."

Diana peered out at the inn, which featured a mixed theme of old-time West and old-time railroad. A massive black locomotive engine sat before the three-story inn. The Whistle Stop's entry was flanked by two oversized cigar store Indians. Diana couldn't help but find it revolting.

"Yes, isn't it?"

"Okay, just one more. . . ." Lev Voloshin crouched low with his camera and worked to frame the great Diana French, posing as directed with arms crossed and face stern in the dramatically empty coal tender hitched behind the Whistle Stop's train engine. Voloshin adjusted his Hasselblad's focus and position and clicked off a shot.

"Perfect. Grand."

Andromeda, standing off to the side with Will, Kathleen Saunders, Howard Clark and Rayna Higgins, smiled with impatience.

"Now can I say hello?"

Voloshin brushed his long black hair from his face and nodded as he waved his crew to let down their lighting bounce boards.

"But of course."

Andromeda moved to Diana French and gave her a long hug.

"I'm so glad you came."

Tensing as Andromeda held her, Diana tried to muster an equal hug in response.

"How could I not?"

Clark clapped his hands to get everybody's attention.

"Okay, now, who all do we need to go on this?" He addressed Will. "Do you need to go or are we done with you?"

Having spent the past two hours changing outfits as Clark's Lithuanian ordered him to pose like a model and look serious when he felt ridiculous, Will shook his head.

"I'm all shot up. I have to get back anyway. I'll see you all later."

Will met the eyes of his sister as he turned to make his exit. He quickly averted his gaze and moved past. As he stepped to his truck, he could tell Andromeda suspected something of his inner turmoil. Andromeda's brow furrowed in worried concern. Closing the door to his truck and turning the ignition, Will knew that if he couldn't get rid of his doubt completely, he would at least have to work harder at concealing it. A last glance at Andromeda and he saw she still looked at him with a questioning gaze. Will sent her a meaningless smile and put his truck in gear.

Voloshin quickly spun on Andromeda, obviously eager to get to work. He looked her perfect figure and face up and down.

"You are gorgeous! I will tear your clothes and cover you with mud. You will still be gorgeous, even more gorgeous!"

Higgins raised her hand and one of Voloshin's crew drove over with a passenger van.

"We better get going. We've got a lot of shooting to do."

Andromeda showed her nervousness. Clark noticed.

"You okay?"

"I'm just excited."

"Try to save it. The real excitement hasn't even happened yet."

Andromeda smiled brightly.

"It will."

FORTY-TWO

WE THE PEOPLE

*T*hey *can see through it; I know they can. They're just pretending they can't. They're talking about me. What are they saying? What are they saying about me?*

Janice Piasecki, sitting in her office and staring out her see-through mirror at the sneaking strangers who ate her food and talked behind her back but pretended not to, scratched her itching neck and stood. She scrambled over her desk, kicking papers and pens to the floor, and stood facing the see-through mirror, now an inch from her face.

In the large hall of Piasecki's Polecat Pub and Eatery, families ate burgers and fries, drank soft drinks and shakes, played video games, sat at the bar and drank beer, shot pool at the pool table and generally had a good time. Not one person was looking Piasecki's way.

But they wanted to; Piasecki was sure of it.

Piasecki knew they were purposely trying not to look her way because they didn't want her to know about their conspiracy. They didn't want to reveal their plan. But they already had. Piasecki already knew. She knew they were against her. They were planning to take what she had.

"Liars, thieves . . ."

A family getting up from a nearby table did what so many families had done before. They stood at the mirror and checked themselves out. They checked their dress and their teeth. They checked their hair.

They were spies and they were spying.

"Get away. Don't look at me."

But the family kept primping and staring.

"I said get back!"

Piasecki slammed her fist into the glass and the family on the other side stepped back.

"Get out!"

Piasecki kicked aside her desk and lifted her office chair. The family now seemed to hear her as well. They retreated farther. Other patrons were now looking toward the wall mirror.

Piasecki had unmasked them. The spies, liars and thieves were all looking at her now. The conspiracy was out in the open.

If they would not leave, she would force them out.

She lifted the office chair over her head and threw it with enraged power into the glass.

"Get out!"

In the dining hall the huge wall mirror shattered in a massive crash of metal against glass as the scream from the office was followed by a chair. People sitting nearby covered their heads and scrambled to get out of the path of the tumbling chair and the spray of sharp shards. Janice Piasecki, her face red in fury, leapt through her broken wall mirror and waved her arms at everyone in sight.

"Get out!"

She set her haunted gaze on her traitorous workers.

"You too! Liar spies! Get out!"

To speed the process of herding out the spies and liars, Piasecki began kicking chairs and overturning tables. Pitchers of soda, half-eaten pizzas, plastic baskets with ketchup puddles and hard french-fry leftovers spilled to the floor.

"I know who you are! Revealed! Seen! Traitors!"

Carl and Eric and Betsy and the bartender and all the other workers quickly rushed out the front entry along with the terrified customers as Piasecki's rage came closer. By the time she kicked and overturned her way to the front doors, she was the only one left in the building.

"Whores!"

She slammed shut the doors and spun the locks. Yanking down the shades, she slapped off the lights and rushed far back in the room. She bent and lifted in each hand a sharp and menacing shard of broken mirror. Satisfied, she spun around to judge her status.

"No one but me is going to win this one."

. . .

Denny watched her through a twelve-hundred-dollar pair of binoculars.

Lying low behind a bush at the top of an abandoned rock quarry carved deep into the Kansas earth, Denny watched in telescopic flatness an image, somewhat jittery due to his excitement, of Andromeda Wiley in a body-hugging velvet gown. She was lying across a bulldozed mound of rocky earth, caressing in a seductive fashion the shaft of a dirty old shovel. A photographer with long black hair kept blocking Denny's sometimes excellent view, circling the prone Andromeda to click off shots. Other people Denny didn't know held white circles of fabric to bounce light on Andromeda. Howard Clark, whom Denny knew well and despised, stood close to the Wiley temptress for the best view.

Denny could tell from the absence of seams under Andromeda Wiley's skintight velvet gown that she wore nothing but the gown. He kept hoping she would move in some way that might give him a glimpse of what lay beneath, but she never did. After forty minutes of watching, having quietly followed the troupe out of town in a nondescript cargo van owned by the Savings and Loan, his cell phone suddenly rang. In the binocular image he saw a few heads suddenly turn. He ducked lower and quickly pulled out the cell phone to silence it by answering the call. He spoke in an annoyed whisper.

"What? What is it?"

Lois Knowles's voice came through, full of sarcastic suspicion.

"Did I disturb you at something, Denny?"

"Uh, no. . . . I was just . . . What do you want?"

"You have to come back and close up."

"Handle it; I'm busy."

"I can't. Closing up is your job. I don't do work I don't get paid for."

Denny took a look through his binoculars to see if anything had changed. Andromeda Wiley was still fully dressed. Denny spoke back into the phone.

"I'll be right in. Don't ever call me on my cell phone again."

"You're the boss."

"Janice! Now, open up in there!"

"Forget it! Go away! You didn't vote for me!"

Sheriff Austin stood at the front door to Piasecki's Polecat Pub and

Eatery with Fred Zinneman and tried to reason with a woman who had obviously gone insane.

"Janice, listen. I did vote for you and no one is out to get you! You're just imagining things!"

Inside Piasecki's Polecat Pub and Eatery, Janice Piasecki jammed another table into the Gordian knot stacked at her entry to further barricade the front doors and windows. A pile of chairs and tables nearly twenty feet high prevented anyone from getting in to take what she had. The traitors and liars and spying whores would not succeed in their conspiracy.

"I'm imagining things, am I, Austin? She looked through my mirror! Did I imagine that?"

Piasecki threw the last free chair onto the massive pile and stepped back into her now-empty restaurant.

"Tell the thieves they won't win this one!"

Outside the barricaded entry Sheriff Austin lowered his head in tired dismay. He waved for Carl, still dressed as Buffalo Bill, to come closer.

"You've worked with her; she knows you. You talk to her."

Carl shook his head.

"She called me a pig-fucking-rat whore. I'm not going anywhere near her. She's crazy."

Fred Zinneman piped up.

"We know that, Carl. The question is, is she a danger to anybody else, or even herself?"

"I don't think so. She's alone in there. That's how she seems to want it."

Sheriff Austin lifted his head.

"Fine, I'm sick of this shit. First Randy and Pat and then Cullman and now Janice. If she wants to stay in there, let's just leave her."

Zinneman protested.

"We can't just leave her."

"Why not?"

"I don't know. Can we?"

"If we take her out of there, where are we going to put her? In a cell, that's right, and then we have to hear her screaming and ranting all night long. I'm not going to get all cut up just to do that. We'll call the white-suit boys tomorrow and have them come get her. In the meantime, tape this section off and ask the locals to keep an eye open to see if she tries to come out." Sheriff Austin stepped down from Piasecki's Pub and climbed in his car. "I'm going home. Anything else happens, you take care of it."

Fred Zinneman strung up yellow police tape around the front of Piasecki's Polecat Pub and Eatery as Sheriff Chuck Austin drove off in his cruiser. Carl moved to Zinneman and spoke in a whisper.

"I heard Randy Vale whacked off at his brother in front of the Straight Line. Man, that's sick."

"I am oh-so-glad I did not see that one."

"Both those Vales . . . One time him and Pat just punched me in the gut for no reason. They deserve whatever they get."

"That's exactly what somebody else said about Cullman Shermer."

Carl pulled free his Buffalo Bill beard and recited his Uncle Nick's favorite line.

"Yeah, well, good things come to those who wait."

FORTY-THREE
THE WATCHERS

Lisa sat a stone's throw from the Wileys' main house in the barn loft apartment she shared with Will, watching her lover pacing the length of the high-ceilinged room.

"You know what I think? I think you're jealous."

Will stopped pacing.

"That's ridiculous."

"Is it? Before Andie came back, you got all the attention—not just of your parents but the whole town. I think you might be a little jealous that Andie's stealing some of your thunder."

"Lisa, I don't need the psychoanalyst crap. I'm not jealous of Andie."

"Then maybe you're just being territorial. She's like an intruder on your turf. Maybe you think she needs to rough it a bit before you put out the welcome mat."

Will huffed in exasperation.

"You just don't get it."

"I'm trying to. Why did you even bring it up if you won't explain it to me?"

"How can I explain it? It's just something I feel."

"That Andie is hiding something?"

"Yes."

"Something bad."

"I don't know. . . . I don't know if it's bad."

"But you're sure she's hiding something. You're sure because she said something to a known prick and he decided right at that moment to take a dive off the deep end. You're sure because she was the last person to see

Shermer alive. Honestly, I don't even know what you're saying. Do you really think Andie somehow caused those two things to happen? And how did she do it? Drug them? I guess she drugged Shermer's horses, too."

Will knew his standing on this issue was tentative at best. He did not want to appear as even more the fool to the woman he loved. But Lisa was the only person on earth he could confide in. He exhaled completely and spoke more slowly.

"I'm not saying she caused Randy Vale to do what he did, and I'm not saying she made those horses stomp Shermer."

"Thank God for small favors . . . "

"What I am saying is, why Andromeda? Why was she at the two most surreal events to happen in Wishbone since she fell in that shaft?" Will plopped into a chair. "She's my sister and all but . . . " He felt himself gritting his teeth. "I just don't like weird shit like this."

"Especially the kind you imagine."

"Can't you at least fake some support?"

Lisa chuckled as she rose and moved to Will. She sat in his lap and put her arms around his strong shoulders.

"I never fake anything with you, baby." She lowered her face to force Will to look her in the eyes. "You do know you're acting like a preschooler, don't you? Come on, think about how Andie must feel. She must think she's cursed or something."

"She said she thought she might be jinxed."

"There, see? Is that what somebody who has something to hide would say? She's as bothered by what happened as you are." Lisa stood. "Anyway, your mom wants us to eat dinner in the main house tonight. We should get going."

Will did not move from his seat.

"I'll be down in a minute."

"Whatever you say, chief." Lisa began descending the loft steps. She stopped halfway down and looked back up to Will. "If you just watch Andie, if you look a little deeper, I'm positive you'll see you're just imagining this whole thing."

As Lisa disappeared down the steps, Will decided she was right about one thing.

Andromeda needed to be watched.

If she had something to hide, Will was determined to find it.

. . .

Denny had waited and waited for good things to come.

Under a blanket of stars, in the cool night air, he had cautiously crept closer to the back of the Wiley home, having purposely dressed in dark clothing. Reaching a point as close as he dared go, he lay on his potbelly between the harvested rows of corn and propped himself on his elbows to scan the Wileys' lit windows with his twelve-hundred-dollar binoculars.

Minutes turned to hours and still she did not show.

In that long stretch of time, his mouth grew dry with anticipation, an anticipation that was disappointed multiple times as lights flashed on and figures entered rooms, only to turn out to be Peter Wiley, or Sandra, who was fully dressed, or Will and his girlfriend, Lisa, also fully dressed.

But his long wait was finally rewarded. As the lights downstairs went out, as the lights in the rooms he knew belonged to Peter and Sandra went out, as Will and his girlfriend left the main house and disappeared into the barn, the lights in another room came on.

Andromeda appeared and the curtains were wide open.

For a long time she dropped out of sight of the tall bedroom windows. Denny guessed she was either in her bathroom or sitting off to the side and could not be seen. But finally she did reappear.

She lay on her bed, still dressed, and read a book far longer than Denny liked. At one point she kicked off her shoes and socks, and Denny's hopes shot up. But she did nothing else to follow the action. She just lay on her stomach or on her back and read and read.

Well after midnight, just when he was beginning to feel she would never stop reading, when he was feeling so parched and achy that he could take no more and knew he would have to leave, he saw her set her book down on her bedside table. She stood and stepped closer to the windows. Denny tried to hold his binoculars tightly as he shivered in voyeuristic excitement. He could see her entire glorious body from her knees up.

For a long time she just stared into the night.

"Come on . . ."

Denny was shivering from both the cold and his voyeuristic excitement. His long wait was rewarded.

Her hands drifted down to her pants. Her precious fingers unzipped her pants so teasingly. She took hold of the top of her pants, and slightly wiggling her hips, she slid them to her feet, stepped out of them, and tossed them to the side.

"Oh, God . . ."

Then she reached up and slipped off her shirt, also tossing it to the side. She stood absolutely naked.

Her nude body was everything Denny imagined.

Suddenly she started doing things. She slid a hand down her flat belly. She slid her hand between her legs. Denny saw her stiffen.

She was touching herself, right there before his eyes. It was the most incredible sight Denny had ever seen. It was a holy grail vision from Denny's sexual nirvana.

In its witness he lost control.

"Ohh . . . ohh . . ."

Denny's eyes rolled back in his head as he felt himself go. He glanced down at his crotch to see the pool of liquid staining his slacks from within.

It had never happened before. Not ever.

He had never had an orgasm without touching himself or having himself touched. It was a sign that this vision of erotic beauty was as special as he had hoped.

He looked back to the object of his ecstasy.

The room was dark, the light was off.

The curtains were drawn. The show was over.

"No . . . no."

Denny waited for fifteen minutes to see if there might be an epilogue, but it was all dead silence at the Wiley home.

Dejected and wanting more, he crawled back and began moving for his car, parked at the distant edge of the Wileys' expansive holdings. He only took two or three steps before his foot suddenly caught on something and he tripped, falling flat on his face.

He heard something break.

Pushing himself up on his hands, he saw he had landed on his treasured binoculars. The lenses, which tinkled out into the rich soil, had completely shattered.

"Fuck. Shit."

He looked to see what had tripped him. A root the thickness of his thumb curled up out of the soil in an arc. Denny pulled his foot free and stood in rage. He reached down and grabbed the root and began yanking to tear it free from the soil, to punish it. But it was stronger than Denny. It

would not budge or break. Huffing and tired but deciding he still needed
to do something, Denny kicked the root as payback. He grabbed the remains of his binoculars and shuffled for his distant car. His only consola-
tion was that the binoculars had served the purpose for their purchase far
better than expected.

He had seen her and she was everything he hoped she would be.

Now more than ever, he had to find a way to get inside.

Peering through her darkened curtains, Andromeda watched as the
hunched figure of Denny Sharf trudged under the starlit sky across the
hundreds of rows separating him from his car. She let the curtains fall
back and she climbed under her sheets, accepting the embrace of darkness.

She stared into the dark, her ally, with one last thought.

Only two more days and it would all be over.

FORTY-FOUR

THE GUARDIANS

"**T**his is the first time we've ever been able to talk, just you and I."

Diana French sipped the *latte* set before her by Sandra Wiley and nodded.

"That's true. I hadn't realized that, but you're right. We've always had a bit of an entourage."

Diana smiled at Sandra and looked out the large window of the Wileys' farm home. Outside, Howard Clark, Lev Voloshin and the crew set up a shot of Peter Wiley looking strong and proud as he stood on a beefy combine. Twelve of Wiley Organics's regular workers surrounded the base of the combine, also looking proud. The pose made Peter look regal and fatherly.

Will, Lisa and Andromeda stood nearby, making faces to try to crack Peter up. He tried not to notice but often failed, losing his composure more than once. He jokingly frowned for his children to behave.

Sandra returned Diana's smile.

"It's been a long ride, hasn't it?"

"For both of us. But you've come through it nicely, Sandy."

"I have?"

"Don't give me that; you know you have. The way people talk about you in town, it's clear that you've become Wishbone's leading lady."

"I suppose there are worse things I could be."

"Well, you've handled everything as well as anybody could."

Handled things.

Sandra had definitely handled things.

Sandra recalled Baby Carlotta. She recalled thinking how the accident that had forever changed Carlotta's life could in retrospect be seen as beneficial. Looking out to her beautiful, healthy and brilliant daughter, she felt it might be safe to say the same of Andromeda. In retrospect it could be said her falling in that hole was the best thing that ever happened to her.

When Andromeda fell, Sandra worked hard to hold it together through the agonizing rescue operation. From minute to minute she felt a nervous breakdown was one straw away, even as she worked with Howard Clark to orchestrate the wooing of the national press. And even when Andromeda had been pulled to safety, there had been months of private anguish over the trap of Sandra's design. But Sandra did not believe, as Peter did, that talking about it was the way to heal the wound. She could heal her guilt only by forgetting her guilt.

But now, knowing how well Andromeda had turned out, Sandra felt she could safely embrace the positive aspects of the experience. It had changed Andromeda's life for the better. Why should Sandra feel guilty for that?

Andromeda had everything Sandra never had. She had the love of a concerned family, she had financial security, she had the respect and admiration of many and she had unlimited educational opportunities. Andromeda had been all over the world. Sandra could not say the same. At twenty Andromeda was young and full of life. At twenty Sandra had lived without friends in a house deserving demolition. At twenty Andromeda was the envy of all. At twenty Sandra had been the envy of none.

So what did Andromeda have to complain about?

Nothing.

If Sandra had not proposed the trap to Peter, if Andromeda had not fallen in that hole, then she would probably right this minute be a poor young mother with no prospects and no means of creating any.

Because of Sandra's trap, Andromeda lived a better life.

Sandra felt her tongue swell as a flush of envy passed through.

Andromeda had everything Sandra now had, but she had it twenty years sooner, when all the doors were still open. Andromeda was more beautiful than Sandra had ever been. She was more refined, she was more clever, she was more intelligent and insightful. She was better at controlling her emotions. Sandra had no doubt that Andromeda was probably even better at art. Why shouldn't she be? She had everything going for her. She had everything going for her because that's how Sandra arranged it.

Having her more impressive daughter around so often over the past few days, Sandra caught herself fighting a burgeoning resentment. Sandra received the second glance now when for so many years she had received the first. She lived in Andromeda's shadow. It was only one part of her resentment.

The rest of her resentment grew out of the fact that Andromeda would never have to know or understand the desperation that drove Sandra and Peter to find that shaft and rig that trap. She would never have that fear in her life. Her life was lived on a happy cloud that hovered above the world of shit that was Sandra's birthworld.

However much Andromeda had suffered, Sandra had suffered far more, and almost all of her suffering was done on Andromeda's behalf. Sandra felt she wasn't completely unreasonable to think that Andromeda owed her something. But the thing Sandra wanted most—the rewinding of her clock to give her twenty more years of youth, to give her the beauty Andromeda casually took for granted—was something even her brilliant daughter could not give.

Diana finished her *latte* and set down her cup. She followed Sandra's gaze out the window to Andromeda, who was now trying to arm wrestle Lisa Benson while Lev Voloshin raced around the two young women and snapped shots.

"You've done so well with her, Sandra."

"We've both done well with her, Diana."

"I suppose we have." Diana watched as Andromeda defeated Lisa Benson in the arm wrestle. Andromeda stood and took a bow as Lisa called for a rematch. "That girl has the whole world in her hands."

Sandra bit her lip.

"She certainly does."

FORTY-FIVE

BOBBY

Ask any child in Wishbone which house was haunted and which house had ghosts and skeletons and probably murderers too, and nearly every child would mention the decaying abode that Andromeda stood prepared to visit. Looking at the ruin, she decided the time for that visit was well past ripe.

The Ford sedan parked in the driveway was so ingrained with dirt, it was clear it had not been driven for several seasons. A former lawn was now a field of tall brown grass, dried milkweed, thistle and puffed dandelion. The trunk of a formerly pruned crabapple tree was now a mass of suckers. The uppermost branches of the tree were shriveled and dying. Unclipped arborvitaes billowed over curtained windows. Vine roses consumed a trellis and pulled it from its mounts. Screens and shutters leaned against forgotten storm windows on the leaf-covered front porch. Christmas lights, none lit and most broken, still draped the gutters. A bird fountain was now tipped and cracked.

The house looked abandoned.

Andromeda pulled the tilting picket fence up straight to pass through the sagging gate. She navigated the walkway littered with old rolled-up newspapers, tossed by a paperboy unaware that the occupant had long ago canceled his subscription. Stepping onto the hollow-sounding porch, she pulled open the creaky screen door and knocked on the paneled oak. She waited for an answer.

It didn't come.

Andromeda stepped to the curtained picture window separating the inside living room from the outside porch. She leaned into the glass and cupped her hands around her face to block the glare of the day. Through the narrow split between the curtains she could barely make out interior details. There seemed to be a great deal of stuff in the room. But one thing she could make out was a running television. The Weather Channel occupied the screen. Somebody wearing a terry-cloth bathrobe sat in an armchair watching the dull report with his back to the picture window. Andromeda knocked on the glass.

"Bobby? Mr. Timms?"

Bobby Timms moved his head slightly. Andromeda was encouraged. She spoke louder.

"It's me! It's Andromeda!"

Timms moved even more. He turned his face to look toward his window. When Andromeda saw the face of Bobby Timms, she stifled a gasp.

Timms was completely white. His hair was white, his skin was white, the haphazard stubble dotting his face and neck was white. Timms had no color at all, as if all his blood and life had emptied out. The only color Andromeda saw in his face was in his mucousy yellow and bloodshot eyes. He limped up and pushed aside the curtain. Squinting into the assault of light, he tried to focus on Andromeda as she stepped back to allow him a fuller view.

Timms's face gained an almost imperceptible amount of color as he saw in the young woman on his porch a memory of a face he once knew clearly.

"Andie? Andie Wiley?"

Timms gestured to the door and both he and Andromeda moved to it. Andromeda heard lock after lock unlatching and then the door finally swung open. Bobby Timms, looking shorter and smaller than Andromeda remembered, but mainly looking too many years older than the fifteen that had lapsed since she last saw him, pushed open his creaky screen door and worked his face into a surprised smile.

"You're a woman."

"So they say. I came by to say hi."

"Huh? Oh, that's great, that's really . . . Would you like to come in? Or maybe—"

"Yeah, I'll come in, if that's okay with you."

"Uhh . . . sure, come in."

Timms limped aside and held open the door as Andromeda entered.

Andromeda quickly absorbed the sights and sounds of a lasting depression. The odor of cat piss was strong. Several male cats, none seemingly neutered, slept or trudged about the house. The carpeted floor, which should have been blue, was almost gray from the quantity of embedded cat hairs. Hanging plants drooping by the windows were so long dead that a layer of dust an inch deep covered their curled leaves and branches. Long drapes of dusted spiderwebs filled the ceiling corners, and the formerly white walls, yellowed with age, were speckled with the feces and brown urine of flies and cockroaches. A glance into the kitchen revealed a garbage can overflowing with used TV dinners and cat food cans. The only part of the kitchen floor not covered by a layer of grime that only a scraper could remove was the path trodden by Bobby Timms to the cluttered sink, the filthy stove and the grubby fridge. A table in the kitchen was overloaded with vitamin bottles. In the dining room, where there should have been a table and chairs, stood a weight bench with one barbell, and mirrored tiles were stuck to the wall. Bobby Timms saw Andromeda looking at his puny exercise set-up.

"I get a couple minutes in each day, try to keep in shape."

He shut the door and the house grew more grim.

"Let me clear you a seat."

Timms limped to his sofa and threw magazines, books and old jazz records onto the floor. He brushed the cat hairs from the cushion and offered the seat to Andromeda. She smiled gently.

"Thank you."

Andromeda sat and Timms limped back to his armchair. He plopped down and hit the mute button to silence the weatherman. Setting down his remote, he turned back to Andromeda.

"Andromeda Wiley. I never would have thought it."

"If it hadn't been for you, I never would have thought it either."

"Fifteen years, that's how long it's been. Went by fast. . . . That was really something, wasn't it? A hundred feet down there in that hole, you a little girl like you were, all those people coming in from all over. That was really something."

Bobby Timms nodded as he fell into remembrance. He made it clear as his gaze shifted to watch the muted weatherman on TV that his social skills were much atrophied.

Andromeda could not believe this was the same Bobby Timms who had been so full of vim and vigor, who took charge, who got things done. She heard herself saying it when she thought she was just thinking it.

"Bobby, what happened to you?"

Timms swung his gaze back to Andromeda. He knew what she meant. "This."

He made a weak gesture to encompass his grim hermit world. Andromeda nodded at his damaged leg.

"Does it hurt?"

"Sometimes. I got medicine for when it does. I still get around."

"When did you quit the department?"

"Few years, a few years after your thing. I'd been doing it for sixteen years; they offered me full disability. . . . You know Mona left me? Did you know Mona? Maybe you didn't. Anyhow, she took Susie, Jake, the twins and Alex—all of them went to Arkansas. She married a doctor. He's a proctologist. I guess he knows how to fly. Takes the kids for rides, or *took*. . . . I guess they're your age now." Bobby Timms smiled blankly at Andromeda. "Well, I'm glad to see you. I'm shocked, but glad. Are you in town long?"

"Long enough."

"Did I hear they're throwing a parade for you and Will?"

"For all of us; you too."

"Me? No one invited me. Parades . . . Nope, not for me. Besides, like I say, I'm not invited."

"I invited you. You have to be there. You're Bobby Timms. You saved me."

"Will saved you. Chuck Austin saved you. I wasn't even there then."

"You almost died for me."

"Andie, fact is, and don't take this wrong, but I didn't think much of that whole business. I mean, it wasn't some defining thing in my life or anything . . . "

Andromeda's eyes drifted to a dusty pile of Velobound booklets. The titles said, *Anatomy of a Rescue.* Bobby Timms continued.

" . . . so it's not really all that important to me if I'm in some parade or not. I don't need things like that to make me happy. I got what I got and that's what I like. You understand, don't you?"

"Sure."

"You're doing just fine without Bobby Timms and anyone can see that's the case. So good luck on your parade and thanks for coming by."

"I'm not going yet."

"Well, sorry, but . . . you need to because I have things to do. . . ." He let his eyes drift back to the Weather Channel. Now the weatherman was showing satellite shots of a storm off the coast of Java. "I really don't have time for guests."

Andromeda stood and walked to the windows. She yanked aside the curtains.

As light streamed in and illuminated the complete panorama of Timms's spiritual entropy, clouds of displaced dust billowed into the room. She coughed as Timms coughed. He shielded his eyes from the light as if he were a melting vampire.

"Close those! I don't want them open!"

Andromeda lifted open the windows and the fresh air outside sucked away the dead air within. She turned to Bobby Timms.

"They're open. They stay open."

"Andie, I didn't invite you in to make a mess of—"

"No more talking." Andromeda moved to Bobby Timms and knelt to his level. She looked him in the eyes and Timms stopped talking.

Andromeda refused to accept what she saw.

"This is over."

She grabbed the remote and clicked off the TV. She yanked the batteries from the remote and shoved them in her pocket. She stood towering over Timms.

"Stand."

Bobby Timms stood.

Andromeda was firm. "Clean up. Let these cats outside. Mow the lawn. Tomorrow you'll be at the parade, dressed for work. You're Bobby Timms. No one looks down on you."

Timms could see he was going to do exactly what she had just said.

"Okay, thanks for coming by Andie. See you tomorrow."

Andromeda moved to the door and propped it open with Timms's one iron barbell. The cats, spotting an avenue to that other world they had glimpsed only through cracks in the curtains, timidly began moving out onto the porch. Timms began picking up trash as Andromeda stepped out the door and looked back.

"You deserve better than this."

He watched her from the bushes. He watched the bitch who had ruined his life as she left the run-down piece of shit Bobby Timms called home.

He still had no idea how she managed it, but Randy Vale was positive the only reason he wanted to kiss and screw his brother in front of half the town was because the Wiley bitch made him think it was what he wanted to do. How she had accomplished that feat, he still had no idea. He just knew she had. He knew she was the one who had planted the sick urge in his groin.

Forget the fact that Pat would go through months of healing before he could walk again, Randy's respected reputation, cultivated over more than three decades, was wiped out. He now had no rep. He was instead the laughingstock of the county.

Randy had a new urge.

Randy had an urge for revenge.

He considered kidnapping her and driving her to some remote site where he would beat the hell out of her before making her do things she would never willingly do. Knowing he would never be able to set her free after such an episode, he thought out how he would finish her off and dispose of her body. But all his plans remained nothing more than plans. There was something in the idea of having to actually face her and spend time with her that caused him great discomfort. He was somehow aware that if he looked in her eyes again, his plans would not succeed.

What he needed was a fast strike. He needed to do something to Andromeda Wiley so sudden and unexpected that she would not have time to react or look him in the eyes. Randy had to be gone before she knew what hit her.

In the trunk of the unassuming car pinched from his father's lot, he visualized the jar of sulfuric acid, pinched from his father's shop. Wearing gloves, he would uncap the jar, rush from whatever hiding place he would choose when the time was right, and splash the Wiley bitch in the face. Her skin would bubble and peel and she would be hideously scarred for life. She might even be blinded. Randy smiled at the thought.

Andromeda Wiley would soon have the rest of her life to regret fucking with Randy Vale.

FORTY-SIX

SIGNALS

As Andromeda drove into Wishbone and passed Piasecki's Polecat Pub and Eatery, she saw Sheriff Austin and Fred Zinneman out front with three men in hospital uniforms. An open ambulance waited nearby. The door to Piasecki's was wide open, and teens Andromeda recognized as employees there walked out carrying smashed tables and shattered chairs.

Andromeda pulled up to the stop sign. Will stepped off the curb and jumped in.

"Check that out. Janice Piasecki barricaded herself in her place yesterday, fully bonkers, smashed her mirror and kicked out all her customers. They broke in to take her to the funny farm, but when they opened the place she wasn't there. I guess she wiggled out a hole somewhere. How weird is that?"

"It's totally tabloid. Where are Mom and Dad?"

"They're at the Whistle Stop with Diana and Clark and everybody. You want to head over now?"

"No, I have some business downtown. Why don't you take your truck. I'll meet up with you later."

Andromeda pulled over and climbed out. As Will took the driver's seat, he leaned out to Andromeda as she stood on the street.

"Andie, are you all right?"

Andromeda turned to her brother, slightly perturbed.

"I'm fine, Will. Why do you keep asking me that?"

"Because of the Vale thing and then Shermer. Because of all of this. I just want to know if you're okay."

"I'm okay, seriously, and if I'm not, I promise you'll be the first to know."

Will continued watching Andromeda as she crossed Main Street and stepped up on the opposite sidewalk. He watched her until she moved down the sidewalk and stepped into the Wishbone Savings and Loan. His brow furrowed in doubt.

"I hope so."

Will put his truck in drive and pulled away.

Upon entering the Savings and Loan, Andromeda headed straight for New Accounts.

"I'd like to open an account."

Lois Knowles looked up from her desk and realized who her customer was. She stood and shook Andromeda's hand as Andromeda read Lois's nameplate.

"Andromeda Wiley. How the hell are you? Man, you look great."

"Thanks, Lois. Didn't you use to run the Easter egg hunt?"

"Yeah, but I couldn't participate; conflict of interest."

"I went once. I found a dead bird and a half-full can of Miller."

"You did well. So what are you here for?"

"Savings, checking, the works."

"No problemo, can do, can do. Have a seat."

Suddenly a voice piped up from behind Lois. Denny leaned out his office door.

"I'll handle this one, Lois, thank you. Miss Wiley, won't you come in?"

"I had it handled, Denny."

Lois sat and Andromeda headed into Denny's office. She smiled back.

"We'll talk later."

"Watch your step."

Denny closed his door behind Andromeda as she entered his office.

"Please, have a seat."

Andromeda sat. A short section of bare skin separated her delicate shoes from her tight slacks. Denny made a large arc around his desk and tried to look graceful as he sat in his leather desk chair and faced the object of his desire.

"Did I hear you'd like to open a savings and checking account?"

"Yes, could you do that for me?"

"Of course. How much would you like to start with?"

Andromeda pulled two cashier's checks from her dainty clutch. She en-

dorsed them and handed them over to Denny. She pulled out identifica-
tion to accompany the checks.

Denny was appreciative of the amount.

"Nice numbers."

"So I've been told."

She didn't seem to mean money.

Andromeda laid one of her legs over the knee of the other and began
rocking it up and down as she leaned back. She put her chin to her chest
and looked to Denny with a conspirator's smile, nipping the nail of her
thumb. Denny wondered if she was saying what he thought she was saying. He decided he had to risk it.

"I can see that they would."

"Oh? How? Tell me. What do my numbers say . . . Denny?"

Just the way she said his name.

"That you're a complex woman."

"But my needs are so simple."

"What are your needs?"

"What are anybody's needs? What are yours?"

She lifted a pen. Opening her mouth she tapped the pen on her lower
lip. She still smiled at Denny. She uncrossed her legs and parted them
slightly.

Denny remembered how he had seen those same legs—and more—
naked less than twenty-four hours ago. It was an image he would never forget. It was an image he had to see again but without binoculars in the way.
He decided he would risk much if he might see it firsthand.

"I'm like any man. The basic things, I guess . . . needs, I mean."

"Like?"

"You know . . . "

"Like food?"

"I need food, so, yeah. Food, I guess."

"It's such a funny word, *food*. Doesn't sound real. . . . What else? Besides food. What else do you need? There must be something you really,
really, really need, something you think about all the time, something that
gets your juices going."

Denny could picture what he really needed: to strip this seductress
naked right there and lay her across his desk to take her completely.

"There's a few things, yeah."

"I'm sure there are. Me, I know what I need."

"What do you need?"

Andromeda responded with her most Cheshire smile. Then she teasingly changed subjects.

"I like that attraction you built about me. How's it going, getting in my shaft? Whoa, that didn't come out right. Pardon my faux pas. You know what I mean."

Denny tried to be suave.

"Sure . . . Deets'll be done tomorrow. We'd like to time it so when the parade ends at Andromeda's Tomb, we want it to open on camera."

"Sexy idea."

She said it first. *Sex.* And *shaft.* She'd said that too. Denny saw the door to opportunity opening wider.

"Sexy, how?"

"You're revealing something hidden, shedding layers, exposing what's within. It's very erotic. The earth as it opens is showing its womb." As she said it she made a sort of wave right past her crotch. Andromeda again smiled the Cheshire smile. "Do I get a choice in cloth?"

"Huh?"

"For my checkbook. I can't take vinyl. I mean, I'll buy a cloth one somewhere else if I have to; I'd just rather do everything through you. I feel like I know you. I like it better that way."

"It's better for everyone to know each other better."

"It's the only way. . . . You have a house right on the land where our old house used to be, isn't that right?"

"Uh . . . "

"Don't worry, I'm not mad. I'd like to see it. I think it might be neat."

"You want to see my house?"

"Yes, can I? Please?"

"Sure, maybe tomorrow or . . . or how about tonight?"

"What time?"

"Eight?"

"Later is better for me. Is midnight too late?"

Denny thought midnight, two in the morning, five in the morning, anytime was just right.

"No, I'm always up reading."

"Oh, I read too. So you'll take care of this for me?"

"You mean the accounts?"

"Yes, my dear."

"Done. You also get a safety deposit box at no charge for depositing a sum this size . . . and for being such a lovely customer."

"*Enchanté,* monsieur, but I don't need that box. I've got nothing to hide." Andromeda stood and trotted for Denny's door. "So I'll see you at midnight and you'll keep this between us? It's more exciting that way."

"I'll be waiting and I won't say a word."

Andromeda left Denny's office and he sat back down at his desk.

It was a dream come true.

She was giving him the signals. The signals were there. She wanted it, she practically said so. She said more when she wasn't saying anything than some women do babbling out loud their entire lives. She was saying she was ready. Denny wanted to make sure he was ready too.

He called his wife, Laura, and asked her to make a run to Wichita to pick up a needed box of bank forms. He told her to stay at whatever hotel she wanted. Knowing Laura would see a stupendous chance both to spend money and hook up with her doctor lover, he was not surprised when she said she would be leaving within the hour. The main obstacle was out of the way.

He would have to stop at the liquor store for beer, wine, champagne and some harder stuff in case that's where her tastes ran. He thought he might also try to get some marijuana from some of the skateboarding teens who always smelled of it. He had never smoked it himself, but he thought it might be a good idea to have some handy in case pot was the aphrodisiac that would get Andromeda Wiley's juices flowing.

Whatever it took to see her juices flow.

Except for Bobby Timms, all the people who mattered were there.

Lev Voloshin set up the group shot in the conference hall at the Whistle Stop. In a dense semicircle before strobes, flags and silks, Andromeda, Will, Peter and Sandra stood or sat with the rest of the principals. Diana French, Mary Downes and Denny Sharf posed next to Sheriff Austin, Fred Zinneman and Bart Currie. Behind them stood Julie Fletcher, Howard Clark and Rayna Higgins. Mayor Tommy Vale, Frank O'Connor and Kelly Mahon were in back and stood the highest. The lighting was dramatic and Voloshin worked his subjects with a master's touch. They gave him everything he wanted.

As Voloshin looked into his viewfinder, he raised his hands to conduct the group's movements.

"Mayor in more, Clark out more. You, Sharf, stand more straight."

"I am standing straight."

"Get him quarter apple to stand on."

One of Voloshin's crew grabbed a thin rectangular wooden box and set it down for Denny Sharf to stand on. It raised him two inches. Voloshin closed his fingers into an "okay" sign.

"Ready and . . . beauty! One more!"

When the photo shoot wrapped, the group opened beers and sodas and finalized plans for the following day's celebrations.

The mayor held a gold foil-wrapped box about six inches square. He held it as if it had heft. As he absently tossed the box up and down, Sheriff Austin nodded at it.

"Is that . . . ?"

"Cullman Shermer, what's left of him."

Howard Clark pointed at the box in Tommy's hands.

"I want a shot of that!"

Tommy tipped his head before turning back to Peter and Sheriff Austin.

"Me and the council were planning to scatter the ashes as soon as this bit's over, but now with Piasecki on the loose . . . You think she's dangerous?"

Sheriff Austin shook his head.

"She's been unstable before and she's always been harmless. I wouldn't worry. Any word on Randy?"

Tommy could barely hide his anguish.

"Nothing. He took a car off the lot, grabbed his clothes and went who knows where. Have you heard anything?"

"Currie is pretty sure he saw Randy passing him on Route Three, so my guess is, wherever Randy went, it isn't far."

Howard Clark consulted with Andromeda and Rayna Higgins.

"So at the end of the parade they'll open the second shaft to meet up with Andromeda's shaft. I don't know how you feel, but I think it would be incredible if Andie here was the one to break through."

Overhearing and trying like everyone else to avoid Denny Sharf, Mary Downes leaned close.

"Isn't that a little tacky, even for you, Howard?"

"It's not tacky, it's fun. The whole point of this story is to show how Andromeda has changed. So that's what we show, the change. She's not afraid to open that shaft and be the first to visit the spot where she was trapped. It's also about how the town has changed. I want to show how individual events heavily focused on by the media . . . how there's this whole life-of-its-own thing that takes over. It's about all the little detours people take because of an experience like that. How did it change Andromeda? How did it change Wishbone? It's not tacky, it's fantastic. Take Bobby Timms—pure pathos. I hear Bobby Timms has become a sort of . . . "

Mary raised an eyebrow.

"What?"

"Loser? I'm going to send a crew over to his place and get that whole deal covered. It's like unrequited love—people eat up that sad shit."

Andromeda turned to Howard Clark.

"Howard, leave Bobby out of this."

"Andie, he's part of your story and I want to show how he's changed, whether he's become a drunk or what; I don't care. People want to know the whole picture, the good and the bad. Timms is one of the only ones who actually lost something in the rescue. That's basic. That's the meat."

"I don't want you bothering him. Besides, he'll be at the parade tomorrow. If you want to interview him or whatever, you can do it then. So please, for me, leave him alone."

Howard Clark turned to Rayna Higgins.

"What do you think?"

"I'd like to see what's up with Timms. If he's been castrated by the experience, I'd like to see the cut." Rayna Higgins smiled at Andromeda, somewhat impatiently. "It's a lot to ask us not to cover an important element of this story. We lose our balance. The way you want us to write this thing it'll give the impression that when a girl falls in a hole, everybody wins."

Andromeda saw Denny Sharf sending her a nervous attempt at a sly smile.

"Not everybody. I see plenty of losers when a girl falls in a hole."

FORTY-SEVEN

ON THE EVE

It wouldn't go down in history as the tidiest scattering of ashes.

As Clark and Voloshin stood ready with cameras in hand, Mayor Tommy Vale, Frank O'Connor, Kelly Mahon and Reese Vosker struggled to open the well-sealed box containing the charred remains of Cullman Shermer. A pocketknife was produced and a slit was made. Tommy Vale peeled back the cardboard flaps and undid the wire twist that kept the contents of the inner plastic bag airtight.

"Ready?"

Frank O'Connor looked at his watch.

"Yeah, let's go."

The men stepped to the little bridge on Main Street that spanned Wishbone's creek, and Tommy Vale held out the open box. He waited until Clark and Voloshin were in position with their cameras.

"Okay?"

Clark gave the thumbs-up signal.

"Go for it."

Mayor Tommy Vale tipped the open box of ashes, expecting as the others did that Cullman Shermer's bone bits and gray powder would trickle out in a sort of heavenly veil to settle like a gray blanket over the gently frothing waters of the creek. Instead, the moment he tipped the box the entire plastic bag slid out of the cardboard box and plunked into the creek. It quickly sank. There was no scattering whatsoever.

For a moment there was some discussion about retrieving the plastic bag and trying again, but nobody wanted to risk slipping down the muddy bank and sullying their dress shoes and suits. They decided it was the thought that counted.

Howard Clark decided the shot of the mayor's face and those faces of the city councilmen stupidly looking over the railing to watch the bag of ashes sink was priceless.

They said their good-byes, and the nonceremony intended to celebrate Cullman Shermer's life was over.

From her hiding place under the bridge, on a three-foot-wide strip of dry dirt to the side of the creek that was her sanctuary from the spies, Janice Piasecki watched what they had done to Cullman Shermer. Wild-eyed, with disheveled hair and clothing, Piasecki kept to the dark confines of the low culvert that cut beneath the street. Janice Piasecki, Wishbone's newest troll, vowed that what happened to Cullman Shermer would not happen to her.

"No one puts me in a bag. No one throws me in a creek."

Minutes after the inept ash scattering, Howard Clark sat in his suite at the Whistle Stop typing fast thoughts into his laptop. Rayna Higgins, wife and business partner, sat in bed typing fast thoughts into her own laptop. Neither looked up to speak.

Higgins was the first to break the *clack-clack*ing drone. "Regardless of what she says, I'm not leaving out the fact that Bobby Timms took a dive after Baby Andromeda's rescue." She lifted the velobound booklet given to her by Julie Fletcher. Its title read, *Anatomy of a Rescue.* "Did you start reading this yet?"

"Haven't had a chance. How is it?"

"It's juvenile, there's no through-line, the grammar is terrible, he has one whole chapter devoted to his family and how holding together the family is the reason behind everything—it's an incredibly pathetic plea for attention from a wife who evidently didn't care. So I love it."

"Then, his castration started in the home and not during the rescue."

"He only spends about three pages on the rescue. There's a few hints about what went on under the Timms family sheets. From what I can tell, he pursued her madly to marry him, she finally relented, he adored her, he did everything for her and it bored her to tears."

"Like it would you."

"Who wants a lapdog? Where's the romance in that? So she left."

"Old Bobby Timms, fire chief, a strong leader in public, willingly pussy-whipped in private."

"That's about it. It didn't matter that everybody else thought he was a hero, he wanted his ex to think so too." She resumed typing at the same fast speed as her husband. "You're not having doubts about getting past the surface on this, are you? Because if you are, this story is over right now. Without the overview, it's just a touchy-feely chronology. Tell me you want blood."

"I need blood. I don't owe these people anything. I had to put up with their hicky 'howdy's and 'saints be praised's for a year and a half. That's about the same sentence for first-time robbery. Besides, we'll be long gone by the time this shows up in *Insight*. If anybody's feelings are hurt, they can write me and I'll relay their complaints to the shredder."

Higgins smiled. She closed her laptop and set it aside.

"You're bad."

Clark closed his laptop and stood. He moved toward Higgins on the bed and began to remove his shirt.

"That makes two of us . . ."

Kathleen Saunders worked the phones.

"That won't work. We need to be in San Diego on the ninth; from there we have our retreat in Sedona. You'll have to shuffle your speakers if you want us, and I've told you that from the very beginning. . . . Yes, I understand. Now *you* understand: This is not how Diana French operates. We do not adjust our schedule for you, you adjust your schedule for us. . . . Uh-huh. Tell you what. I'll be returning your advance. Good luck and bye-bye."

She hung up. Diana French, dressing for the evening, stood at the closet mirror and looked at the reflection of her capable assistant as she sat at the veneered dining table. Katheleen doodled on a complimentary stationery pad.

"Five, four . . ."

The phone rang. Kathleen lifted the receiver.

"Hello, Dr. French's office. Kate Saunders speaking. How may I help you? . . . Uh-huh, I see. You'll rearrange your speakers to fit us in? Well, thank you for your help. We appreciate it. . . . Uh-huh, looking forward to seeing you too. Okay, bye-bye." She hung up again. "San Francisco is on."

Diana sighed.

"I am so tired of this."

"That's not true; you enjoy speaking."

"Speaking, yes. I'm tired of this. This." She waved her arms at their room in the Whistle Stop. "I want this to be over."

"I've booked a flight for tomorrow night. We'll leave as soon as the parade is over."

"If it hadn't been for that bastard Clark . . . If I hadn't shown up for this ridiculous ceremony, he would have made me seem like the ice queen. I just don't need this right now. This Baby Andromeda thing has been my ball and chain long enough."

"You really didn't want to come, did you?"

"If I never see Andromeda Wiley again, it'll be too soon."

"Pardon my 'whoa.' "

Diana turned, softening.

"I know, Kate, I'm horrible. But I hate her. Okay, I said it. I hate her. And don't you ever repeat any of this."

"You know I wouldn't. What did she do to you?"

Diana recalled hundreds of discussions with Andromeda. She recalled a typical one, in which she addressed Andromeda in her most professional and adult manner. "Andie, you need to allow yourself to trust me. When you accept your vulnerabilities, you'll be able to trust what I say, you'll be able to do as I say." She recalled seven-year-old Andromeda smiling back and saying, "Now, are we talking about me or are we talking about you?"

Diana pulled on her suit jacket.

"She's who she is and that's enough."

FORTY-EIGHT

ENCOUNTER

As Will and Andromeda walked side by side along a forested path that skirted Wishbone's muddy waterway, formations of geese flew high above, squawking their way south for the winter. The twilight breeze blowing through the tall elms tore loose dying leaves to blanket the path ahead. Large white clouds lazily drifted over the gurgling stream that had recently accepted the compacted ashes of Cullman Shermer. The scene was idyllic.

Neither Will nor Andromeda paid heed to the postcard scenery. Both walked with eyes aimed at their feet.

Flustered by Will's silence, Andromeda spoke first.

"Will, we've walked nearly a mile. You keep acting like you have something to say, but every time I think you're ready to say something, you just clam up." Will remained silent and Andromeda sighed in exasperation. "Look, you're obviously upset about something. My guess is it has to do with me." She turned to Will and waited for elaboration. It did not come. "So you're really going to make me play fifty questions. Okay, is it animal? Is it vegetable? Is it Gummy Bear?" She watched as Will broke a small smile. Reaching out, she pushed his smile higher. "That's better. Now, will you tell me what's wrong?"

Will gently pulled Andromeda's hand from his face and submerged his smile. He looked to his sister and wondered how to explain his concerns without damaging their still tenuous relationship.

"I just wish I could read your mind."

"I'm an open book, Will. If you want to know something, just ask."

Will breathed in deep to calm his nerves. He exhaled.

"I want to know why you went to see Shermer."

"I told you why, to say thanks."

"At night when no one else is around? Why not during the day? Better yet, why not wait until the parade?"

"Why not . . ." Andromeda stopped abruptly in the path and turned narrowing eyes on Will. She took a long pause before speaking. "I don't believe it. Do you . . . do you think I had something to do with Shermer's death?"

"I . . . I don't think that . . ."

"You do. I can see it in your eyes."

Will averted his eyes. He took a few steps farther down the path, but Andromeda did not move. Will slowly turned to again face her.

"First Randy and then Shermer, all on the same day."

"Oh my God. So I made Randy Vale attack his brother too?" Andromeda began to pace. "Will, how could I have anything to do with either of those things? I mean, what else do you want to accuse me of? Earthquakes in China? Famine in Africa? The hole in the ozone layer?"

"I don't want to accuse you of anything."

"Like hell you don't!" Andromeda's pacing intensified along with her evident fury. "I come back after fifteen years, you barely say anything to me the whole time I'm gone, and now, just because I'm around when a couple odd things happen, you blame me for it? How many times do I have to prove myself to you?"

She glared at her brother and he felt his resolve withering under her stare. With his thoughts now jumbled, Will was hard pressed to deliver a reasoned response.

"Ever since you fell in that hole, you've changed."

"And how can you tell? You haven't lifted a finger to get to know me."

"I feel it."

"The only thing that's changed is the way you treat me. One day we're inseparable, five days later I'm a leper. In case you haven't noticed, dear brother, I've paid my fucking dues!"

Andromeda turned and stormed off down the path. Standing mute for a long beat, Will gulped. He watched as Andromeda disappeared around a bend.

"Ah . . . goddamn . . ."

Moving slowly out of embarrassment and a sudden sense of shame, Will took up the chase.

. . .

The bitch was alone and she was not paying attention.

The moment he had waited for had finally arrived.

It was time for payback.

Randy crouched low near the forest path that ran to the creek from behind Holson's Deli and hefted the hunk of one-inch oak doweling. He had paralleled the bitch and her brother through the creek woods for over an hour, waiting to see if he would get a chance with her alone. After witnessing an argument between the Wiley brother and the target, Randy felt warmed inside as she stomped off by herself.

She was now only a few feet away and she had not noticed Randy. Her cheeks were wet from crying and she kept her eyes aimed at the ground. Feeling the jar of acid between his feet, Randy thought with deep satisfaction that he would wipe away her tears along with her face.

He held the oak rod tight and stayed silent as Andromeda Wiley took two steps past. Then he stepped from the bushes.

Andromeda reacted too late as Randy stepped out from the forest undergrowth and swung the doweling. With a thudding impact, he smacked the back of her head. Her eyes closed and she fell without resistance to the forest floor.

Tossing the dowel aside, Randy quickly grabbed her arms and began dragging her into the woods. As he pulled her toward the spot where he would shred her beauty with the burning liquid, he couldn't help but wonder if he shouldn't enjoy that beauty one last time before it was gone forever.

Will rounded the bend, expecting to see Andromeda somewhere on the long, straight section ahead that led to the back of Holson's Deli. Yet he saw nothing. Wondering if she had decided to sprint this last section of path, and deducing that meant she wanted to get away from him as fast as possible, he almost missed the drag lines running into the dense undergrowth.

Will's well-honed instincts suddenly called for caution.

He parted the undergrowth and stepped into the forest. Thirty steps farther he saw Andromeda, lying unconscious in a heap and partially covered by decaying leaves.

"Andie?"

Forgetting their fifteen-year divide, Will rushed forward to save his sister.

He suddenly felt a shaft of cold steel press against his neck.

"That's far enough, dickie."

Will froze and knew the voice in an instant.

"Randy Vale . . ."

As Will carefully turned, Randy's twisted smile came into view.

"That's my name. Don't wear it out."

Will glanced to Randy's gloved hand. In it he held a blue-black revolver. His finger rested on the trigger. He kept the gun aimed at Will's head as he backed up a step. Will tried to sound calm.

"What's that for? What are you doing?"

"I overheard your little spat. You think she made me go after Pat. If you think she's a mind-fuck too, then I know I'm right. I mean, who can do shit like that? Only witches and shit."

Will watched as Randy revealed a glass jar. A clear liquid filling the jar sloshed against the cap.

Randy answered Will's questioning stare.

"You ever pour salt on a slug? Watch it melt? That shit's got to hurt, man. Your bitch sister hurt me; she hurt me bad. Time she feels my pain."

Keeping his gun trained on Will, Randy moved closer to Andromeda until he was right above her. He held the jar over her unconscious face. As Randy spun off the cap, Will received a whiff of a familiar substance.

He was suddenly very worried.

"Randy, come on, man, what are you going to do with that?"

"Gonna watch Baby Andromeda burn. . . ."

As Randy began to tip the jar, Will felt his leg muscles spring into action before his mind knew it.

"Don't!"

Will dove for Randy. But the dive was a miss. Randy sidestepped Will, slammed the pistol butt down on Will's temple, and Will crashed into the musty turf. He struggled to keep from joining his sister in forced slumber.

Will lifted a dazed face to Randy as he brought the pistol even closer—now inches away and aimed right at Will's forehead.

"D . . . don't . . ."

Randy chuckled.

"Right."

Randy began to squeeze the trigger. Anticipating the coming impact, Will began to close his eyes. He stopped when he saw movement behind Randy. He saw Andromeda open her eyes and glare at Randy's back.

She spoke with perfect calm.

"I'll bet you're thirsty."

Randy's finger suddenly froze on the trigger.

"N-no . . ." He stood and tossed aside the gun. He grabbed the open jar of acid with both hands even as they began shaking. In seconds his face was wet with cold sweat. "No!"

Still clutching the jar of acid, he rushed back onto the path and ran at high speed toward Holson's Deli.

Will locked eyes with Andromeda and felt chilled by her total serenity.

Forcing himself to his feet, he snapped up Randy's gun and staggered off in pursuit.

Lois Knowles, anticipating an evening of beer and canasta with friends, stood at the counter at Holson's Deli and tried to decide on meat cuts for the group sandwich. Behind her, a line of anxious patrons pondered their own sandwich choices. In the midst of this slow-moving ritual, the back door to Holson's Deli suddenly banged open and Randy Vale, out of sight for days, rushed in to make a bold appearance. His eyes were wild in frenzied torment.

"I'm really thirsty! I'm really fuckin' thirsty!"

Holding aloft an open jar of some clear liquid, Randy stood before Lois and the stunned deli crowd and began gulping down its contents. As an acrid smoke started rising from Randy's mouth, as his lips puffed and bubbled and as he began convulsing violently, Lois was the first to state the obvious.

"Hey, that isn't water!"

Quickly emptied, the jar dropped from Randy Vale's hands and crashed to the floor. What little liquid remained was corrosive enough to instantly etch pits and holes in the linoleum.

Everyone watched speechlessly as Randy stood in a tottering spasm, his terrified eyes open to their widest. The entire area around his mouth was now a red, pink and white landscape of bursting lesions.

The last, tortured exhale Randy Vale would ever make exited his scorched lips. He fell dead into the salad bar, and its contents tipped to the floor.

Quick-thinking mothers and fathers averted the eyes of their little ones as other patrons cut loose screams to match the horror. No one thought as yet to approach Randy Vale as his corpse shuddered through its final throes.

As radishes and broccoli chunks skittered helter-skelter, as salad dressings and carrot slivers cascaded over the body of Randy Vale, Will rushed in the back door. Still holding the gun and seeing its reason for being had just expired, Will shoved it into his pants and covered it with his loose shirt. He stood staring at the body of Randy Vale with as much shock as any. The horror reached its apex as the acid burning through Randy's midsection split his belly and spilled his smoking innards over the pocked tiles. Lois Knowles was one of the few who did not faint.

Will suddenly felt a cold presence behind him. He knew right away that he had felt this chill before, and the memory returned with full impact.

It was the chill from their old basement.

Spinning around, he saw Andromeda standing just outside the door in the back lot of the deli. She said nothing and she made no gesture but Will felt drawn to her. He felt drawn to the chill.

Exiting the deli, he moved to his sister and tried to figure out which question to ask first. He chose the most obvious.

"How?"

Andromeda brushed out the wrinkles in her clothes and stood looking none the worse for wear.

"A better question is why."

"Why?"

Andromeda's perfect lips turned up in the slightest of smiles.

"Why not?"

Without another word, she walked back into the forest. Will watched her disappear in the growing dark.

As a bright moon rose on the horizon and as the evening wind picked up, he stood frozen, realizing his familiar fear had become reality. Andromeda was more than who and what she appeared to be.

Then what is she?

Will was soon led to an even more frightening question.

What does she want?

FORTY-NINE
THE FEAR

Will drove from town with bloodshot eyes unblinking. His hands grabbed the steering wheel of his truck so tightly that his knuckles grew white. He failed to notice as he ran stop signs, and the honks from narrowly avoided collisions never reached his numbed consciousness.

In his lap sat Randy Vale's revolver.

It gave him little comfort.

He possessed a weapon for an unknown defense, but lacked any knowledge of Andromeda's whereabouts. The thought twisted his guts. Knowing where she was and knowing what she was up to was the one piece of information Will absolutely needed to know. Yet he had run from maintaining that knowledge. He had run from Andromeda because it was the only thing his mind and body would let him do.

When Andromeda casually walked back into the forest after Randy Vale's provoked suicide, Will knew he should pursue her. He knew he should stop her and wrest free the answers he needed. But his feet would not move. In abject terror, he was incapable of following his little sister into the darkening woods. All he could do was stand mute as she vanished in the dark, his ears hearing only the screaming witnesses to Randy Vale's liquefaction. So he sped from the scene. Yet distance did not lessen the power of what he had seen. As he brooded further, he was drawn closer and closer to a single image that eventually dominated all.

Andromeda's eyes.

They were the windows into a soul he now knew was beyond imagining. To know that soul, to discover its heart, to learn its intent meant Will would have to look into those eyes. He would have to peer deep for his answers. He would be forced to face his fear.

As he reached down and took hold of the cold, steel pistol, he knew that he would first have to find Andromeda.

FIFTY

FACE-OFF

Lisa jumped as Will stormed into their barn loft apartment.

"Holy shit! You scared the hell out of me."

"Have you seen her?"

"Who?"

"Andie. Did she come back?"

"I don't know; I've been here all day. Besides, I thought she was with you."

"She was." Will began an agitated pace down the length of the loft. "So you haven't seen her."

"No, I have not seen her. Will, what's going on? Did something happen to Andie?"

Will suddenly saw in vivid detail a perfect image of Randy Vale dropping dead into Holson's salad bar. He felt he could still smell the foul odor of acid-seared flesh.

Will stopped pacing and shook his head in dismay.

"She killed him. She killed him. . . ."

"What? Who? Killed who?"

"Andie. She killed Randy Vale."

"Randy Vale is dead? Oh my God, how?"

"She made him drink acid. . . . She . . . she . . . "

Lisa rose as Will struggled to find the words. Moving to Will, clearly seeing his torment, Lisa spoke calmly.

"What do you mean she made him?"

"She made him drink a fucking jar of acid! He burned his guts out right on the floor of Holson's Deli! Jesus Christ! I . . . I don't even know what she is!"

"You mean *who*."

"I mean *what*! That thing, whatever she or it is . . . that is not my sister!" Lisa felt tears of fright blurring her sight.

"Will, please, you're really scaring me. What's wrong with you? You're not making any sense!"

"There's nothing wrong with me. It's her, that thing that says it's Andie." He looked blankly into space, as if to find something capable of providing an answer. "I don't know what to do. . . . What do I do?"

"Please tell me what happened."

Will breathed deep to calm his nerves.

"We were walking along the river and we had an argument. Andie walked off and when I went after her I saw her lying in the woods—she was unconscious. Vale stepped out and put a gun to my head. He was going to shoot me, and then he was going to pour acid on Andie's face—"

"Oh God, Will—"

"—but she came to, and all she said was 'I bet you're thirsty.' Vale dropped the gun and ran into Holson's and then he drank the acid and I saw the whole thing and now . . . and now . . ."

"And now what?"

"Now I don't know what to do. I don't know what to do about Andromeda." Lisa stood mute a long while before stepping back from Will. She frowned in silent concern as she looked on her lover. Will acknowledged her concerned look. "You don't believe me."

Lisa fought back tears.

"You come rushing in here and . . . and you tell me Randy Vale is dead and . . . and then you say Andie did it, but then you tell me all she really did was say 'I bet you're thirsty' when he was getting ready to kill you and burn off her face. . . . It's all so horrible and unbelievable, but . . . I mean, if it really did happen and Randy Vale really is dead, well . . . how can you stand there and blame Andie for it? What has gotten into you? You keep saying you don't know Andie anymore. Well, who are *you*? You're her brother but you keep making these crazy accusations. How can you even think those things about her? You don't know *her*? I'm beginning to think I don't know *you* at all."

Will's face suddenly drained of color.

"You know me. I'm your Will."

Lisa released her tears as she passed the breaking point.

"I don't know shit! What's happened to you? I just don't get what you're trying to do!"

Will moved to Lisa but she took another step back.

"What . . . are you . . . are you scared of me?"

"I . . . I don't know." She thought for another moment. "Maybe I am."

"But it's her. It's not me, it's her!"

"Stop it! Stop saying that! Goddammit, what has gotten into you! How can Andie do these things? You're not thinking right. People don't just say things that make other people kill themselves. That doesn't happen!"

"It does happen. I saw it!"

"You don't know what you saw. You've been trying to find a reason to keep hating Andie since the day I met you, and now that she's here you blame her for every fucked-up thing that happens in this fucked-up town!" She let out her breath, wiped her eyes and tried to look at Will with patience even as her mind raced. "You need help. You're not thinking right. We need to find you some help."

Will stood like stone and flexed his jaw.

"You mean someone like Diana French."

Lisa moved to Will and took his hands as she stared into his eyes.

"She might be able to help you. You're not well, baby."

Will pulled his hands free and stepped from Lisa for the first time as an opponent.

"I know what I saw. Andie killed Randy Vale just like she killed Cullman Shermer. How, I don't know. What I do know, since you won't believe me, is I'm all alone on this."

"But I can't believe you. It's too much. You're not being fair—"

"What's fair? When has any of this shit been fair? Practically my whole life I've had to deal with one thing or another that has to do with Andie falling down that fucking hole! And now what do I find out? I find out what I've always suspected is true. I find out whatever it was that I pulled out of that hole was not my sister."

"If she's not Andie, then what is she?"

Will stepped past Lisa and started down the steps.

"That's what I plan to find out."

"Will, wait!" Lisa rushed after Will as he went down the steps two at a time. She caught up to him as he reached the door at the bottom of the steps and began to draw it open. "What are you going to do?"

"I know what she's not. I have to find out what she is."

Will swung open the door and froze solid.

Andromeda stood before him with a tender smile.

"Hey, you guys about ready for dinner?"

Will stood staring at Andromeda for a long beat, unable to find words or action. Lisa broke the impasse.

"Andie, what happened to Randy Vale?"

Andromeda turned a disappointed gaze on Will.

"Jesus, Will, you weren't supposed to tell."

Lisa responded before Will had a chance.

"So something did happen . . ." She questioned further: "Andie, I need to know what it was."

Will found his voice.

"So do I."

Andromeda turned to Lisa with a face filling with distress.

"You have to promise not to tell our mom or dad, or anybody. We don't need to get involved in this mess."

"I won't tell; I promise."

Andromeda let out a sigh as she prepared to speak.

"Me and Will . . . we were walking at the river and we had . . . we had a little spat, I guess. I ran off, something hit me in the head, and the next thing I know I'm lying on my face in the woods and Randy Vale is five feet away with a gun to Will. He had this jar or something in his hand and . . . I thought he was going to kill Will but then, I don't know, he just flipped or something, like someone flicked a switch in his head. He dropped the gun and ran up to Holson's Deli. Will ran after him. By the time I got up to Will, Vale was . . . he was . . ." Andromeda shook as if with a heavy chill. "I-I don't want to talk about the rest . . ."

"Is Randy Vale dead?"

"Is he? I don't know. All I saw was that his mouth was all . . ." She gestured to Will. "Will saw all of it. What does he say?"

"He says you killed Randy Vale."

Andromeda's open jaw matched her widening eyes in stunned shock. "What?"

"He says you said something to Randy that made him drink from that jar."

Andromeda closed her jaw and looked on Will with a face laced with disdain.

"You just can't stop, can you?"

Andromeda suddenly turned and began heading back to the main house. Will called after her.

"You know what you did! And you know I saw what you did!"

Andromeda stopped cold in her tracks and slowly spun to face Will and Lisa as they remained standing in the doorway of the barn loft.

"I know that I killed Randy Vale? Cullman Shermer too? Is that what you want to hear, Will? A confession? Okay, fine. I did it. Now can we eat?"

She again turned toward the main house and began walking off. Lisa glanced at Will and her eyes became slivers of fury. She pushed away from him and followed Andromeda.

"You have to keep trying to ruin it."

"Lisa, wait—"

"Don't even talk to me!"

Will stood alone in the loft doorway and watched as Andromeda and Lisa disappeared into the main house. The familiar sounds of crickets, distant hounds and far-off freight trains barely broke the silence of the night. But within Will, the raging sound of his torment was a roar growing louder by the second. It threatened to deafen all reason as he considered his lonely position as the only person on earth who knew a monster had switched places with his sister. The only sound he now heard in his head was the voice of his own resolve.

The monster would be revealed.

The monster would be revealed tonight.

FIFTY-ONE

THE CALM BEFORE

"**P**ass the salt."

Lisa grabbed the shaker and handed it to Peter, who sprinkled his freshly buttered corn. He talked as he munched.

"How does it work? We give a speech and then there's a parade?"

Trying hard to act unflustered, to seem normal, Lisa shook her head.

"There's a parade into town. The parade stops at Courthouse Square Park, so you guys can give some speeches from the bandstand, and then Will and Andromeda get on a float as the parade heads out to Andromeda's Tomb."

Sandra finished her glass of red wine and frowned.

"I hate that name. It's not a tomb. Andie didn't die down there."

Andromeda patted her riled mother on the hand.

"They call it that for the tourists, Mom."

"You mean Denny Sharf calls it that. I especially don't like that."

The side door opened and Will walked in. He stood staring at the dinner scene for a moment before moving to a seat directly opposite Andromeda. As he sat, as brother and sister stared across the table with barely concealed venom, Lisa cautiously changed subjects.

"Did anybody . . . did anybody hear about Randy Vale drinking a jar of acid in Holson's Deli?"

Peter nodded.

"We heard the sick bastard killed himself. Didn't hear he drank acid. I didn't want to mention it because I'm tired of hearing about those two. I never could stomach those Vale punks."

Sandra was miffed.

"Now, is that the charitable thing to say? He was obviously a troubled soul."

"If he didn't do it to himself, he would have done it to someone else. That Randy especially—I always thought he had murder on his mind."

Will looked across the table to Andromeda and their eyes met. He suddenly felt disoriented as she looked to him with softer eyes. She was now sending Will a look that was pleading and hopeful. In the face of her wordless sincerity, he fought to remain in opposition. She was not what she appeared to be and he was determined to remember it.

But like a calming opiate, Andromeda's look began to quell the storm of suspicion within Will. He blinked and turned his gaze to his food.

Sandra moved forward with her train of thought.

"I'm not condoning the things those Vales did. Everyone knows they were a bad pair. I'm just saying we should be even more thankful for what we have when we see how others live their lives."

Andromeda set her eyes on her mother.

"And what do we have, Mom?"

"We have everything. We're all here, we're all healthy, we're all happy. We're still a family. I know this sounds horrible, but I wonder sometimes if we shouldn't thank your whole experience, Andie. I mean, where would we be now?"

Will spoke with sourness.

"We'd be a normal family."

Andromeda looked to Will.

"No, Mom's right. Our lives would be nothing right now if I hadn't spent almost a week in a hole, scared to death, thirsty, starving, peeing in my pants, having worms and bugs crawl on me, having dirt fall on me, not being able to sleep, having nightmares, thinking I was about to die. What's five days of hell in exchange for a lifetime of heaven?"

"You don't mean that."

"Yeah, I mean it. It sounds like a pretty good deal to me. In fact, if I was broke and starving, maybe homeless, with no future, and somebody told me if I spent five days in a hole then my whole life would change, that I'd get a house and cars and new clothes and new friends and fifteen years later they'd throw me a parade, I'd say show me the hole. Right, Mom?"

Andromeda turned on Sandra. Sandra and Peter suddenly stopped eating.

"I . . . I don't know if I would go that far, honey. . . ."

"Well, I would. If I was in the position you guys were in—two kids, nowhere to go—I'd sure think about it." Andromeda finished her meal and stood. "Well, that was great, as usual. I'm off to take a drive."

"Where to?"

"I don't know. Around. Don't wait up."

Shaken, Peter could not believe how close Andromeda had come to the truth.

"Honey, is everything okay?"

"I don't see how things could be any better."

"Okay. Well, just be careful."

"I've already fallen in my hole. That sort of lightning doesn't strike twice."

As Andromeda headed down the hall for the front door, Will stood. Lisa reached out and tightly squeezed his wrist.

"Where are you going?"

Will pried Lisa's hand from his wrist.

"I'm just going to talk."

Will followed Andromeda down the hall and out the front door. As he pulled it shut, Sandra turned to Lisa with a worried expression. After Andromeda's comments, feeling like a traitor on the verge of being revealed, Sandra sought reassurance.

"Everything is okay, isn't it?"

Lisa turned back to the table and struggled to squelch her concerns.

"Yeah. Yeah, everything's fine."

"Really? Because I want everything to be right."

Lisa answered with total conviction.

"Me too . . ."

In the cool night, brother and sister once again faced each other as strangers.

"We have to talk."

"I'm through talking. I need some air."

As Andromeda began walking off, Will reached out and grabbed her arm. She spun on him and her turmoil was evident. Looking into her eyes and feeling the familiar chill, feeling a fear of the unknown, Will suddenly thought it wiser to avoid provoking her. He had seen her kill Randy Vale with her voice. What else she was capable of, he didn't care to know.

He let her arm slip from his hand, and shoved his hands in his pockets to appear less threatening.

"It's just you and me now, so don't try to deny it. We both know you killed Randy Vale. I want you to tell me about Shermer."

"Shermer had fifteen years to change for the better. So did Randy Vale. They failed."

"So you killed them."

"They got themselves killed."

"A lot of people haven't changed for the better in the last fifteen years. Are they about to get themselves killed too?"

Andromeda kept silent but did not retreat further. Will pressed on.

"What happened to you in that hole?"

"You said it yourself, Will. I changed."

"Into what?" Now it was Will who examined Andromeda. "What . . . what are you?"

Andromeda was suddenly angry.

"I'm me! I'm Andie! I'm skin, I'm bones! I'm hair, I'm teeth!" She lifted an arm and pinched some skin to prove her point. "I'm your little sister. I always have been and I always will be."

"You're not. You can't be."

"Of course I can because I am! What else could I be? You think I'm a ghost? You think I'm a bogeyman? You think I'm some kind of monster from the deep? Here, touch me. Come on, take my hand." Will did not move to take Andromeda's hand as she jutted it out. Andromeda's eyes closed tighter. "I said, take my hand."

Will cautiously reached up and took Andromeda's hand in his own. He could feel her soft skin in his calloused palm. He could feel her warmth and he could feel the pulse of her beating heart.

Andromeda again softened.

"Is that the hand of a monster?"

Will stood still a moment, fighting his internal battle. On one hand he fought to convince himself Andromeda was not human, that she was some other being who had switched places with his long-gone sister. On the other hand, he found he wanted nothing more than to believe everything Andromeda said. He wanted his sister. He wanted her back more than anything.

Will continued holding Andromeda's hand.

"I don't know. I don't know anything anymore. People can't do what you do!" He let Andromeda's hand fall from his own. "All I know is, my Andie wouldn't kill."

Andromeda took her time responding as her eyes grew moist.

"Your Andie died a long time ago, Will. She died in that hole. You've known it all along."

As Andromeda's voice quavered, Will felt his internal battle being won by the desire to have her back. She stood before him with naked emotion and he suddenly felt protective.

"I think she's still here. I think she just lost her way."

A tear raced along the outside of Andromeda's cheek and dropped from her chin. She began backing up toward Sandra's Mercedes. As she opened the door, she looked to Will with ancient sadness.

"Some people never find their way back from the dark."

"Let me help. I saved you once. Let me save you again."

"You only get to be my hero once. . . ."

Andromeda slid behind the wheel, closed the door and started the car. The Mercedes kicked back gravel as she turned the car up the drive and disappeared into the night.

She did not turn on the lights.

Will could only hear the car as it grew more distant in the darkness.

"You have to turn on the light . . ."

Peter sat in bed and waited for his wife to finish her nightly duties. Impatient, he called into the bathroom, "Come in here. I can't discuss it like this."

In the bathroom Sandra sat on the closed toilet. She wore the face of a shoplifter who has not left the store and who believes she was spotted.

"You said we weren't going to talk about it ever again."

"That was before. That was before tonight."

"What about tonight?"

Tired of waiting for his wife to leave the bathroom, Peter tossed aside the covers and walked in to face her. He sat against the sink counter as she spun on the toilet seat to avoid his direct gaze.

"You heard what she said. I don't think she was talking idle chat. I think Andie knows something."

"How could she know anything, Peter? She doesn't know. What's to know? There's nothing to know. She's my daughter, she thinks like me— that's all it was. Thinking."

Peter looked down at Sandra. He just couldn't understand.

"All these years all I've wanted is for you to say you feel bad about what we did. That's it. I haven't been asking you to join a nunnery or spend a year in prison or carry stones on your back. I just need to know you feel as bad as I do."

"About what, for God's sake! You just go on and on about it! We didn't do anything, Peter. It was an accident. She fell in a hole. We did not dig that hole. That hole was there. If we did dig it, then maybe . . . maybe . . . But it was there, it was there already. She fell and . . . and . . . you just have to ruin it every time it starts getting good between us, don't you?"

"What am I ruining? What am I ruining if we can't even admit we feel bad or possibly even terrible about what we were planning to do to Will but did to Andromeda instead? Why is it so hard for you to just say it?"

Sandra turned to Peter and her face showed genuine grief.

"Because I didn't mean for her to fall in that hole. I don't know why I should hate myself the way you hate yourself because of an accident." Sandra was crying now. "I felt like dying when Andie called up out of that place. How much worse do I have to feel, Peter? How much is enough? I'd give everything away if I could go back in time and stop her from falling in. I just wanted her to be happy!"

Feeling his usual compromise coming on, Peter sighed and knelt to lay a hand on his crying wife's shoulders.

"I know all that. I know you want her to be happy."

"Well then, what? She *is* happy; everyone can see that. We can be happy too. Why shouldn't we be? I just can't take you hitting me with this anymore. I want to forget it forever, Peter. It just hurts too much to remember."

"I know it hurts."

"So stop, then. She doesn't know. She's just a smart girl."

"She is smart."

Sandra sniffled, yanked off some toilet paper and wiped her nose.

"Of course she is; she has you for a father."

"And you for a mother."

Sandra faced Peter. She put her hands around his neck and pulled his forehead to hers. He soaked in her warmth. "Andie is happy. I guess that's what matters." He pulled away from Sandra and stood. The argument was over. "You coming to bed?"

"In a minute. I have to do my eyebrows."

"All right. 'Night."

Peter left Sandra. She closed the door shut and wiped the last tears from her eyes. She stood at the mirror. Lifting her tweezers, she began pulling out errant hairs that threatened to ruin the graceful arc of her eyebrows.

"We should all be as happy as Andie. . . ."

FIFTY-TWO

MIDNIGHT RENDEZVOUS

Andromeda drove through the pitch-black countryside for twenty minutes with her headlights off. In the dark of those twenty minutes an old memory rose to fill her thoughts.

She was back in the hole, held tight by the roots. The *poom-poom* was close and loud. It was all she could hear. It was all she could feel. She was drawn into the void and her body was dying.

But just as she began to give up, as she prepared to surrender to the void, a hand reached into the darkness and pulled her into the light. A familiar voice caused her to open her eyes, and the first thing she saw as her life started anew was the face of her brother.

Now, fifteen years later, Will was again trying to pull her from the dark.

She knew it was possible to let him. Will could again be her hero, or at least he could be allowed to think he was. Andromeda had the power to live the life that Will and their parents hoped she would. But to live that life, she had to give up the dark.

It would be like giving up her heart.

As she blindly drove through the still night, the hopes and needs of her family battled her newer impulses. She considered trying to live life the way Will expected, and she began to tremble. Every muscle in her body twitched and torqued, letting her know she would suffer a thousand little deaths every day she fought her instincts.

For Andromeda, the idea of it was as unnatural as breathing underwater. She would choke on the light. She would find herself fighting horrendously to act like the others, to think like the others, to live and love like the others. But she would lose the fight because she was not like any other. The light was no longer her world.

The dark was her new world.

The dark was her new sanctuary.

She shouted out to no one in particular, "I . . . I can't!"

Her car straddled the white dashes dividing her from what little opposing traffic she had encountered in the darkness. As headlights from an approaching van broke the night ahead and flashed on her darkened Mercedes, and as a blaring horn shattered the silence, Andromeda yanked the car back into her own lane. She finally realized she had not turned on her headlights.

Andromeda flicked them on to pierce the darkness. The first object that came into view was a large, colorful billboard. It showed a beautiful home in luxurious surroundings. Elegant letters told Andromeda she had reached Royal Oak Gardens.

She was home.

Shoving down on the brake pedal, she skidded the Mercedes onto the graveled shoulder. With the engine still idling, she looked back to the four-lane paved road with landscaped center divider cutting into the new neighborhood. From her father's letters she knew the entry road lay exactly where her family once had their gravel drive.

She looked down the road bordered by full trees and trim abodes and tried to picture the placement of the run-down shack she had once called home. Without landmarks it was impossible to tell. Only Denny Sharf, who had overseen the construction of every home, had that power.

Andromeda shook off Will's conception of who she should be and remembered why she had come back to Wishbone. She remembered what she had come to do.

She checked the Mercedes's clock and saw it was midnight.

Andromeda put the car into reverse, backed up and turned into the drive. Passing stately homes, she stopped when she reached Denny's address. It was a large two-story house. Through the tall plate glass of the entry she could see a long chandelier of smoked-glass rectangles. The yard had not a leaf out of place, and as she pulled into the drive the sprinkler system burst on.

Andromeda left the Mercedes and walked down the mortared cobble path to the front door. Pushing the doorbell, she heard a grand chime echo within the house. The sound of steps grew closer and Denny Sharf opened the door. The heavy scent of cologne wafted out after him. He was freshly shaved, and what hair he had left on his head was slicked down into a vague semblance of style. He wore an unused outfit plucked from a catalog: corduroy slacks, wool shirt, cotton turtleneck underneath and deerskin slippers on his feet. He held a scotch on the rocks in his hand. He smiled a knowing smile.

"Come in."

"I think your sprinklers got me a little bit wet."

Denny led Andromeda into his home and shut the door. He glanced out the windows to see if anybody was watching. Satisfied, he turned back to Andromeda and led her farther in as she tilted her gaze from ceiling to floor.

"You got wet? Do you need to dry off . . . or anything?"

"No, I . . . " She stopped as she saw through the family room patio door a well-lit pool in the backyard. "You have a pool."

"Just like the one at your house. The same contractor—"

"Show me."

"Of course. This way."

Denny escorted Andromeda through his family room to the patio door. He slid the door aside, and she stepped out onto the deck encircling the underlit waters. The entire backyard was ringed by an eight-foot-high fence. No other house could be seen. Andromeda moved to the pool and dipped her hand in the water.

"It's a little cool, but still warm enough."

"Did you . . . I mean, would you . . . "

"Are you asking me if I'd like to take a swim, Denny?"

"If that's what you'd like."

"I don't know. I didn't bring a suit." Andromeda looked at the backyard perimeter. "Doesn't look like anybody could see in, though."

"Nobody can see anything."

"What're you drinking?"

"A scotch on the rocks."

"Make mine straight."

"Be right back."

Denny moved back into his house without removing his eyes from the three-dimensional fantasy of Andromeda Wiley. He quickly made his way to his wet bar and fumbled open a bottle of Glenfiddich. Pouring a good-sized straight shot he walked back out to Andromeda at the pool. She stood where he had left her, filling those lovely tight slacks and staring into the inviting, clear depths of the mildly heated pool. Denny handed her the glass.

"Here you go."

"Thanks." She took the nearly full shot glass and tipped it back, swallowing its contents in one gulp. She handed back the empty glass and wiped her mouth. "Whew, that was just what I needed."

She shook her body as if to toss off a chill and then she began to stretch just like Denny had seen her do in her bedroom. Denny sat with his drink to watch. He looked at her chest and remembered the erect nipples of her perfect breasts. He remembered the flat plane of her toned belly. He remembered the dainty patch of down at the split of her legs. He remembered his spontaneous orgasm and he struggled to keep his building erection from repeating the action. Given the fact that she was here and had hinted that she was willing to try things, he felt it was okay to openly watch.

Andromeda closed her eyes and raised her arms over her head.

"Where was our old house in all this?"

"Right here. The pool is where your basement used to be."

Andromeda froze with her legs slightly apart and her arms over her head. She opened her eyes and looked at the pool.

"Right here? Your pool used to be our basement?"

"Yep. That's why I put it there—didn't have to dig another hole."

"Wow . . . " Andromeda suddenly smiled teasingly at Denny. "Nobody can see in here, can they?"

Denny could feel something happening. The smile she was sending him meant something.

"It's as private as it gets."

"I don't know . . . "

"What don't you know?"

"I don't know about taking a swim."

Once again Denny wondered if he was reading her signals right. He thought he should probably offer something to make her feel more secure if she was having doubts.

"If you need a suit, you could probably use one of my wife's. She's a little bigger than you but . . . If you want."

"But you said nobody can see us here."

"That's right. Nobody can see us."

"Then I don't need a suit. . . ."

And right before Denny's eyes she took hold of her shirt and lifted it over her head. Suddenly nude from the waist up, her beautiful breasts were right there for Denny to see, even without binoculars. Andromeda kept her eyes locked on Denny as she kicked off her shoes and unzipped her pants. She stepped out and stood stark naked on Denny's deck. Denny's erection flamed to full strength as he stared at the patch of hair barely cloaking the object of his ultimate desire. The light from the pool cast a rippling glow on Andromeda's perfect skin. She ran her hands over her body as she spun, showing Denny her sensually trim butt and strong back, before turning to face him. She smiled more deeply.

"This feels good."

Andromeda locked eyes with Denny. Her smile grew more intimate. Her hands drifted to her breasts. One hand stayed in place, massaging her breast and teasing her swelling nipple. The other hand slid down farther. She slid it between her legs. She moaned.

"Ohh . . ."

Not six feet from Denny a naked Andromeda Wiley was touching herself as he had witnessed through her window. His mouth was hanging open.

Andromeda coyly bit her lip like Denny had seen her do before. It had the same electric effect.

"This is all you've ever wanted to see, isn't it? No mountains, no oceans, no other worlds. Just this. Just this shape, my shape, doing this."

"Nothing else . . . just you . . . "

"Would you be my first, Denny?"

"Your . . . your first?"

"My first ever." She let out another little moan of pleasure as she moved her fingers and swayed her body. "You like me?"

"I love you. You're incredible."

"This is only half the picture. Meet the real me?"

"Yes . . . *yes.*"

"Run inside, count to one hundred and come out naked."

"Huh?"

"Do it."

Denny nearly tripped as he rushed into his house. He kept his eyes on naked Andromeda as long as he could. She yelled from outside with a voice begging for what Denny was dying to offer.

"Start counting, lover! Hurry!"

Denny rushed into a bathroom and tore off his clothes.

"One, two, three . . ."

He was naked by the time he reached ten.

"Eleven, twelve, thirteen . . ."

What was waiting for him outside was beyond a *Penthouse* "Forum" moment. This was pure and real heaven. Denny would have paid ten thousand dollars and more to even see what he was seeing. And here she was offering the whole tour for free.

In the mirror he checked out his profile even as he massaged his painful erection. Attempts to suck in his belly were futile; there was too much of it. His arms drooped flab and his skin, dotted with moles small and large and covered with a sporadic mat of curling hairs, was a pale greenish yellow. His posture was extinct. Denny knew he was practically hideous, but that fact might be exactly what turned on the hot and ready beauty touching herself out on his deck. She was probably so jaded by great-looking guys coming on to her that she had grown attracted to the opposite.

And she was a virgin.

Denny would finally screw a virgin.

He had previously thought that feat could be accomplished only by flying to Thailand and buying a ten-year-old girl from her junkie parents before the girl could be sold off to a prostitution ring in exchange for a weeklong high. But here he was getting set to enter not just a homegrown virgin, but the most beautiful woman Denny had ever seen. And she had said nothing about a condom. There would be no plastic to stop him from feeling her juice and her warmth. He would give her his essence flesh to flesh; he would plant his seed deep inside her or maybe in her mouth or maybe somewhere else.

"Sixty-three, sixty-four, sixty-five . . ."

She would taste him. It would last for days. Maybe it could include Laura. Laura might think more of him if she saw what he was getting ready to do right now. Denny Sharf was going to have sex with Baby Andromeda, virgin.

"Ninety-eight, ninety-nine, one hundred."

He again tried to suck in his gut. He stroked himself vigorously for a moment to assuage a quick flush of excitement. Then he stepped out with his precious boner in hand.

"Here I come!"

Denny stepped out onto the pool deck. Andromeda was not to be seen. He heard her voice.

"Over here."

He turned, still holding his stiff boner, and saw that Andromeda was dressed. She sat with her legs crossed in a chair next to the bubbling Jacuzzi. Denny didn't get it.

"What's going on?"

"First you see me, then I see you."

Still not sure what was going on, Denny much preferred the idea that he would just come out with his raging boner to find Andromeda still naked so he could get her on her knees and slide his boner inside her to screw her fast and hard. But she was dressed and he was not, and now his boner started to shrink. Andromeda grabbed a towel, stood and walked toward him. She began circling him to size up his naked body. Denny suddenly felt examined and powerless. His boner grew even softer. Andromeda whispered in his ear.

"Dance for me."

"Dance?"

"I want to see you move."

As out of shape as a man could get, Denny tried to dance in a way he thought might seem sensual, even though there was no music to help. He tried to dance a seventies dance, something that at one time went well with Bachman-Turner Overdrive or Average White Band, but all he could do was jerkily wiggle his fat back and forth. Still, Andromeda didn't seem to mind. She smiled.

"What do you think of me, Denny?"

"You're . . . you're amazing."

"Well, I want you to take some credit for that. If you hadn't arranged for us to move out of our house, I never would have fallen in that hole. Who knows what I'd be now? Probably just some normal, everyday girl."

Denny, getting tired but continuing to dance, huffed out his reply.

"You . . . you're not just . . . an everyday girl."

Andromeda took a moment before responding.

"No, I'm not, am I? But when I lived here, right *here*, in fact, all I wanted was to be a normal, everyday girl. Because of you a normal, every-day girl was something I never got to be."

Denny sensed a subtle change in Andromeda's tone. His dancing slowed.

"Are you—"

"I said dance!"

She snapped Denny across the butt with the towel, firmly enough to make a point. Denny liked it. It was a little bit of Mistress Wanda. He danced with renewed energy. His boner returned and he began playing with it as he danced. Andromeda continued circling him.

"Move closer to the Jacuzzi."

Denny danced his way closer to the Jacuzzi. The water bubbled fero-ciously and steam rose into the cold night. Andromeda moved to stand right before him. His back was to the bubbling water of his custom hot tub, shaped like a big clam. The inviting water steamed resolutely as Denny's own steam started running out. His breath grew short.

"I don't . . . I can't dance . . . much more."

"Would you rather sit in the tub?"

"Yes."

"Then sit."

Andromeda pushed a finger into his bare chest. The force of it was enough to cause Denny to fall back into the hot tub and its bubbling water.

As he gladly fell he flashed on the impending scenario. He would sit in the soothing caress of the swirling waters; Andromeda would stand above him and again slip out of her clothes. She would again stand naked before him. Then she would take a step into the tub. She would let the water wash over her body and it would glisten on her naked skin. She would move to Denny. Under the water she would take his boner in her soft hands, squeezing and stroking it. Then she would straddle him. She would guide his boner inside her tight virgin opening and she would let him bite her nipples as she rode him to mutual ecstasy.

Denny thought all of these thoughts in the four feet of air that separated his standing position and the bubbling water's surface. He was just sec-onds away from the greatest sexual experience of his life. And then he hit the water.

He instantly knew something was wrong.

The Jacuzzi's water was not bubbling because the jets were turned on. The water was bubbling because it was boiling.

Denny shrieked in invincible agony as he went under. Hot enough to cook an egg in three minutes, the water immediately began cooking his body. He thrashed and screamed underwater, and the bubbles from his scream merged with the boiling bubbles of hot air rising from the floor of the tub.

He flailed to the surface, convulsing in excruciating torment, speechless in shock. Through singed eyes he saw Andromeda looking down at him in deep concern.

"Oh my God! Quick, jump in the pool!"

Denny's mind, feeling so much pain—torture pain, dungeon pain, like needles under the fingernails or holes drilled in teeth or electric shocks to the testicles but all over and all at once—somehow heard Andromeda's suggestion. The water of the pool was cool. It would save him.

He scrambled out of the hot tub and finally let loose a crying scream.

"Nayyaagghhh!"

"Jump in the pool!"

Denny staggered to the pool and dove in the shallow end.

Expecting instant relief, he was stunned as the pain suddenly doubled.

Tearing open his eyes as he sank, he watched in horror as sheets of skin began cleaving loose from his body. A familiar mole from his arm drifted off as his skin from wrist to elbow ripped free like wet tissue. Pink droplets of blood and yellow droplets of fat escaped forever as all of Denny's skin, superheated then suddenly cooled, sloughed off and clouded the waters. He felt a flap of skin from his left eye to his chin peeled away. He felt his formerly excited boner split, as even that favored flesh abandoned his body.

He was peeled like a boiled tomato, and his newly exposed nerves felt all there was to feel.

All there was to feel was total agony and unspeakable pain.

Denny suddenly flashed on his terrible experience fifteen years ago in the basement of the Wiley home, on the day of repossession, when he was temporarily trapped. This pool occupied the very same space where he had collapsed to his knees, crying in self-pity because his perversion was on the verge of being discovered. He was back in that basement. He felt that fear. He felt much worse.

Somewhere in his sudden and unexpected hell, his mind told him to stand before he drowned. His ravaged muscles and tendons found the strength, and he staggered upright in the shallow end of the pool. The chilled air raking over his seared and exposed nerves multiplied the pain. He sucked in a sharp breath.

"H-he . . . help . . . "

Andromeda stood at the edge of the pool looking down at the flayed and disfigured creature dripping flesh, fat and blood that was once Denny Sharf. She noticed he had lost an ear and most of his scalp. The other ear looked like it would soon go too. Denny looked up at her with terrified and agonized eyes. He raised an arm and a fold of skin hung down eight inches. Even his fingers were peeling back.

"P . . . lease . . . he . . . lp . . . me."

"I don't think anything can help you now, Denny."

Denny suddenly realized what was going on.

She was killing him.

Andromeda Wiley was killing him on purpose.

He was nothing more than an appetizer to a spider. Her sex was the bait and Denny's life was her prize.

He felt himself sinking into the waters. He knew he would soon suck in a lungful and drown. He would die. But as he saw the last moments of his life quickly playing out, as his knees began to buckle, he forced himself to ask of this beautiful monster who had killed him the last question on his mind.

"Wh . . . why?"

Andromeda thought about the life she would have lived if she had not fallen into that hole.

"Because all I ever wanted to be was an everyday girl."

FIFTY-THREE

THE HAPPY DAY

The weather cooperated and the turnout was better than Wishbone could have hoped.

Tourists from all over came to see the parade, to hear the speeches, to down a pitcher in the beer gardens, to test their skill at skittleball and see how the girl in the hole had turned out. Many who came with family and friends had firsthand stories about Andromeda and the Wileys.

"I helped man the sump pumps when her brother pulled her out. She stared right at me, first thing she cleared that hole. Looked me right in the eyes."

"Our church group donated a bunch of clothes to the Wileys, and I know for a fact Sandra Wiley wore a jacket of mine on TV."

"We buy their produce for our restaurant. They have the best cherry tomatoes anywhere."

"My mom was in the hospital where they brought Andromeda. She got a bunch of the extra flowers people sent in."

"I wrote a letter and sent five bucks. They sent me back a printed thank-you note."

But most had no personal attachment to the saga and were present mainly to have a good time. Up and down Main Street and on the streets encircling Courthouse Square Park, people standing, leaning, sitting on coolers, beach chairs and on seats yanked from vans filled the sidewalks five to ten deep. Children squatting on their parents' shoulders waved American flags or Wagoneer pennants. Teens flirted and slipped through crowds of seniors wearing souvenir straw hats and green visors. Boys riding bikes were warned by Sheriff Austin and his deputies to step down and walk. Vendors pierced the crowds selling sodas, ice cream, cotton candy, Mylar windmills, balloons, peanuts and peanut brittle. Empty avenues separated the sidewalk crowds, and a few clowns engaged in goofy antics to give the folks something to look at before the parade got under way. Two stiltmen did a dance that delighted all.

It was that expectant lull before the festivities, when everyone staked out their turf and latecomers grumbled about how there were no good spaces left. Many of the luckier locals took up positions on building rooftops or hung out of second-story windows. Guests in the various hotels fronting Main Street and Courthouse Square Park received the same bird's-eye view.

Main Street, at least, was ready.

They couldn't say the same at the other end of town.

At the far east end of Main Street, out at the Little League field, all the parade entries lined up in an organized spiral. In line, two of Wishbone's finest fire engines gleamed brightly. Vintage cars in pristine condition were followed by souped-up hot rods in equally fine shape. The Wagoneer High marching band was placed right in front of the Kiwanis, who dressed like Arabs and drove tiny go-carts. A faction of Cherokees in period outfits were ready to strut right in front of members of the Daughters of the American Revolution, dressed as prairie pioneers. Right behind the Kiwanis, Roy Crawford and his Broncobusters tried to keep their dancing horses calm as workers ran here and there to put finishing touches on the floats representing most of Wishbone's major businesses.

At the float for the Wishbone Savings and Loan, made to look like a whale whose blowhole spouted a fountain of fake money instead of water, Lois Knowles fought a hangover and stared at her watch in consternation. One of her coworkers, Gail, walked up with her hands in the air.

"He's not home. Got his answering machine."

"That idiot Denny. Twenty to one he doesn't show until after we've done all the work."

"I work for him too. I'm not taking that bet."

The float for Vale's Chevrolet, looking like a huge Conestoga wagon pulled by papier-mâché Chevy trucks and cars instead of horses, was having trouble with its carburetor. Dressed like Wild Bill Hickok, Mayor Tommy Vale, bravely participating in the parade even in the face of his tremendous grief over Randy's suicide, tried to adjust the carburetor's air flow. Nearby, his red Hummer sat idling, and three Wishbone Wagoneer cheerleaders sat on its roof holding pom-poms, chewing gum and looking bored. The Wileys' old pickup was also running, and in the back six salesmen with ready supplies of brochures for Vale's Chevrolet sat in cowpoke outfits watching their boss struggle with the float engine.

Tommy had to fight back tears as he turned the carburetor's fuel valve.

"Goddammit, this is what Randy should be here doing."

At the float for the Pony Express Hotel—which was made to look like an old-time brothel front, with windows that opened and girls hired from town to show some cleavage and smile lasciviously as they flashed their bloomers—Reese Vosker and his wife, Rita, dressed as a slick gambler and a slicker madam, sneered at Frank O'Connor's entry.

"Look at that; he didn't even get dressed up."

Frank O'Connor, dressed in a suit and tie, adjusted a painting on a stationary easel set up on his "float," which was nothing more than a low flatbed towed behind his Lincoln. On the carpeted flatbed were several displays of artwork from O'Connor's gallery. The price tags had been enlarged so people could more easily see his outrageous prices.

There were many other entries, floats big and small from the Cobbler's Nook, the Whistle Stop, the Fourth Street Bowlarama and Ben Franklin. There were floats from almost every business in town. All were made of colorful papier-mâché and/or flowers, and all attempted to echo some common theme tying them to Wishbone.

Some radically failed, like the float for the pet store owned by Widow Palozi's son, Steve, a man who inherited her miserly instincts. Steve Palozi pulled his float for Pet Stuff, purchased from a neighboring town a week earlier for pocket change, straight out of mothballs without a single alteration. He swept off the dust and paint chips from a float displaying a large Easter bunny surrounded by happy kittens, puppies, fish, birds and frogs emerging from cracked Easter eggs. A big banner on the side still said, HAPPY EASTER 1992.

Kelly Mahon, acting as the parade director, stood on top of the home-team dugouts and spoke to the chattering throng through a lime-green plastic Wagoneer megaphone.

"Okay, everybody, listen up! I said listen up!" The crowd quieted. "Now, you all know the route, so we're going to be pulling out in a minute. I just want to make sure everybody knows to keep it tight but not too tight.

We don't want gaps but we don't want to run over anybody's toes. Okay? So let's have some fun!"

As Mahon climbed down nobody was thinking of fun. Right now the parade was still pure work. Everybody instantly went back to doing exactly what they were doing before—panicking about some figure's nose falling off or trying to get some motor that powered a papier-mâché ballerina working or trying to get a lunky float engine started. Paint was applied to missed spots as Mahon waved the first float onto Main Street.

The parade was under way.

Peter, Sandra, Will and Lisa stood as one knot in the lobby of the court-house. Standing in a second knot, Howard Clark, Rayna Higgins, Kathleen Saunders and Diana French discussed their impending roles in the day's celebrations. Everyone made certain no hair was out of place or strand of lint clung to dress or suit. Will looked from his watch to the courthouse door and then back to his watch.

Lisa pulled Will out of earshot from the others.

"Where is she?"

"She'll be here. She's running late. She was out late." Lisa stood silently and Will was drawn to look her in the face. "What?"

"You tell me."

"There's nothing to tell. We talked."

"So tell me what you talked about. Don't bring me into this thing with Andie and think I'll sit by and take whatever crumbs you feel like tossing me. That doesn't fly, Will. You have to tell me how you and she stand." Lisa's eyes betrayed her deep concern. "You have to tell me where *we* stand."

Will could palpably sense the fragile state his formerly strong bond with Lisa had reached. All it would take was a tiny shove in the wrong direction and their union would be severed. No matter his continuing doubts, losing Lisa was something he wished to avoid at all costs.

It was time for a retreat.

"I was wrong."

"So you don't think she's some kind of monster? You don't think she killed Randy Vale and Cullman Shermer?"

"No, and I'm sorry I ever said it. I'm sorry I ever thought it. But I'm mainly sorry I included you in it. I won't be surprised if I've lost your trust."

Lisa's eyes grew moist at hearing the news she prayed to hear. She reached her arms around Will and drew herself to his chest.

"It might be a little bruised, but it's not broken."

Will looked thankfully into Lisa's upturned face and kissed her deeply. As they heard the courthouse door open, they pulled out of the kiss. Andromeda strode in dressed in the height of chic and cracked a bold smile.

"Let's get this party on the road."

Diana French handed her purse to Kathleen Saunders.

"My stomach is feeling queasy. I'll be in the bathroom."

Andromeda watched Diana head down the long tiled hallway to the distant ladies' rest room.

"I should go too. Wouldn't want to have to pee in the middle of my speech."

Will stopped Andromeda.

"Did you . . . did you think about what I said?"

"I did."

"Then you know it's not too late. You can still turn back."

"Will, I thought about everything—"

"And?"

Andromeda gently patted his hand.

"And you don't have anything to worry about."

Will watched as Andromeda followed Diana down the hallway and into the bathroom.

Somehow Andromeda's assurance failed to relax him. He still flexed his jaw and he continued to bunch his shoulders. He considered Andromeda's comment and began to wonder—even if he didn't have to worry, should somebody else?

Inside the bathroom, all steel and white tile and clean beyond clean, Andromeda stepped to the counter and emptied makeup supplies on the hard surface. She began touching up her eyeliner as a toilet flushed in one of the closed stalls. The door opened and Diana French stepped out. She stopped when she saw Andromeda.

"Oh."

"Hello, Diana."

"Hello, Andie." Diana stepped closer. "Ready for another day in the sun?"

Andromeda finished her eyeliner application and closed the pencil case. She spun to face Diana.

"Tell me something; when you first heard about my troubles down under, which did you think first: 'I can help that poor little girl' or 'I can help myself'?"

"Don't try that game on me anymore. I don't have to stand for it."

Andromeda moved to block Diana as Diana moved to exit the bathroom.

"And what did I have to stand for? In fact, what did I stand for? A book? Is that what you thought I was good for the first time you saw me? Were you thinking, 'Chapter one: Hello, my name is Diana French'?"

"I helped you. I gave you years of my life."

"You helped yourself to years of my life."

"You came out okay."

"You don't even know how I came out. Have you ever really tried to find out what's inside me?"

"I tried to find out every single day of your stay at The Campus, and don't you stand there and belittle my teachings anymore—I won't have it!"

"Calm down, Doctor."

Diana huffed in and out a few breaths.

"If you wanted me to find out what was inside you, all you had to do was tell me."

"I'm telling you now."

"Well, now is not the time. You are no longer my patient, Andie. As you reminded me time and time again, you don't need me. You're doing just fine without having to hear what I have to say."

Andromeda moved closer to Diana.

"Seriously, I need you to know what's inside me."

Disturbed by Andromeda's approach, Diana began backing up.

"I told you, this isn't the time."

"This is the only time we have left, Doctor."

Diana backed into the door of another closed toilet stall, and the door swung open. She continued moving back as Andromeda closed in.

"Maybe later. Now, please . . . let me by."

Andromeda stepped into the stall, backing Diana up to the toilet wall.

"How come you seem so afraid?"

"I-I'm not afraid."

"Oh, you're afraid. If there's one thing I know, it's fear. Boy, oh boy, don't I know what it's like to be afraid. Look, you're shaking."

"Let's discuss this later. Now, please . . . let me by."

As Andromeda moved her face closer to Diana's, Diana pressed herself as far back as she could. Her breath came in agitated bursts. Andromeda moved still closer, until her face was inches from Diana's.

"Find out what's inside me. It's something you should share."

"No. I don't want it. I don't want anything from you. Now, please . . . move back. You're frightening me." Her eyes widening, Diana looked past Andromeda for an escape. "I—I can't breathe in here . . . please! Get back!" She could take no more. "*Move!*"

Diana lunged forward, aiming for the sliver of space to the side of Andromeda that would allow her past and set her free. But Andromeda caught her midstride. She slammed Diana into the side wall of the stall and held her tight.

"Not until you find out what's inside . . ."

Andromeda suddenly planted her mouth over Diana's. Diana struggled against Andromeda's manic kiss as Andromeda's breath filled Diana's lungs. Andromeda pressed harder. Diana was lifted from the floor and her feet dangled.

Suddenly Andromeda let go, pulling her mouth away. She stepped back. Diana slumped to the floor, drained and breathing hard.

Andromeda backed into the bathroom and returned to her purse. She pulled out a tube of lipstick and applied another layer, checking out her coverage as she puckered her lips toward the mirror.

Diana staggered to her feet. She eased herself out of the toilet stall and stood with disheveled hair. Her eyes shot deep hate toward her former patient.

"You monster."

Andromeda closed up her purse and turned with a smile.

"And I say the nicest things about you."

Andromeda walked out and the door swung shut behind her.

Diana French moved to the mirror and looked at her ravaged hairstyle and lipstick. As she worked both back into place, she felt her stomach boil with spite.

Andromeda Wiley was the most hateful creature ever to stand on two legs. That Diana had once thought she could do any good for that demonic soul now seemed the height of naivete.

Andromeda Wiley was beyond hope. She would go through life bringing misery and ruin to every person she touched. She was a monster.

Diana stared into the eyes of her reflection.

She did hate Andromeda Wiley and she knew she was right to hate her. But a new feeling took root. Diana began to feel that Andromeda had to be stopped.

Whatever it took to end the hate.

Howard Clark, the one-time lowly cub reporter, told war stories to seven camerapeople and their attached reporters.

" . . . When you interview fanatic dictators you have to forget they're insane. If you can get past that, you'll realize they're actually pretty easy to talk to. I'll bet Hitler could tell a good joke."

Rayna Higgins cocked her head as Andromeda walked down the hallway from the bathroom.

"That's her."

Cameras swung to seven shoulders and seven bodies jockeyed for the shot. One cameraman said what the others were thinking as the beautiful woman in a designer outfit with such long and slender legs drew closer and closer.

"Wow."

Andromeda moved up and video lights flared to life. The courthouse hallway was suddenly ablaze in light. Andromeda blinked in the glare.

"Hey, geez, can't you bounce that or something?"

Clark gestured to the seven crews.

"Meet the press."

CNN took the lead.

"Could you tell us what it's like to know that fifteen years after your accident, so many people are still following your story?"

"I think it's encouraging. I owe a lot to a lot of people. I hope the folks I never got to thank hear me thanking them now."

Fox network went next.

"We were told you were on the . . . well, they said you were attractive. Any interest in acting or modeling?"

"Little ol' me? Hadn't thought of it. Of course, stranger things have happened."

"Like what?"

"You mean besides spending five days in a hole ninety-six feet deep?"

"Well, what would you consider strange?"

"Probably the same things you do. If I said that Howard and his wife here will fall into a hole in the ground in the next twenty minutes, you'd probably think that was strange, or I was strange, or both. Strange is relative." Toying with the closest camera, Andromeda pointed right into the lens. "That's for you to decide."

The news crews were charmed. Howard Clark and Rayna Higgins chuckled at her joke.

Will walked back in from outside. Sandra, Peter and Lisa stood behind him.

"Andie, the parade's almost here. You should come out and take your place."

The NBC reporter gestured to Will as he and his family walked down the courthouse steps, crossed the street, entered Courthouse Square Park and headed for the bandstand.

"That was Will, right?"

Andromeda nodded.

"It was, but listen, save your tape for the real action."

"Can we have both of you, then?"

"You shoot whatever you want, mister."

Andromeda exited. Howard Clark and Rayna Higgins followed.

The news crews filmed Andromeda heading down the steps. She smiled and waved back. Suddenly a perturbed voice spoke from behind the reporters, echoing off the walls of the courthouse lobby.

"Out of my way!"

The crews turned as Diana French, her hair and lipstick back in place, pushed her way through to the courthouse doors. She was recognized.

"You're Diana French."

"And you're in my way; now, move!"

Diana pushed past and moved down the steps toward the street. The dismissed reporters chose not to video her backside.

"My opinion? The shrink is crazier than her patient."

The parade participants in their costumes, riding their go-carts, prancing their horses, driving their floats and marching with their bands circled the block and surrounded Courthouse Square Park. The Wagoneer marching band entered the park and took up position in an arc in front of the bandstand. They played "Louie, Louie" and "Shock the Monkey" and "Celebrate" as the sidewalk crowds hustled into the park and filled it to capacity.

The TV crews mounted their cameras to tripods and took up position to catch the action.

The ornate wrought-iron bandstand stood in the center of a colorful mass of humanity. People climbed trees where possible, and the steps of the courthouse across the street were filled with local teenagers eager to watch while remaining hip and aloof.

Tommy Vale, in his jet-black Hummer with the three pom-pom-waving cheerleaders on top, honked his way up the park pathway, annoyed in his grief by all obstacles in his path. Counting on one hand the few people who had offered condolences for the death of his favorite son, Tommy said under his breath, "Sons of bitches can all go to hell." His horn played "Cielito Lindo," which Tommy only remembered as being the theme song from an old Frito-Lays commercial. The throng parted to let Tommy and his urban assault vehicle past. Parking to the side of the bandstand, Tommy sluggishly stepped out in his Wild Bill outfit and climbed without passion onto the covered platform of the bandstand. The Wiley family, Sheriff Austin, Fred Zinneman, Bart Currie, Howard Clark, Rayna Higgins, Diana French, Kelly Mahon, Frank O'Connor, Julie Fletcher and Mary Downes sat at the back of the bandstand as Tommy scowled his way to the podium and tapped the mike.

"Is this thing on?"

Tommy's voice bellowed out of PA speakers attached to the top of the bandstand. The crowd answered his query in unison with a raucous, "Yes!"

Seeing the difficulty Tommy was having keeping with the spirit of the day, Sheriff Austin stepped up and whispered in his ear, "You sure you can handle this, Tommy? I mean, I can take over for you if you'd like."

"I'm the fucking mayor and this is my fucking job. Why don't you do yours and sit your ass down?" Resigned, Austin shook his head and returned to his seat as Tommy paused a moment to shake off his glare. When he turned back to the mike to face the crowd, he smiled as if he were the most carefree man on earth. "Well, howdy, howdy, howdy ladies and gentlemen and otherwise. My name is Tommy Vale, and as the mayor of the great town of Wishbone, Kansas, I'd like to welcome you all to today's celebration! Now what'd you come to see? Well, let me tell you . . ."

As Tommy blathered on about the wonderful things to see in Wishbone, Andromeda stepped close to Mary Downes and whispered, "Would you do me a favor?"

"Name it, Andie."

"When I'm through speaking, would you stay here on this bandstand for a little while?"

"What for?"

"I'd feel better if you didn't go anywhere."

"All right, I don't mind resting my dogs."

Andromeda gave Mary a slight smile as she went to sit back down. They both turned to watch Frank O'Connor stepping up to give his speech.

"Good afternoon—oh, excuse me, it's still good morning. My name is Frank O'Connor, city councilman and proprietor of O'Connor's Gallery of fine art located at 347 Dakota Street . . ."

Mary ventured a glance at Andromeda as she and the rest of the assembled speakers listened to O'Connor droning on about vast improvements made to the sewer system and the street lighting since he had become a councilman. Mary couldn't help but notice a sad wash on Andromeda's face, a sadness unprovoked by O'Connor's boring dissertation. Too much a student of human expression, Mary could see Andromeda was suffering some sort of emotional distress that she was holding back from the public eye.

Scanning the rest of her fellow invites, Mary glanced at Diana French and was shocked to see her staring at Andromeda with the most hateful frown. Noticing she was being watched, Diana flicked her eyes to Mary and then abruptly turned to face forward as Kelly Mahon stepped to the podium to rattle off a welcome list to all the new businesses that had arrived in Wishbone over the past year.

Sitting between Andromeda and Peter, Sandra turned to her daughter and also noticed the sadness in Andromeda's face.

"Is there something bothering you, honey?"

Andromeda turned to her mother and took a long time answering.

She let her eyes play over the face of the woman who had brought her into the world. She saw in her mother so many features she saw in herself. She could remember the times before her fall when her mother would read to her or rock her to sleep, singing "It's a Small World." She could remember times afterward when her mother came to see her at The Campus to tell her what language she was learning or how Will was doing or what plans Peter had for the farm.

Andromeda took her mother's hand and squeezed it.

"Everything's fine, Mom."

Sandra smiled.

"I'm glad."

She was now a spirit being, one who is invisible.

She was a shadow warrior and she walked among the clouds on a superior plane.

But right now back on earth, Janice Piasecki, her hair and eyes wild, her body caked head to toe in dried mud, worked to open the nozzle lock of a shiny chrome gasoline tanker parked at the curb a block from the action. As she broke loose the hose latch and dragged the hose to a nearby storm drain, feeding in its open end, she moved back to the tanker truck's control panel and opened the tanker's flow valve. The hose swelled and stiffened as thousands of gallons of high-octane premium gas flowed down the hose and into the drain. It ran under the streets to overflow cisterns, to lay a deep river of gas throughout the intersecting pipes feeding into the main drain.

Janice Piasecki breathed in the fumes deeply, as if the smell of gas were a fragrance from the finest bouquet.

"That's the smell of winning."

Grabbing up a bucket of the honey-colored fluid, she slunk off to continue her campaign against the spies.

Howard Clark, Rayna Higgins and Julie Fletcher stepped to the podium as they were introduced and began their short talk about being in the right place at the right time.

Peter elbowed Sandra and they switched places so he could sit next to Andromeda.

"So, what do you think?"

"I'll be glad when it's over."

"You want to get everything back to normal, huh?"

"I just want everything back."

Sheriff Austin, Fred Zinneman and Bart Currie stepped past for their turn at the mike. Peter set his hand over his daughter's as she rested her hand on her knee.

"We're so proud of you, Andie. You're one in a million."

Andromeda thought with a hurtful pang that the ratio was much higher.

Sheriff Austin and his men finished their short speech and Tommy Vale, master of ceremonies, introduced Mary Downes. Mary lifted herself up and walked to the mike to say simply, "I did what I could to help. Sometimes the person you help most when you give a helping hand is yourself."

The crowd appreciated her comment and clapped as Mary returned to her seat. Tommy turned to Diana French, on the verge of introducing her, when he saw she was vigorously shaking her head and silently mouthing the word *no*.

"Uhh, and moving along, it's time to introduce two people who put the organic in organics—Peter and Sandra Wiley!"

Andromeda and Will shared a mutually uncertain look as their parents stepped to the podium. Peter began, "I'm not too good at this. Probably a lot of you don't know me or Sandra—well, more people know Sandra; I don't get out as much." The crowd chuckled. "We weren't doing too well before Andie's accident and, well . . . you know, maybe I should shift this duty to my wife."

Sandra leaned to the mike as Peter stepped aside.

"He does the same thing when it's time to take out the garbage."

The crowd chuckled again. They were liking these Wileys. It was good to know they had not driven miles to see a family of snoots. These here were down-home folks who talked in ways they understood.

Sandra continued.

"Those were hard times, not just for us, but for a lot of folks up and down farm country."

Farmers in the crowd nodded and said, "Ain't it the truth."

"Just about the only thing we had was our family. So when Andie fell in that hole . . . that was just about it for us." The crowd could see this was bringing up hard memories for Sandra Wiley. "We were thinking, why us? Why Andie? And then you people . . . You were just great. You came from all over, you wrote us letters. You gave us back our daughter. Now, I don't want to start crying so . . . So I just want to say thank you, for me, for Peter, for Will and especially for Andromeda. You're not just what makes this country so fine, you're what makes the world the place it ought to be. Shoot, I *am* going to start crying. . . ."

Peter took over as Sandra tried to hold back tears.

"Thank you, thank you all so much. We'd be nothing at all without you and, well . . . we just want to know you have our deepest thanks. Thank you."

Peter led Sandra, who was now crying openly, back to their seats as Tommy returned to the podium.

In the crowd, affected by Sandra's kind words, there were many wet eyes. It was clear that most, including some of the newspeople, were touched and glad they had come. Except for the speeches by Frank O'Connor and Kelly Mahon, the crowd had been getting everything they hoped to get from the day. And there was still more to come. They had yet to hear from Will Wiley and Andromeda herself. And following that, they still looked forward to the exciting moment when Andromeda would break into the shaft where she spent those five awful days.

It was total satisfaction all around.

Tommy introduced Will Wiley, who nervously made his way to the mike, uncertain if he should leave on or take off his baseball cap. He decided to keep it on.

"Howdy." The crowd howdy'd back and the news crews made sure to get the focus right. "I don't know what else I can add to what my mom and dad just said. I was just eight when this whole thing happened, about as old as that little guy right there . . ."

Will pointed down into the crowd to a boy standing with his family. The boy didn't realize at first that Will was pointing at him. But when he did his eyes lit up and he said, "Me? He's pointing at me?" People nearby smiled to see how happy the little boy was at the simple acknowledgment.

Will continued.

"It's a great age for jumping off rope swings or building a tree fort, but it's not the best age to know what you can and can't do. Good thing too. I told Sheriff Austin I'd been in holes tighter than the one Andie was down. I lied."

Will turned back to Sheriff Austin and smiled. Austin waved his hat at Will and joined in the joke. The crowd laughed at the back and forth.

"I saw through that years ago!"

"Yeah? So then you also know I was the one who teepee'd your house three Halloweens ago."

"Now, that I didn't know. We'll be talking later. . . ."

"Uh-oh." Will turned back to the laughing crowd. "Well anyhow, going headfirst down that shaft to pull out Andie was fun in a way, at first. . . ." He suddenly remembered Andromeda's cold stare from the bottom of the hole. Flashing forward, he saw the tortured and dying face of Randy Vale. He felt the dark unknown threatening to divide him from Andromeda. He felt the chill of old fears. Not wanting to lose momentum, he sped past. ". . . and there she was and we yanked her out and you know all the rest. I don't like to think I'm some hero or something. I just did what any brother would do for his little sister." Will turned to look back at Andromeda and their eyes met. "I love my sister, and I feel like all of us here had a part in making her into the person she is today. So thanks for everything and God bless."

It was such a rich experience for the crowd to watch these honest and good people sharing their hearts so freely that many who cried wondered if they could stand another tear-jerking speech. But the main attraction, the person they had come to see, was next on the roster. They quieted in anticipation as Tommy Vale stepped to the mike to introduce her.

"And without further ado, I'd like you all to meet our Baby Andromeda . . ."

Andromeda stood and intercepted Will as he returned to his seat. She grabbed him and hugged him tightly. Surprised at the strength of her emotion, he hugged her back. The audience and Tommy Vale waited as brother and sister embraced.

Andromeda, struggling with deep-felt emotion, brought her lips close to Will's ear and whispered, "Don't ever forget that I'll always love you." She gave Will a last tight hug, kissed him on the cheek and spun to face the crowd.

As Will sat, again feeling that knot of worry, Andromeda stepped to the podium. The audience, most of whom had never seen her and who had driven miles to do so, now got a good look at her. They were universally impressed.

"What an absolutely beautiful girl."

"I think I'm in love."

Andromeda smiled gently at the expectant faces looking her way.

"Hello. My name is Andromeda."

The monster.

There she stands, talking to a crowd of fools. They smile at her and think isn't she lovely? But I know better. She's the evil one. They should stop smiling. They should throw stones. They should throw knives.

The monster should die.

Then the hate would end.

Diana didn't hear as Andromeda spoke to the crowd about the tender care she received while at The Campus. She didn't hear when Andromeda faced the cameras and said Diana French was the person who brought her back from the brink. Diana heard none of it, she heard nothing at all. The only working sense she had at the moment was sight. And using that sense, she saw one thing only.

The gun in Sheriff Austin's holster.

It was less than two feet in front of Diana. She had reasonably good reflexes. She felt she could easily reach out and yank the gun free. Then she could swing it up and aim it at the devil who was fooling the fools. A gun was much more effective than stones or knives. She could fire six hot slugs into the monster's back. The monster would die. The hate would end.

The entire world would be saved.

Diana looked up and saw Andromeda turning to look back at her. In those hateful eyes, so coldly pale and blue, Diana suddenly saw a flash. It was the signal that the hate would now spread. The hate would consume the crowd. The crowd would go to their homes in their little towns or cities and they would infect others with the hate. In a matter of weeks the hate would take over the planet. Diana would be able to see the hate when she flew to London or Tokyo. She would even find the hate in her beloved Sedona. She would never escape it.

It had to be stopped.

It had to be stopped here.

Andromeda turned back to the crowd.

" . . . because of Diana's constant guidance a heavy weight was lifted from my heart . . ."

Diana stared at the gun. She stared at Andromeda. She stared at the gun.

The hate had to stop.

"Monster."

Sheriff Austin had no idea until it was too late.

Diana reached out and yanked Sheriff Chuck Austin's nickel-plated .38-caliber revolver from his holster. Kicking back her chair, Diana leapt to her feet and aimed the gun at Andromeda's back. She screamed.

"Hellhound! Back to hell!"

As not just the whole crowd but especially those on the bandstand realized something was up, Diana pulled the trigger. Nothing happened. She continued to pull the trigger. From the crowd Kathleen Saunders shouted out in horror, "Diana, no . . . What are you doing?"

Andromeda stopped talking and calmly turned to face Diana.

Sheriff Austin cried out to Diana as he leapt to his feet and saw the good doctor waving his very own gun.

"Put down my gun!" Seeing that Diana would not put down his gun, and recognizing her clear intent to shoot Andromeda, the sheriff had no recourse but to yell for help. "Zins!" He spun back to Diana. "Doctor, put down my goddamn gun!"

Fred Zinneman and Bart Currie yanked free their own pistols and swung them on Diana French as she suddenly realized she had not clicked off the pistol's safety. "Silly me." She clicked it off now and put her finger back to the trigger. "This is the end of hate."

"Diana!"

As Diana French again trained the pistol on Andromeda, this time with the safety off, Sheriff Austin knew this surprise crisis had reached critical mass. He waved his men to fire.

"Go! Stop her!"

Fred Zinneman and Bart Currie opened fire on Diana French.

As bullets ripped through her pressed outfit, as blood splashed out holes in her back to color the wrought-iron posts of the bandstand, as she danced and jerked with each concussion, Frank O'Connor leapt off the bandstand and rushed for safety in the now screaming, fleeing and ducking crowd. Kathleen Saunders covered her ears as she ducked and held her breath, twitching at each loud blast killing her lover.

Diana French dropped the pistol as Fred Zinneman and Bart Currie ceased firing. With glazed eyes she stumbled back to the railing. She looked out and saw Andromeda.

"Andie? What . . . happened?"

Then she fell over backward, over the railing, and plunged to the concrete walk at the base of the bandstand. Her neck snapping with the impact, she lay twisted in death in a spreading pool of her own blood.

It was an instant melee.

Kathleen rushed for her fallen friend and partner.

The crowd screamed and cried. Most decided the party was over and many fled with their children in their arms. Still, there were plenty of gawkers, both amateur and professional. The news crews rushed to the corpse of Diana French for the full-color record as Kathleen Saunders took the dead doctor in her arms and cried out her grief.

On the bandstand, those remaining sat stunned and gasping in horror. Sandra looked down at her dead friend as Lisa Benson rushed to Will. "Oh my God, Diana . . ."

Returning his stolen gun to his holster, Sheriff Austin refused to believe what had just happened. He yelled out to whoever would listen, "Let's get an ambulance over here!"

Sandra, Peter and Will turned to Andromeda as she walked to the railing and looked down at the body of Diana French. Even though Andromeda seemed emotionless, Sandra was crying.

"Oh, honey, honey . . ."

Will looked to Andromeda and she to him. He saw the cold depth in her eyes. It was back.

And it was stronger than ever.

"Andie, what are you doing?"

"I'm saying my thanks." Will felt his chest tighten as Andromeda turned those hard eyes on their mother. She spoke in a voice loaded with disdain. "And you mother . . . I know what you did."

"Wha . . . what are you talking about?"

"The hole. You put me there. You made me fall in on purpose. You found the hole, you set it up and you trapped me."

Will sent a questioning gaze to his parents and then one to Andromeda. "Andie, that's crazy."

"Too bad it's true. We needed money—Mom came up with the plan, Dad found the hole and I fell in it. And then everybody in the whole wide world felt so darn sorry for us that they had to send us the money we needed. Isn't that about right, Dad?"

Peter and Sandra were both trembling. Neither could believe what they were hearing. But it was true. Andromeda knew. Peter felt instantly nauseous.

"Andie . . . Will . . . we didn't—"

"Honey, you weren't supposed to be the one. It was supposed to be—"

Andromeda finished her mother's sentence.

"Will? It was supposed to be Will?"

Sandra looked at Will. He felt his legs growing weak.

"You made Andie fall down that hole? And . . . and . . . you meant it for me?"

"We were so poor, Will; we were losing our home—"

"So you thought the best thing to do would be to make one of us, me or Andie . . . You set the whole thing up? This was all a lie?"

Sandra's eyes darted all over, trying to grasp what clues she might have overlooked that would have warned her that in a split second, her whole world would shatter.

"It's not a lie. We changed our minds. We weren't going to do it. But Andie . . . she found it and she . . . she fell. I don't . . . Andie . . . Will, we . . . we . . ."

Sandra suddenly swooned and collapsed. Peter caught her and dropped to his knees. He looked up to his coldly staring daughter and son and had no idea how to respond. Two minutes earlier life couldn't have been better. Now it couldn't be worse.

"Will, I'm so sorry. Andie, please . . ."

The mayor, frantic at another horrible turn of events that had ruined a day that had been going so well, came running up, shaking as he tried to express his confusion to the guests of honor.

"I . . . I don't know what to say. She pulled Chuck's gun. She . . . what else could he do? My God, Randy and Pat and then this. I've never seen such a nightmare."

Andromeda spun to face Mayor Tommy Vale, father of Randy and Pat and the king of callous.

"You haven't seen a nightmare until you've seen mine. See it now."

He suddenly froze like a deer in headlights. All the color drained from his face and a wet spot quickly spread down his pants. As his bladder emptied its contents down the inside of his pants to pool in his shoes, Tommy suddenly screamed and ran from the bandstand. He flailed his arms wildly as if trying to ward off a swarm of invisible bees.

Will spun accusing eyes on Andromeda.

"You're doing this. I know you are. You're doing all of this! You have to stop. You have to stop it now!"

Andromeda stood as an eye of calm in the stormiest of seas.

"No, Will. They have to learn you don't get something for nothing."

Frank O'Connor, having made good his escape from the park, stood on the sidewalk before the Pony Express Hotel. Two of Cullman Shermer's hayride buckboards, fully hitched and ready to roll, were parked before him on the street. He stood oblivious to the fact that three stories straight up, on the rooftop of the hotel, Janice Piasecki, bridge troll, purposely drenched from head to toe in cleansing gasoline, held her open bucket of divine deliverance directly over his head. She sneered down at her number-one traitor.

"Liar, thief, spy. I see you."

Janice poured out the contents with perfect aim.

Frank O'Connor didn't know what it was that hit him until he smelled the gas. Soaked by the sudden downpour of flammable liquid, he coughed past the fumes to glance up at his attacker.

On the rooftop Janice Piasecki held up a trio of kitchen matches.

"The truth will set us free, Frank!"

She struck the matches to the wood of the hotel's cap rail and they flared to life. So did Janice Piasecki. In a flash she was consumed in flame. She stepped on the cap rail and jumped.

Those below, including Sheriff Austin, who had noticed Piasecki on the roof, looked up to see a human ball of flame streaking down toward the street. Frank O'Connor suddenly knew his danger.

"Oh God . . ."

Janice Piasecki landed smack in the middle of the fluffy haystack sitting in the buckboard. In an instant the hay burst into flame, and the flames leapfrogged to the hay mound of the neighboring buckboard.

Startled by the sudden proximity of so much heat, the hitched horses of the two buckboards reared and kicked. In their frenzied fear they snapped the straps holding them to the horse rail, and the buckboard infernos shot off, one down Main Street and the other in a veering path that cut across the park, sending sparks and flames fifteen feet high and thirty feet back.

Janice Piasecki rolled off the hay to the street as the fire consumed her. She began rushing for Frank O'Connor.

"Liar, liar, pants on fire!"

O'Connor, as out of shape as any, huffed in terror as he began to run.

"Help me! Somebody help me!"

No one was stupid enough to help no matter where O'Connor turned, and the gruesome foot chase gave the crowd another reason to panic. Sheriff Austin and his deputies fought against the new wave of terrified tourists.

"Out of the way!"

They drew their guns for the second time in five minutes and hopelessly tried to get a bead on Janice Piasecki as she ran burning after Frank O'Connor.

Hobbled by his girth, O'Connor could sense Piasecki getting closer. One touch and he would be a ball of flames too. As he neared the Wishbone Savings and Loan, hoping to duck inside, he looked back to see how close she had come.

She was too close for O'Connor to make it.

He screamed at the unfairness of it all.

"Not me!"

Janice Piasecki used a last burst of strength to leap on Frank O'Connor. O'Connor shrieked as the flame from Piasecki's embrace shot up and down his gas-soaked frame. Their momentums combined, Piasecki and O'Connor crashed through the picture window of the Wishbone Savings and Loan and landed in New Accounts.

Brown nylon carpeting and olive green curtains were instantly ablaze.

Before five seconds had passed, a five-alarm fire was out of control in the Wishbone Savings and Loan.

Down Main Street, having opted to forgo the speeches and sitting in the dark and cozy confines of their Pony Express Hotel float drinking from a private stash of champagne, the Voskers believed the series of echoing reports they had heard minutes earlier were from firecrackers. But as they now glanced out the driving slit to see people running past, they guessed there might be something more going on. Rita Vosker looked straight ahead and saw something more.

"Reese, back up. Back up!"

In an image borrowed from the Apocalypse, the horses still hitched to the intense inferno that used to be one of Shermer's buckboards made a direct bead for the Pony Express float.

"Oh Lord." He started the engine, but in his panic Reese Vosker couldn't get the float in gear. "I—I can't . . . I can't get it to work!"

The buckboard tore loose from the two horses and began to roll. Reese and Rita saw the gigantic fireball bouncing end over end and heading their way.

It arrived.

Rita and Reese shrieked as flames impacted through the flimsy shell of the papier-mâché float and made their way into the tiny driving compartment. In an instant their lungs took in heat hot enough to melt iron.

The flames reached the gas tank.

The entire float detonated in a massive nova of sound, debris, heat, smoke and the Voskers' dying agony.

Smoking and burning chunks of float and buckboard, propelled sky-high by the eruption, landed on balconies, rooftops, cars and other floats. Each seed of flame sprouted a healthy crop of its own.

In seconds fires were burning up and down Main Street.

But it was a simple bit of flaming float dropping into one of the storm drains, where high-octane premium gas from the emptied tanker sat in pools, rivulets and deep lakes everywhere under the besieged town that lifted the disaster to new heights.

The gas was ignited. Its ignition raced through the subterranean passages, and the concussion of the underground blasts, spreading here and there and shooting flames hundreds of feet into the air from every drain opening, burst open the roads as pipes were sundered and cisterns erupted with the force of a hundred grenades. Manholes all over town shot skyward like iron missiles, shattering whatever lay in their path on the way up and on the way down.

Car after car screeched out at the same time, only to ram every other car bent on fleeing. Mediocre drivers became terrible drivers as they tried to flee the cataclysm sucking down the town of Wishbone.

Everywhere, light poles and stop signs fell crazily, creating further obstacles to escape. Humps of shattered asphalt rising a foot high and more from the underground explosions laced the once beautifully paved roads of Wishbone.

People who had no idea where to run decided to run everywhere.

It was pure and total chaos.

At the bandstand Howard Clark, Rayna Higgins and the news crews didn't know where to shoot next—there was too much to see. The raging fires caused a dark pall of black and gray smoke to blot out the light of day. Particles of ash drifted down to obstruct clear views. The odor of wood and plastic and even burning flesh seared their nostrils.

Peter, still holding his delirious Sandra, looked to Andromeda with wet and pleading eyes.

"Andie, we didn't want this but . . . but it's done. What can we do?"

Andromeda didn't answer. She moved with determination for the front of the bandstand. Mary Downes, having witnessed the spectacle of Diana French's hail-of-gunfire death, Janice Piasecki and Frank O'Connor's incineration, along with the admission that Peter and Sandra Wiley had purposely caused their daughter to fall down that hole, stood and stepped in front of Andromeda. When Andromeda swung her gaze her way, Mary saw in Andromeda's eyes something new—a cold, cold fire.

"Andie?"

"I told you to stay here. So sit."

Mary found she could not help agreeing that it was the most sensible suggestion of all time. She sat.

Andromeda continued to the far bandstand rail and watched Howard Clark and Rayna Higgins just below, leading the news crews to the action. In their path down the wide park walkway lay an overturned bench.

Andromeda stared at the small of Howard Clark's back.

"Mustn't forget the reporter."

Clark, Higgins and the rest of the crew froze on the wide concrete pathway as across the street the Pony Express Hotel suddenly blasted wide open. Trapped pockets of gasoline fumes, which had backed up inside its many toilet and sink drainpipes, had found their spark and released in one great chorus all their stored energies. Porcelain toilets and sinks went airborne. The ceramic projectiles split the supports holding up the building and it collapsed into its foundation, sending into the air a blindingly brilliant shower of dust, burning embers, ash and shards of the Voskers' lost dream.

Clark and Higgins were both belatedly thinking the same thing.

"We should get out of here."

They were allowed only one step.

The wide concrete pathway directly before Clark and Higgins split and dipped as the ground beneath was rocked by another bursting pocket of fumes. As if on an upper pivot, an entire eighteen-foot section of the path suddenly dropped ten feet. As the pathway dipped down toward a split in the earth where a river of flame coursed from one severed sewer line to its many cousins, Clark and Higgins slid with it.

"Howard!"

Dropping to her stomach on the now precarious slant, Rayna Higgins reached up and grabbed her husband's pants leg. Inches below her feet the flames swirled and boiled, occasionally sending up a scout to lick at her legs. Also on his stomach and slipping as he tried to find a handhold in the tilting slab, Clark looked past his wife to the draft of billowing flames in the wide maw of the boiling sewers. The overturned bench slid into the hole and was consumed, the flames devouring its wooden slats and torquing its iron. He then looked up out of the fiery pit that threatened to consume himself and his wife. The news crews stood at the hole. More than a few kept cameras to shoulders to capture the action live.

"Stop shooting! Get some fucking rope!"

Veterans of combat coverage, regaining their wits, rushed to snap up a long coil of TV cable.

Higgins shrieked up to her husband as her feet and legs traveled from first-degree to third-degree burning. Her soles were on fire.

"Howard!"

Clark began shaking his leg.

"Let go, you're pulling me with you!"

Suddenly the slab tilted more.

Clark frantically clawed at the concrete with his fingers as he and Higgins began sliding. Where he clawed, his broken skin left bloody streaks.

"No! *Not me!*"

The crew members with the TV cable rushed back to the hole and tossed down the free end. They were too late.

Rayna Higgins and Howard Clark slid howling into the bright morass of fire. As they shrieked their last shrieks, the flames stripped them of clothing and flesh, sucking them into the gaseous, lavalike flow. They vanished and the concrete slab slipped in to follow.

The camerapeople who had not stopped filming pulled eyes from eyepieces and looked about sheepishly. Those who had tried to help just stared into the fiery pit, stunned by what they had seen.

But when another explosion erupted down the street, they forgot Howard Clark and Rayna Higgins and rushed to the next photo opportunity.

Mayor Tommy Vale battled unseen demons. Seized by a terror that had nothing to do with all that was happening to the rest of the town, he rushed for his beloved Hummer. The three cheerleaders, too terrified to move, still sat on top. Tommy barked at them.

"Off!"

"No!"

Tommy leapt into the safe confines of his urban assault vehicle, revved the engine and hit the gas. With a rig capable of climbing a three-foot-high wall, he opted for the direct approach to escape.

He gunned the Hummer forward and blasted through a hedge, sweeping the cheerleaders from his roof. Jumping the sidewalk, he plowed the Hummer over the knot of honking cars now blocking the intersection of Main Street and Dogwood. As families and individuals scrambled from their uselessly gridlocked transports, Tommy drove over hoods, rooftops and trunks, reducing every car in his path to junkyard fodder.

The Hummer blasted over the congestion, navigated a downed building front and handily made it over the road humps. Yet even as Tommy sped from the downtown sector over smooth roads beyond the ruin, he continued to scream in utter terror.

"Leave me alone! *Leave me alone!*"

An impartial observer would see upon witnessing Tommy's rapidly serpentine exit from town a man reacting to nothing. Tommy saw much more.

What Tommy saw as he raced toward one of the giant wishbones at the distant edge of town was a calamity without peer.

Instead of a smoke-blackened sky, Tommy saw a vast dirt tunnel rising straight up to an infinite distance, confining in its base the town of Wishbone. Emerging from the tunnel walls for its entire length were writhing roots as long and wide as skyscrapers. The roots dove down aggressively, attacking like cobras to gouge out massive chunks of town—ripping up trees, houses, cars and whole streets. Tommy could see beneath and beyond the approaching concrete wishbone a land more familiar—a peaceful pastoral setting of farms and slow tractors. Gleaming at the end of this straight strip, the wishbone was a gateway exiting this horrible shaft, a gateway that promised to lead Tommy back to his world.

But other sights worked to distract Tommy from his goal.

Beasts worthy of any painter's vision of hell's inhabitants slithered, flew, leapt, chewed and clawed at everything that drew their fancy. Creatures like scaly and diseased grubs the size of school buses trailed wide swaths of slime as they munched and gnawed on petite homes and picket fences. They had appendages like hands and disturbingly humanlike faces, and they lunged and growled at Tommy as he sped past.

Smaller beings the size of dogs raced in packs alongside Tommy, their barks sounding like fingernails clawing down blackboards as they tried to clutch his Hummer. They had four legs and a body but no head or tail. They had no fur, just albino skin that hung in fleshy folds, and their feet were jointed like those of a massive insect. Three of the creatures managed to leap on and pierce the steel skin of the Hummer. They began climbing toward the driver.

Tommy screamed from the bottom of his soul.

The wishbone drew nearer. The creatures drew nearer. But Tommy grew convinced he was going to make it. He could see the open stretches of farmland beyond the gateway of the wishbone arch. He could see the turnoff to Slauson's Ferry, he could see the distant intersection with Route 291 East, and he began to feel a renewed confidence.

Tommy smelled victory.

"Goddammit, I'm going to make it!"

And then the pastoral land beyond suddenly disappeared. In its place was the jagged edge of an asphalt cliff. Beyond the arch the road suddenly dropped into the open mouth of another incredible beast. Horrified at this mouth and open throat, lined with waving flagella like those found in intestines, Tommy knew he would be devoured whole if he did not stop his approach.

He slammed down on the brakes and yanked back on the emergency handle.

The Hummer fishtailed and turned off-road as its tires locked, grinding rubber into the pavement in a fantail of gray smoke. Tommy screamed and shielded his face, seeing that he was now headed straight for one of the two support posts of the concrete wishbone.

The impact was immediate and final.

The Hummer was utterly destroyed as it wrapped itself around the concrete support. Glass, steel and rubber forever lost their original form as velocity met unyielding resistance.

In the aftermath, Tommy sat dazed in the protective interior. He tried to shake off the effect of the crash as he lifted his head. Opening his eyes, he expected to see hell closing in. But it was not.

Everything was normal.

The farms were still there, the houses were not being eaten by giant grubs, headless and hairless dog creatures were not giving chase and there was no immense shaft rising above him that lowered skyscraper-sized roots to tear up the town. Tommy opened his door and staggered out.

"I'm alive." Feeling overwhelming relief, having completely forgotten his poor, dead son, he stepped into the center of the lane and decided to rejoice. "I'm alive!"

Then he heard something crack.

As he turned to the source of the sound, he suddenly wished he had listened to the archway contractor when the contractor suggested going beyond code for the arch's steel reinforcement.

"No fucking way . . ."

The giant wishbone, cracked at its base by the impact with the Hummer, fell his way. Tommy held up his arms as if it might make death hurt less.

The force of several tons of metal and concrete landed right on Mayor Tommy Vale. In a sick crunch of stone and bone and an accompanying liquid burst, it flattened him to a thickness of one inch.

Where Mayor Tommy Vale had stood to breathe his final breath there now lay the shattered remains of a broken wishbone. The splat that seconds earlier had been Tommy Vale, mayor of Wishbone, lay at the point of impact like a fly in the sweet spot of the swatter.

And in the distance the town of Wishbone continued to burn.

Sheriff Chuck Austin couldn't hold on much longer.

The pit had blasted open right in the middle of Main Street. A little boy, just four years old, bawling and stumbling about alone, had tripped into the pit. Sheriff Austin climbed into the cavity to rescue the boy before he fell into the flames below. But the boy slipped farther, with Austin following, and they were now both depending on Austin to keep them from falling all the way as he gripped the boy in one hand and a tiny handhold with the other. Austin knew he would not be able to hold on much longer, but try as he might he could not lift the boy high enough for the boy to climb out.

Austin felt his fingers slip. He tried to get the child to focus.

"Climb on my shoulders! Grab on where . . . grab where my hand is holding!"

With the last of his strength Sheriff Austin lifted the boy above his head so the boy could buy a few more minutes hanging from the handhold. But suddenly the boy was lifted out of Austin's hand. Thinking he had dropped the child, he then saw someone on a rope in a yellow fireman's outfit pulling the boy free.

When the boy was lifted out of the way, the face of Bobby Timms looked down at Sheriff Chuck Austin.

"Need a hand?"

Bobby Timms pulled Austin up and out. Once back on his feet, Austin turned to Timms with amazement.

"Where'd you come from?"

"I keep asking myself, Where have I been?" Timms grabbed two teenagers who were standing around looking confused. "What are you two doing?"

"Man, we don't know."

"Then get on that hydrant and man that hose!"

Timms pushed the two teens to a hydrant, where a hose was already attached. In the distance other citizens worked side by side with Wishbone's fire crews to put out fire or dig out rubble. As the teens opened the valve and began dousing a fire of their own, Austin shook Timms's hand in his own.

"I am so glad to have you back."

"Only half as glad as I am."

With barely a limp, Bobby Timms joined forces with Sheriff Chuck Austin to stop the end of the world.

Will raced up in his pickup, dodging pits, debris and fires to fishtail it through the park to the bandstand. As Will leapt out from the driver's seat, Andromeda rushed down from the bandstand.

"Put Mom in the front!" she cried. Will moved to grab Sandra. Andromeda opened the driver's door and slid behind the wheel. "Come on, hurry!"

Will and Lisa helped Peter guide the still-dazed Sandra into the front seat. Andromeda looked over at her father as he lifted Sandra inside.

"You shouldn't have done what you did."

"Andie, we weren't going through with it."

"You shouldn't have even thought it."

"We were so desperate."

"You don't know what it was like down there."

"We don't know."

"That's right, you don't, but you will . . ."

Andromeda hit the gas. The pickup shot away and the passenger door slammed shut.

"Andie, wait!"

Lisa, who was beginning to think Will was right in his suspicions, asked the question needing the most immediate answer.

"What is she doing?"

Will knew exactly what she was doing.

"She's taking Mom to the hole."

FIFTY-FOUR
BELOW

Wayne Deets, master excavator, road builder and mover of mountains, knew there were only about four inches of soil left between the new bottom of the secondary shaft and the shaft that had captured Andromeda Wiley fifteen years earlier. He was tempted to just push his hand through but he knew doing so would ruin the whole purpose of the stunt—to see Andromeda Wiley do it herself. Deets was proud of his work and he was anxious to show it off, but the parade was now forty minutes late and he was growing concerned that the stunt had been called off. He hoisted himself back up out of the pit.

Crossing through the cavern rooms, he knocked on the door to the ticket booth. Laura Sharf opened the door and leaned out.

"Yeah?"

"Where are they? Where's Denny?"

"I don't know. I just got into town a couple hours ago and I came straight here. So don't ask me."

Laura shut herself back in the ticket booth.

Deets pushed open the glass double doors and stepped out into the lot. It was totally empty but for his van and Laura Sharf's baby-blue Mazda. In the lot, hundreds of chairs were set out to face two huge video screens of the kind used in big concerts for the benefit of distant ticket buyers. Two live images were on the screens. One screen showed a shot of the top of the secondary shaft. It could be seen that a seat was outfitted to a rope and motorized pulley rig that hung from the ceiling directly above the secondary shaft. The tiny bridge and the Plexiglas cover had been removed, as had all the date markers and the mannequin at the bottom of the hole. The dangling seat hung over a straight drop eighty-three-feet deep.

The second screen image was a live shot from the bottom of the secondary shaft showing the tunnel created through the labors of Wayne Deets. Deets's tunnel angled down to the dirt wall that enclosed the place where Andromeda had been held captive fifteen years earlier.

Deets crossed the lot and walked up the shallow slope to the two-lane road heading east back to Wishbone. When he reached the empty road and looked east, he saw that the entire horizon was black with smoke.

"Oh, man, what the holy majolies . . . ?"

Suddenly Deets saw a pickup truck heading his way, west out of Wishbone. It was the only vehicle on the road and it was moving fast. As it approached, Deets could see it meant to turn into the lot at Andromeda's Tomb. He started back down the drive, hoping to learn from the occupants what was going on in town.

When the truck took the corner and sped into the lot, Deets saw it was Andromeda Wiley herself behind the wheel. Somebody else, a woman, sat in the seat beside her, apparently asleep.

Deets moved to the truck as it stopped. Andromeda hopped out. Deets smiled in his gregarious way.

"Hey-howdy-ho, where is everybody?"

Andromeda hadn't noticed Deets until he spoke. She noticed him now.

"Are you the only one here?"

"Nah, Laura's in the booth."

"Tell her to come out."

As Deets passed through the concrete tubes to the ticket booth, Andromeda moved around the truck to the passenger door. She opened it as her mother worked to open her eyes. Feeling drugged by the strain of all that had happened, Sandra looked to Andromeda in confusion.

"Andie . . . What are you doing?"

Andromeda did not speak. She reached in and pulled her mother from the truck. Half walking, half carrying Sandra, Andromeda moved past the damaged drill and headed for the structure of Andromeda's Tomb.

Deets and Laura stepped out. Laura wore a tight sweater that showed much cleavage.

"What's up?"

Andromeda moved closer. She looked to Deets.

"Why don't you go sit in your van and stay there for a couple hours?"

"Okay."

Deets walked to his van and climbed in. He shut the door behind, lifted a magazine from the seat, put his feet on the dash and began reading.

Andromeda turned to Laura.

"You're Denny's wife?"

"Yeah, I guess."

"In that case, do something you should have done a long time ago."

"Yeah, what?"

"Run." Laura, suddenly frantic, looked in all directions. Andromeda pointed north. "That way."

Laura spit out her chewing gum and took off into the scrubby fields surrounding Andromeda's Tomb, running as fast as she could. She headed due north at a fast clip.

Sandra struggled against an oppressive weariness, trying to bring herself back to full consciousness.

"No . . . not this."

"You should have been saying that before you put me in the hole."

Andromeda moved with her mother into the innards of Andromeda's Tomb.

Reaching the secondary shaft and Deets's rigging, Andromeda reached out for the dangling seat and pulled it to her mother. She set Sandra in the seat and strapped her in. As she let the seat and Sandra swing out over the shaft, Andromeda planted her feet on either edge of the seat and straddled her mother. She grabbed the control box for the pulley motor and pushed the down button. The seat holding both Sandra and Andromeda began descending into the shaft. The earthen sides rushed past in a rapid and smooth descent.

They quickly reached the bottom.

Andromeda stepped off and unstrapped her mother. Bright lights were strung along the length of Deets's new tunnel.

Andromeda dragged Sandra some fifteen feet down the slanted shaft, where it ended at the dirt wall. She set down her mother and played her hand over the smoothed surface. Pushing in slightly, she could sense it was not thick.

Sandra, who was aware where they were but who could not fully awaken no matter how she tried, began crying.

"Honey, no . . ."

Andromeda's eyes narrowed.

"It has to be this, Mother."

She shoved with both hands and the dirt gave way.

Fifteen-year-old air wafted out from the little chamber at the bottom of the old shaft. Ahead, illuminated by the string of lights in Deets's tunnel, the mesh of roots sat waiting, still pale and moist white, but unmoving. The little bits of burlap, the old newspaper, the cup, the twigs, the square of wood and Peter's contraption, which had entombed Andromeda those five days, were still present. They were unchanged in this protective environment, unaltered artifacts of a little girl's hell.

Andromeda stepped into the little chamber and pulled her moaning mother in with her. Sandra's eyes, still heavy from the cloud of fatigue that refused to lift, opened wider to witness this new horror. She felt herself settling into the fibrous den as the roots entangled her feet, her waist, her arms and her chest. Her mouth opened to release a scream. But all that emerged was silence as she felt the mitt of roots clutching tighter and tighter.

They were back where it all began.

But for Andromeda, she was where it would all end.

Tommy Vale's mechanics had thankfully done a good job getting the old Wiley truck running, because it was the only accessible vehicle Will had been able to find.

As he raced west in the old truck heading for Andromeda's Tomb with his distraught father, skirting flaming fissures, road humps and panicked tourists, Will tried to make sense of everything that had happened.

The revelation that his parents had purposely arranged for him to fall into the shaft that had instead taken Andromeda was enough of a shocker to last a lifetime. But there had been a banquet of shock this day. Diana French, Janice Piasecki and Frank O'Connor, Howard Clark and Rayna Higgins—it seemed like just about anybody who had selfishly profited from Andromeda's experience was shaking hands with the Reaper.

And suddenly Will knew that was the idea.

"She's getting back at all of us. Randy Vale, Cullman Shermer, Frank O'Connor . . . all of us. She's taking everything back."

Peter lifted his head in misery.

"How?"

"I . . . I don't know. I just know she is." Ahead, a gigantic red-and-yellow arrow that read YOU ARE HERE pointed into a parking lot. Will slowed the old truck to a stop and looked into the lot from the two-lane country road. His new truck was parked near the drill. "She's here."

Will's mouth was dry. He had no idea what lay ahead.

Peter had no idea either, he just knew whatever was happening had to be faced. What he and Sandra started had to be finished.

"Pull in."

Will turned the wheel and drove into the lot.

It seemed so peaceful and calm.

He began to wonder if maybe the only thing happening inside was an argument between mother and daughter. The fact that a man was sitting in a nearby van casually reading a magazine suggested that there had not been any calamities here, at least. He parked the old truck, got out and walked to knock on the window of the man's van.

Deets rolled down his window and gave the young man facing him a smile.

"What can I do for you?"

"Did you see my sister Andromeda and my mother here?"

"Andromeda Wiley is your sister? Then you must be Will."

"That's right. Did they go inside?"

"Yeah, maybe five minutes ago."

"Did they seem okay?"

"I couldn't see anything wrong."

"Well . . . could you come inside with us?"

"Sorry, have to stay in my van for"—Deets looked at his watch—"another hour and fifty-two minutes. That should make it a couple of hours."

"What? Look, we need as many people as we can get to go in there with us. Just come out and come with us."

"I told you, not for another hour and fifty . . . one minutes, and don't expect Mrs. Sharf to go with you either. She's long gone. Fast as she was going, I'd say she's two or three miles out by now."

Will looked in the direction Deets pointed. The landscape was empty all the way to the horizon, without a soul in sight. Will turned back to his father as he stood waiting at the old truck.

His face drained, Peter evidenced his guilt in the slump of his shoulders and the shattered confidence in his eyes. His demeanor suggested an open plea.

"I have to be a part of this."

Suddenly a face appeared on one of the large monitors. It was Andromeda's. She stood before the camera at the bottom of the secondary shaft. Her voice boomed out the speakers lining the screens.

"Hello, Father. Hello, Will. You shouldn't have come. But now that you're here, you might as well come on in."

As Andromeda cleared the frame, Will and Peter were treated to a clear shot down Deets's tunnel, through the now-pierced dirt wall and into the little chamber. They could see the bits of flotsam; they could see the roots. And they could see Sandra. She was almost completely submerged in the root mass. Her wet and wide eyes spoke volumes. She was scared to death.

She was not alone in her fear. Peter was shaking with her.

"Sandy . . ."

Will felt his heart fall to his feet.

In a live shot on a big screen for all the world to see was the tangible object of his fifteen-year nightmare. The roots that had held Andromeda, the roots Will believed had placed that alien stare in his sister's eyes were right there in full video color, and now they held his mother. But somehow they fell short of Will's memory of a monster. In appearance they were just simple roots from any familiar plant. They were not moving on their own, they were not wrapping themselves around his mother like some Jack in the Beanstalk fantasy. They were just lying there like roots, and his mother was simply lying within their mass.

Will had always wanted to blame some outside agent of change for turning his little sister into the malevolent beast she had apparently become. But now, staring at the hated roots that sat so inertly, Will felt himself losing the focus of his blame. Was it something that had always resided in his sister that had driven this terrible day, something that lay dormant until her fall into the shaft had set it in motion?

There was only one person who had the answer and she was waiting inside.

Will moved to his own truck, opened the door and opened the glove compartment. Laying inside was Randy Vale's revolver. Hesitating a moment, Will lifted it and shoved it into his waistband. He looked to his father and began moving toward the trap of Andromeda's Tomb.

"Let's go."

They passed through the concrete tubes and moved toward the open turnstile. With each step, Will conjured images of those terrible days fifteen years past. His memories were accompanied by smells that the area still retained. The oil-slicked earth was still present. The dried weeds and grasses had a familiar scent. Even the still air reminded Will of those days.

They passed through the turnstile and entered Andromeda's Tomb.

Andromeda stood at the top of the secondary shaft. She had dismantled Deets's rigging. The secondary shaft was now an unimpeded, eighty-three-foot-deep straight drop. Peter's face, already drained of color, lost even more when he saw what his daughter held. It was the two-by-four and corrugated sheeting contraption he had used to trap her. Andromeda looked to her father.

"Hello, Daddy. I believe this is yours."

She tossed the device to the ground before Peter's feet. The dirt from the metal sheeting, encrusted for fifteen years, broke off and dirtied the floor.

Peter looked up from the physical icon of his endless guilt. He could barely meet his daughter's hard gaze.

"Andie . . ."

From the depths of the eighty-three-foot-deep shaft, Sandra's voice called up, cracking in fear.

"Peter! Oh God, Peter! Get me out of here!"

Andromeda smirked.

"Seems I've heard that line before. . . ."

Will didn't know where to begin. He felt like a novice trying to defuse a master's bomb. He had no idea which wire to cut to keep it from exploding in his face. Will looked his sister up and down.

"I won't even pretend I know what's going on here or how you did all that back in town. I just know you did. I need to know why."

"I'm finishing what Mom and Dad started."

She fixed her glare on Peter, and he felt the last of his resistance wash away. If she asked him to jump in that hole, to plunge eighty-three feet to a certain death, he would not hesitate. Anything to end this hell.

He had not looked deep enough when Andromeda returned after her fifteen-year absence. He hadn't asked the right questions. He hadn't discovered who she was or what she hid. He went easy on himself; he said, Maybe it's okay for me to be happy, wanting it so much that he easily grew proud in how his daughter carried herself and how people spoke of her. He could say she was doing fine because it would allow him to be happy.

But the horrors she hid.

The horrors she had now shared with the entire town.

The final horrors she reserved for her family.

There were things in Andromeda greater and more powerful than anything credited to the great mystics, gurus and spoon benders. Andromeda had shaken a town to its roots. Wishbone, Kansas, would never be the same.

It appeared that the Wileys of Wishbone would not be spared the upheaval, because here Andromeda stood and, one hundred feet below, Sandra lay caught in a net of roots. It was a situation that cried out for resolution. As much as he feared it, Peter had to know that resolution.

He looked to Andromeda and hoped to find his little girl in the determined woman who had taken control of their lives.

"Andie . . . We . . . we didn't want you in there. We didn't . . . It was a mistake, that's what it was. A mistake." Peter began sobbing. He saw Andromeda would let him continue. "You have to believe us. We never wanted this to happen to you."

"I know—you wanted it to happen to Will."

Peter had to ask the question that had haunted him since Andromeda first revealed her knowledge.

"How do you know that?"

"I know lots of things. I know things no girl my age should ever know. I know things you could never know if you lived a hundred lifetimes. How's this for a tidbit? Your Baby Carlotta? She committed suicide when she was sixteen. Put a shotgun in her mouth. Painted her head onto the wall of her parents' garage. Doesn't look like her experience turned out to be the best thing that ever happened to her, does it?"

"But why this?"

"Because you said yes. You said, I will build the trap. And you built it. There it is right there. You went that far. You brought us right to the door." Now it was anger. "That's saying, 'I'm doing this . . . I'm really building a trap for my child! I'm really willing to see my child in the bottom of a hole for five days!'" The anger peaked and then subsided. "You and Mom were everything to me. To know you would do such a thing to me or Will . . ." She paused for a long moment. "That's why you're here. To know what I know, to see what I've seen. Especially Mom. She's going to live with the real me for a while."

Peter asked a second haunted question.

"When did you know?"

"I knew right away."

Peter flashed back to the image of Andromeda screaming for him when she came out of her silent stare those fifteen years back, in the hospital in Wichita. He flashed on the desperate look she sent him as he rushed into her room to see her waiting with arms open. To know that even then, in that special moment, Andromeda was aware that he and Sandra had purposely constructed the trap that had held her for five days bit deeper than any sting to date.

It meant she always knew. Every Christmas, every Thanksgiving, every phone call and letter—it was always there. The knowledge. The knowledge that her two parents had been the generals coordinating her lifelong nightmare.

"I don't know what else to say. What can we do?"

"You can leave."

Will could not accept that option.

He could feel that this crisis was building to the moment when the novice would have to choose his wire. The bomb would defuse or it would explode. In his gut Will felt certain he would choose the wrong wire. But he *had* to choose. He had to choose between his parents and Andromeda. He had to ask himself which life he valued more—the lives of his two parents, two people who had stupidly put in motion the sequence of events leading to the current nightmare, or the life of his sister, a woman who had wrongly lived with an indescribable horror for three quarters of her life?

The choice was unacceptable either way.

Andromeda made it for him.

"Time's up. Time for you to leave."

Will knew that on the surface, he should easily be able to overpower Andromeda. But Andromeda was no ordinary girl. He had no idea what she was capable of. He felt certain that if push came to shove, he would be the one to hit the tarp first.

"We're not leaving Mom in that hole, Andie."

On cue, Sandra yelped from the bottom of the shaft. "Andie . . . please!"

Andromeda didn't flinch.

"She stays. You go."

Will's mind raced for a winning strategy.

"You know I can't do that. I'm not leaving without Mom! Now, god-dammit, get her out of there!"

"You can't win this one, Will. You can't be the hero here. This time, it really is too late."

"What are you going to do to her?"

"I told you, she gets to meet the real me."

"And who is the real you? Who are you that you can kill a whole town? And Mom too? Who's next? Me?"

"No, never you, and not Mom either. You can't understand this, Will, at least not yet, so don't try. Just go!"

"You know I can't do that. You won't listen to me, you won't stop . . . All I can do is stop you. . . ."

Will pulled the gun from his waistband and aimed it at his sister. With sweaty palms and an unsteady grip, he tried to give the impression that he was capable of pulling the trigger.

Andromeda raised a single eyebrow as she glanced at the pistol in her brother's hand.

"What are you going to do with that? Shoot me?"

"If that's what it takes."

"Will, even I can't stop what I'm doing. Now, throw down the gun."

Will was determined to keep his edge.

"I won't throw it down."

"But you already did."

Will looked to his hand and saw it was empty, and then he saw the gun lying at Andromeda's feet. He had obeyed her command without even knowing it.

As Andromeda kicked the gun into the open shaft, Will grew desperate.

"Andie, you can't leave her alone down there!"

"I wasn't alone when I was down there. Mom won't be either."

"What do you mean?"

"You think what you see, you think this is all there is? This is just the shell. The real life is where no one looks. Up here is the icing, down below is the cake." Andromeda began retreating toward the open pit of the sec-ondary shaft. "Did you know you can drill three miles deep and still find colonies of bacteria? Did you know there are plants growing just under the surface that spread out for miles and miles? One plant, the size of a county? Pretty amazing, huh? Some trees live for thousands of years and people are oh-so impressed. Well, there are things down under, things you wouldn't believe, still alive and still growing, that knew the step of the mastodons. You can learn a lot, living underground for twenty thousand years, almost as much as you can in five long days." Andromeda continued moving back until she stood right at the shaft edge. "Mom's not alone, she'll never be alone. She'll always have me."

With a sinking heart, Will understood.

"You're going back."

Andromeda was suddenly softer.

"I've been everywhere and I've seen all there is to see. My time in the light is over."

His torment reaching its zenith, Peter knew he could not live above knowing what was happening below.

"Take me instead. Take me."

Andromeda smiled bittersweetly.

"No, Dad, not yet."

Will could not stand it any longer.

"Fuck it! This is insane! I'm getting Mom out of there."

Will made a move forward and the ground suddenly shook with the force of a notable quake. In Denny's display cases, items from the rescue tumbled off their shelves and pictures hanging in frames slipped to crash to the floor. The jolt came and went in a heartbeat, but it was enough to make Will pause. Andromeda reacted as if the jolt were the most usual thing.

"I told you not to try."

Will took another step forward. Again a jolt shook the structure but this time with a force strong enough to crack one of the walls. The crack extended up the wall and over the ceiling. Foam and plaster stalactites snapped free and dropped to the floor. The glass in many of the display cases shattered and the mannequin of eight-year-old Will tumbled out. When the head of Will's mannequin rolled from its shoulders and came to rest at Andromeda's feet, he took it as a sign. He stopped.

"Andie, I can't lose Mom. I can't . . . I can't lose either of you."

"You aren't losing us. You want us, just follow your nose."

"What does that mean?"

"You'll know." Andromeda fixed her gaze on Will. She smiled so gently, and in that moment she was the tender and kind sister Will had missed for fifteen years. Will's heart was squeezed by instant grief. She was going away again but there wasn't a thing he could do about it.

Andromeda let out a soft sigh as she smiled sadly.

"Just remember—my favorite color is blue."

And with that Andromeda took a step back and fell into the hole.

Will dropped to his knees as Peter half fainted, crashing into the glass of another case.

"Oh God, no . . . "

"Andie!"

As Will again surged forward, believing there was still something he could do despite the fact that no one could survive an eighty-three-foot drop to hard earth, another shock shook the building, but one that refused to subside. Large chunks of ceiling dropped to the floor and the walls cracked open wide to let in the light of the day. With each new jolt, following no pattern, just an unerring build to inevitable destruction, more and more of Denny Sharf's Andromeda's Tomb was ripped from the foundation. As a piece the size of a refrigerator fell from the ceiling to block Will's view of the secondary shaft, Peter regained enough of his senses to yank his son from the building before they were both lost.

Peter pulled Will out into the lot, finding it difficult to walk a straight path as the ground shook and tossed. Rushing into the lot, father and son fell into the now bouncing chairs and looked back toward Andromeda's Tomb.

The ground opened up to swallow the concrete tubes and pillars, the roof slabs and the gift shop with its T-shirts and shot glasses. As a giant cloud of dust rose to obscure the continuing devastation, Will glanced at one of the large video screens, the one displaying the view down Deets's tunnel.

She stood there bigger than life.

It was Andromeda and she was alive.

As she moved toward the tiny chamber at the bottom, toward their mother, she turned for a moment and looked back, directly into the jittery lens. From the cracking speakers her voice called out one last time before image and sound were cut off.

"I'll always be here."

She blew Will and Peter a kiss and then they saw no more. The screen went blank and the speakers fell silent.

The quaking slowed, slowed more and then stopped completely.

As Peter cried in anguish, sitting amid a tangle of chairs and lost to reality, Will stood and faced the ruin.

The dust cleared and he saw it had all gone away. There was nothing. Just a flat patch of bare soil. Everything had been devoured by the quake. The only evidence that anything approaching a tourist trap had ever been there was the cartoony sign jutting up from the soil at a dramatic angle. The only word still visible was ANDROMEDA.

Deets rolled down his window and called over as he tapped his watch, oblivious to the destruction of Andromeda's Tomb, which had happened mere meters from his face.

"Hey, I'm only supposed to stay in here for a couple of hours but my goddamn watch stopped! How long would you say I've been in here?"

"Long enough."

"That's great to know. Thanks."

Deets put his feet back on his dash, lifted his magazine and continued reading.

Will turned to his father and lifted him from the chairs.

Peter bawled in shock.

"I didn't . . . Andie . . . Sandra . . . No."

Will slid his father into the truck's passenger seat, moved to take the wheel, started the truck and put it in gear. He drove to the road and turned on the blinker that would send them east. Looking both ways, he saw no traffic. No one was coming.

No one would ever come again.

He pulled the truck out of Andromeda's Tomb and headed home, back to Wishbone. He glanced in the rearview mirror. The huge arrow that said YOU ARE HERE now pointed to nowhere.

Will turned his eyes forward.

The horizon was full of white smoke. The fires in Wishbone were being put out. Tomorrow the clean-up would begin.

He drove and thought about the halving of his family.

He thought about Andromeda.

He had learned many impossible things about her but the one she seemed to want him to remember most was that when he followed his nose, whatever that meant, he should remember her favorite color was blue.

It was something he vowed he would not forget.

• • •

Sandra lifted her head as the darkness took over.

She could feel herself going; she could feel herself giving up. To her surprise, she found she no longer cared.

It was over, the whole run. In a mere forty-one years she had come to her day of reckoning. But it was the end she deserved and she knew it.

This was not a place she would move past. She would not carry on with the life she had built, and without the serene rituals of society dinners and copying the styles of Monet and Degas, Sandra's life had no meaning. She felt empty. She felt worthless. For once she felt she had to make a sacrifice.

She would sacrifice her life because it was the only thing she had left.

She felt Andromeda moving close even as her body grew numb.

"Andie?"

"Yes, Mother?"

"What's going to happen?"

"You'll see things you could never have seen before."

"Will it hurt?"

"Don't worry, Mom. It won't hurt a bit."

Andromeda moved close to her mother. Feeling her own body numbing, she offered Sandra the world of experience that had been her solitary domain for fifteen years. She could sense the acceptance as her mother's breathing quieted, as her fears fell away. As if washed by a richly pervasive wave of sentience penetrating her every cell, Sandra suddenly saw what Andromeda saw, felt all that Andromeda felt and knew all that Andromeda knew.

She had lived a life so superficial, yet Sandra in that instant truly knew life at its deepest. Memories and experiences, moods and torments, joys and conquests came pouring into the shallow spaces of her shallow soul to fill her with the knowledge of life. With an embracing satisfaction, she intimately knew lives lived everywhere spanning thousands of years.

In that moment Sandra remembered mastodons.

Andromeda lay with her mother in the dark cocoon and felt herself filling with the essential self she had missed for fifteen years, since the day Will pulled her from the hole. She felt complete again and more.

She felt universal.

As much as she once desired it and in ways still did, Andromeda would never be just an ordinary, everyday girl. She would not hang out with friends and chat about relationships, she would not commiserate on alleged slights, argue politics or talk religion or seek out the help of friends to find her life's soulmate. Andromeda would never have a soulmate. She would not marry, she would not bear a child. She would not grow old and walk her golden years holding the hand of her graying life partner. She would not do any of these things as Andromeda Wiley.

She would not do any of these things because she had done them millions of times as other souls, souls she knew so fully that she could remember banquets and battles and loves and voyages, vast experiences from the surface so richly implanted into her consciousness during her last day in the hole.

In the dark, much that had happened in the world, the answers to mysteries great and small, were shared with Andromeda by things ancient and unseen living in places where man set no foot. Suffused with the experience of living, watching and absorbing the march of existence year upon year, they had shared what they learned with the thing that moved, the little girl named Andromeda, when she fell from the light to land in their dark world.

In their touch Andromeda had seen much beauty but she had also seen so much horror. She had seen the worst man and beast could offer. She had offered it herself. She had offered the horror to an entire town. But because of her change, or perhaps because those who had perished so horrifically deserved their punishment, she felt no remorse. Their deaths were footnotes to the panorama of constant and inescapable mortality.

Denny Sharf, Janice Piasecki and all the others had lived small lives yet they died great deaths. In the end they would achieve an immortality of sorts because none living would forget how they took leave of the world.

For her mother Andromeda offered something else. She offered truth. Sandra would learn the truth about everything that lived, from the tiny to the giant. What was seen and felt by that life, Sandra would also see and feel, as if she had lived that life herself. The grand tapestry would be revealed, seen from the rarest perspective—the perspective of total understanding.

What had seemed like a punishment was the greatest of gifts.

Andromeda shared with her mother the answer to the question that had troubled philosophers, saints and poets for centuries.

Why?

Andromeda knew why and now Sandra did too.

As Andromeda gave herself to the darkness, she sensed her mother's new awe as life bid her welcome. In that moment Andromeda felt closer to her mother than she had ever felt before. In the history of the world there had never been a mother and daughter so close.

They were the ultimate family and they were finally home.

And when it came time, Peter and Will would come home too.

FIFTY-FIVE

THE FAMILY FARM

It had been eight months.

It had been eight months since the town of Wishbone believed Andromeda and Sandra Wiley had been killed in a tragic collapse of Andromeda's Tomb. Where the tragedy had occurred, there was now nothing more than a field of weeds surrounding a memorial stone paid for by Will Wiley.

Living the life of a survivor, Will looked out on his land.

The first cabbage was ready to harvest. The corn was chest high. The squash, the beets, the radishes, carrots and onions were all just about ready to pluck. From the front porch of the Wiley family home, the sight of nearly thirteen hundred acres of deliciously edible, organically grown vegetables was there for the taking. It wasn't quite thirteen hundred acres for one reason: Since Andromeda's step back into the darkness, Will had decided to let fifty acres grow a new crop.

It was a crop that could never be picked.

Covering a fifty-acre patch at the heart of the Wiley family farm, close to the farmhouse, in view of the kitchen, the grasses of a lost world grew where they had not for over a hundred years. In this patch of earth, at least, fifty acres of native prairie was winning.

Will walked out to the patch and strolled through the tall grasses under the warm June sun. Puffy clouds crossed the sky and a single-engine plane droned lazily high above. The slightest breeze rustled the grasses.

It was the most peaceful of scenes.

A passing observer would survey the landscape, taking in the postcard-perfect tableau, and come to the conclusion that this was one of the quiet places where respite of body and soul could be had for free. Such an observer might think that not much happens in such a place.

They would be wrong.

On the inside, where most of the world was, down where the materials of life were gathered, at that primordial band where magma became crust, the real action was happening. This was where the seeds of life sprouted new crops, sending them off to futures lasting milliseconds or millenniums.

Every step, every moment of every individual existence on the outside was lived above an unseen mass of living beings outnumbering those above by hundreds to one. Most were just single-celled creatures unchanged since the planetary brew rang true and life sprang into being. But others were more complex. Some had lived so long they faced evolution in a single lifetime.

Andromeda and Sandra were now part of that evolution.

They were part of the creation.

Will considered how scientists in the rain forests were constantly discovering new species of plants, insects and animals on almost a daily basis, only to warn of their inevitable extinction the following day as entire ecosystems were wiped clean, shunted aside so cattle could be raised, made into patties and served in Happy Meals all over the globe. If that was true on the outside, might it also be true down below? How much of the life below had humanity failed to encounter? What else might be living down there besides ants and worms? How much had they missed?

Will guessed that Andromeda was probably right. They had missed most of it. There were creatures in the crust still undiscovered that had been allowed millions of years to evolve in unchanging environments. To what point they had evolved, none could say.

Andromeda seemed to know.

Andromeda had emerged from her trauma with the ability to do things no one else could. Whether her abilities had come from contact with a creature living its existence far from animal eyes, or whether she had become something more than human by a mechanism of her own making, Will could not say. All he could say was that she had changed. In the end she had taken their mother to the place of her change.

Will sat in the grass and created a hole. He reached through the blades to a delicate flower growing in their midst. Looking something like a rock lily but with a woodier stem and larger flowers, the overhanging light-blue flowers with their upturned pistils were targeted by bees all over Will's mini-prairie.

Will ventured a sniff.

Its fragrance was intoxicating. It soothed and it comforted.

It was a most familiar fragrance, yet until the flowers suddenly appeared in this fifty-acre patch four months earlier, he had never inhaled it before.

Now he inhaled it often.

When the flowers first appeared and opened their blooms, Will had thought to pluck them to make way for a crop of hops. But one whiff of the supremely serene fragrance sent him to the library to discover the flower's name. After intensive research he discovered the flower had no name. It was a completely new species and it had made an appearance at only one place on planet earth.

The Wiley family farm.

Will decided to give the flowers a closer look.

The flowers had the most delicious fragrance he had ever encountered, and that's how he knew. They were colored a translucent blue, almost crystalline in its ability to refract light, that was a perfect match for Andromeda's eyes, and that's how he discovered the truth.

The flowers were Andromeda's creation.

A wispy tendril of the flower gently wrapped itself around Will's finger. In the gentle squeeze of his finger he could feel the pulse of its life. He could feel it saying hello.

Poom-poom.

Poom-poom.

Poom-poom.

In eight months Will had not been able to find a name for the flower. He still called it Andie. He guessed he always would.

Andromeda had taken herself and their mother from the light and into the darkness. Yet he couldn't help feeling he would see them again. He couldn't help feeling they were somehow waiting for him.

When the time came he would try to be ready.

Under his care the family flower would thrive. It would bloom and it would survive.

It would spread.

Lisa called to Will from the edge of the prairie, taking care not to crush any of the special flowers she believed her new husband had planted.

"Will, dinner's ready! You want me to bring down your dad?"

"Yeah! I'll be in in a minute!"

Will watched Lisa turn back into the house. He could picture her moving upstairs to coax Peter from the chair in Andromeda's room, where his father sat every day, thumbing an old Mickey Mouse nightlight from one hand to the other. Will had hoped to help heal his father's loss over Andromeda and Sandra. He thought the flowers might help. As the fragrance had eased his own pain, Will felt certain it would do the same for his father. Yet try as he might, he could not convince Peter to take a stroll into the prairie to sample the fragrance for himself.

One day Peter would take that stroll, he would bend to the beautiful flowers and smell their perfume. And then he would understand that what he had thought lost forever lived a new joy right before his eyes.

Will stood and began walking back to the house.

He was aware of the grasses bowing under the pressure of his step. He spoke silent apologies. These days, every step reminded him that life, the soul of a living being, was everywhere he tread.

He tried to step light.

Will never told Lisa the final details of what had happened to Andromeda and his mother. To the world and the recovering town of Wishbone, the whole disaster, which had destroyed half the town and had swallowed Andromeda and Sandra Wiley along with the entire structure of Andromeda's Tomb, was all some freak accident that could be dealt with and forgotten. The wagon trains would ride again.

Will stepped into the home he shared with Lisa and his father and looked back at the healthy prairie.

He would never move. He would never let the field fall into other hands. He would live here, in this house, to stand guard over this prairie and its special flowers for the rest of his life.

It was what any brother and son would do for his family.

MARTIN SCHENK is an Oregonian living in Los Angeles. He has worked in the film industry for the past decade. A graduate of the USC School of Cinema/Television, he has worked as a cartoonist for *National Lampoon* magazine and has sold an original screenplay to Disney. He is currently at work on his second novel.